To Lee,

DEAD MAN SINGING

DEAD MAN SINGING

Steve Couch

The Book Guild Ltd

First published in Great Britain in 2023 by
The Book Guild Ltd
Unit E2 Airfield Business Park,
Harrison Road, Market Harborough,
Leicestershire. LE16 7UL
Tel: 0116 2792299
www.bookguild.co.uk
Email: info@bookguild.co.uk
Twitter: @bookguild

Copyright © 2023 Steve Couch

The right of Steve Couch to be identified as the author of this
work has been asserted by them in accordance with the
Copyright, Design and Patents Act 1988.

All rights reserved. No part of this publication may be
reproduced, transmitted, or stored in a retrieval system, in any form or by any means,
without permission in writing from the publisher, nor be otherwise circulated in
any form of binding or cover other than that in which it is published and without
a similar condition being imposed on the subsequent purchaser.

This work is entirely fictitious and bears no resemblance to any persons living or dead.

Typeset in 11pt Minion Pro

Printed on FSC accredited paper
Printed and bound in Great Britain by 4edge Limited

ISBN 978 1915853 233

British Library Cataloguing in Publication Data.
A catalogue record for this book is available from the British Library.

For my dad,
who loved music deeply and loved his family more.

part one

TURNING OF THE TIDE

MARCH 1990

CHAPTER ONE

He strode onto the tiny stage in the poky, smoky, barn of a room, met with a smattering of applause rather than full-throated cheers. Taking up his round-backed Ovation acoustic – the only ovation his shows started with these days – he plugged in and stepped forward: showtime. He had nothing to say to this crowd, not yet anyway. The hum of chatter from the bar hadn't dipped at all; this audience needed winning round.

His left foot tapped out the tempo, and he launched into the opening number. One from his early days: a treat for any old fans but with enough swagger to get the attention of the unconverted; that was the plan anyway. Through the glare of stage lights he could make out some heads nodding to the music. Those opening chords used to get a bigger reaction.

By the end of the first song, there was some life at the front. He saw a few younger guys, but mostly it looked like long-serving fans, what was left of his faithful following. The back of the room – never mind the crowd at the bar, out of his sight in this bizarre L-shaped space – was still talking, though, ignoring the legend in front of them.

'Good evening, Oxford, it's great to be here at the Jericho.' That was a lie, but he could hardly say he considered a two hundred-capacity venue beneath him. It was basically a pub gig and he wasn't even filling the room; when had that stopped being a surprise? 'I'm Dave Masters, and if you didn't know that, either you're in the wrong place or I am. That was "Midnight Rolling", from my very first album, and here's one from my most recent one. This is "Stagefright".'

It sounded better with a full band – it just wasn't the same without the piano introduction – but it still worked now that he was reduced to these solo acoustic shows. With the tiny rooms that Tony was getting for him these days – Bristol Louisiana yesterday, the Jericho tonight – there wasn't enough money for a band as well. Most of the audience would know it was a cover version, but he didn't go out of his way to advertise that fact for the ignorant ones. Unlike the man in the song, he wasn't afraid of the spotlight, but playing live just didn't feed him like it used to.

When he got to the solo, one of the younger lads at the front lit up; probably a player himself from the way his eyes were glued to the strings, taking in the finger work. Dave turned ever so slightly to his left, giving his young acolyte a better view. The song went down well. Pockets of the crowd were warming up now, but there were still plenty that seemed to regard him as an unwelcome distraction. Why pay for a ticket if you don't want to listen?

By the end of the night, the atmosphere had improved. He had always been more of an album act, so his few hit singles had to be spread sparingly through the evening, saving "Trouble on My Mind" to the end as his best chance of getting back on for an encore before the applause stopped. He had always mixed his own songs with a few cover versions, but these days the covers helped to maintain the interest of the unconverted. "I Saw Her Standing There" was a turning point halfway through, and then an old Traffic song pushed the energy levels up again at just the right time. Whatever else the years had seen him lose – along with a sizeable part of his audience – he still knew how to pace a show and win over a crowd.

'This is my last one; join in if you recognise it.' He broke into the familiar opening riff of "Trouble on My Mind". Fifteen years ago he'd been playing it on *Top of the Pops* and touring proper venues, like Hammersmith Odeon, Manchester Apollo and Leicester De Montfort Hall. His biggest hit – the one people always asked for – was "Let You Go", but that was from his early '80s days, when he had been persuaded into a lush, synth-drenched sound in the name of commercial success. It had worked on "Let You Go", but it wasn't really his taste. He tended to play it in the first half of the set, just to get it out of the way, and to stop people calling for it all the way through. "Trouble on My Mind" did its job tonight, as usual, not that he risked waiting for too long in the wings.

He picked up the guitar again and stepped up to the mic. 'Thank you, Oxford. Back when I started, singer-songwriters were required by law to do a Bob Dylan cover. Here's mine.' With that, he strummed the opening chords of "It Ain't Me Babe". He'd recorded an exuberant, barrelling band version on *Songsmith*, his first album, but now he was playing something closer to Dylan's laid-back acoustic original. Over the years, Cath had scathingly described it as his theme song: a man brazenly admitting his inability to step up to responsibility. She had a point, but it went down well with an audience, which was all he really cared about.

Ten minutes later, he was sitting in the dingy dressing room, pulling on a bottled beer and wiping himself down with a towel. He'd turned things round tonight after a slow start, but maybe he was too old to keep slogging round the circuit for such diminished returns. At least it wasn't a stupidly long drive to get home tonight. The club manager arrived, cash in hand, and they exchanged pleasantries as he counted out Dave's fee.

'I thought it was more than that. My manager said £300.'

'That was for selling at least seventy-five per cent of the tickets. Half full means half payment.'

'First I've heard of it.' Dave was standing, squaring up to the bloke now. He was taller than the manager, but they both knew it wouldn't come to actual violence.

'Well, that's what was agreed. Take it up with your manager. It's a shame we couldn't get a few more in, you really got them going tonight – it was a good show.'

Dave accepted the money and the olive branch. It had been a good show in spite of the low numbers.

'I loved that Traffic cover,' said the manager. 'Didn't Joe Cocker do a version?'

'"Feelin' Alright"? Yeah. I've got a band version on my live album.'

'And which Cocker album is it on?'

Dave sighed. '*With a Little Help from My Friends*.'

'Ah, right. I'll have to look out for a copy.'

'Or you could buy my live album, seeing as you enjoyed my version. It would make up for stiffing me on the fee – and it's not as if Joe Cocker needs the money.' The manager shrugged and turned away, refusing to rise to the bait and wishing Dave a good trip home. Dave resisted the temptation to point out that you wouldn't catch Joe Cocker playing a dump like this; he wasn't sure the comparison really worked in his favour.

He slept in the next morning, waking up after midday. Post-gig adrenalin was still pumping after the relatively short to trip home to Surrey, so he'd put records on and played some pool in his den while he decompressed, getting to sleep the right side of 4am after the gold records on the wall had finished sneering at him, taunting him with past glories. Time was he'd still have been partying when morning broke, but that was a lifetime ago in the days of major tours and full houses; the days of hotel rooms and groupies. His house was the last sign of his previous success. It wasn't exactly a rock-star mansion, but it was bought and paid for, and the six bedrooms were five more than he needed anymore.

Early in the afternoon, the phone rang. It was Tony, his manager.

'Dave. How was last night?' Even a casual greeting sounded overly formal with Tony's plummy intonation.

'The usual – a bit slow starting but we got there by the end.'

'Full house?'

Dave snorted. 'Hardly. More than half, but only just. I only got a half fee – what's all that about? Why am I playing tiny pubs and clubs and not even filling them? Remember when I could sell out multiple nights at Hammersmith Odeon? Where have all those fans gone?'

'If I could answer that, Dave, I'd still have you playing those venues, you know I would. Listen, I have a treat for you.'

'Phil Collins wants to produce my next album?'

'I wish. No, sadly it's not a career thing – well, not yours anyway – but I think you'll enjoy it. One of my other acts has a gig tonight and I think you should come along.'

'Why would I want to do that? Who are they?'

'It's who they're supporting that you should be asking me about.'

'Who are they supporting?'

'Your hero, Richard Thompson. He's doing a solo acoustic show at Hackney Empire. I wondered if you wanted me to get you added to the guestlist.'

Dave didn't even need time to think about it. 'Absolutely, thanks, Tony. What time is the show?'

'Doors open at 7.30, Thompson probably isn't on until 9ish. Try to get there for my lads, though, I'd value your thoughts on them. I'll see you there.'

Dave promised he'd try. For one thing, he'd been with Tony a long time and even if the level of gigs he was playing had declined in recent years, at least Tony had kept him working. Plenty of his peers had failed to ride out the purging fire of punk, but Tony had helped him survive and flourish in the years after. They had been together for twenty years or so, and he was certainly entitled to ask a favour – particularly when the favour involved a free Richard Thompson show.

Approaching the venue, he was unable to shake off a feeling of anxiety, of potential humiliation. He was sure Tony wouldn't have let him down, but it would be embarrassing to be turned away, particularly if anyone recognised him. Then again, maybe being turned away and no one recognising him would be worse.

'Hi,' he greeted the girl in the box office. 'You're holding a comp for me.'

'What name?' she replied, instantly and without enthusiasm. She didn't even look up (which at least gave Dave an excuse to cling to for any lack of recognition).

'Dave Masters.' This time it stung a bit that there was no reaction other than to rummage through the named envelopes.

'Here you are.' She almost smiled as she passed him his ticket without making eye contact. 'Enjoy the show.' Somehow he suspected she wouldn't be regaling her mates with stories about her latest brush with celebrity.

Dave made his way through the Empire foyer and headed straight for the smoke-filled bar. Collecting his pint, he found standing room next to one of the doors and settled himself to some people-watching while he drank. At one point he noticed a couple nudging each other and looking in his direction. The man, rather presumptuously, waved in his direction. Dave was about to react when a voice from over his shoulder called a greeting and went over to join the couple. False alarm, they had been looking straight through him. At least no one had noticed his humiliation, not this time. He was never sure whether he minded being recognised or not being recognised more. Either way, it was a pain; fame was great up to a point, but sometimes he thought anonymity would be better than where he was now: a faded has-been, constantly unsure whether his name or face would ring a bell.

It was tempting to stay in the bar and just skip the support act. Then again, maybe they would be good; Tony had struck gold at least once in the past (with him) so this could be a chance to see something special, someone who might even give his career the leg-up it so desperately needed right now. Reluctantly, he downed what was left of his pint and headed for the stalls.

It was a magnificent venue: an old music hall with plush blood-red velvet seats, sweeping galleries and an ornate proscenium arch which put the bare boards of the Jericho into perspective. As he made his way to his seat – fairly near the front, out towards the left-hand side of the stage: could be worse – he noticed that most of the seats were still unoccupied, although he didn't doubt that would change once Richard Thompson came on. The early birds made up a good mix of ages: from grey-haired bank manager lookalikes to scruffy students and everything in between. The one person he couldn't see was Tony.

The house lights dimmed and three earnest-looking young men made their way out onto the stage to a smattering of applause. One of them had an acoustic guitar, but the others were more exotic in their choice of instruments; there were some ethnic-looking drums and one of the trio set himself up behind what looked like a hammered dulcimer. Maybe this was going to be more interesting than the usual identikit support acts.

In truth, they weren't bad. Dave enjoyed the music, particularly the ethereal air of the dulcimer. The lyrics were hand-wringingly worthy, though – a song about domestic abuse, another about the evils of capitalism; he had no problem with message songs, but did you really want to be told how to think when you were on a night out? Where was all the boy-meets-girl-loses-girl stuff that people could relate to their own lives? Every song in their set laid out what was wrong with the world and how it was his fault. Where was the fun in that?

The battle between musical form and lyrical content meant Dave lost interest by the end. As the stern-faced frontman said,

'This is our last one,' he decided to beat the rush to the gents. By the time he got back to his seat, the house lights were up and a familiar figure was in the previously empty seat to Dave's left.

'Evening, Tony, you made it then. I thought you'd stood me up.'

Tony turned and gave a broad smile, showing his teeth as he stood to greet Dave with a hug. In contrast to Dave's jeans and collarless shirt, Tony's designer shirt spoke of someone trying just a little too hard to be effortlessly cool. His overly gelled hair was fixed in place as permanently as his smile.

'As if. Did you catch my lot? What did you think?'

'Different. The music was good, but they were a bit po-faced and preachy. They need to decide whether they want to be rock stars or social workers.'

Before Tony could reply, the house lights dimmed again. Moments later Richard Thompson strolled easily towards the mic stand, acoustic guitar in his hands, with warm applause greeting his every step. He plugged in and without a word started on his opening number, "Turning of the Tide". The lively up-tempo tune belied world-weary lyrics about the inevitable passing of glory days. Thompson had the audience in the palm of his hand – no winning round required here. The lyrics struck a chord with Dave. The tide had turned on his own career, and right now he couldn't see any way of turning it back.

When Thompson got to the guitar solo, a chiming, lyrical flourish effortlessly laid on top of his own accompaniment, Dave shook his head and drew a breath. Despite a resolute lack of hit singles, Thompson was as good as it got. Dave had been a bigger draw than him once upon a time; that had all changed now, though.

'I see why you like him,' said Tony. 'Do you think he needs a manager?'

'He'd want someone who can book him into better rooms than the Jericho.'

'Touché.'

It was a great gig. One of Dave's favourite songs, "Withered and Died", even got a rare outing. Occasionally Dave played a version in his live shows but had somehow never got around to recording it. These days the title was too much of a gift to hostile reviewers looking to dismissively sum up his career.

It was time for Thompson to introduce his next number. 'This one is inspired by all those acts who struggle unappreciated for years, only to find that their career takes off spectacularly once they die; something that I'm keeping in mind. It's written by John French – Drumbo from the Magic Band. Anyway, this is "Now That I Am Dead".'

Thompson picked a jauntily rhythmic melody, then started to sing in a voice comically wrapped in mock-melodrama. The lyrics were clever and fun, with some nice rhymes about record sales that increased now he was deceased, and dying in order to make a living. Dave couldn't help but run the figures through his head. Hackney Empire held 1,250; he used to fill bigger rooms than this and now he couldn't sell out venues a fifth of the size. It wasn't even as if Richard Thompson was part of the younger generation who had pushed Dave aside – he was around before Dave got started, and here he was still ploughing his own furrow and playing to decent-sized, adoring crowds without having to compromise his music. He even mixed up full-band shows with solo acoustic ones like this. Why hadn't Dave been able to sustain things in the same way?

At the end of the night, Tony and Dave found themselves tucking into burgers – mad cow in a bun, as Tony insisted on calling them – in an all-night greasy café.

'What happened to me, Tony? Where did it all go wrong?' Tony raised a quizzical eyebrow, encouraging Dave to elaborate while chewing on a mouthful of health risk. 'I mean, when we started together, it was onwards and upwards all the way. Now I can't even fill the bloody Jericho.'

Tony shrugged. 'The new album could change everything. If it does well, we can put you back in bigger venues. We could get you out with a band again.'

'Let's hope so. The songwriting was a real struggle for this one, though; I just don't seem to be able to get them out these days.'

'It'll come, don't worry. How close is the album to being finished?'

'Nearly. I think I need one more track. I might have to do another cover version to finish it off, but I'm working on it.'

'Okay. Well, hurry up – the record company have been asking for it. They're getting impatient.'

'Impatient in a good way? Like they can't wait to hear what I've done?'

Tony's frown answered before his words did. 'More like a what's-taking-so-long, has-he-lost-his-touch way, to be honest.'

'Lost my touch? Bloody cheek. Let them wait – this one will be worth waiting for.'

'It'll have to be. Anyway, if it doesn't set the world ablaze, I've got a plan B.' There was a playful twinkle in Tony's eye.

'Go on.'

'You heard that dead song tonight – if all else fails, we can kill you off. That'll make everyone realise just how talented you are and get the old records selling again.'

'Yeah, but I won't be around to see the benefit, will I?'

'Ah, that's the clever part. If we fake your death, we can ride the wave of sympathy and nostalgia back up the charts and find a whole new audience. I could get the old albums reissued, maybe a *Best Of*. You'd be rolling in it.'

Dave started laughing, then saw something in Tony's expression. 'You're not even joking, are you? You're serious about this!'

A smile played around Tony's face. 'Well, only if the new album doesn't do all that we're hoping, and only if you're happy to walk away. There's not much point in faking your death if you don't disappear to make it convincing. What do you think?'

'I think you're mad, Tony, that's what I think. We'd never get away with it.'

'Maybe. Or maybe I just need a bit of time to work out the details. Leave it with me.'

CHAPTER TWO

The next day, Dave hit the road for another regular gig: Tesco's. He had no one to shop or cook for him anymore; his marriage had died around the same time his career started to decline in the '80s, although to be fair to Cath her departure wasn't anything to do with that. She was no gold digger; she just heard one too many excuses and got fed up with a husband who spent most of the year succumbing to temptation on the road.

It was rare that he got bothered in the supermarket now. Occasionally, like today, he'd notice men of a certain age nudging their wives and surreptitiously pointing in his direction. It just underlined how far he'd fallen. Back when his second album, *Flying Wild*, heralded the arrival of the big time, visits to the supermarket became impossible – he was too busy and too well known to do it safely. That tour had been great; his first time headlining decent-sized venues like Nottingham Rock City and the Rainbow. He'd played them before, but only as a support act to the likes of Traffic, Free and the Faces. He even played a few dates with Paul McCartney and Wings. That was when Dave first added "I Saw Her Standing There" into his set, partly after Vince, his drummer, dared him to play it without telling Macca first. Fortunately, the great man approved of their version, after calling Dave a cheeky sod.

So how had he gone from hobnobbing with a Beatle to glorified pub gigs? He was off trying to conquer America in '76 and '77 when many of his peers were dismissed as dinosaurs. A live album – *Live Masters* – recorded mostly on those American dates reintroduced him to the UK, and then in the synth-ridden '80s, he hit big with "Let You Go" then managed sporadic appearances in the lower reaches of the singles chart. But drink had dulled his songwriting and the albums began a slow but steady decline, both critically and commercially. He was still capable of catching lightning in a bottle from time to time, or so he tried telling himself, but he had to churn out a lot of dross to find the gold.

As he pushed his trolley back to his car, it started to rain. Dave turned his collar up and quickened his pace. He just felt like going home. A lyric floated across his mind, a memory of an old song that bassist Phil had played endlessly back in the day. How did it go now?

Once he got home, he dumped the shopping bags in the kitchen without a thought for his frozens and headed straight to the den and his record collection. Phil's copy had been the B-side of a Charlie Rich single, but Dave had a version of the song on an old Rita Coolidge album. Maybe this would be the track he needed, the last piece of the jigsaw? By now he was lowering the needle to the vinyl and listening. He could already hear what he wanted to do with the song – a sparse arrangement, no drums for the most part, just his guitar and maybe a bit of organ giving it a hint of gospel-blues. As soon as the track finished, he replaced the needle and listened to it again, picking up his guitar and starting to work out his part for it. Yes, this was going to work.

Recording "Feel Like Going Home" went really well. Clive, the producer, approved of Dave's instinct to keep it simple and the vocal was one of the best Dave had put on tape for years: yearning and broken without becoming mawkish. The electric guitar solo – the richer tone of the Gibson rather than his usual Strat – had

Clive positively purring. Maybe this was the hit single he'd been hoping for. As long as he put one of his own compositions on the B-side for the songwriting royalties, that would be okay. Time was he wouldn't have even thought about that, just gone for a couple of great songs regardless of who wrote them, but show business is still a business, and he had to make sure he got paid.

A couple of weeks later, he was sitting in a meeting room at Ultimate Records with Tony and a cluster of suits, who had replaced the suits who sat in judgement on his previous album, who in turn had replaced the suits before that. Tony was in gregarious form, working the room the way Dave worked an audience. He was every bit as much of an artist as Dave, in his own way. Eventually it was time to play the tapes.

The first track was one of his, probably the best song he'd written in the last few years. "Blood and Rust" was a brooding take on getting older, with a driving rhythm and some muscular guitar towards the end. Dave was hoping it would be picked for a single, but the suits made little response. One of them said that blood and rust didn't sound very hygienic, and that was as much discussion as it seemed to warrant.

Next was a cover, a '60s classic: "I'm Not Your Steppin' Stone".

'Isn't this the Monkees?' asked one of the suits.

'Paul Revere and the Raiders originally,' replied Dave.

'Nah, it's the Monkees, definitely.'

'I used to love the Monkees,' piped up someone else, and the discussion veered away towards childhood memories of Saturday-morning television.

'How about an album of Monkees covers?' someone suggested. 'That would give us an angle to push for the marketing.'

'How about you leave the thinking to the grown-ups?' growled Dave, shaking off the restraining hand Tony laid on his arm. 'How's this for an angle: the new album from acclaimed singer-songwriter Dave Masters?'

'Yeah, 'cos that worked so well on the last album,' came the sneering reply. 'And the one before that.'

A couple more of Dave's songs fared no better than "Blood and Rust", then it was the next cover: a version of a Steve Winwood single from two or three years earlier which drew comments from the suits.

'I remember this. Where are the synths?'

'I went with an earthier feel, more piano, more guitar.'

'But people think of you with synths – "Let You Go" was great. Synths would sound better.'

Things didn't improve from that point. Dave's carefully chosen cover versions – Gene Clark, Leon Russell – were dismissed, with the suit who had suggested the album of Monkees covers reminding Dave that the whole point of a cover was to take advantage of a song that was already popular, not to do something nobody knows.

'That can work,' soothed Tony before Dave could reply. 'But Dave has always enjoyed introducing his audience to great songs they might not have heard.'

'Well, if Dave wants to introduce people to great songs, why doesn't he try writing some?' It got a good laugh from the rest of the room, while Dave forced himself not to react. He hated these people. What did these parasites know about it anyway? They were businessmen, nothing more, but they sat in judgement of artists.

By the time they reached the final track, "Feel Like Going Home", Dave had almost given up hope. Suddenly, the mood in the room shifted. Everyone seemed taken by the melancholic organ and heartfelt vocal. Dave felt goosebumps forming on his skin. Damn, this was the best thing he'd recorded in years. When the guitar solo cranked the emotion up another notch, even Monkeeman was smiling. Dave had caught the lightning and even these idiots could see it.

'Now that's more like it,' said Nigel, the chief suit, as the song finished. 'That's fantastic.'

'What do you mean, "That's more like it"?' spluttered Dave. 'The whole album is bloody great.' Again, he felt Tony's hand on his arm and bit his tongue.

'This could get Dave back into the singles charts, back into the limelight,' said Tony. 'Back to serious sales figures.'

'Well, there's certainly something for us to work with in that last track,' admitted Nigel. 'We'll put our heads together and see what we can do.'

Tony tried to put the rest of the meeting in a positive light as they drove away, but Dave knew that apart from "Feel Like Going Home", it had gone badly.

'Don't worry, I'll sort it,' said Tony. 'That's my job. I'll get on to Nigel and we can plan a marketing campaign. They're not wrong about "Feel Like Going Home" – it's great. We need something livelier as the first single, just to soften the ground. After that, as long as we get the airplay, we could have a huge hit on our hands.' He paused for a moment, before adding, 'I hadn't realised you had done so many covers – almost half the record.'

Dave shifted uncomfortably. 'I told you, my writing has dried up. The best of the new ones were written a couple of years back.'

'Ah, don't worry about it, you'll get your mojo back soon. "Steppin' Stone" and "Feel Like Going Home" could be just the singles to get you back up the charts where you belong.'

'Not "Blood and Rust"?'

Tony shrugged without enthusiasm. 'Maybe. I think "Steppin' Stone" will get more airplay, though. Lots of people like the Monkees.'

The next day, Dave was woken by the ringing telephone. He stumbled through the house to answer. It was Tony.

'Do you know what time it is?' he grumbled.

'It's nearly midday.'

'Is it? Well, that's still too early. What do you want?'

'You're not going to like this. You know that side project Mark Knopfler was working on, the Notting Hillbillies?' Dave knew: the Dire Straits guitarist had hooked up with two musician mates from way back. The three guitarists had apparently been working on an old-school country rock album.

'Yeah, I've been looking forward to it, sounds like fun.'

'Well, it came out today. You'll never guess what they've done: they've covered "Feel Like Going Home".'

'Who's singing?' Please be Knopfler; he's a great player, but I can out-sing him standing on my head. Please be Knopfler.

'Brendan Croker.'

Damn, he's got the pipes for the song. 'Is there a guitar solo? Who plays the solo?' Please not Knopfler, any of the others, but not Knopfler.

'Knopfler.'

Damn. 'Has Nigel heard about it yet?'

'I don't think so, but we'll have to tell him. Look, leave it with me – just because they've released a version, doesn't mean you can't have it on your album too.'

'And as a single, don't forget.'

'We'll see.'

There was no word from Tony for a couple of days, and Dave still hadn't heard anything as he loaded his gear into the Fiesta Estate for another gig. This was a much longer trek than Oxford: the Georgian Theatre in Stockton-on-Tees. Trips like this one made him miss the old days of a proper tour bus, with a driver and bandmates to banter with. Flicking through his in-car collection of cassettes, he rejected the first two Dire Straits albums: he still hadn't forgiven Mark Knopfler for stealing "Feel Like Going Home". *The Who by Numbers* ate up the early miles, although some of the songs – "Success Story", "How Many Friends" – rankled a bit given his own recent experiences of the music industry. Once his career started to decline, it was amazing how many "friends" had stopped returning his calls. It was as if they were afraid that whatever had made him lose popularity would rub off on them.

The M1 traffic started to get bad round about Northampton, so he switched to something more laid-back to help him relax. Jackson Browne's *Late for the Sky* was working well, but the other side of the cassette, *Running on Empty*, was a whole album about the love-hate relationship between the performer and the road. Why did he put himself through it? He tried telling himself that he owed it to his fans, that the buzz when he connected with an audience made it all worthwhile, but deep down he knew that it wasn't the same anymore.

He ground to a standstill shortly after junction 17, and it took him more than an hour to crawl his way to the next junction. Being Dave Masters, rock star, had lost its appeal, but he wasn't sure Dave Masters, ex-rock star, would be any better; the endless didn't-you-used-to-be-famous conversations. Maybe he'd be better off if he was just a nobody; if no one ever recognised his face or name, wouldn't that be better than the constant uncertainty, inevitably followed by another minor humiliation whichever way things turned out? He tried to shrug the thought off; all he needed was to get a good gig under his belt and he'd soon be feeling on top again. Hopefully tonight would be one of those nights where everything clicks.

Eventually he made it to the venue, a lovely old-fashioned building which, in a better mood, he would have appreciated a lot more. It was still another tiny room, though.

He found a payphone and called Tony to let him know all was well.

'Any word yet from Ultimate?' There was no answer. It was a crackly line, so maybe Tony hadn't heard him. 'I said, have you heard anything about the album?'

'Yeah, this morning. I wasn't going to tell you until after the gig, but seeing as you've asked… they're pulling it. They've rejected the whole thing. Nigel said the only good track was "Feel Like Going Home", and he's not confident that your version will stand up commercially against the Notting Hillbillies.'

'But nobody has heard of the Notting bloody Hillbillies.'

'No, but they've heard of Mark Knopfler. His name recognition means column inches and airtime.'

'What about my name recognition?' The resulting pause was longer than Dave was expecting.

'Look at the venues you're playing now – you don't have the same reach anymore, you must know that. Look, Dave, I love your music, always have, but I can see Nigel's point. It's just a shame you missed the original deadline and we didn't get this out a couple of months ago, beat Knopfler to the punch.'

'So are they expecting me to re-record the whole album?' The emotional effort of starting from scratch loomed heavily over Dave, not least with his songwriter's block showing no sign of clearing. He wasn't sure he could face it. Tony took another uncomfortably long pause.

'No, not exactly. They're cancelling your contract, dropping you from the label.'

'What?! I've been with Ultimate my whole career. How can they just dump me?'

'It's business, Dave, what can I say? I've tried talking Nigel round, but they don't see you as a good investment anymore. Look, I'm negotiating the details of the release. We'll get to keep the master tapes and the rights, and I think I can get them to write off the advance. Once that's settled, I can take the album around some other record companies. Take a few days, think about making a few changes – maybe do some more in the style of "Feel Like Going Home" – and we can reconvene once you're back from the frozen north. Have a good show, mate.'

Dave slammed the phone back into the cradle, prompting a concerned look from one of the venue staff.

'Everything all right, pal?' he asked.

'Yeah, bloody marvellous,' replied Dave as he stomped off to the dressing room.

It hadn't been the ideal preparation, and he really wasn't in the mood, but he was a professional so the show must go on. The Georgian Theatre was a similar size to the Jericho, but the manager said it had sold well, close to capacity. Hopefully they were his crowd, the ones who used to pack out the nearby Newcastle City Hall for him.

He waited for the house lights to dim, then walked out onto the stage and launched into "Midnight Rolling". The manager was right; it was a good-sized crowd, but they didn't seem to be going for it yet.

'That was "Midnight Rolling", from my first album, back in 1971. Here's something from my last album.'

'I hope it bloody well is your last album!' shouted a voice in the crowd, prompting a ripple of laughter. Dave ignored him and started up the riff for "Stagefright".

'Get back to the '70s, you old hippy!'

He attacked the vocal with more ferocity than normal, letting his frustration out in his performance. He got a decent round of applause at the end, but suspected he hadn't heard the last of the heckler. "Feelin' Alright", as it increasingly did these days, took on new meanings for him. Despite the deceptively positive feel, the lyrics leant towards something darker and the need to make changes. Did he really need this life anymore?

Sure enough, the interruptions kept coming all through the show. Dave tried to channel his growing anger into his performance. Some of the crowd were with him, but one or two others joined the heckler in baiting Dave at every opportunity. Trying to turn things around, Dave decided to bring out his new trump card.

'This is an old Charlie Rich number.' He picked out the opening notes of "Feel Like Going Home" and the crowd fell silent. Even without the organ, the brilliant old song was working its magic, Dave could just feel it. Then, as he sang the title line at the end of the first verse, his hecklers surfaced again.

'Well, why don't you piss off home then? We won't stop you!'

'See ya, hippy!'

The spell was broken. The crowd was divided between those who were laughing and those who had been enjoying the performance and were on Dave's side.

'Look,' began Dave, abandoning the song, 'just what is your problem? You've paid good money to see a gig. Why bother if you're just going to take the piss?'

'You're the one taking the piss, man. You've been stealing a career for too long. Nobody cares about you '70s hippies anymore. Move on. It's over. No one cares.'

'Stop calling me a hippy. If you want to step up here, I'll show you I'm not all peace and love.' Before the heckler could respond, the bouncers arrived and started to drag him towards the doors. In truth, Dave knew they'd arrive before his bluff could be called, but part of him would have been quite happy to get into it. One way or the other, the violence – given or received – would have been a form of release.

The gig never really got going again after that. The atmosphere was flat and uneasy, and Dave didn't even bother coming back for an encore. It was a five-hour journey and the post-gig euphoria he had been counting on to sustain the long drive home had never materialised.

Five hours turned out to be optimistic. He stopped for a quick kip in a service station car park somewhere near Derby, then got going again an hour or so later. He flew past junction 18, reflecting that this stretch would at least be quicker than on the way up, but he spoke too soon. Moments later he heard a knocking noise from the engine, a rattle that was definitely getting louder. Suddenly, smoke was billowing from under the bonnet and the car lost power. He eased off the deserted motorway and coasted to a halt in the layby. He found a torch, pulled his jacket over his head to protect himself from the rain and went to peer at the engine, not that he knew what he was looking for. His examination left him none the wiser, so he put the hazard lights on, locked the car and trudged back towards the nearest emergency telephone. By the time the AA man reached him a couple of hours later he was soaked through to the bone and his black mood had engulfed him just as thoroughly. Half an hour of poking and prodding brought the conclusion that the car was beyond a roadside fix. In fairness to the bloke, he didn't bat an eyelid when he heard how far Dave would need towing, but a trip to London and back probably wasn't what he'd had in mind at the start of his shift.

'So, what were you coming home from?' asked the AA man as they drove away.

Dave, really not in the mood for chat, toyed with ignoring the question, before grunting as brief an answer as he felt he could get away with. 'A gig.'

'Oh, right, that's good. Anyone I might have heard of?'

He was about to say he was playing the gig, not just attending, but decided against it. He didn't want to admit to who he really was. 'Dave Masters.'

'Oh, I remember him. I didn't know he was still around, mind. Was it worth the long journey?'

Dave knew the answer but couldn't bring himself to say it out loud. He half-turned in the seat and pretended to drop off to sleep.

When the AA man dropped him off at his house, the sun was already up and the birds were singing. As his rescuer started his long journey back up north, Dave went indoors and walked straight to the telephone. He dialled Tony's office number, knowing there would be no one to answer at this time, and left a message on the answering machine.

'Tony, I've had enough; I'm done. That plan of yours, plan B: I'm in. I don't want to be Dave Masters anymore.'

CHAPTER THREE

When Dave woke up, things didn't look any better. The message for Tony had been, in part, just a big dramatic gesture to round off a far-from-perfect night, but on this side of the morning it made a lot of sense. What was left in his life anyway? He had long since lost contact with his family, distance proving an easier option than constantly butting heads with his dad once he had struck out on his own. There was no one who would miss him; the only reason to carry on was for his music, and where was that getting him these days? The things that used to come naturally, effortlessly, had dried up and he couldn't see how he was ever going to get them back. The lippy heckler's words had struck a nerve and Dave suspected that the kid was right: no one cared about his music anymore. He'd had a good run; twenty-plus years since cutting his teeth on the local scene in Birmingham. He remembered how thrilled he was when his teenage band, Tin Biscuit, got a support slot at Mothers not long after it opened. Later he'd see bands like Pink Floyd and Fairport Convention – with a young Richard Thompson, already a mesmerising guitarist – treading the same boards; proper musicians on the same stage he had played. That had helped convince him to give music a go. When his band couldn't get a repeat booking at Mothers, he knew something was missing. He wasn't sure if it was him or the others who weren't good enough so he started playing solo, trying to prove to himself that he wasn't the weak link. Gradually, he found collaborators with a bit more talent than his school-friends. Performing as the Dave Masters Band they worked steadily in pub venues and even made it back to Mothers with a residency on Wednesday nights. After one Mothers gig, a posh lad with a southern accent introduced himself as Tony Broadway, bought Dave a pint and offered to become his manager.

Tony had the right connections, and when he didn't he could quickly convince people that he did. He persuaded Dave to ditch his bass player, pointing out that it was a ruthless business and that anyone who wasn't delivering had to be removed. In came Phil Chambers, newly available after the break-up of local scenesters Habeas Porpoise, and soon the Dave Masters Band was moving up in the world. A three-record deal was secured and the rest was a road paved with hard work and ever-increasing rewards. Phil, Vince, Simon on keyboards and Davey the rhythm guitarist (he had been known as Dave too, but Tony insisted there couldn't be two Daves in the band) were happy as sidemen. Dave was the undoubted leader: writing all the songs, singing and playing lead guitar. It was his name on the posters, but it was a real band; they all contributed musical ideas and they stuck together. That camaraderie on the road was what he missed most of all, even more than decent-sized crowds. One by one, his old bandmates had disappeared. Davey barely made it out of the '70s before the drugs took him. He died on the same day as John Bonham, which meant poor Davey got only a passing reference in the news. Vince, Simon and Phil were all still out there somewhere. Phil had given up the business and moved into teaching sometime in the mid '80s, Simon left around the same time, trading up to tour with the likes of Eric Clapton and Phil Collins, while Vince had stayed with Dave right up until the point Tony said they couldn't afford to keep a band on the road. Dave had Vince's number but never used it; guilt over cutting his old friend adrift stopped him from keeping the friendship alive.

Well, now the business was cutting him adrift. He was fed up and although he had no mortgage to worry about, he was far from rich. Music was all he'd ever known and now even that had left him. If Tony's plan meant a golden handshake from the industry, that wasn't asking too much, was it? It wasn't even the money that bothered him; he just wanted a bit of recognition for his body of work. Tony's plan would give him that and bring an end to his current misery.

Once Tony had made sure that Dave was serious about the message, he told him to keep a relatively low profile while he made arrangements. They cancelled Dave's remaining gigs, agreeing that it wasn't worth replacing the car for a few weeks. Dave changed his will, putting all income from his musical rights into a trust fund that Tony would operate. Tony would pay a regular stipend from the fund to Dave's new identity. Dave had asked why he couldn't just make himself – his new self – the owner of the rights and manage his own money, but Tony persuaded him that they needed a bit more distance, just in case anyone started sniffing around.

For a few weeks, nothing happened. On Tony's instructions, Dave sorted out his house, choosing the possessions he wanted to take with him, mainly records and a couple of guitars – his Ovation and one of his Strats; the rest could go into storage after his "death", ready for rock memorabilia auctions in a few years' time. Tony had forced him to limit himself on his records – there was no way he could take his entire collection, so he had to pick and choose. Tony brought round four record cases, enough to hold about twenty-five albums each, which he maintained should be plenty for a normal person. A hundred albums represented a fraction of Dave's collection. How the hell was he supposed to whittle it down to that? How do you sum up an artist in just one album, or even two or three for the privileged favourites? What albums to sum up the Beatles? Or Dylan? Did he go for albums of sustained brilliance, or particular songs that he couldn't bear to be without? In the end, he went for a mixture of the two, but couldn't escape the feeling that he was leaving too much behind. The one complete back catalogue to make the cut was his own; even though he was walking away from life as Dave Masters, he couldn't bring himself to leave the music behind altogether, even the '80s stuff. He wondered which album someone else would choose to represent his career: *North Face*, perhaps, his third album and the one that produced "Trouble on My Mind", or maybe his live album; certainly not anything later than '79's "Don't Walk, Run". What had been the point of the last ten years?

Despite the frustration at Tony's restrictions, Dave was impressed, as ever, at the detail of his planning. The obituaries were apparently already written, ready to offer to newspapers; the label's decision to cut Dave free from his contract would give Tony a much stronger hand for negotiating a lucrative release of the last album with its oh-so-prescient final track. Dave got the feeling that his manager was quite looking forward to killing him off; Tony got the same pleasure from deal-making that Dave did from playing.

They had argued about where Dave should live. His first suggestion – a tropical island – was dismissed by Tony: it was going to cost serious money to set up a new identity, and even though the sale of Dave's house would comfortably cover those costs, it made sense to be frugal until they knew the extent of the post-death sales boom. Tony had suggested a quiet village somewhere, maybe Cornwall or Devon, where Dave would be out of the way, but Dave wanted access to the London gig scene. Tony wasn't wild about the idea, afraid that it would increase the chance of Dave getting recognised, but he reluctantly gave way once Dave agreed to grow a beard and cut his hair short, anything to make him look less like the public image of Dave Masters.

Dave stayed in as much as possible. He started growing the beard but held off with the haircut until Tony said everything was ready. Then, one morning in mid-April, the phone call came.

'Right, we're on. Everything is ready. I'll be round at yours in half an hour. Make sure you've got your driver's licence and a phone bill or something like that.'

Tony arrived in an unmarked white van, helped to load up Dave's luggage and then drove Dave past a car rental place before heading into a car park down the road.

'Go back and rent a car. Try to be vague, as if you don't care about the details. When they look back on this, we want you to seem like a man with no plans for the future. Once you've got the car, meet me back here.'

He felt that he'd done a good job of acting distracted. He asked for a car without specifying any preferred make, and he agreed a twenty-four-hour rental period with what he felt was a suitably haphazard air. Typically, the young lad behind the counter didn't even react when he gave his name.

Once reunited with Tony, he was instructed to hand over the car keys along with all the ID he had on him. In return Tony gave him the keys to the van and a large brown envelope.

'Right, Dave Masters is about to come to an untimely end, but that's not your problem. You are now Tom Mulvaney.'

'Tom who? Don't I get to choose my new name?'

'The people I had to deal with didn't exactly give us much choice. They can't just invent an identity, they had to wait for something suitable to, well, to come available – and I wasn't about to ask what that involved. I've written the address of your new flat on the envelope, and you'll find the keys inside, along with Tom Mulvaney's driver's licence, national insurance number, bank account details and birth certificate. Once you look suitably unlike you, take some photos and use the rest of it to get a passport. Other than that, you're a blank canvas. Oh, I've put some cash in as well, just to tide you over, but I'll make regular payments once the trust fund is up and running. I'll come to collect the van in a few days. There are some hair clippers in the glove compartment; make sure you use them before you move in to the new place.'

'Where am I meant to do that?'

'I don't know, anywhere between here and the flat. As long as you don't turn up at your new place looking like Dave Masters I don't care. Good luck, Tom. You've got my number if you need anything, but for God's sake be discreet.'

Dave shook Tony's hand and watched him drive off, then glanced at the envelope. The address was in Barnet. He'd never lived in North London before, which was probably why Tony chose it. Checking the A to Z in the van, he saw that it was as far north as Tony could have got while giving him access to the Tube network. He really had reached the end of the line – the Northern Line.

Dave took the clippers into the toilets at South Mimms Services, almost at the end of his run round the M25; it was the first time in twenty years that his hair hadn't been at least over his collar. The radical cut made the grey stand out: he hadn't dyed it in a while and the roots that were previously just beginning to show were now noticeably prominent. With his beard growing in nicely, he wasn't sure he would recognise himself from old album covers and publicity shots. A lyric from "Stagefright" flashed though his head, as he wondered whether his new disguise would hold up for him. As for his eyes – his best feature, Cath had always said – they had long since lost their sparkle. The eyes looking back from the mirror now were sad, bordering on dead. Maybe he'd escaped his old life just in time; maybe it wasn't too late for them to shine again, eventually. He scooped the hair from the basin and dumped it in a bin, symbolically drawing a line under his past life. Goodbye Dave Masters, hello Tom Mulvaney. What kind of a life are you going to carve out? He really was a blank canvas – as blank as the page when he last tried writing lyrics. At least that was all behind him now.

Dave parked the van outside the building and started relaying his stuff up the stairs. It was a pokey little one-bedroom flat, with stained patches on the carpet and a kitchen, dining area and living room all crammed into one tiny open space. It was a big step down from six bedrooms but Dave didn't mind. He wasn't likely to be here for long.

He was finishing his third trip up the stairs, carrying a couple of record boxes, when the door of the flat opposite opened.

'Oh, hello, are you just moving in?' She was short and slim, younger than Dave. He guessed she was around thirty, maybe a little more, which gave him ten years or so on her. There was something about her face – not tired, something deeper than that – but when she smiled her eyes seemed undefeated, twinkling from under a low-hanging blonde fringe. It was a very different sight to his own eyes in the mirror at South Mimms.

'Yeah, that's right. Does that make us neighbours? I'm D…' He had to pause, just briefly, to stop himself from saying his real name. '…Tom, Tom Mulvaney.' This was going to take some getting used to.

'Nice to meet you, Tom. I'm Cindy.'

'Incidentally?'

She grinned impishly, dimples forming around her cheeks, the one on the left slightly deeper than its counterpart. 'I wish – as if anyone would write a song about me. Love that one though.'

'I toured with the Faces.' It slipped out before he could stop himself. It was only when he saw Cindy's eyes widen that he realised what he'd done. 'I mean, I used to follow them, get to as many of their gigs as I could, back in their heyday.'

'Wow, that must have been amazing.' She nodded towards the record case in his hands. 'If that's an indication of your taste in music, I might have to borrow some of those sometime. Anyway, can't stop, I've got to get to work. Nice to meet you, Tom.' He watched her down the stairs, admiring the view and cursing himself. Day one and he'd almost blown it – twice. Hopefully the deception would get easier as he got used to it.

He set about unpacking and organising his new flat. It was already furnished, though most of the furniture looked as past its best as his career. He'd bought a record player to bring with him (Tony wouldn't let him remove the state-of-the-art system from his old place, saying they wouldn't be able to explain its absence), so setting that up was a priority. He dug through the record cases and regretted that the only Faces album he had selected didn't have "Cindy Incidentally" on it. He put the album on anyway, nodding along to the opening riffs of "Bad 'n' Ruin". When the vocal kicked in he found himself wondering whether or not his mum, God miss her, would recognise her son these days.

He filled the kettle for a cup of tea and went to the fridge, only to realise that it was empty – no milk; if it came to that, no tea bags. He took the needle off the record, grabbed his coat and headed to the corner shop he had noticed around the block.

Taking a basket as he went in, he picked up a few essentials – milk, tea, bread – to see him through until he could do a proper shop. Radio 1 was on in the background, playing some Stock, Aitken and Waterman rubbish when he entered, but at least it was followed by something a bit better – real instruments; pop-rock with a bitter-sweet, cynical lyric: something about kissing this thing goodbye. He didn't recognise the singer, but he was enjoying the song.

There was no queue, so he made his way to the till to pay for his shopping.

'Oh, hello again – we must stop meeting like this.' He hadn't recognised her at first, but it was Cindy from the flats.

'Hi, Cindy. I'm not stalking you, honest.' Why had he said that? Why mention stalking at all? She'd think he was a nutter now.

'Who said I'd complain if you were?' She flashed him that crooked smile again and nodded at his basket. 'I see you're the last of the big spenders.'

'Yeah, well, you know how it is. I was going to buy caviar but you seem to have sold out.'

Her eyes sparkled. 'I know – we've had a run on it just lately. It's flying off the shelves.'

The song finished and the DJ back-announced the singer as someone called Del Amitri, before handing over to the news reader. Cindy had just finished putting his shopping through when a familiar name on the news report caught Dave's ear.

''70s rock star Dave Masters is reported to have gone missing. He recently cancelled live appearances and his agent, Tony Broadway, says he hasn't heard from his friend and client for days. He is concerned about Masters' state of mind and says that if anyone sees him, they should contact the authorities.'

'I always quite liked him,' said Cindy. 'What was that big hit he had?'

'"Let You Go"?' offered Dave. That was always the one that people meant.

'No, there was an earlier one: "Trouble on My Mind", that's it. I didn't even know he was still playing; hope he's all right.'

That's why I'm in this mess, he thought, everyone has forgotten me. At least now people were thinking about him again. As he walked towards the flat, he thought of another plus: he had met one of his neighbours and she seemed to have good taste in music. Even better, unless he was misreading the signs, she seemed to have worse taste in men.

CHAPTER FOUR

Apart from doing a full shop at the bigger supermarket in town (hopefully Cindy wouldn't feel he was cheating on her), Dave laid low the next day. He spotted a record shop and promised himself a visit once he was out of hiding. He kept one eye on the TV news, with the sound turned down, leaving both ears available for his record player. That evening, there was a knock on the door. Dave hesitated; no one knew he was here, and Tony had said he'd stay away to make sure no one saw them together. Had something gone wrong already?

He opened the door to find Cindy, holding a bottle of wine.

'Housewarming present,' she said, peering from under her fringe. 'Carefully selected from the extensive range available at work. I thought it might swing me an invitation to nose through your record collection, you know?'

Dave grinned. 'Fine by me, but you'll have to bring a bottle opener from yours. I forgot mine in the move.'

A few minutes later, she was sitting by his vinyl, head at an angle reading the spines.

'I haven't heard of half of these people. The ones I've heard of are great, though; I thought you'd have good taste.'

'What kind of stuff are you into?'

'Oh, all sorts. Oooh – the Faces; is this the one with my song on it?'

'Sadly not. I left that one behind.'

She turned to look quizzically at him. 'Left it behind? Why?'

Damn, he'd slipped up again; better think quickly. 'I, er, had to downsize. I've got a much bigger record collection than this but I knew I wouldn't have room for all of them here. I had to pick out some favourites that I couldn't bear to be without.'

'That makes sense – I noticed that you've only got one or two for most of the bands here. Although you must be really into Dave Masters – you've got loads of his.'

How to explain that? 'Yeah, I got into him early on and just kept going.' He tried to arrange his face into a casual expression but wasn't sure if he was pulling it off. 'I'm a big fan.'

'Has there been any more news about him?' She looked genuinely concerned for him, as if he was dealing with a missing family member or something.

'No, nothing. Not that I've heard anyway.'

'So... how come you're downsizing? Was there a Mrs Mulvaney until recently?' For a moment Dave wondered what she meant by Mrs Mulvaney, then remembered that he was Mr Mulvaney now.

'Umm, yeah, something like that.' How was he meant to explain without getting into uncomfortable territory? 'It's a bit touchy, to be honest. Can we talk about something else?'

'Yeah, of course.' She pulled a record off the shelves. 'As long as we do the talking after you've put this one on.' It was Springsteen's *Born to Run*, a choice which met with Dave's approval.

To avoid any more awkward questions, Dave focused on finding out more about Cindy. For once he had a good reason not to talk about himself. He'd asked if there was a Mr Incidentally, finding out in the process that her actual surname was O'Hara and that she was single again after a long-term relationship. Her ex had hated Bruce Springsteen – more of a Pet Shop Boys fan – and never let her play that kind of stuff.

'You're well rid of him then – never trust a man who prefers synths to guitars.'

'I'll drink to that.'

Cindy noticed his guitars and asked if he played. Dave admitted to "playing a bit", but managed to change the subject. When *Born to Run* finished, Cindy asked him to pick the next record. Dave never needed an excuse to educate a woman's taste in music. A Pete Townshend solo album was first, with Cindy particularly enjoying "Let My Love Open the Door", although Dave baulked a bit when she pointed out that the backing vocals sounded like ELO. After that, Dave tried to shift the mood into something a bit more laid-back. The wine was going down easily and who knew where the evening would end up? The first of his chosen accomplices was Sandy Denny. Cindy loved "It'll Take a Long Time", which gave him the chance to enthuse over Richard Thompson's playing. Sadly, the wine ran out too quickly and his next choice, Joni Mitchell's *Blue*, didn't maintain the desired effect. Cindy seemed to enjoy it at first, but during the third track, "Little Green", she went very quiet for the first time all evening. A few minutes later, when Dave got up to turn the record over, she made her excuses and left. He wasn't sure what he'd done wrong, but maybe it was for the best. There was always another time, and a one-night stand might have made for some awkward encounters on the staircase in the coming weeks.

The Dave Masters story kept rumbling on in the news, with details slowly leaking out, in line with Tony's carefully co-ordinated media plan. The events from that Stockton show were picked over at length, although some accounts had Dave leaping from the stage and exchanging blows with the heckler until security pulled them apart, rather than merely brandishing strong words. The news that he had rented a car and failed to return it was stated repeatedly as an ominous sign.

A couple of days later, Dave hit the front pages. The rental car had been found abandoned near Beachy Head, prompting speculation that he had almost certainly committed suicide. Tony was all over the telly, looking like a man struggling to keep his emotions in check – he really should have been an actor, he was that convincing – saying that the discovery of the car didn't necessarily mean anything, and that if Dave was out there somewhere to please, please get in touch to let him know he's okay.

Dave nipped out to the phone box on the corner and dialled Tony's office number. Tony didn't have an assistant, so there was no risk of anyone else answering.

'Hello, Tony Broadway Representatives.' Tony was masking his grief well, sounding clipped and business-like as usual.

'Hi, Tony, it's… Tom Mulvaney. Just getting in touch to say I'm okay.'

'Ah, you saw me then. Which channel?'

'BBC.'

'Okay. Try to catch the ITV appeal – I choked up a bit more convincingly on that one.'

Dave chuckled. 'I'll look out for it. Everything seems to be going well.'

'Absolutely, I thought a drawn-out discovery would get better coverage than announcing your death straight away. Don't be surprised when they find your body in a day or so. Oh, and I've got to return the van by next Tuesday. It's better if we don't actually meet up, so just leave the keys hidden under the wheel arch.'

'Righteo. Oh, yeah, is it too soon for you to bring me some more of my records?'

'Too right it is, and far too risky; I'm more recognisable than I've ever been thanks to all the news reports. The last thing we want is for the two of us to be seen together.'

After arranging a time for the van to be picked up, Dave headed back to the flat and put the television on. The BBC had Paul Gambaccini summarising his career.

'Dave Masters was never quite in the rock elite, but he was a great songwriter and guitarist who hit a rich vein of form in his 1970s recordings. His '80s output was more hit-and-miss, but 1982 brought his biggest hit, "Let You Go". After that, he seemed to lose his way musically, which possibly contributed to this week's events. He was a great interpreter of other people's songs, and at his best playing live – *Live Masters* from 1978 is one of the great live albums, and if you've never heard his take on the Beatles' "I Saw Her Standing There", you should really check it out. One of the tragedies of his career is his poor timing. If "Let You Go" had been a couple of years later, or if Live Aid had come along a couple of years earlier, he would surely have been on the bill and with his live prowess may well have enjoyed as big a career boost as the likes of Queen and U2.'

Ah, Live Aid. He'd discussed it with Tony but they'd decided not to go for it. Dave had never been that keen on charity gigs – what did other people's problems have to do with him? – and Tony had an aversion to Dave playing without getting paid. To be honest, they had both thought it was going to be a bit of a disaster and best avoided. He wondered how differently things might have been if he'd pushed for a place on the bill.

Gambo was wrapping things up now: 'All in all, he was an extraordinary talent who probably didn't get the appreciation he deserved.'

It was slightly odd to hear himself being talked about in the past tense. So, he was "an extraordinary talent", was he? He wasn't sure about that, but he'd certainly not got the appreciation he deserved. If Tony's plan worked, that was about to change.

Cindy called in later, still in her supermarket uniform.

'I heard the news. Are you okay?'

'Yeah, I'm all right. Still a bit numb – I'm not sure I've taken it in yet.'

She reached out her hand and placed it gently on his upper arm. 'Let me know if you need anything. This is the last thing you need just now on top of your break-up. My friend Amy was in bits when Phil Lynott died.' Dave reassured her that he was fine, and she half-turned towards her front door before pausing. She looked like she was weighing up whether to say something else. Tom decided he'd be up for a sympathy shag if it was offered.

'One more thing – and say no if you want – but could I borrow one of your Dave Masters albums? I've only ever heard his singles and all this talk about how good he was makes me feel I'm missing out, you know?'

The next day, April 21st, they found his body. It was a surreal experience for Dave, not least as he was one of the few people in the world who knew that it wasn't actually his body. Dave wondered whether the corpse, which was found with Dave's ID, was the real Tom Mulvaney, or just some random dead person of approximately the right height and build. It also occurred to him that Tony's contacts may have taken things into their own hands to cause a death rather than waiting for a suitable body to turn up. He hadn't thought that anyone else might have to die for him to disappear and it didn't sit easily with him. It was done now, though: Dave Masters was dead – officially – and he had to make the best of things as Tom Mulvaney.

It suddenly hit him that this was real, not some game he could walk away from. He was officially, legally, dead. He'd get to hear all the nice things that people only say once it's too late, but he'd never be able to go back. His old life as Dave Masters, faded rock star, was a thing of the past; what kind of life was Tom Mulvaney going to have? He might have to get a job, but what the hell was he qualified to do? He had been so focused on the idea of getting free – escaping the diminishing returns of the live circuit, the mile after mile of solitary driving, the meetings with arrogant kids in suits who cared more about bank notes than musical notes – he hadn't considered what he wanted in its place. What had he been set free for? He should be feeling relief, but what he felt most of all was lost. All he'd ever known was the road and the studio. Creating his music and playing it to as many people as possible had been his entire adult life. It had been brilliant, then frustrating, then soul-destroying, but it was him. How was he meant to do something else? Where to even start? He may not always like Dave Masters, but he certainly knew who he was. Who the hell was Tom Mulvaney?

The day after the body was found, the papers all carried his obituary. Some of them used Tony's pre-prepared copy, which carefully dropped in that Dave had finished recording an as-yet-unreleased album shortly before his death, while others drew on their own music critics to sum up his years as a recording artist. There were lots of nice things, including comments from some of his peers. If you judge a man by the level of star that is quoted in his obit, he hadn't done too badly: No Paul McCartney, but Denny Laine shared the story of Paul's reaction to him playing "I Saw Her Standing There". Ian McLagan from the Faces remembered their time on the road together fondly, and even Mark Knopfler, the man who had unwittingly sabotaged his big come-back, said nice things about his guitar-playing.

He made another phone call to Tony and discovered that the funeral had been arranged for the following Tuesday, close to his former home.

'And you're not coming!' insisted Tony. 'Everything's going great and I'm not having you mess it all up by wanting to see everyone crying over you.'

'Oh, come on – how many people get to go to their own funeral? You'd want to see yours given half a chance.'

'Typical rock star – the only thing that eclipses your talent is your damned ego! No, absolutely not; you'll ruin everything. All it would take is for one person to recognise you, one awkward question, and we'll both be in handcuffs before you can say Elvis lives. You're not coming and that's final.'

Final, is it? thought Dave. We'll see about that.

CHAPTER FIVE

Cindy called round that afternoon, on her way back from an early shift in the shop. She said she had almost cried when she heard about them finding the body. Dave had to keep reminding himself that as far as she was concerned, he was just a devoted Dave Masters fan, not the man himself.

She had another reason for calling in, other than seeing how he was coping. One of the local pubs did a monthly music quiz, and some of her friends from work often got a team together. The next one was that night; did he fancy joining them? It sounded like it might be fun – and it was definitely a good excuse to spend some more time with Cindy – so Dave quickly agreed. Cindy said she'd call for him on her way out, around 7.30.

In the meantime, Dave thought again about the funeral. He was torn between Tony's caution and – he'd admit it – his own ego. Tony was right that there would be people there who mustn't recognise him, but how could he stay away? Back in the day he had joked that when he died, he wanted Tony to hire a handful of glamourous models to look hot and cry at the funeral; he'd never expected to be in a position to see if Tony went through with it. Maybe he should see how tonight went at the pub. If his disguise was holding up for a night out, maybe he could risk the funeral too.

7.30 arrived, and Cindy with it. She was wearing a bit more make-up than Dave had seen her in before, and looked great in tight jeans, ankle boots and a low top that forced Dave to concentrate on maintaining eye contact rather than let his gaze slip downwards. The outfit was completed with a faux-leather jacket and a brown fringed handbag: quite the rock chic. The pub was a short walk away. On the way round Cindy was talking about how good the Dave Masters albums she'd borrowed were. She'd taken *North Face* (with "Trouble on My Mind") and *Live Masters*.

They soon found Cindy's friends in the crowded pub. There were three of them tucked in the corner, all in their twenties by the look of them, making Dave and Cindy the old-timers. They had only managed to save one extra chair, so Cindy shoved onto the bench by the wall next to the only other woman, who was introduced as Nicky. The others were Robin, a confident young man with no time for self-doubt, and Dunc, a big grinning lad with a flat-top haircut who offered Dave a cigarette. Dunc worked at Quicksave with the girls, while Robin was one of his old school-friends who had badgered Dunc into roping the others into the quiz team. Nicky reminded Dave of a young Chrissie Hynde but without the bullet-proof self-confidence, if you could imagine such a thing. Dave had done *Top of the Pops* with Chrissie once, miming to "Let You Go" while the Pretenders were in the charts with "I Go to Sleep". He'd always quite fancied her but, unusually for him, he'd been too intimidated to try his luck. Dave checked whether anyone needed another drink, then went to buy for himself and Cindy. The sound system was playing a Squeeze single, the one with the chorus about being tempted.

By the time he got back, someone had brought round some answer sheets, which Robin had taken possession of. Two of them – respectively headed "'80s" and "1s and 2s" – were blank apart from spaces for answers to questions that hadn't been asked yet, while the other (which Robin was carefully scrutinising) featured poorly reproduced photographs.

'Details from album covers,' explained Cindy. 'They always have one round that people can get started on before the first questions.'

'I've got most of them,' added Robin, drawing on his cigarette and passing the sheet across to Dave. 'Any ideas on the others?'

'Number three is the Rolling Stones, *Let It Bleed*.'

'What, the one with the cake?'

'Yeah, and you've got number five wrong.'

Robin visibly bristled. 'I don't think so.'

'The one with the piano. You've said it's Elton John, but that's Supertramp; *Even in the Quietest Moments*.' He went to change the answer, but Robin stopped him.

'Hold on, mate. You don't just go changing it until we've all agreed. What do the rest of you think?'

He looked defiantly round the table. Dunc quickly fell into line and parroted Elton John, while Cindy, bless her, stuck up for Dave.

'I've seen his record collection – Tom knows his music, particularly '70s bands.' Robin turned to face Nicky, leaning over her and putting himself as much between her and Dave as he could. God knows Dave hadn't always treated women well in the past – Cath would vouch for that – but only in terms of being unfaithful. There was something about the way Robin was intimidating Nicky that he really didn't like.

'What do you think, Nicky? Who's got it right – me or the newbie? You know I know this stuff; you've only just met him.'

Nicky dropped her head and squirmed in her seat for a moment, before shrugging and quietly saying, 'Elton John, I suppose.' She looked apologetically at Dave, who smiled back in spite of his growing irritation at Robin.

That set the pattern for the rounds that followed. Dave made a couple of contributions to the '80s round, although lots of the questions were about acts he either hadn't heard of or simply didn't care about. He knew a question about Genesis, largely because Tony – always the bigger prog fan of the two – had tried to get Dave on the bill for one of their '80s tours, and another about Robert Plant, but apart from that he wasn't any threat to Robin's control over the team. The "1s and 2s" was more hit-and-miss. The question master named a single, and the teams had to guess whether it had reached number one or number two. Robin insisted, against Cindy's protests, that Ultravox's "Vienna" – a classic apparently – was a number one, and nobody believed Dave when he assured them that Dave Edmunds had a number one with "I Hear You Knocking". As the evening went on, Dave came to realise that he had to get his answers in quickly; once Robin had suggested something, he wouldn't back down, even if he was only guessing.

The quizmaster told everyone to make sure their team name was on their answer sheets and swap papers with another team. Dave's team (The Rockin' Robins) swapped with Thin Quizzie and waited for the answers. Dave noticed that Thin Quizzie had agreed with him on Supertramp, although he thought better of pointing it out to Robin.

After going through the answers, the quizmaster announced that they would take a ten-minute break before the second half of the quiz, to give everyone the chance to get another drink while he totted up the scores. He put a record on (Springsteen's "Glory Days": not bad at all) and Dunc got a round in. Another record (something by the Pet Shop Boys – Dave and Cindy shared a playful grimace when it started) came and went, and then the scores were read out. Team of Four Head, a bunch of long-hairs in the middle of the pub, were in the lead with twenty-three out of thirty, closely followed by Thin Quizzie and 668 Neighbour of the Beast. The Rockin' Robins were in fifth on a respectable nineteen out of thirty, though Dave reckoned that they could have been tied for the lead if Robin hadn't been so intractable. The next three answer sheets were handed out: "'70s", "'60s" and "Featured Artist".

Once again, Robin took charge. 'Now, don't forget: '60s and '70s are our weakest rounds. If we haven't got a clue, guess Smokey for the '70s and Procol Harum for the '60s. Agreed?'

'Only if we haven't got a clue,' added Cindy. 'Tom probably knows a lot more about the older stuff than the rest of us.' Nicky and Dunc seemed happy with that, though Robin scowled at having his authority challenged.

Dave did pretty well on some of the '70s ones, although he struggled with the questions about punk and new wave acts. In the '60s round, he really shone. For the first time all evening, he was aware of Dunc and Nicky looking first to him for an answer, as questions about Traffic, Cream and the Small Faces all fell nicely.

'Question eight,' said the quizmaster. 'Who had a hit single with "A Whiter Shade of Pale" in 1967?'

'That's the Beatles, isn't it?' said Robin.

'Procol Harum,' responded Dave.

'No, we only put that when we don't know one. We know this one's the Beatles.'

Dave decided to put his foot down. 'No, that one really is Procol Harum. It was their biggest hit.'

'Go on, Robin, put Procol Harum – Tom's on fire in this round.' Nicky and Cindy were fighting his corner now, and even Dunk wasn't supporting Robin, who reluctantly gave in.

The "Featured Artist" round turned out to be about Status Quo. Whoever won the quiz got to pick the featured artist for next time, and Team of Four Head (Dave got the reference now) had evidently won the right to celebrate the champions of no-nonsense heads-down boogie. Dave chipped in with an answer about their earlier, psychedelic-era material, and another naming their original drummer. Dave and Robin had another stand-off over who founded the group with Francis Rossi (they eventually went for Dave's answer of Alan Lancaster, rather than Robin's Rick Parfitt). When the answers were given out, they had done well on the '70s, almost perfectly on the '60s and made a good showing on Status Quo, including the point for Alan Lancaster.

'We're in with a chance here,' said Robin. 'I told you my Procol Harum standby would come up trumps one day.'

A team called E=MC Hammer were last, and as more and more teams were announced, the Rockin' Robins were still in the running. The major shock came when Team of Four Head were announced in third place, despite a strong showing on the Quo round, leaving just Thin Quizzie standing between the Robins and victory.

'There's only one point in it, but tonight's winners are…' They were all leaning forward, as if to usher the words into their ears a fraction of a second sooner. Robin's fist was clenched, his eyes gleaming with glory so close at hand.

'…Thin Quizzie, with forty-two out of sixty, just ahead of the Rockin' Robins on forty-one.'

Robin slumped back into his seat, muttering, 'So close.'

'That's the best we've ever done,' said Nicky. 'Do we win anything for second?'

'Ten quid, I think,' replied Dunc.

'It would have been fifty if we'd won,' moaned Robin. 'Just one point out.'

'Well, maybe you should have listened more to Tom in the first few rounds – we missed out on lots of answers that he knew.' Robin glared at Cindy while Dave said nothing; he was quite happy to let her fight this one for him. Robin went up to the quizmaster to claim their runners-up prize (and to argue about the Supertramp answer). He got back to the table and grabbed his coat.

'Oi, what about the tenner?' said Dave. 'It'll cover another round.'

'Yeah, but I don't want to stay and watch that lot celebrating.' He nodded in the direction of the victorious Quizzies, who seemed delighted with their £50 winnings.

'Okay, but why do you get to take it all? The rest of us are staying, so hand it over.'

'Why should I miss out? We'd never have come second without me.'

'He's right,' added Cindy. 'We'd have come first.' Robin silenced Dunc's laughter with a glare, while Nicky contented herself to a sneaky grin.

'So stay then, have a drink and share the winnings with the rest of us.'

'I told you, I'm going home.' He was glaring aggressively now, though he took a step back when Dave stood up.

'Tell you what,' said Dave, pulling two pound coins from his jeans pocket and slamming them onto the table. 'Here's your share. Now give us the ten quid and clear off, if you're so determined to run out on your team.'

Dave could see Robin bristling – he didn't like being confronted – but was confident that he'd back down. Sure enough, Robin picked up the coins, tossed the ten-pound note onto the table and skulked away scowling. None of the others were in a hurry to leave, and with the tenner subsidising their drinks, everyone was in a good mood. Dave managed to avoid too many questions about what he did, and Nicky seemed a lot more relaxed and chatty now that Robin wasn't dominating the conversation. Dunc seemed all right; not the brightest spark but a nice enough bloke. One of the barmen was working his way round the tables, reminding people that there was live music on the following week, someone called Chris Breslan.

When closing time arrived, it turned out that Dunc lived in the opposite direction to the others, so Cindy asked Dave if he minded the two of them walking Nicky home. It didn't take them too far out of their way, and frankly Dave was enjoying the company of the two younger women. Back in his touring days, he'd have made a play to get both of them back to his hotel room. Back then, he punched seriously above his weight due to the added sexual allure provided by a guitar, a stage and a couple of thousand excited fans. Somehow, he didn't think tonight's performance in the '60s round would have quite the same effect.

'Do we know anything about this Chris Breslan bloke?' asked Dave.

'Just one of the locals, I think,' said Nicky. 'Nothing special, but it might be fun.'

'Shall we give him a go?' asked Cindy.

'I'm up for it, how about you, Tom?'

'Yeah, why not? It'll be nice to see some live music again.' He hadn't been in an audience since that Richard Thompson show, which seemed like a lifetime ago. And in a sense it was.

They dropped Nicky off, then walked another ten minutes to their block of flats. Cindy wanted to know what Dave had made of the others, and agreed with his assessments. She got on well with Nicky, who had been badly treated by men in the past – 'Haven't we all,' she added – and was usually quite shy in groups as a result. Dunc was a bit of a workhorse with the heavy lifting at the shop. Neither her nor Nicky were all that keen on Robin, but as the quiz team had been his idea, they felt stuck with him.

'Well, here we are,' she said as they reached their shared landing. 'I'm glad you came – it was fun seeing someone put Robin in his place.'

'I enjoyed it. Maybe he'll be more willing to listen next time.'

'I doubt it. Goodnight.'

Dave lingered briefly on the landing after Cindy's door closed. He toyed with knocking, trying to get invited in. He could say that he had remembered she wanted to borrow another Dave Masters album, and once he was through the door, who knew where things would end up? It wasn't a threesome with groupies, but he was sure that Cindy liked him. Then again, he was enjoying being normal with Cindy and her friends, so why risk upsetting the apple cart? He put the key in his own door, went in and put a record on (an early Traffic album, a direct result of the '60s round). As Dave

Mason and Steve Winwood sang their hearts out, Dave's thoughts turned to next Tuesday: no one had recognised him tonight, so he was determined to go ahead and gate-crash his own funeral.

CHAPTER SIX

After successfully negotiating the pub quiz with his identity intact, Dave decided to start venturing out a little more. He spent a happy hour in the record shop, rifling through the racks before handing over £10 for four second-hand albums, including the Faces one with "Cindy Incidentally". Ultimate Records had re-released "Let You Go" and it was getting some serious airplay – Radio 1 were playing it to death. When the charts came out, it was straight in at number eight; Tony's plan was working and Dave's music was suddenly finding favour with people who wouldn't give it needle time a month earlier. Even with his music ever-present, his disguise seemed to be holding up well. Dave had promised Tony that he wouldn't turn up at the funeral, but now he had no intention of keeping his word. Anyway, it wouldn't be Dave turning up, would it? It would be Tom Mulvaney.

The funeral was being held near his old home, which involved a tube and train journey of a couple of hours. He had freshly shaved his head, as his original severe crop was starting to grow out by now, and added some coloured sunglasses to a charity-shop suit. He'd read somewhere that your eyes are the most recognisable feature, so he thought it was worth covering them up. The face in the mirror had grown more familiar now, but he remembered how strange it had looked at first; to anyone else, there was no reason to associate this man, this face, with the late Dave Masters.

The turn-out was an anti-climax. Dave deliberately arrived at the last minute, slipping into the crematorium just before showtime and finding a seat at the back. The press had been speculating on which of Dave's rock-star peers would turn out for him, mentioning some of the big names he had toured with over the years. There was no sign of McCartney, Winwood or any of the Faces; no gaggle of glamourous models either. Dave spotted Cath, who looked fantastic – not exactly happy given the circumstances, but she seemed to be in a good place. He was glad; she had deserved better than him, and he hoped she'd managed to find it.

There were a few members of his family – cousins, his dad – but he hadn't had anything to do with them for years. He had adored his mum, but she died when he was a kid. If she had still been around, he couldn't have put her through this, but he doubted his dad would even care. They had fought every step of the way through his teenage years, and once his music career gave him some independence, he was out the door without looking back. Cath had tried to keep the lines of communication open between the two of them, but this was the first time Dave had seen his father since the divorce. Dad looked just the same – uptight and tense – and Dave felt all the old resentments flaring up again.

Tony was there, impeccably turned out and chatting with the vicar. Dave quickly looked away when Tony turned in his direction. At last, he spotted one of his musical peers, his old drummer Vince Preston. He was surprised at the sudden surge of emotion. Vince was the last of the classic line-up, the one who had stuck with him right to the end. Well, until Dave had cast him aside because Tony said they couldn't afford to keep a band on payroll. Vince had filled out a bit, having always been on the chunky side of things, and had lost more hair than Dave remembered. His wife, Mary, had come with him and was clinging to his arm as Vince sniffed into a crumpled tissue. Seeing how upset Vince was made Dave realise how much he missed his friend.

There was some churchy stuff, including a hymn that Dave didn't join in with, just in case someone recognised his singing voice. After a Bible reading, something about choosing the narrow gate because broad is the way that leads to destruction, the vicar stood up to speak. He said that he had never known Dave, other than through his music (he didn't look like a rock fan, but he was the right age, so who knew?), so he was going to hand over to someone who knew him better than most. Tony walked slowly to the front and stood behind the lectern.

'Dave was never a great one for religion,' he began. That was true – Dave had always thought it was a load of rubbish: one of the many battle lines with his dad. 'But he would be pleased to see this gathering – he was always at his best with an audience.' Not much of an audience, Dave thought; some things hadn't changed.

'I first met Dave twenty or so years ago. I was looking to get into the music industry, and I had heard about a talented singer-songwriter working the pub circuit around Birmingham. I went to see him, and I was blown away – he could sing, he could play, he could write. There was so much potential. More than that, when I introduced myself after the gig, I was struck by his hunger to get out there and taste it all. Would I have taken him on if I hadn't liked the guy so much? Probably, but I don't think I'd have carried on working with him for anything like as long. Dave's success changed my life professionally, but, like many people here, he changed my life personally too. He was a good friend, and I miss him. The story that's been repeated a lot on TV in the last week, about him playing a Beatles song when supporting Paul McCartney, sums up Dave's sense of fun. What hasn't been reported was that McCartney's road manager was furious and wanted Dave kicked off the tour. The following night, Dave had to be talked out of playing an entire set of Beatles covers, including a lurid – and entirely fictitious – reworking of "Penny

Lane", with new lyrics casting Denny Laine in an X-rated starring role. If I hadn't threatened to kill the mics myself, he would have gone through with it too. Life on the road can be a grind, and it takes a lot of the good ones. Life on the road with Dave was full of laughter and full of love. I know that the boys who played with him felt they had one of the best jobs in music.' Vince was nodding. And, Dave noticed, crying now.

'The '80s were hard for Dave, professionally and personally. I don't think any of us saw the signs that he was going to take his own life. A few weeks before his death, he finished recording a new album which includes some of the best work he'd done in years. He had so much left to give. It's easy to blame ourselves, but Dave was Dave right to the end. He knew his own mind, and if he had decided he didn't want to carry on, no one was going to talk him out of it. He was always his own man and always stayed true to what he believed. I miss you, mate.'

Was it Dave's imagination, or did Tony deliver that last line while looking directly at him? Had he been spotted? Tony would have something to say about it if he had.

The vicar took over again and said that as Dave's body made its final journey, Tony had requested that they play the last song Dave ever recorded. Dave faked a sniffle to mask his laughter: even a funeral was a marketing opportunity for Tony. The crematorium didn't have a concert-level sound system, but as the organ and guitar opening of "Feel Like Going Home" gently swelled, the song took hold of the room. He had to admit, the lyrics were perfect for the occasion; he hadn't been remotely suicidal when he recorded it, but it certainly sounded like the words of a man who had lost all hope.

From what he could see, just about everyone was in tears now. Damn, he'd got it so right on that song. If it wasn't for Mark bloody Knopfler, all this deception wouldn't have been necessary. Then again, the record-buying public were notoriously unpredictable (translation: bad) in their taste. These were the same people who were buying pre-packaged teen dross and relentless dance music that was heavy on beat and missing anything he could recognise as a song. Without the prompt of a celebrity death, they would probably have overlooked "Feel Like Going Home" and sent another soap star up the charts instead.

After the service, people were milling around outside the crematorium before a wake back at the house, which Tony hadn't yet put up for sale. Dave hung around, listening in to conversations. He stayed out of Vince's sight – if anyone was going to recognise him it was Vince, after all the years they had spent on the road together. Even so, what was the point in coming along at all if he wasn't going to hear what people were saying about him? Vince was talking with Dave's dad, so he edged closer to listen.

'I can't believe he's gone, Mr Masters. He was so full of life – it doesn't seem possible that the man I knew would commit suicide.'

'Well, you knew him better than me, lad. David and I didn't always see eye to eye, but he was a good judge of character. The fact that he kept you with him all those years says something about what he must have thought of you.'

'He was a great bloke – well, when he wasn't being a twat.' Both men laughed, and Dave tried to suppress a smile. 'He gave me so much, just being my friend. I just wish I could have paid him back somehow.'

'I'm sure you did, lad. I just wish I'd got to know him the way you did, that I'd managed to make things right between us before he passed. I loved him, you know; that never stopped, even if I couldn't find a way to let him know.'

This was a side to his dad that he had never seen during his teenage years. Or had he chosen not to see it? On reflection, it can't have been easy for the old man, grieving for his beloved wife while trying to bring up a rebellious son. Dave wished they could have made things up before it was too late, but it would take too much explaining for him to come back from the dead.

'Hi,' said a familiar voice from over his shoulder. 'I don't think we've met. How did you know my ex-husband?' Dave turned and saw Cath, the slight smudging of her mascara the only sign that she wasn't in complete control of her emotions.

'I, er, live around here. I knew him from the pub. I hope you don't mind me coming, I just wanted to pay my respects.' Dave was far from a regular at the local. At first he'd avoided it because he didn't want to be bothered by fans, then because he didn't want to face the fact that the locals didn't care who he was. He did most of his drinking alone in the house, not down the pub, but this was the first cover story that came into his head and he'd blurted it out without thinking. He peered at Cath, looking for any sign that she saw through it.

'Well, it was meant to be a private ceremony, but you're hardly paparazzi, and I'm sure Dave would appreciate the sentiment. Are you coming back to the house afterwards? You're very welcome.'

Dave declined politely and left, quitting while he was ahead. Anyway, that singer was on at the pub tonight, and an evening of live music – and Cindy – sounded much more fun.

When he got to the pub with Cindy, there were mic stands set up on the small stage. By the look of things, Chris Breslan didn't have an electro-acoustic, so they were just pointing one mic at the guitar with another for him to sing into. It was a bit amateur hour, frankly.

There was no sign of Nicky, so Cindy got the drinks in – she reminded Dave he had bought the first round last time – while Dave found a table close to the front. Nicky arrived after a few minutes and they chatted happily, the two girls exchanging work gossip and talking about people Dave didn't know. He didn't mind though; he had put some money in the pub jukebox so the background music was better than last time. While he waited for the show to start, he reflected on the funeral. His dad's words had surprised him, made him wonder whether there might have been a chance for the two of them to make things up, but Vince had surprised him even more; it hadn't occurred to him that his so-called death would affect anyone but himself, that other people would be genuinely hurt as a result.

Just after Dave's selections finished, Eddie the landlord turned off the jukebox, went to the mic stand and called for quiet.

'Thank you for coming, ladies and gentlemen, and now let's give a warm King's Head welcome to Chris Breslan.' With that, he vacated the stage and left it for an awkward looking man, maybe ten or fifteen years younger than Dave, with a cheap acoustic guitar. There was something familiar about his face, but Dave couldn't work out what.

'All right?' he started, looking slightly uncomfortable on the stage. 'You all in the mood for some music?'

'Get on with it!' shouted someone, to general amusement.

'Will do,' the performer replied. 'Here's a Beatles song.'

A bit of an obvious start, thought Dave, until he realised that the lad had delved a little deeper than the ubiquitous standards. "I've Just Seen a Face", from the *Help!* album, just about survived Chris's rudimentary acoustic treatment and Dave couldn't help but smile at the way the lyrics fitted his growing fondness for Cindy. As much as Cindy was enjoying the song, bopping in her seat next to him, he couldn't help but think he could do a much better version of the song.

Nevertheless, the opener did its job and got everyone going. The next one was better, Creedence Clearwater Revival's "Have You Ever Seen the Rain", followed by a straightforward rocker, a Bryan Adams song called "One Night Love Affair" which Dave hadn't heard before. Dave was enjoying himself, and he realised that his amateur-hour assessment was both spot on and a bit unfair. This *was* an amateur act; Chris Breslan was perfectly decent by that standard. As a guitarist he was more cut out for rhythm than lead, but his voice had a warm, likeable quality to it. He seemed to have a range of influences that went beyond his years, which was always a good sign.

Next was a Mike and the Mechanics song, "The Living Years". Dave knew it all too well, largely because Tony's love of prog extended to over-produced pop spin-off solo projects. Fresh from seeing his father at the funeral, the lyrics hit Dave in a way they never had before. Unlike the song's protagonist, he still had time to make things up with his father as they were both still alive. However, his own dead/not dead status put him in the worst of all worlds: there was nothing to stop him reaching out to the old man, and yet it was impossible. How would he even begin to explain the last few weeks, never mind the wasted years between them?

For the next song, Chris reached down into his open guitar case for a harmonica brace, slipping it over his neck and putting a harp in place. The Creedence track encouraged Dave to hope for some Dylan, or maybe Neil Young. No such luck.

'Here's a single from last year – not mine, obviously – which should have gone a lot higher in the charts.'

The song opened with strummed guitar and a nice wailing harmonica line. It felt naggingly familiar, but Dave couldn't place it.

'Oooh, I loved this one,' squealed Nicky.

'Me too,' added Cindy. It wasn't until the lyrics started that Dave realised it was the Del Amitri song from the supermarket. The extra colour of the harmonica made it a bit less one-dimensional than Chris's other numbers and there was a decent round of applause at the end.

'Thanks. I'm going to do one I haven't played live before, just because it seems like the right time to be doing it. This is for Dave Masters.'

Cindy glanced at Dave, who was working hard at not revealing anything on his face. He recognised the chords – he'd played them enough times – of "Let You Go" and found himself mouthing the words in spite of himself.

'I thought we'd run forever, you and me,
Take on the world and leave them in our dust.
But now I fall behind as you surge away from me,
I can't help feeling everything is lost.
You're blazing like a comet, I'm fading like a scar,
You're moving up, I'm stuck here down below.
I loved you then, I love you now, but I lost you long ago,
And now I know I have to let you go.'

The singer was building to the chorus now, reaching for the emotion required by the power ballad. Dave wasn't sure that he quite pulled it off, but it was an honest effort.

'Got to let you go, I've nothing left to give.
I want to walk beside you, but I know you're gonna leave.
I would have given you the world, but now I've come to know
All you want from me is freedom, I have to let you go.'

Everyone at the time had said what a vulnerable, honest lyric it was. Truth was, he'd written it about his relationship with Cath but from her point of view – he was the blazing comet, her the one left behind; any vulnerability was totally fake. By the time it was a hit, he had realised what an arse that made him, but by then he was stuck with having to play it for the rest of his career. At least he was rid of that particular albatross now.

'Rest in peace, Dave,' Chris whispered into the microphone as the generous applause died down; Dave had to stop himself from laughing at that. He saw Cindy glance in his direction and covered it by pinching the bridge of his nose and looking like he was filling up. She put her hand on his arm and squeezed.

'This is my last one. If you enjoyed the set, tell Eddie the landlord so he'll book me again. If you didn't, well, drown your sorrows in more beer, which will also make Eddie happy. This is a Pretenders track.' Dave couldn't resist glancing at Nicky, who he was already thinking of as the local answer to Chrissie Hynde, as Chris bashed out the opening chords to "Back on the Chain Gang". The audience was enjoying it, with a few even providing the 'ooh, ah' backing vocals in the chorus. Dave couldn't help wondering whether he had escaped from a chain gang, or whether he was back on one now that he was anonymous again. Glancing to his left and seeing Cindy bopping away, he decided that this particular chain gang didn't seem all bad.

Later on, when Chris was packing away his gear, Dave wandered over for a chat.

'All right, mate. I enjoyed that.'

'Ah, thanks. It was the first time I've been out on my own. I used to be in a band, but the lead guitarist got married and his wife made him give it up. Not that we were going anywhere; it was just a hobby thing, making the nine-to-five bearable.' He looked up at Dave, then did a double-take. 'Hang on, you look familiar; where have I seen you before?' Dave froze, his mind racing to find a response if Chris said he looked like Dave Masters. 'Aren't you that bloke from the pub quiz the other week? We never used to worry about the Rockin' Robins, but you lot gave us a real run for our money this time.' Dave exhaled with relief, and now he knew where he recognised Chris from: he was one of the Thin Quizzie boys.

'Yes! And now I know why I recognised you. I'm Tom, Tom Mulvaney. You lot certainly know your stuff.'

'Thanks. The quiz team is what's left of my band. If ever you feel like dumping the Robins, you're welcome to come and join us. With your '60s knowledge, we'd be unbeatable.'

Dave promised to think about it, though he knew there was no way he was going to switch without Cindy. When he got back to the table, Cindy and Nicky were enthusing about their shared love of Del Amitri – who, it turned out, were a group, not a bloke called Del. Nicky was offering to tape their album for Cindy, and she agreed to do a copy for Dave too.

As before, they walked Nicky home, although Dave let the girls do most of the chatting. He had really enjoyed the gig, but he was realising that before music had been a job for him, it had been a bit of fun, like it was for Chris. He just couldn't focus on the girls' conversation, so when Cindy accepted Nicky's offer to come in, Dave made his excuses and went on home. If only there was some way he could get back to playing music for its own sake. Maybe he should see about getting a job at a pub like the King's Head; at least then he could be close to events like tonight's one more often.

CHAPTER SEVEN

Dave didn't sleep well that night, thinking about Chris's set at the King's Head. Why couldn't he do something similar? Low-key local gigs for beer money, all covers and none of his own songs: where was the harm in that? Tony wouldn't see it that way, but who said he had to know? He got up and started pulling out records, checking the track listings and putting together a possible set list. At around 9am the doorbell rang. It was Cindy, freshly laundered after her night on the sofa at Nicky's. She looked past him to the many albums strewn across the floor.

'Blimey, you've been busy.'

Dave grinned sheepishly. 'Seeing the gig last night, got me to thinking why don't I give something like that a go? I'm at least as good a player as that bloke.' Yeah, and then some. 'I was looking for songs.'

'Oooh, that sounds exciting. Can I be your official groupie?'

Dave paused for a moment, trying to read whether this was a serious offer or just joking about. He suspected the latter, more's the pity, but you never know.

'Well, I have very exacting standards – perhaps we can arrange an audition?'

Cindy laughed and playfully hit Dave on the arm. 'Behave.

I'm not that kind of girl. Well, not often. I've got something for you.' She put her hand in her pocket and pulled out a cassette. 'Nicky recorded that Del Amitri album for you.'

'That's great. Say thanks when you see her. Tell her I owe her one.'

'There's something else. What do you think?' She thrust a crumpled, photocopied flyer into his hand. It said "Live at the Harlesden Mean Fiddler, Red Stewart and the Two-Faced Faces perform the music of Rod Stewart and the Faces".

'It's a tribute act,' she explained. 'They're playing tomorrow, and my shift finishes early enough that we could make it in time for the show. I know you saw the real thing lots of times, but I never did. This is as close as I'm ever going to get.'

Dave wasn't sure about the idea of a tribute act – it seemed a bit parasitical. If they were any good, why not make their own music instead of leeching off other people's talent? Then again, the Faces were always a great night out (even more so if you hung out with them after the show), and it was another chance to spend time with Cindy.

'Yeah, why not?'

Once Cindy had left him and headed off to work, he made some coffee and thought more about the gig. The Mean Fiddler was a decent venue – a big step up from the rooms he'd been playing at the end. It would take five or six hundred if they filled it; they must be doing all right, this tribute band. Who knew that so many people would pay for something they knew wasn't the real thing?

After getting some breakfast inside him, he headed round the corner for the phone box.

'Tony Broadway Representatives.'

'Hi, Tony, it's… Tom.'

'Hi, Tom, how are you doing? It must be, oh let me think, all of a day since I saw you last.'

'Ah, I thought you'd spotted me. Nice bit of promotion for "Feel Like Going Home", by the way.'

'Stop changing the subject. It was a stupid risk – I even saw you talking with Cath at one point. What if she had recognised you?'

'She didn't, though. Admit it, you only recognised me because you were on the lookout; everybody else thinks I'm dead, so they don't expect to see me.'

Tony sighed. 'Maybe, but it was still a stupid, egocentric, vainglorious thing to do.'

'Well, what do you expect? What was the phrase you used – something about me always knowing my own mind and being my own man?' Dave sniffed a couple of times before mimicking Tony's end to the eulogy: 'I miss you, mate.'

'Oh, piss off. Anyway, things are going well with the record company. With sales of your back catalogue on the up, they want to buy back the rights to your last album. Their plan is to put out a *Best Of* compilation and to stick "Feel Like Going Home" on it as the lead single.'

'What about the Notting Hillbillies? I thought I couldn't compete with them commercially.'

'That's all changed; you've got the golden ticket – you're dead. That's publicity even Mark Knopfler can't generate. I'm pretending to talk to a couple of other companies, just to get a better deal out of Ultimate, punish them for not staying loyal when you were alive, but it makes sense to stick with them. They've still got the rights for your old stuff, and I think this compilation is a great idea.'

'Will I have a say in what goes on it?'

'Well, that's the trouble with being dead: you can hardly turn up for the meetings, can you? You'll just have to trust me to look after your best interests, as ever.'

'Thank God I never did that prog album you wanted me to try – you'd be packing the *Best Of* with twenty-minute sagas about elves and lost unicorns or something. Seriously though, it has to really be my best work – I don't want it full of naff '80s stuff.'

'Tell you what, as long as you don't take more than a couple of days to get your thoughts together, you give me a track listing and I'll do my best to get something that you'll be happy with. No promises – they won't give me the final say – but I'll see what I can do. Anyway, apart from gate-crashing funerals, what have you been up to? How is life back in the real world?'

'It's all right. I've made some friends, been to an amateur pub gig.'

'Anyone I should be checking out?'

Dave laughed. 'Hardly. Nice bloke, decent voice, but doing it for the love rather than the money, and just as well. Oh yes, and I'm off to a proper gig tomorrow night. Well, I say a proper gig: it's a tribute act, the Faces, playing at the Mean Fiddler.'

'The Faces, crikey, that takes me back. Do you remember that tour I got you with them?'

'You know what they say: if you can remember a tour with the Faces, you weren't really there. What do you know about tribute acts? What should I be expecting?'

'To be honest, it's not something I've ever looked into. Let me know how it goes – I'm always on the look for fresh talent, particularly now that my number-one client has gone and killed himself.'

Dave put aside the plans for the covers set and threw himself into selecting tracks for his compilation. As soon as he got back to the flat, he pulled out his old albums and started making notes. He knew this material better than anyone – which songs worked best in concert, which ones connected with his audience (back when he had an audience). His main aim was to shift the public perception away from the '80s synth years, remind them of his true musical identity. He had tried to get back to it with his last couple of albums, but the sales figures marked them as the worst of his career. They had a few good songs that deserved a second chance, though. He was tempted to leave "Let You Go" off the record altogether, but he knew the record company would never go for that, particularly now it was a hit all over again. He really was stuck with the damn thing.

As he flicked through the albums one by one, scribbling down song titles in two lists headed "definitely" and "maybe", it occurred to him that there was enough quality material to warrant a double album. He'd have to mention that to Tony. It felt good to immerse himself in his own songs, although it was a bittersweet feeling: after all, he'd never get to play them in front of an audience again. Had he been too hasty in closing the door on being Dave Masters?

The journey to the Mean Fiddler took about an hour on the tube, giving Dave and Cindy plenty of time to chat. He was still dodging questions about his past and what he did for a living. Cindy was excited by the idea of him playing a pub gig, and pleaded with him to include "Cindy Incidentally" on the set list. It wasn't a bad idea; "Stay with Me" was possibly a better-known Faces track, but there was a nasty edge to the lyric that reminded Dave too much of the way he had treated women over the years. As good as the song was, he didn't really want to celebrate that part of his life anymore. Not that it was his life – Tom Mulvaney had never done anything like that, as far as he knew. This wasn't just a clean start professionally; he was going to do better with his relationships too. He was glad that things with Cindy were still going slowly. He was becoming fonder and fonder of her and realised that he wanted more than just a one-night stand.

'What about a Dave Masters track?' Cindy asked once they changed onto the Bakerloo line. 'You're such a big fan, and you saw how well "Let You Go" went down the other night.'

'Maybe, I'm not sure, though. It's only the discerning fans like the two of us who get how good he really is – I mean, was.'

'I don't know about that; since he died, he's been all over the radio. Not just "Let You go". I heard one called "Jack of Hearts" the other day, it was pretty good.'

'Yeah, from his second album. Not his first single but his first hit.' And one that Dave wouldn't leave off the compilation even if he could. He had a lot of affection for that song; would it do any harm to include it in the covers set?

They got to the gig, bought some drinks and waited. Cindy kept asking him what the real Faces had been like live. He said they were a tough act for this lot to follow – one of the best live outfits he saw back in those days. If the tribute band was half as good, it should be a good night.

It was a fantastic night. Red Stewart and the Two-Faced Faces strode onto the Mean Fiddler stage with all the swagger of their namesakes, and right from the first note their set had the laddish playfulness that he remembered. They included a mixture of Faces favourites and Rod solo singles, but nothing after he sold his soul to spandex trousers in America. They didn't take themselves too seriously, and band and audience alike seemed committed to having a good time. They even got a John Peel lookalike to come on stage miming with a mandolin for "Maggie May", in honour of the famous *Top of the Pops* appearance. In short, everyone left fully satisfied. It wasn't the Faces, but it was the next best thing. There was lots of singing along from the audience, and Dave made a point of singing directly at Cindy when they played her song, which reduced her to giggles. When they played "Ooh La La", Cindy sang along with the bit about wishing she'd learned life's lessons when she was younger, then leaned over to Dave and said, 'Forget "Cindy Incidentally", this should be my song.'

They tumbled out of the venue and waited for their tube, chatting and laughing. Once their train came and everyone piled on, they had to stand. At one point, the train juddered suddenly and Cindy lost her balance. Instinctively, Dave reached out to catch her and stop her from falling. She didn't seem in any hurry to extricate herself from his arms, which was fine by Dave. All in all, it was turning into a great night out.

They lingered at Cindy's door, and she looked coyly out from under her fringe.

'Thanks for tonight, it was great,' she said.

'It was your idea – I should be thanking you.'

'Do you mind if I don't invite you in? Not just yet.'

That wasn't what Dave had been hoping for, but the last three words held out hope for the future – there was no need to rush things. And anyway, she hadn't seen him play guitar yet. How could she resist him after that?

'Sure, whatever you want.' He raised his eyebrows in what he hoped would come across as a light-hearted follow-up. 'Of course, if it makes it easier, you could always come in to mine instead – anything to help.' She hit him, but her smile made it clear that she had got the joke.

'Stop it. It's just that… well, in the past I've rushed into things and it's never worked out well. I really like you and—'

Dave cut her off. 'It's okay, I don't mind. And you don't have to explain anything. When – if – you're ready, I'll be here.'

'No, I want to. It's just that… I don't know anything about you, you're a closed book. I know about your break-up – well, I know that it happened, but nothing more than that. I don't know what your job is or how you earn your money. I don't know where you used to live or what you did there. I know more about your record collection than I do about you. You're a mystery, Tom Mulvaney. It scares me how much I like you and how little I know you, you know?'

Dave stepped back half a pace. 'Fair enough. I have been pretty closed off. I don't think I'm ready to open up just yet, but soon. I promise.'

She stepped forward and gave him a long hug, eventually lifting her head. For a moment Dave thought she was going to kiss him, in spite of everything she had just said. Maybe for a moment she was, but if so she thought better of it. Instead, she veered off and kissed him very softly, very tenderly on the cheek, which was almost more wonderful. Almost.

'I can wait,' she said. 'Just don't take too long.'

It wasn't the end to the evening that Dave had been anticipating and it had given him lots to think about. What the hell was he going to tell Cindy about his past? He certainly couldn't tell her the truth.

CHAPTER EIGHT

Dave didn't get a lot of sleep that night, and not for the reason he had been hoping earlier. His last conversation with Cindy was proving a lot harder to reconcile with the facts of his life. If he told her – or anyone – who he really was, everything could collapse quicker than a heart-throb's pop career. Was pretending to be dead against the law? Was it fair on Cindy to lay that kind of secret on her? Was it even smart? But Cindy was the first good thing to happen to him in years. If he couldn't share something real with her, they didn't have a chance. The question was, did Tom Mulvaney have anything real to share?

When he wasn't agonising over Cindy, his mind kept circling back to the gig. It was one of the more enthusiastic crowds he'd seen in recent years. Even if their guitarist wasn't as good as Ronnie Wood, their bass player as lyrical as Ronnie Lane and their keyboard player was a poor man's Ian McLagan, the crowd reacted like it was the real thing. People wanted to relive their memories, or – like Cindy – to experience bands they missed first time around. Judging by the turn-out, there was money in the tribute game too. If he was going to go back to performing, why not go the whole hog and play his own songs as a Dave Masters tribute act?

Maybe the idea was crazy, fuelled by frustration, wishful thinking and lack of sleep, but it all seemed to make sense. He could tell Cindy that he used to be a musician – session player, no public profile to speak of – and he was looking for the right project to get back into the game, a project he'd just found thanks to her. It would make her feel he was letting her in – most of it was true; the only lies were the low-profile history (and, of course, the fact that he had faked his own death and taken on someone else's identity, but best not to sweat the small stuff). Giving up on the idea of sleep, Dave got up and went to find his list of songs for the compilation. He decided to have another go at the running order. After all, this album may well provide the bedrock of his set list for the foreseeable future.

After an hour or so, Dave had a list of twenty-six songs from across his entire career, including "Feel Like Going Home". It was weighted heavily towards his '70s heyday, with seventeen tracks from his first five albums, including four each from *North Face* and *Live Masters*. The rest of the albums provided a couple of songs each, apart from 1984's *Fork in the Road*, which just about managed one (and even that had only scraped in).

Finally, with daylight bleeding through the curtains and what sounded like an audition for a birds (not Byrds) tribute act filling the skies, Dave went back to bed with enough peace of mind to finally sleep.

Morning broke, but not for Dave. It was another post-noon start for him, and he found a note pushed under his front door when he dragged himself out of bed. It was from Cindy, just checking he was okay. She was a sweet kid. Who was he trying to fool? She was great. If he let this one slip through his fingers, he was a bigger idiot than anyone had previously realised. He went to find some paper and wrote a reply to push through her door. 'Slept in late – nothing to worry about. That's just what us men of mystery do. Done a lot of thinking – all of it good.' How to sign off?

"Love" felt premature, but "Cheers" a bit too detached after the conversation the night before. How about just signing his name? As with a song, sometimes less is more. Add a kiss? Why not. Dave re-read the note he had just written and froze on the spot. He crumpled it up and started again. He'd only gone and signed it "Dave" instead of "Tom". Cindy may have said she wanted him to open up, but that was a bit too honest.

If one half of his problem was someone who wanted him to be more up-front, the other was someone who wanted him to fade into the background and stay hidden. There was no way Tony would go for the suggestion of Dave becoming his own tribute act. He had to get on and do it, then present it as something that could earn Tony some money. First of all, he had to prove that the concept worked, then he had to find a band to play with him. He had an idea of how he was going to do both of those things.

While the rest of the world was out at work, Dave popped down to the King's Head in the afternoon, hoping to find Eddie behind the bar. When he walked in, Eddie was polishing glasses with only a couple of domino-playing pensioners to keep business ticking over. Dave greeted him, ordered a pint and sat down on a barstool.

'Will you have one yourself?' he asked.

'That's very kind; don't mind if I do.' Eddie poured another pint before adding, 'You've been in here before, haven't you? I'm usually good with faces.' Not too good, I hope, thought Dave.

'Yeah, I was in for the pub quiz the other night, then again for the gig the other Tuesday.'

'That's right – you were with that stroppy bloke who complained about coming second.'

'Yeah, sorry about him. He's a friend of a friend; that was the first time I'd met him. I've got to say, this is great little boozer. I know the pub quiz is a monthly thing, how often do you put on gigs?'

'No fixed pattern really. I try to do something most weeks, just to pull in a few more punters. Did you enjoy it then?'

That was a tricky one to answer: he was trying to get on the landlord's good side, but he also wanted to present himself as a superior option for future bookings.

'Yeah, I thought he made a decent fist of it. I was chatting with him afterwards and he seems like a nice lad. Thing is, I reckon you could get more people in with someone better.'

Eddie seemed to see where Dave was leading him. 'And I suppose you could direct me to that someone, could you?' Here was where Dave had to start filling in Tom's blanks.

'Funnily enough, I could. I'm a musician – guitarist. Thing is, I've just moved to the area and I'm working up a live set as a tribute act.'

Eddie looked interested. 'Go on. Who do you do?'

'Dave Masters. People have always told me I sing a bit like him, and although my natural playing style is a bit different, I've been in the game long enough to adapt – if you're not flexible, you just don't get the work. Anyway, since he died you can't turn on the radio without hearing his songs, so I reckon it's the perfect time for someone like me to get out there and help someone like you sell more beer.'

Eddie chuckled. 'Well, that's the goal at the end of the day, isn't it? But how do I know you're any good? And more to the point, how do the punters know you're any good? Chris is a regular and he's got mates who come along to support him. No offence, but if no one round here knows who you are, how can I be sure you'll bring in a thirsty audience?'

Dave had expected that one. 'Funny you should ask. I've got a proposal that won't cost you a penny and will give you a chance to sample the merchandise.'

Later that day, list in hand, Dave phoned Tony. He explained his reasons for wanting the compilation to be a double album.

'Yeah, I'd been thinking the same thing. Once we've put "Let You Go" and "Trouble on My Mind" on an album, plus "Feels Like Going Home", of course, there won't be enough big-hitters left to make a subsequent volume two look attractive. The best way to maximise revenue from your back catalogue is with a double.'

Dave was offended. 'Maximise revenue? I was thinking about making it a worthy summary of my whole career – on a single album too many tracks that deserve a place would be pushed out by the ones that have to be there.'

'Well, you keep thinking about worthy summaries, and I'll keep thinking about the bottom line. When we both stick to what we're good at, that's when the magic happens. Anyway, I've agreed a deal for the last album. If "Feel Like Going Home" flops as a single, I don't think they'll release the album at all, but if that and the compilation are both hits, they'll have it out for Christmas.'

'Great. When does the single come out?'

'As soon as they can organise getting it pressed. They might wait until they're sure they've squeezed "Let You Go" for all it's worth, but they won't want to risk the Notting Hillbillies beating them to the punch. Anyway, how was that tribute band?'

'Do you know what? They were great, really good. I was a bit sceptical at first – I only went because of some girl – but the crowd loved them.'

'And the girl?'

Dave paused, would Tony object to him letting someone get close? Better play the innocent. 'She loved them too.'

'That's not what I meant. After the gig, was she forthcoming? Did you get some?'

'Tony, please. A gentleman never reveals such matters.'

'You *have* changed. I'll take that as a no then.'

Dave didn't rise to the bait. He had got what he wanted out of two conversations today. Tony's news from the record company meant that conditions for his return to performing were likely to be perfect in the next couple of weeks, and Eddie had agreed to his plan to prove his appeal. Now all he had to do was practice the rust away. That and find a way to convince Cindy that he was worth the risk.

The first of those was easy to achieve. He worked his way through the songs on his proposed album track listing, spending more time on some than others. He hadn't decided yet which would make his first set, but if everything went well he'd need to be up to speed on most or all of them before long. As for Cindy, that was going to take a lot of careful thought and a little preparation.

A few nights later, Dave was seeing to the final touches when he heard the much-anticipated knock at the door. He was wearing his smartest non-stage gear (though stopping short of a tie, obviously). He opened the door to reveal Cindy, looking fantastic in a clingy top with the kind of scarf that Janis Joplin used to carry off with aplomb. Janis never looked half as good as Cindy, though.

'The note said dress to impress – how did I do?' She smiled, almost managing to hide her nerves.

'Consider me impressed – you look amazing.'

'You've scrubbed up pretty well yourself, and something smells great.'

'Well, you said you wanted to get to know more about me, so how's this for starters? I am a hugely limited cook, but I've been told that my chilli con carne is a masterpiece. Are you okay with spicy food? I've done a milder one as well, just in case.' Fortunately Cindy was happy to give the full-strength version a go, although Dave had toned it down a little bit. He wanted everything to go just right.

'Here's the deal,' he said as they sat down at his kitchen table; he hadn't got a tablecloth, but he had managed to rustle up some candles. 'Tonight you can ask all the questions you want, and I'll answer them. If you don't like what you hear, well, at least we've given things a go.'

Cindy smiled, her face lighting up. 'Thanks, Tom. I get that this isn't easy for you, for whatever reason. I really appreciate that you're going to all this trouble.'

'Trouble? It's a pleasure – how often do I get to enjoy the company of a beautiful lady *and* the finest chilli this side of the Thames?'

She had lots of questions. She seemed to buy Dave's story about being a session musician. She wanted to know more about Cath and why he had relocated. Dave had spent a lot of time thinking about what to say when that came up, and he'd decided to tell the whole truth. It was risky, but on balance it was more of a risk to add extra lies when he was already covering up such a whopper.

'Okay, here's the bit that doesn't make me look good. I wasn't a very good husband. I was too young and I was in love with the rock 'n' roll life. Let's just say that I didn't behave myself and she was very forgiving about it, right up until the point when she wasn't. I don't blame her for leaving me; if anything she should have got rid of me a lot sooner.'

Cindy was very quiet at that. Dave knew it was a risk telling his potential girlfriend that he had history as a cheating louse, but she said she wanted open and honest.

'Wow,' she said at last. 'I wasn't expecting that. Would things be different now?'

'Absolutely. It's like that Faces song about wishing we knew better when we were younger. I've learned my lesson. I don't intend to lose an amazing woman again.' He reached out his hand and took Cindy's, squeezing it gently. She didn't pull away.

Cindy was the first to break the silence. 'The thing is, my ex.'

'The Pet Shop Boys fan.'

She grinned. 'That's the one – you love bringing up his faults, don't you? He used to cheat on me, and then make me feel it was my fault. I didn't have the sense of your Cath and I stayed with him until he left me for someone at his work, someone younger with a prettier face and bigger tits.'

'Not possible.' A stunned look flashed across Cindy's face, prompting Dave to clarify: 'The face. I meant the face. I wasn't talking about your… I meant your face.'

Cindy was trying to suppress a laugh now, enjoying Dave's discomfort rather than taking offence. Eventually she let him off the hook and carried on.

'Anyway, the point is that I promised I'd be careful if I met someone else, that I wouldn't get involved with anyone who might treat me like that again.'

'Well, I don't expect you to trust me just yet, but the fact I told you my less-than-impressive past will hopefully count for something – if I was just trying to get into your knickers, I'd have kept that particular character flaw to myself.'

'True.'

'And whatever else I've done in the past, I have never – ever – made anyone listen to the Pet Shop Boys.'

CHAPTER NINE

Cindy didn't stay the night, but Dave hadn't expected her to. He didn't want to mess this up, and if that meant taking it at her pace, he could live with that. He told her about the Dave Masters tribute act idea, and she even came up with a great name he could use. He got a proper kiss as she was leaving, though, soft and warm and just long enough to feel like it was lasting forever and that it ended far too soon.

"Let You Go" started to drift down the charts, having stalled at number two. Dave's regret at missing out on his first number-one single was tempered with relief that it hadn't been with that bloody song. Thanks, Adamski, whoever the hell you are, for keeping it off the top spot. "Feel Like Going Home" was quickly released, with a marketing push promoting it as the last song Dave Masters recorded, the one that reduced everyone to tears at his funeral. By the time the next quiz night at the King's Head came round, it was in the top ten and moving up the charts.

Chris and his mates were there again, this time playing as Quizzie Little Thing Called Love. Dave went over and said hello before the quiz started, and said he had an idea to put to them afterwards if they didn't have to hurry away. He checked a couple of things with Eddie and introduced himself to the quizmaster.

By the time he got back to the table, he had missed a successful coup. Robin looked sulky as Cindy clutched the team pen, refusing to yield either it or the early starter sheet – lyrics this time – to Robin. As a result, it was a much more democratic process with everyone able to contribute. Robin was still argumentative, but he had lost control.

The quiz started properly, as before, with the '80s round and the team thought they'd done okay. Next was an intros round, and Dave almost choked on his pint when the driving riff from "Trouble on My Mind" featured in question four. Robin tried to convince everyone that it was The Eagles, but when Cindy said Tom had all Dave Masters' albums, that settled the matter.

They were doing better than last time, but Quizzie Little Thing Called Love stayed narrowly ahead of them, and a team called This Is Not a Drill, Please Evacuate the Pub were also in contention. As suggested by their name, Chris and his mates had chosen Queen for the featured artist round, a band Dave remembered crossing paths with in his early days. His breakthrough had come before theirs, but he couldn't dispute the fact that they'd done better than him over the long haul.

After papers were swapped and answers read out, the quizmaster announced they were going to do something a bit different this week.

'Instead of me playing records while we tot up the scores, we've got some live music for you.' Dave was already out of his seat and heading to the stage. 'Some chancer has asked for a gig and Eddie wants to see if he's any good before booking him. So, let's have a big welcome for Tom Mulvaney.'

By now Dave had his Ovation plugged in and was staring into the face of an audience for the first time in a couple of months.

'Good evening. Tonight, Leslie, I'm going to be Dave Masters.' There was some applause – most notably from Cindy, Nicky and Dunc, and a little laughter at his *Stars in Their Eyes* reference, but as he started strumming the opening of "Feel Like Going Home", the pub fell silent. He felt the mood change when he started singing. He didn't know what they had been expecting, but he was sure it wasn't for him to sound as much like himself as he did. He couldn't recreate the record perfectly – he'd have killed for that organ – but he had worked up a pretty good acoustic version of the song. The hushed pub lapped up the emotive, picked solo that took the place of the more rounded electric one from the record and he knew the song was landing long before the enthusiastic applause at the end.

'I've only got time for one more, so here's one from the *Live Masters* album. I think you'll all know it.' With that he launched into "I Saw Her Standing There", and long before the end the room was tapping, nodding and bouncing along, even joining in with the singing in places. He'd nailed it: the applause was rapturous, coursing through Dave like a drug he had forgotten he needed. One final comment into the microphone – 'Thank you very much, and I hope I've passed the audition' – and he unplugged his guitar and was off. Eddie followed him to the microphone.

'That was Tom Mulvaney. Would anyone like to see him play a full set of Dave Masters songs next Tuesday?' The cheer was an emphatic yes. 'Right, next Tuesday it is then. Bring your drinking money.'

Dave's team, this week called The Quicksave All Stars, had scored better than last week – forty-four out of sixty – but only finished third, behind Chris and his mates and eventual winners Trivia Newton John. Robin tried to start an inquest into where they had gone wrong, but the others only wanted to talk about Dave.

'If I closed my eyes, I'd have thought it was really him,' said Dunc. 'Rather than some old beardy bloke in a pub.'

'None taken,' replied Dave, laughing. He excused himself and headed over to Chris's table.

'Bloody hell, Tom, that was amazing,' said Chris. 'I feel embarrassed now – you must think I'm useless.'

Dave shrugged, 'I've been doing this a bit longer than you, I expect. No, fair play, you held your audience, and that's not nothing. You did a good gig.' He looked around the table, including the others in the conversation. 'Chris tells me you boys used to be in a band together. Next Tuesday I'm playing solo and acoustic, but after that I'm looking for a band. How about we get together to rehearse and see if we're a good fit? I think we can make a few quid and have a good time doing it.'

They didn't need persuading. Numbers and addresses were swapped – Dave really had to get a phone put into his flat – and a rehearsal date and venue was pencilled in. He arranged to meet up with Chris first, to walk him through a few songs so he could teach them to the rest of the band. Nobody was committing to anything yet, but Dave could see that Chris's mates were excited. He went back to Cindy and the others, read the question in her eyes and simply said, 'They're in.'

Dave was rehearsing hard for the solo show, and was surprised at how much he was looking forward to it. It had been a long time since he felt like this about playing live; it had become so commonplace, not quite just a job but certainly getting that way. Now that he'd had time away, he was remembering everything he loved about it.

On Sunday evening, a couple of days before the solo show, Chris came round with his guitar and the two of them set up in Dave's flat. They worked through half a dozen numbers and Dave pumped him for more information about the band. While Dave's music wasn't an exact fit with what they had played before, it wouldn't be a huge stylistic stretch for them to play his material.

'They get what this is, though, yeah? It's about recreating Dave Masters' sound rather than creating something new of our own.' It felt weird discussing his music as if he was someone else.

'Sure, sure. We'd been talking about what we could do to get back into playing again since Richie left, and we knew we needed a lead guitarist – you've already seen it was never going to be me. We never imagined we'd find someone as good as you, so we just want to run with this and see where it goes. We were only a covers band anyway; we've no delusions about having a unique sound.'

That sounded hopeful, as long as the others all saw things the same way; the last thing Dave wanted was a power struggle with some ambitious kid. If this was going to work, they had to stick closely to Dave's old material. Before Chris left, Dave gave him a cassette of songs to pass on to the others before their first rehearsal together.

'Will do, Tom,' said Chris. 'Good luck on Tuesday – we're all coming.'

The night before the gig, Cindy had invited Dave to come round to hers. She said she wanted to return the favour and cook for him. Dave accepted enthusiastically. Possibly too enthusiastically, as Cindy looked flustered.

'I mean, it really is just for a meal. I still need time before…' She petered out and Dave gave her what he hoped was a reassuring smile.

'I know, it's okay. A meal sounds wonderful.'

She looked relieved. She told him not to worry about getting dressed up; she'd really appreciated the effort he went to, but she'd rather have a relaxed evening if that was all right with him. Dave would have agreed to anything at that point – anything short of the Pet Shop Boys providing the soundtrack: a man has his limits. They settled on Monday night, the day before his big return gig. Cindy thought it might help him to take his mind off things and not get too nervous. He didn't argue, though he knew that a touch of nerves always helped.

She answered the door, standing coyly in jeans and a simple top but still looking fantastic, those irresistible eyes peeping out from under her fringe. Dave handed over the bottle of wine he had brought and decided to take his chances with a kiss on the cheek.

She didn't recoil, which was a good start. Once inside, he could see that the layout of her flat was much the same as his, yet she had made it much more homely. Photos and nick-nacks were scattered around; flowers and carefully draped scarves added flashes of colour. There was nothing substantial he could pin down, but it made all the difference. At best, his flat was an okay place to crash; hers was a home.

She told him to pick out something from her record collection, or fetch something from his if he preferred. Dave didn't need a second invitation to check out her taste. There was a definite overlap with his – Springsteen, Clapton, Beatles and several acceptable *Best Of* albums – Queen, Blondie, the Pretenders – although compilations were often a sign of a casual rather than committed fan. He noticed the best of The Eagles, and made a mental note to introduce her to the Ozark Mountain Daredevils sometime. There was also a lot of stuff that he knew of but had never really listened to, post-punk acts like Elvis Costello and U2, as well as the likes of Kate Bush and several names that meant nothing to him.

Dave asked her to pick something he wouldn't know but might like. She scanned her albums and made her choice: an album by someone called Hothouse Flowers. The cover had long-haired blokes with acoustic instruments – guitar, mandolin, even an accordion – which was encouraging. As she lowered the needle onto the record, Dave realised how much he wanted to like it, for Cindy to impress him with her taste. The first track started with a basic guitar riff, with the other instruments adding deftly judged flourishes before the whole thing exploded joyously about a minute in, reminding Dave of early Van Morrison. The lyrics seemed to be a man apologising for treating a woman badly. He wasn't sure whether it was a deliberate dig from Cindy, but if it was it somehow made her selection even better. She was the perfect woman: beautiful, funny and with great taste in music. Could it get any better than that?

It could: the food was wonderful. Cindy was a much better cook than him, having rustled up a three-course meal which made his chilli look unimaginative. There was home-made soup, followed by the most delicious pork ribs Dave could ever remember tasting (no mean feat considering he had eaten barbeque on tour in Texas in the mid '70s). There was even a home-made banoffee pie for dessert.

'Wow, just wow,' said Dave. 'It's a good job we're taking things slow; I'm not sure I could do myself justice tonight – after all that food I can barely walk, let along anything else. How come you're such an amazing cook?'

Cindy shrugged. 'I had a good teacher. My mum said cooking is a great way to show people how much you care for them. I think that was one of the reasons I was so touched when you wanted to cook for me.'

'Tell me about your mum.'

'She was an old-fashioned London girl. She saw through my ex, of course. It's just a shame I wasted three years not seeing what she spotted straight away.'

'You said was – past tense. What happened?'

'She died a couple of years ago, not long after my ex left me. I think the two things together knocked me hard.'

'I'm sorry.' Cindy shrugged away his condolences, and he decided to risk a dangerous question. 'What do you think she would have made of me?'

Cindy paused before answering, fixing Dave with a forensic look that made him feel exposed. 'I think she'd like you, probably.' She paused again. 'Funny, charming, good-looking. She'd warn me to be careful, though. "Leopards don't change their spots, Cinders", that's what she always said.'

'Well, I've changed mine, but I can't blame you if you're not convinced yet.'

'How long were you with your ex? Do you mind me asking about her?'

'No, you're all right – new era of openness and all that. We were married for six years, but we were a couple for six or seven years before that.'

'That's a long time. Did you have any kids? You've never mentioned any.'

'No, no kids, and thank God for that: at least it was only the two lives I ruined. Well, no kids I know about anyway; with all those casual on-the-road flings, there could be some out there somewhere, but no one ever got in touch.' It would be ironic if there were: Cath had wanted kids, and Dave had reluctantly gone along with trying, despite dreading the responsibility that fatherhood would demand of him. When, eventually, they found out that Cath couldn't have children, she was devastated, but he hadn't been able to hide his relief. That had been another factor in the break-up: the sensitivity and support she had needed from him was more than he was capable of providing. In retrospect he felt more ashamed of that than of all his flings put together. 'What about you? Were you ever tempted to have kids?'

Cindy looked down behind her fringe, pausing before answering. 'I'd have to find the right man first. I thought for a while that me and Pet Shop Bastard might end up with a family, but… well, you know how that worked out.'

They talked for a bit, swapping memories of their late mothers. Dave was happy to stay late (or even to stay over, though he wasn't going to be the one to suggest it), but Cindy insisted he went back to his flat before it got too late. 'Big day tomorrow,' she had said, as if he was a kid getting ready to start school.

Dave got to the King's Head early to make sure there were no problems with the sound system and stuck his planned set list to the floor by his mic stand. He only had forty-five minutes, so he'd picked songs that always went down well. "Feel Like Going Home" was still going up the charts – up to number three, with no sign of sales slowing – so if he kept that till the end, it should get him an encore. He didn't just want a good gig; he wanted to smash it out of the park. Chris and the others were coming, and he wanted to impress them. It was fun to be playing a small gig like this, but the more he thought about it, the more he reasoned that if that Faces tribute act could fill bigger rooms, why couldn't he work up to that level again? He wanted to impress Cindy too, for different reasons.

He was opening with "Trouble on My Mind", something most of the audience would know. He followed his usual practice of getting the first number out of the way before actually speaking to the crowd. He could see Cindy and Nicky sitting together near the front (he had reserved them a table), grinning like teenagers at their first school disco. It was just as well he had kept seats for them, as the pub was packed. The room was warming up nicely as he cranked out the final chords of his old hit. He had planned to say something at this point, but on instinct, he crashed straight into "Feelin' Alright". The way the song gathered momentum always helped to give the set a sense of propulsion, and the energy in the room went up another notch – even more so once he let loose on his solo. He saw Chris and his mates whispering excitedly to one another at the bar.

'Hello, King's Head. Enjoying it so far?' A good response. Already the audience was right where he wanted them. 'I'm Dave ReMastered. Any fans of the real Dave Masters in tonight?' Another big cheer. 'Anyone who was a fan before he died?' A few cheered (including Cindy), but more people laughed in recognition of their newbie status. 'Well, I've been listening to Dave Masters for as long as I can remember.' Technically true, if a bit misleading. 'And if you like what you're hearing, I can heartily recommend his albums – not that I'll see any of the royalties.' Very misleading, that one; still, not as big a lie as the one he was living every day. He had planned for "Let You Go" next, to get it out of the way, but with the energy so high he shifted his running order around. 'Here's the title track from his last album. This is called "Steel Strings".'

It was another cover and a bit less driving than the opening two numbers, so "Let You Go" made more sense after it. Next came "Vagabond Life", which would have been a single if he'd had his way back in '72, then "Jack of Hearts" and "Stagefright", each better received than the one before. It was going perfectly.

'This is my last one, and you knew you'd be hearing this tonight. There's plenty of time for drinking after I finish, so no need to rush away, but as for me, I "Feel Like Going Home".'

Cindy and Nicky weren't alone in swaying along; one bloke even held his cigarette lighter aloft. Dave wrung as much emotion as he could out of the solo and felt himself going to that place where it just flowed. He could still deliver on the nights that didn't happen, but when it did he knew to just go with it. He was slightly over his forty-five minutes – very unprofessional – but nobody seemed to mind. He took a final bow to rapturous applause, set his guitar on its stand and stepped off the back of the stage. The applause went on and on, and Chris and his mates started a chant of, 'We want more.' Dave made eye contact with Eddie, who gave him the nod. To loud cheers, he took the stage again and plugged in.

'Thank you very much. Any requests?' He knew what they'd ask for; in fact, he had deliberately left it out of the main set for this very purpose. 'Okay, but I'm going to need you to join in on the high bits.' With that, he launched into "I Saw Her Standing There", making eye contact with Cindy as much as he could, particularly with the line about not dancing with anyone else. He meant it too; he felt like a different man to the one who had serial-cheated on Cath all those years ago.

As he drank his complimentary post-gig pint, with his fee from Eddie warming his pocket and Cindy glowing with pride alongside him, Dave politely chatted to several punters who came up to ask him about his plans for future gigs. There was no doubt about it: Dave ReMastered was up and running. As good as tonight was, it would be even better if he could get this band together. Talking of which, he was meeting Chris and the others for a first run-through tomorrow evening.

CHAPTER TEN

They were meeting at Chris's house, his garage being the band's usual rehearsal space. Dave arrived to find the others already there, equipment set up and ready to go. They exchanged a few pleasantries, but he could tell they just wanted to get on with it.

'Okay, let me just say this up front,' said Dave. 'Let's treat this as an audition – for all of us. I haven't heard most of you play and I don't know what you're like; you've seen me play, but you've got no idea what I'm like to work with. I need to see if you're any good and you need to decide whether I'm a complete dick. Let's play, then see how we feel at the end of it. I mean, I'm pretty confident that I'm not a dick, but that's for you to decide.'

At Dave's suggestion, they started with one of the songs from their old band. It would let them ease into the session comfortably and give Dave the chance to see them at their best. They opted for one of the songs Chris had played at the King's Head, "One Night Love Affair", with Chris again on lead vocals. With the additional musicians, the song took on a rockier feel and Dave soon found room for his Strat, adding texture and then cutting loose with a wailing solo at the appropriate moment. Judging by the looks he saw the others exchanging, they liked what they heard.

'Very nice, lads,' he said after the extended jam came to an end. 'Shall we try some of my songs now?'

'Your songs?' asked Shaun the keyboard player. 'I thought we were doing Dave Masters covers – has the plan changed?'

Damn, he'd done it again. 'That's what I mean, something from my set of Dave Masters songs.' He had got away with it, but he really couldn't afford to keep doing that.

'How about "Trouble on My Mind"?' suggested Chris.

'Works for me. How well do you guys know it? Do I need to teach it, or shall we just dive in and work it out?'

'I think we've got it,' said Chris. 'We had a pre-rehearsal rehearsal, to make sure we didn't show ourselves up.'

'Right, well, I'll expect this to be perfect then. A-one, two, three, four.' It wasn't perfect, but it wasn't half bad. The drummer – Jonjo – was a bit heavy-handed, but he kept time okay. Shaun had a nice touch which would have more room to show itself in Dave's material than the likes of "One Night Love Affair". Chris's rhythm guitar made more sense with a band to share the load, but the star of the show was Martin on bass. His languid, fluid lines added a melodic touch that caught Dave's ear immediately. It was the bass he had been most worried about; Phil Chambers' playing had been such an important part of his band's original sound, and based on what he was hearing now, he reckoned Martin could handle it.

Dave called out a couple of instructions as they played but saved most of his comments to the end. He was being pickier than he had intended, but only because the first run-through was so much better than he had expected. These guys had the chemistry of a group who knew each other's playing and enough musical know-how between them to adapt to his material. This could work.

After blasting their way through a few songs ("Vagabond Life" was a particular favourite, particularly with Shaun, who got to take a solo on it), Chris went off to put the kettle on.

Dave took the opportunity to sidle up to Martin. 'Some nice playing there. I thought I'd have to show you the bass part for "Out of My Depth", but you nailed it first time.'

'Thanks. I've been working on the songs ever since Chris passed on your cassette. I hadn't realised Dave Masters had such a good bass player – he's great, isn't he?'

'Yeah, Phil Chambers is one of the best. You've got big shoes to fill, but you're making a good start.'

'*I've* got big shoes? Coming from the man who has to play Dave Masters.' Flattery will get you everywhere, son, thought Dave.

By the time Chris arrived with tea and biscuits, Dave had moved on to Jonjo.

'So, who are your favourite drummers?'

'Neil Peart, obviously. Keith Moon.' It wasn't what Dave was hoping to hear. Great drummers, sure, but heavy on either technique – particularly Peart – or pyrotechnics. Dave preferred drummers with a bit more subtlety and feel.

'What do you make of Ringo?'

Jonjo laughed. 'What was it Lennon said? Ringo wasn't even the best drummer in the Beatles.'

'He never said that – and if that's what he thought, why did he use Ringo on so much of his solo stuff afterwards? Go back and listen to Ringo again. He's not a technician like Peart, but his sense of what the song needs, when to hold off and when to push, is second to none. Vince Preston had a lot in common with Ringo. You could learn a lot from him.'

Jonjo scowled. 'Are you saying I'm not up to it?' He looked pissed off.

'Not at all – you've been great so far. It's just that we need to get every part of the sound right, and the drums are vital. Also, listen to Ringo again – listen to *Abbey Road* – just for your own sake; he's phenomenal.' That seemed to placate Jonjo, but Dave decided to change the subject and talk with the others before he put his foot in it again. Jonjo hadn't been great so far, he'd been okay at best, but there was room to bring him up to speed. He had no worries about the rest of them, though; if only he could sub in the real Vince Preston, this band could go far.

He asked the lads about the gigs they had played in the past: what size rooms, that kind of thing. What he really wanted to know was how experienced they were, how likely they were to freeze once they got in front of a big audience. Apparently, they had a good three years of gigging under their belts, but that probably only amounted to a couple of dozen shows, and all with much smaller crowds than he had in mind.

They tried a few more songs, including "Feel Like Going Home". Chris took the acoustic part, with Dave only singing until it was time for his electric solo. He had to rein Shaun in a bit on the organ, but after some fine-tuning, they nailed it. All in all, Dave was delighted with how they had done for a first rehearsal together.

As the others started packing way, Dave announced that he was going to nip to the toilet and give them all a few minutes to bitch about him behind his back. When he came back, they were all sitting expectantly.

'Well?' he asked. 'What's the verdict?'

'Looks like you've got yourself a band,' said Chris with a grin. 'Next stop, Wembley!'

The next stop wouldn't be Wembley, but Dave knew just the place. There was a two hundred-capacity venue in Camden that he had played a year or so back, the Dublin Castle. When Dave dropped in to talk to the manager, he remembered the bloke and hoped that he hadn't been too memorable himself.

'Dave Masters tribute act, you say? Yeah, I could be interested in that. We've just had someone pull out of a gig next month, so there's a gap in our schedule. Could you do Friday 15th?' That only gave him three weeks to fine-tune the band; less time than he had wanted, but it should be enough. They agreed a fee (Tony would have got him more money) and how long they would be expected to play for, then swapped contact details – the first time Dave had given out his new phone number.

'Of course, the real Dave Masters played here last year. Good gig, but we didn't get many through the doors. Now he's dead, he's suddenly popular again. Funny how that works, isn't it?' Yeah, thought Dave. Almost as if it was planned. He couldn't resist finding out what kind of impression he'd made back then.

'What was he like, Dave Masters?'

'He was good: still knew how to put on a show. Hard to like off stage, though: he seemed to think it was all a bit beneath him, like he resented having to play places like this. You could see it was all getting to him; I wasn't surprised when I heard the news – he had demons on his shoulders, if you get my meaning. He was a rock 'n' roll suicide waiting to happen.'

Dave nodded, resisting the urge to argue. It wasn't demons on his shoulders, whatever that meant; it was tiredness. He was knackered after driving all the way from Newcastle to get to the gig – part of Tony's say-yes-to-everything policy at the time. As for resenting the size of the venue, well, after the career he'd had he was entitled to better, wasn't he?

He phoned Chris as soon as he got home, using him as his aide-de-camp within the band, and soon everyone had agreed to rehearsals on Monday and Wednesday evenings, plus all day on Saturdays. Dave would have liked to make it every evening through the week (he was sure Cindy would understand) but some of the boys in the band pushed back against that idea.

At the first of the rehearsals, Dave stuck up a set list on the garage wall. 'These are the songs I think we should get up to speed on. Once we're happy with them we can look to expand our repertoire, but this should give us a good set plus options for encores.' The lads gathered round, making appreciative noises for their respective favourites.

'Can't we add in some other stuff?' asked Jonjo. 'Some other '70s bands – some Who or Zeppelin, maybe, even some Rush.' Stuff with showy drum parts, Dave noted.

'Hardly: we're a tribute band,' Chris reminded him. 'If Dave Masters didn't play it, we don't play it. Simple as.'

'Besides, there are plenty of covers already,' added Martin. 'Maybe Dave Masters didn't have the confidence that his own writing could carry an album or a show on its own.'

Dave bristled at that – whatever his faults, he had never lacked self-confidence. He just liked the idea of curating music in his shows, sharing the stuff he loved with his audience. He bit his tongue, though; after all, how was Tom Mulvaney supposed to know what had been going on in Dave Masters' head? He had to sit on Jonjo a bit in rehearsal, getting him to tone down and play more like Vince, but the rest of them were shaping up nicely. Martin, Shaun and Chris were even getting the hang of the harmonised backing vocals, another integral part of the classic Dave Masters sound. They wouldn't be as tight as he would have liked by the 15th, but he thought they could carry it off.

That meant it was time to make the phone call, the one he had been dreading and looking forward to ever since he started taking the idea of Dave ReMastered seriously.

'Hello, Tony Broadway Representatives.'

'Hi, Tony, it's… Tom.' The name was coming more naturally now, but he still put a pause in for Tony, a brief recognition of their shared conspiracy. 'How's things?'

'All ship-shape and shiny. Ultimate are going with the double Best Of album, and they're rushing it out next week, to make the most of the "Feel Like Going Home" success. Midweek sales figures are putting the single in with a chance of going to number one – we should have killed you off years ago.'

'Yeah, but if we had, I'd never have recorded "Feel Like Going Home", would I?'

'True. I'm sure I'd have found a way round that, though.

They're calling the album *Vagabond Life: The Best of Dave Masters*.'

'That's nice. I wondered if they'd go for "Feel Like Going Home".'

'No, they're saving that for the last album, the one they rejected. It's coming out in time for Christmas. They're afraid that the post-death bubble might burst, so they want to cash in while they can. It's just a shame I can't get you out on the road promoting it all.'

'Funny you should mention that. There's something I need to tell you.'

Tony was apoplectic when he heard about the gig in the King's Head, and even more so when Dave told him about the band rehearsals.

'Look, calm down. I don't look anything like me anymore. Everyone thinks I'm just a bloke who can sing and play like Dave Masters. Why would anyone suspect anything?'

'It just seems like a bit of an idiotic risk if you ask me. Don't forget, it's not just you on the line here. I've done some pretty dodgy things to make this happen – I have no intention of doing time for you.'

Dave hadn't thought about Tony's risk, only his own, but he shrugged the objection away. 'It won't come to that. Everybody knows that Dave Masters is dead, so why would they expect him to be playing as his own tribute act? You're right, it is idiotic, it's ridiculous. The thing is, it's so ridiculous no one will even suspect it.' They argued for a few minutes, and Dave decided it was best to let Tony rant for a while to get it out of his system before he moved on to what he really wanted to say. Eventually, once the storm subsided, he said his piece.

'Anyway, we're playing the Dublin Castle on the 15th. Why don't you come and catch the show? As you said, now's the time to promote the compilation, and playing the songs to paying audiences is the best way to make that happen. If people want to hear those songs live, I'm the closest to the real thing they're going to get. With you managing, it's perfect from a marketing point of view: we make money on the record sales through the trust fund, plus a second income stream through the tribute band; the better each side of that does, the better it is for the other.' Tony said nothing. 'Come on, you know there's money to be made here. You could be the first manager in the business to get a dead artist out on the road. Even if you can't tell anyone, you'll know you've done something not even Peter Grant or Colonel Parker could pull off.'

Tony went quiet for a moment. Had Dave's nod to his professional ego paid off? 'Well, no promises, but I'll try to get along. If I like what I see I'll come backstage and introduce myself. If I do, for God's sake pretend we haven't met before.'

CHAPTER ELEVEN

In between band rehearsals, Dave made as much time as he could for Cindy. He also started dropping in on folk clubs with open-mic nights, particularly ones around Camden. He'd get up, play a few covers, with always at least one Dave Masters number. Before he finished, he'd mention the gig at the Dublin Castle and leave some flyers. Cindy came along when she could, which was fine by Dave.

As Tony had predicted, "Feel Like Going Home" went to number one that week, Dave's first ever chart-topper. Even better, it meant that "Let You Go" wasn't his biggest hit anymore. Everywhere he went, a much younger version of his face peered out from billboards and buses. Ultimate were really pushing the marketing budget for the compilation, far more than they ever had when he was up-and-coming rather than a dead has-been. Tony had managed to get almost all of the songs Dave wanted on the album, keeping the balance of material about right. The inside of the gatefold sleeve was littered with photos from back in the day – including one of a boyish version of himself and his Tin Biscuit bandmates on stage at Mothers – along with images of posters and ticket stubs from old shows. He felt a pang of nostalgia for some of the venues he'd played: Hammersmith Odeon, of course,

Glasgow Apollo, even the Troubadour and Carnegie Hall on the other side of the pond. He'd love to get back to bigger rooms, but for now he was happy just to be playing again. There were plenty of photos of Vince, Phil, Simon and Davey too, making the album of celebration of the band, not just Dave himself, which was as it should be; he knew how big a part they had played in getting him to the top, even if he hadn't been able to stay there. He felt quite nostalgic poring over the images as he listened to the album. The liner notes included a tribute from Ian McLagan, recalling the time Dave spent supporting the Faces and praising Dave's guitar-playing, his showmanship and his ability to connect with an audience. Tony had pulled out all the stops on this. It really was beautifully put together.

He was listening to the album when Cindy called round after work. She was as excited as him about it, and admitted that she'd popped out during her break and bought a copy herself.

'I mean, I always liked his singles, but since borrowing your albums, I've really got into him. It's a shame I never got to see the real thing – not that you aren't a good substitute.'

He couldn't resist fishing for a compliment, one that would work whichever way Cindy chose to answer. 'I bet you wish I was as good-looking as him.'

'I never said that, did I? You can't compete with the younger him from the album covers, but if he was still around I think you'd give him a run for his money.'

Dave took the compliment with a smile. He wished he could let her in on his secret, particularly as he was working so hard on being open with her about everything else.

Rehearsals were going well, mostly. Jonjo was still an issue, but Chris and Martin were gently reining him in (as was Shaun, though with a lot less tact than his bandmates). During a break, the others confided to Dave that Jonjo had tended to overplay in their previous band.

'We even considered replacing him with a drum machine,' said Shaun. 'You know the difference between a drum machine and a real drummer? You only have to punch information into a drum machine once.' If there was one thing that united all bands at every level, it was drummer jokes. Dave thought he'd heard them all, but that was a new one on him.

Dave had brought *Vagabond Life* along, and he showed the lads the photos on the inside of the gatefold. They had been discussing how much effort they should make to look like the original band. They had all quickly agreed not to go down the road of wearing wigs – Dave didn't want to start looking too much like his old self, and the others didn't want to make themselves look ridiculous – but it was worth trying to get the general look right. Dave already knew what he was going to wear, as he had kept some of his stage gear for old time's sake. The others perused the photos, laughing at the '70s fashion choices and commenting on what they already owned that might do the job, with a few jokes about charity-shop rejects, mostly at Martin's expense.

The last thing to establish was the running order. Dave had never run his band as a dictatorship; he expected the final say, but he wanted his musicians to have some ownership of the material too. There were certain songs – "Feel Like Going Home", "Let You Go" (regrettably), "Trouble on My Mind", "Jack of Hearts" and "I Saw Her Standing There" – which were non-negotiable, and others that everyone agreed were among their stronger songs, but that still left room for four or five selections from the others they had rehearsed.

'I still think we should stick in a Who cover,' grumbled Jonjo. 'What about "Won't Get Fooled Again"? There's a cracking drum part in that.'

'What about "Won't Tell You Again", meathead?' replied Shaun. 'It's a tribute act, not a covers band.'

Jonjo wasn't going to let it go. 'I don't know how this Vince Preston bloke stayed with Dave Masters so long; he doesn't get to really cut loose on any of these.'

That was too much for Dave. 'Vince Preston was a fantastic drummer, and a fantastic bloke.' After the briefest of pauses he remembered to add, 'By all accounts. You'll not find anyone better at serving the needs of the song. He could throw down with the best of them if required, but it isn't that kind of music.' Once the Who had been dismissed, they quickly agreed which songs to include. The biggest debate was whether to include "I Saw Her Standing There" in the main set or to hold it back for a crowd-pleasing encore.

Dave woke up around noon on the day of the gig and took a moment to reflect on the day ahead. He was confident in his own ability, but it was big step for the others. None of them had played a venue this size before. Was he asking too much? Had he been too ambitious in taking the early date, rushing them into their first gig together? There was only one way to find out.

Their soundcheck was at 5pm; Shaun was collecting everyone in his transit. Dave was the penultimate pick-up before Chris, and then on to Camden and glory. Dave noticed a card that had been shoved under his door since he got in last night. He opened it and smiled: Cindy. The card had a cartoon guitar on the front and the message, 'You rock my world!' Inside she had written a good-luck message: 'To my very own rock star – the best Dave Masters I've ever seen!' If only she knew.

Dave spent a leisurely afternoon, taking a late lunch and checking over his gear for the show. He put the radio on and, not for the first time that week, heard his live version of "Feelin' Alright" from the compilation album. It was getting a lot of airplay and Tony said it was being released as the follow-up single to "Feel Like Going Home". It was a good choice, even if it was another one where he – or rather, the Dave Masters trust fund – wouldn't get songwriting royalties. It occurred to him that maybe they should change up the set list and start with "Feelin' Alright" to make the most of it.

At about 3.30 – he had told the others to allow lots of time for traffic – the van arrived and Dave loaded his guitars and amp into the back before climbing into the front passenger seat that he'd reserved the previous day, claiming seniority and the fact that his back had a good ten to fifteen years on the rest of them. Shaun was behind the wheel, with Jonjo in the back.

'Where's Martin?' he asked. 'I thought me and Chris were the last two.'

'Yeah, he was only meant to be working a half-day today, but something came up and he couldn't get away. We've got his equipment, but he's meeting us at the venue. He sounded pretty calm about it.'

'Okay, well, no problem. At least it's one less set of farts in the van. Let's get Chris.' Dave's calm exterior masked a mind switching rapidly into risk-analysis and problem-solving mode. They couldn't do the show without a bass player, so he needed a plan B, just in case Martin didn't make it. No one apart from him could handle the lead guitar parts, so Chris would have to switch to bass.

He was going to make a joke of it and let Chris know when they got to his house, but he changed his mind as soon as Chris set foot out of his front door. He was so pale he looked like he was halfway through applying make-up for a Kiss tribute act. Chris smiled weakly at the others and climbed into the back with Jonjo. He asked where Martin was, and Shaun repeated the news. If it was possible, Chris went even paler.

'Ah, it'll be fine. Martin's a pretty reliable bloke, isn't he?' asked Dave, hoping to God that the bass player lived up to the unflappable air he gave off. He diverted any further discussion about Martin's absence by suggesting "Feelin' Alright" as the opener, which the others all agreed was a good idea.

The London traffic was shocking. A journey that should have been comfortably less than an hour took twice as long as it should have done. By the time they got to the gig, it was almost soundcheck time. While the others started to set everything up, making comments – some nervous, some excited – about the size of the room as they went, Dave set out to find the manager. Apart from apologising for their lateness, he wanted to give Cindy and Nicky's names for the guestlist, and to make sure the bouncers knew they were friends of the band and welcome backstage afterwards.

By the time he got to the stage, most of the setting-up had been done.

'What do we do about Martin?' asked Chris, sweat mixing with his paler-than-usual complexion to make him resemble a nervous rice pudding.

'Well, once we've got the levels right on your guitar, you can play the bass for the soundcheck. There's still plenty of time for him to make it before the show, so let's make sure his gear is ready.' No need to worry the lad with the idea of actually swapping instruments for the show itself, not yet.

Jonjo seemed more interested in flailing away at his kit than actually helping anyone with the soundcheck, but eventually they got the levels right on all the instruments. Dave suggested running through "Feelin' Alright", without saying that it was partly so that Chris could start the show with something he'd already played if it came to it. He called out a few chord changes to help Chris, who stumbled over the unfamiliar part a few times. Once Dave was convinced that there was nothing to be gained by playing on, he called time on the soundcheck.

On the way to the dressing room, he called Shaun aside. 'Is Chris always this nervous before gigs?' he asked.

'I've not seen him this bad before, but he's usually the one most likely to throw up, yeah.'

'Okay, keep an eye on him, will you? If Martin doesn't make it, we're going to need him to play bass, and I don't want to stress him out any more than we have to.'

'Leave it to me, boss.'

There was a plate of sandwiches in the dressing room, along with some bottles of chilled beer, plus water and fruit. Not a bad rider at this level, but not a patch on what he had once been used to. Poor Chris took one look at the food and instantly ran to the gents with his hand over his mouth.

'Told you,' said Shaun.

The band sat around waiting – Dave had forgotten how much of playing live consisted of that. He could see that the others were nervous, although they were all showing it in different ways. Chris was constantly standing up, sitting down, talking fifteen to the dozen and rushing off to the gents every few minutes. Jonjo was endlessly tapping his drumsticks on anything that came into his orbit, including at one point the sandwich that Shaun had just picked up, and which was then swiftly thrown into Jonjo's face. Dave wondered if the band was about to self-destruct in a fight before they had even played a note, but Jonjo just laughed it off. As for Shaun, he was asking lots of questions about the typical Dave Masters audience in terms of the male/female split, or about the regular crowd at this venue. Dave quickly realised that each question was a different way of asking how likely he was to get laid. Well, fair enough; like many rock stars, Dave had first picked up a guitar to impress the girls. Things hadn't changed so much, really: there was one particular girl he desperately wanted to impress tonight.

Half an hour to showtime and still no Martin. The clock on the wall seemed to be speeding up: twenty minutes now. Dave decided that he finally had to say something.

'Okay, it's nearly time to go on. I'm going to have a word with the manager here to see how much leeway we've got for delaying the start of the show. We might be able to buy an extra half hour or so, but certainly no more than that. Hopefully Martin will make it anyway, but if he doesn't we'll just have to adapt. Chris: until he gets here, you'll have to move over to bass.'

'But I haven't rehearsed the bass parts, I… I…' Chris petered out, looking like an unwanted puppy who has just been told to get into a sack and go swimming.

'You'll be fine. Shaun, help run Chris through the bass parts while I talk to the manager.' Dave was hoping that his no-stress persona was convincing, because it was about as fake as his identity. This was going to be a disaster. News of a bad show would spread and make it harder to get bookings. More than that, if Tony turned up and it was a shambles, he'd lose his best chance to fast-track the Dave ReMastered Band to bigger venues.

Dave found the manager at the bar and explained the situation. The manager was sympathetic, but they had an absolute curfew on live music as part of their licence. If they started late, it might mean having to cut the show short, which would mean reducing the fee. Dave assured him that they'd be ready on time, with or without the missing bass player.

He walked back into the dressing room, hoping to see that Martin had arrived in his absence. No such luck.

'Okay, lads, we've got about ten minutes to showtime, and we can't put it off – reputation is everything in this game, and we don't want to get tagged as unreliable. Look, I know this is a bigger venue than you've played before, but don't worry about that. I'll take care of the audience; you guys just remember what we've worked on and have fun – let the crowd feed off our enjoyment. Let's get out there and give them the full Dave ReMastered experience.'

The others all nodded purposefully, apart from Chris, who threw up again, this time in a wastebin. Showtime.

CHAPTER TWELVE

Dave was about to open the door and lead them to the stage when suddenly it swung open and in strolled Martin.

'Hi, guys, I'm not late, am I?'

Chris threw himself at the bass player and wrapped him in a hug so intense that Shaun suggested they get a room.

'You have no idea how pleased I am to see you,' said Chris.

'I'm getting a clue,' replied Martin, peeling his bandmate off him and sniffing. 'Have you just wiped sick on my shoulder?'

Shaun grinned. 'He was lined up to play bass instead of you. We were all pretending it was going to be fine, but he'd have crashed and burned. Good to see you, buddy.'

'Never mind all that,' said Dave. 'We're due on stage.'

'What about my stage clothes?' asked Martin. 'I haven't had the chance to change'.

'Too late for that. You'll have to go on as you are.'

'I wouldn't worry,' added Shaun. 'With your fashion sense you look more '70s than any of us.'

It was a good crowd, close to a sell-out; not bad for a brand-new band, albeit one piggy-backing on someone else's fame. As Dave strode towards his mic stand, front and centre of the stage, he spotted Cindy and Nicky near the front, grinning and waving to him. Dave's pre-gig nerves usually vanished once he set foot on stage, but seeing Cindy gave him a brief butterfly sensation in his stomach. He needed the gig to go well for the sake of all his plans, but he really wanted her to enjoy it too. He acknowledged her with a smile and a wink, then turned to check the rest of the band were all in place. After a few nods of confirmation, he launched into "Feelin' Alright".

As he did so, a horrible thought flashed across his mind. Had anyone told Martin that they had changed the set order? Was Martin expecting "Trouble on My Mind"?

Martin was late coming in, having obviously recognised he was about to play a different song to his bandmates, but immediately caught up and played the rest of the song flawlessly. During the guitar solo, Dave edged across the stage towards him and mouthed, 'Well done,' receiving a grin in return.

The audience were really up for it. Much like the crowd at the Faces tribute gig, they seemed to have made up their mind to enjoy themselves in advance. All it needed was a competent performance packed with songs they already knew and the rest would take care of itself. "Feelin' Alright" was followed by "Jack of Hearts", another single that had become better known since Dave's apparent death. Chris seemed okay now, sounding good on rhythm guitar – maybe the relief at moving back to his own instrument helped him conquer his nerves. Whatever the reason, the smile on his face said that he was in the zone now. By the time they got to "Stagefright", Dave was confident that none of his new recruits were going to find it too autobiographical.

The show wasn't perfect. Chris fluffed a couple of guitar parts, but relaxed and got back into the rhythm with the help of a reassuring smile from Dave each time. Jonjo milked the drum break that starts "Midnight Rolling", extending it by a couple of bars before eventually leading the rest of them in. When Dave tried to catch his eye, the drummer studiously looked the other way. But those were small details; overall, the show was going well. After the initial shock of the opening number, Martin didn't put a foot wrong all night, driving the band when the song called for it, adding melodic undertones or just getting out of the way as required. Dave was also coming to appreciate just what a sensitive accompanist Shaun could be, never more so than on "Feel Like Going Home", which they had placed near the end of the show. His organ part was beautiful in its simplicity, setting the perfect stage for Dave's emotional vocal and guitar solo. When Shaun was called on to solo, his fingers flew over the keys in a near-perfect impersonation of Simon Tilley from the original Dave Masters Band. This group wasn't fully formed yet, with some rough edges still to be knocked off, but they had the potential to go far. With a few more gigs, they could really be something. He was enjoying himself too, being back at the helm of a proper band after too many years playing solo. It was great to be able to cut loose on the Strat after so long, and he had to resist the temptation to showboat. This was about recreating the records, he reminded himself, but he indulged once or three times. After all, it was his band and – even if nobody else knew it – they were his songs. During Shaun's solo in "Vagabond Life", Dave moved towards where Cindy and Nicky were dancing. He made eye contact with Cindy and right there her crooked smile made for the perfect moment in a perfect night.

After an hour and a half of whipping the audience up, slowing them down and then ringing them out with "Feel Like Going Home", it was time for the last number. "Trouble on My Mind" reclaimed its traditional place as the show-stopper, and as ever it earned an encore.

'Everybody ready?' said Dave in the wings. 'Let's give them a couple more: "Double Down on Love", and then finish with "I Saw Her Standing There". All good?' Grins and nods answered his question. 'It's going great; let's keep it tight and send everyone home happy.'

They ran back on stage and launched into "Double Down on Love", a rootsy runaway train of a song with lyrics inspired by Dave's licentious on-the-road antics back in the day (Dave made a point of not catching Cindy's eye while he was singing it). The crowd loved it, but not half as much as "I Saw Her Standing There". Thanks to the Paul McCartney anecdote, everyone now associated the song with Dave Masters, and when he launched into the opening riff, the audience roared with delight. It had always gone down well, but Dave couldn't remember this good a reaction even in his heyday. As the final chords died down, Dave and the band saluted the audience and made their way off the stage.

'That was amazing!' Chris was beside himself. 'Did you hear them? They were mad for us!'

'We did it, we bloody well did it!' added Jonjo, gleefully pummelling Martin on the shoulders.

'And Chris got through the show without throwing up again – what were the odds?' asked Shaun.

Dave smiled, enjoying the reaction of his novice bandmates. 'Don't expect to get a lot of sleep tonight, lads. The adrenalin will take a while to get out of your system. But enjoy it – you earned it tonight, all of you.'

Cindy and Nicky were allowed backstage by the bouncers, and as soon as the door closed, they erupted with laughter.

'Cindy was so cool,' gushed Nicky. 'She just went up to the big bloke on the door and said, "We're friends of the band." He asked our names and when she told him he just said, "Right this way, ladies." It's like being royalty – I feel like Princess Di!' Both girls gave Dave a big hug, although Nicky tactfully withdrew, leaving him to Cindy.

'You were amazing,' she whispered into his ear. 'And just a little bit sexy.'

'Just a little bit?' asked Dave.

'That's as much as I'm admitting to. After all, I'm a VIP now – my name was on the guestlist.'

Martin and Chris were chatting with Nicky and offering her a beer from the rider, while Shaun was having a word with the bouncer. A minute or two later, some more girls from the crowd were allowed into the dressing room, and before long Shaun was in the corner with a pretty brunette in a very short skirt.

The door opened again and the bouncer beckoned Dave over. After a whispered exchange, he ushered another visitor into the room. Dave almost forgot to pretend not to know him.

'Great show, lads, I really enjoyed it, almost as good as the real thing,' began Tony before introducing himself to Dave, Chris, Martin and Jonjo (Shaun being otherwise engaged with the girl in the short skirt). 'My name's Tony Broadway and I'd be very interested in representing you. Have you got a manager? Someone to handle your bookings? I think you and I could do some good work together.'

Dave held out his hand. 'Very pleased to meet you, Mr Broadway. I'm Tom, Tom Mulvaney.' The others seemed tongue-tied in the presence of an actual honest-to-goodness rock agent, which was fine by Dave – he didn't want Jonjo or someone to mess everything up. They chatted for a minute or two, dancing the dance with Tony, who was dazzling the newbies with talk of a few shows in London to build an audience and hone their stagecraft, before getting them out on the road and moving up to playing some bigger venues. Dave played it cool, holding off from agreeing anything and promising that the band would talk it over and that he'd get back to Tony soon.

'Don't take too long – after a show like tonight, we've got to seize the moment and fill up your date book.'

'Talk it over?' squealed Chris once Tony had left. 'What's to talk about? This has been the best night of my life; if he can get us more gigs, more of this, let's do it.' The others were just as enthusiastic, with the possible exception of Shaun, who had slipped away to the gents with the brunette. Dave didn't want to speculate on just how enthusiastic he was at that precise moment.

Just as things couldn't get any better for Dave's fledgling rock stars, the club manager came in to pay Dave. He had agreed a share of the door, and the manager counted out £300. When Dave split it equally between the five of them, they just stared at the money. Shaun (back with them by now, with a sly grin on his face and the brunette on his arm) said it was the most they'd ever earned from a gig – their old band was doing well to get £50 between them. It was safe to say that they saw the evening as a success.

Cindy and Nicky had made their own way to the gig, not wanting to get in the way beforehand, but Dave offered them a lift back in the van. Shaun nodded towards the brunette and said that he wasn't heading back to Barnet tonight. Could Chris look after his gear for him? From the rest of the band's lack of surprise, Dave guessed that Shaun made a habit of this after gigs.

Chris drove the van home, with Dave and Cindy joining the others in the back. Dave had suggested Cindy sit up front with him, but she didn't want to abandon Nicky. It was a happy journey, with the band swapping notes on how the gig had gone. Cindy gave Dave's hand a squeeze and leant her head into his shoulder. It had been a great night.

Cindy helped Dave carry his guitars up the stairs to his flat. Although he'd been on his Strat all night, he had brought the Ovation along for Chris to use. He could have carried both himself, of course, but that wouldn't have left an arm to put around Cindy between the van and the stairs.

She carried the Ovation into his flat, and he was pleased to see that she shut the door behind her.

'Fancy a drink?' he asked. 'I've got some beers in the fridge.'

'I've had enough tonight, but I'll have a cup of tea if you're offering. I won't stay long – you must be knackered.'

'To be honest, it takes me ages to come down after a gig – I'll be up half the night.' He paused, wondering whether to risk the next line. 'You're welcome to keep me company.'

Cindy gave him a reproachful look. 'I don't think so; it's all right for you rock stars; some of us have got work in the morning. Besides, tonight was brilliant – you were brilliant – but it scared me a bit.'

'Scared you? You looked like you had a great time.'

'Oh, I did. I loved it, and the fact it was you made it a hundred times better. But then I saw how everyone else reacted to you, and how easy it was for the others to pull.'

'Not all the others, it was only Shaun.'

'Yeah, but he wasn't even the star, was he? If he could hook up with someone after the show, I'm sure you could too.'

Dave ignored the now-boiling kettle and gave his full attention to Cindy. 'Yeah, maybe I could. But I didn't, did I? I'm not saying I never did that kind of thing when I was younger – you know that I did – but I'm a different man now. I want to be with you, not with the kind of tart who comes backstage after a gig.' Dave stepped forward and held both of Cindy's hands. 'I think you're great. I get why you're worried about me straying, but I won't. Promise.' He held her gaze, and then she leant in to him and buried her head against his shoulder.

'I'm sorry,' she whispered. 'I'm just being silly.' She squeezed him again and pulled away. 'Look, I'm going to have a cup of tea with you, then I'm going back to mine – not because I don't trust you, but because I don't trust me: I really do need to get some sleep tonight if I'm not going to be late for work, and I'm not sure we'd do a lot of sleeping if I stayed. You make the tea and I'll put a record on. One more thing.' She put on a look of mock umbrage. 'I came backstage after the gig – does that make me a tart in your book?'

The next afternoon, Tony phoned.

'So, have you and the band "talked it over" yet? That was a bit impudent, frankly.' Dave knew from the tone in his voice that he was joking.

'Yeah, sorry about that, I wanted them to see how cool I was dealing with Mr Big-Shot Manager. We're in.'

'Of course you're bloody well in – *you* asked *me* to come and take a look, remember? Where did you find those boys anyway?'

'Would you believe, one of them played that solo gig at my new local and mentioned that his band had lost their lead guitarist? Last night was the first time they had played that big a room.'

Tony sounded genuinely impressed at that. 'Really? Well, that sounds promising – plenty of room for them to improve. Bass and keyboards were spot on, I thought. I'm not entirely convinced by the other two, though.'

'I know what you mean with Jonjo, but Chris – the guitarist – is all right. He was the worst with pre-gig nerves, but I think once he gets a few more shows under his belt, he'll be fine. He's good at organising the others, kind of the glue that holds the rest of them together.'

'Okay, well, we'll see how they get on when I book some more dates, but if they don't keep stepping up, we may need to bring in replacements.'

'Leave it with me, I'll lick them into shape. Any idea on when you can get us some more gigs?'

'Already working on it. We'll build a following on the London circuit, then move up to bigger rooms and get you out on the road once there's a bit of a buzz. I'm already talking to the Half Moon in Putney, the Sir George Robey and the Rock Garden. How does that sound?'

'Perfect.'

'And another thing. Is that blonde from last night the mystery lady who hasn't handed over the goods yet?'

'Some of us are interested in more than just a few minutes of friction, Tony.'

'Like I said before, I take it you're still not getting any then.'

part two

BACK IN THE HIGH LIFE AGAIN

SEPTEMBER 1990

CHAPTER THIRTEEN

He had slept through his alarm again so was woken by the tender charms of Jym.

'Morning, Tom. Come on, move your arse – you can sleep on the bus.' The words were accompanied by insistent finger-poking. At the start of the tour Dave had tried arguing, but he soon realised it was easier just to give in. He'd missed breakfast, but Jym always made sure there was something for him on the tour bus.

A lot had changed since Camden. Tony had spread the word about their "stunning debut show", and the follow-up gigs were sell-outs. Tony had kept them in smaller venues at first, to send the message that Dave ReMastered shows were a sought-after ticket. Sold-out small shows created more buzz than bigger crowds failing to fill the bigger rooms.

After working the London circuit in July and August, letting the rookies acclimatise to their new level, Tony sent them out on the road for two weeks in September, which was where Jym the road manager came in. A lot of the venues were familiar to Dave, but for the others, the whole experience was a magical new world.

As expected, they quickly tightened up. Chris still suffered from horrendous pre-gig nerves, resulting in a regular pool on how many toilet visits he'd make before the show. Shaun's playing was going from strength to strength, as was his habit of either going missing after a show or bringing girls back to wherever they were staying the night. With a touring party of seven – Jym was assisted by Dink, a burly Neanderthal roadie with a talent for electronics – everyone except Dave had to share double rooms. Whichever unfortunate was paired with Shaun would often plead with Dave to let them bunk in with him when Shaun turned up with company.

Walking onto the minibus – a bigger, newer one that Tony had splashed out on, now that their crew and equipment had outgrown the old transit – Dave saw that the others were all present and correct. Shaun had returned from the previous night's escapades, and Chris, Martin and Ollie were laughing together. Ollie had arrived shortly before the tour began to replace Jonjo, who Tony fired after an unauthorised extended drum solo in the middle of "Jack of Hearts" at the Rock Garden (Martin had offered another drummer joke after the event: why is a drum solo like a sneeze? You know it's coming, you know you're not going to enjoy it, but there's nothing you can do to stop it). Dave had feared some resistance from the others at losing their friend, but no one spoke up; they realised this wasn't a hobby band and that Jonjo simply wasn't the right fit. As Tony had said back in the early days, it was a ruthless business. Ollie was completely different to Jonjo: professional, seasoned and – joy of joys – all about feel rather than flash.

'Morning, boss,' chorused the band.

'You made it out of bed then?' asked Shaun.

'Yeah, you too, I see. Whose bed was it this time?'

'I think her name was Kirsten. Or Christine, something like that. Nice girl, though – very friendly.'

'Now that we're all here, whose turn is it?' asked Jym. They had established a strict set of rules for what music went on the van's tape deck: cassettes only survived by popular consent; vetoes from three of the others would see it immediately replaced with the next man's choice. It could be a fickle electorate, but a prevailing sense of openness to the unfamiliar meant that most albums got at least one track before meeting serious opposition, unless Dink was indulging his taste for metal.

It was Chris's turn, and he passed a cassette to Jym, who slipped it into the slot. Dave wasn't optimistic when a very '80s-sounding piano number kicked in. Dave recognised but couldn't place the lyrics.

'Isn't this a Creedence Clearwater Revival song?' asked Ollie. Of course – "Have You Ever Seen the Rain", from Chris's King's Head set.

'Dunno. This is the only version I've heard,' replied Chris. 'Bonnie Tyler.'

Dave chuckled to himself; perhaps Chris's musical knowledge wasn't as deep as that solo gig had made him think.

'Veto!' shouted Dink, always quick to try to move on to another, hopefully heavier, choice.

Bonnie lasted through a second song, but the third reeked of the '80s in all the worst ways and she barely got through the first verse before Jym and Dave added their vetoes to Dink's.

'Who's next?' asked Jym.

'The old man,' replied Shaun. 'What's it going to be, sleeping ugly?'

Dave passed a cassette forward. 'I feel like something restful. You might like this if you give it a chance.' He knew from experience that Shaun and Dink had a low tolerance to country-folk, but hopefully the others would see him get a few tracks in before something livelier took its place. He passed the cassette forward and Chris read the spidery writing on the box.

'*The Late Great Townes Van Zandt*: never heard of him. Was this released after he died then?'

'Hardly,' replied Dave. 'This came out nearly twenty years ago and he's still alive, as far as I know. Apart from that, spot on.'

'So why that title, if he wasn't dead?'

'A marketing ploy?' suggested Ollie. 'Pretending to be dead to sell records?'

'Maybe he's late because he was as bad at oversleeping as the old man here,' suggested Shaun. 'Perhaps we should start calling him the late, great Tom Mulvaney.' The others laughed, and Dave smiled at the irony. Killed off again; this was becoming a habit.

Dink was behind the wheel, which was always slightly concerning, and they set off for Bristol, where they had a gig at the Fleece. Dave was sitting alongside Martin. Like Shaun, Martin's playing – always good to start with – was getting better and better.

'Sleep well?' asked Dave.

'Yeah, with Shaun away on manoeuvres last night, it was blissfully quiet.'

'Any more thoughts about the future?' Martin had been the most reluctant to join the tour. He had a decent job, and though they'd given him unpaid leave, he had some big decisions to make once they got back to London.

'Still not sure. I mean, I'm loving the gigs but it's all a bit unreal. What if the Dave Masters boom bursts? There's no security in music.'

'Yeah, I know. But you're a good player. If things fall apart Tony could easily get you session work. You're wasted on spreadsheets or whatever it is you do at that office.' Martin shrugged. Despite Dave's best efforts, he just wasn't ready to commit. Dave had hoped that the last couple of weeks might have changed that.

The trip to Bristol would take about three hours. They told Dave later that Townes Van Zandt had lasted for four and a half tracks, but he was fast asleep long before that. He needed it too; he'd been up most of the night writing.

That was another change since Camden. Dave's writer's block had finally shifted. Now that he was firing live ammunition with a real band and enthusiastic audiences, something had clicked and the songs started flowing. Partly he was writing about how good his life was turning out to be (who knew Tom Mulvaney would have such a good time?), but mostly he was writing about Cindy.

Even more than his songwriting and his audience, the biggest change since Camden had been Cindy. Nothing had happened the night of the first gig, but a couple of nights later she had knocked on his door and not left for three days. He'd had his share of conquests – in his day Shaun had nothing on him. Even Cath had just been a shag after a gig at first, but this was different. In a rare experience for Dave, the sense of connection had overshadowed everything else. Cindy had cried afterwards, but insisted they were happy, healing tears. Dave held her and kissed her and told her that he loved her. He meant it too. It was one of those nights where the whole world was reduced to the size of the bed, where the two of them were the only people alive on the planet, the only ones that mattered.

They had spent as much time together as they could, working around Dave's musical commitments and Cindy's shifts at Quicksave. They spent a lot of time listening to music, with Dave taking the opportunity to educate her. She was introducing him to new music too, and being with her was challenging the way he saw the world. One time, when they were listening to a Richard Thompson album, Cindy asked what it was that he liked so much about him.

'Well, for a start he's a great player, so there's that. But there's the authenticity too: he doesn't just copy his influences; he pulls them all together and forges something unique, something that's just him – I could recognise his playing anywhere. He pulls in so many different styles of music, but he doesn't go chasing trends or second-guessing what people want. He plays the music *he* loves without worrying whether anyone else will like it.'

'Is that a good thing?'

'Absolutely. Take Eric Clapton; first he walked away from the Yardbirds because he thought they were becoming too pop. Then, when Cream were set to be the biggest group in the world, he heard The Band's first album and realised Cream were heading in the wrong direction, so he broke them up. That's authenticity. It's a shame he's lost his way a bit now.'

'Do you think? I quite like his last couple of albums.'

'His playing is as good as ever, but the arrangements are too commercial. He says it's the price for keeping his guitar the way he wants it, but art shouldn't be a trade-off; it's an expression of the artist's soul: my music the way I hear it and to hell with everyone else. That's authenticity.'

Cindy had started laughing, which had confused him.

'I'm sorry! I'm not being rude or anything, but you've got to admit, it's a bit funny you going on about authenticity.' She must have seen by his face that he didn't see the joke. 'I mean, you're a tribute act – you make a living pretending to be someone else and you're talking about authenticity.'

Dave laughed. 'Who says a tribute act can't be authentic?'

'What, are you telling me that you're the authentic Dave Masters?'

If only she knew. 'No, of course not. But I'm faithfully recreating his sound. I'd say there's more authenticity in our set than in some of the crap in the charts.' He had meant it too. Even if he had been Tom Mulvaney rather than the actual Dave Masters, this was proper music, written and performed with heart and passion. Tribute or not, it was real.

'Anyway,' Cindy had continued, 'what's so good about not caring what other people think? I get it from the point of view of an artist, but if someone acts like that in real life, we don't call them authentic; we call them selfish bastards. If my ex said that cheating on me was just him being authentically himself, would that make it okay? There's a thin line between not caring what people think and not caring if you hurt them, isn't there?'

Dave conceded the point. The younger him had never given much thought to how his actions affected other people. Cath had borne the brunt of it, of course, but others had suffered for the licence he gave himself. Now that Dave Masters was dead and gone, Tom Mulvaney could do things differently, do them better.

They went out to gigs; they went to the cinema. Part of what made things with Cindy so great was that for the first time in years he felt like a normal person in a normal relationship. He didn't have to worry about people recognising him, and he could just do regular punter things. Usually it was just the two of them, although they carried on the quiz night at the King's Head when Dave's live schedule permitted. Cindy found out about a Del Amitri gig at Hammersmith Odeon later in the year and persuaded him to get three tickets so that Nicky could come along too. She made a joke about hoping he didn't mind a threesome, which made Dave feel a little ashamed of his thoughts back when he first met them both.

Bristol went well. They swapped out a couple of numbers to keep things fresh, but the core of the set was pretty solid. "Vagabond Life" went particularly well, with Shaun's solo probably the best he'd played it yet. They did three encores, indulging themselves as it was the last show of the run. They were heading straight home after the gig, Tony intent on saving money on overnight accommodation for the final night.

Cindy was out at work by the time Dave got up. He ignored his bags, still not unpacked from the night before, and got his guitar out. He had been thinking about Cindy all the way home, remembering the sparkle in her eyes the day he first met her. There had to be a song in that. Picking out a delicate melody, he started improvising words and soon had the beginnings of something he was happy with. The recurring refrain in the lyrics – "Your Eyes Shine" – would make a good title. It still needed a lot of polish, but it had definite potential. If only he still had an outlet for all these songs he was writing again; that was the downside to being dead.

They had a rest day, then the first of two dates that Tony had booked for their triumphant return to London. Both were at bigger venues than the band had played before, and the Chris sweepstake was expected to lean towards the higher numbers. First up was the Mean Fiddler, the same club where Dave had his first tribute experience, and then a couple of days later the famous Marquee Club. Dave had played the old Marquee when he first arrived in London back in the early '70s, and he was disappointed when Tony pointed out that it had moved from its iconic Wardour Street address a couple of years previously. Still, the new Marquee had a bigger capacity, so it would be a better earner for the band, assuming that Tony's theory of the value of sell-outs had worked. Either way, it would be great to play in front of Cindy again – he'd missed seeing her and Nicky down the front of the crowd when they ventured away from London.

The Mean Fiddler was a success on all fronts: a sell-out capacity crowd, an atmosphere that sizzled and one of the tightest shows the band had played yet. If anyone had been at that first Dublin Castle gig and then this one, they would have been amazed at the band's improvement in such a short time. Backstage afterwards, Cindy and Nicky (again, loving their VIP status) were chatting with Dave, Martin and Chris, while Shaun and Ollie tried their luck with a gaggle of young female fans.

'So, the busker outside: your idea or Tony's?' asked Cindy.

Dave and the others exchanged puzzled glances. 'What busker?' asked Dave.

'There was a young bloke with an acoustic guitar singing Dave Masters songs when everyone was queuing up. He had a sign with him, but I didn't get the chance to see what it said. Nicky and I skipped the queue, what with being on the guestlist and everything, you know?'

'Nothing to do with us. Tony didn't mention anything either.'

Martin went to find the bouncer who had been on the main door to see if he could shed any light on the matter. When he came back, he had a puzzled expression on his face.

'Apparently, he was playing Dave Masters' hits on his guitar and telling people that for the best Dave Masters experience in

London, they should forget your show and see him at the pub down the road instead. He was handing out flyers – look.' He handed Dave a crumpled sheet of paper.

Dave took it and read it aloud. '"Vagabond Dave, London's finest Dave Masters Tribute act, plays the Royal Oak, Harlesden. See Dave Masters as he was in his prime, rather than as an old washed-out has-been." Bloody cheek – I don't do Dave Masters as a washed-out has-been.'

Cindy was reading over his shoulder. 'And look at the quotes he's got at the end – there's one from Russell Grant: "I've spoken to the spirit of Dave Masters and he says Vagabond Dave is his true successor."' That at least got some laughter.

'So, if he's London's finest,' huffed Chris indignantly, 'how come he's playing a pokey pub when we're on at the Mean Fiddler?'

'Ah, don't worry about it,' said Dave. 'He's just trying to bark up a crowd, like I did when I was playing the open-mic nights. Mind you, I never trashed anyone else or tried to steal their audience. I'll mention it to Tony. Look, we played a great gig and sent everyone home happy. We don't need to worry about Vagabond Dave and his endorsements from beyond the grave.'

Chris went to find Tony, who was hobnobbing with the club manager, and brought him over. Tony scanned the flyer, chuckling at the Russell Grant line.

'You've got to admire his cheek – this is good self-promotion, I'll give him that. Look, I'll make some enquiries and see what I can find out. I doubt it's anything to worry about, though. You boys have put in the work and started to build a following; it sounds like this is just a chancer with a guitar. Forget about him.'

That night, with post-gig adrenalin keeping him awake, Dave kept thinking about the young upstart. Judging from the flyer, he had deliberately booked himself a gig nearby to clash with their Mean Fiddler show. If he did the same again when they played the Marquee – the band's biggest show yet – Dave wasn't going to take it lying down. Vagabond Dave might find that he's got a fight on his hands if he wants to be London's best Dave Masters experience. After all, if it was a question of authenticity, how could he lose?

CHAPTER FOURTEEN

Dave arrived at the Marquee in plenty of time for the soundcheck. The rest of the band weren't all there yet, though Ollie was limbering up on his kit. Dave nodded his greetings and went to find the bouncers.

'All right, lads,' he said. 'Do you guys know yet who's doing the main door tonight?' The biggest one made himself known. 'Right, could you to do me a favour? There's twenty quid in it for you.'

Soundcheck came and went, along with Chris's lunch: it was their biggest show yet and Chris seemed to be going for a new personal best for pre-show toilet trips. Half an hour before the doors were due to open, another bouncer knocked and poked his head round the dressing-room door.

'Tom? Carl on the door said to let you know: he's here.'

'Great, thanks.' He turned to the rest of the band. 'Who wants to see me teach Vagabond Dave a lesson?' Without waiting for a reply, Dave walked out, collected his Ovation from the stage and headed out to the front of the club. His bandmates exchanged glances and rushed to follow.

Dave reached the door, where Carl pointed down the queue to a young man playing "Trouble on My Mind" on a battered acoustic while his mate handed out flyers. Dave paused to pick out the key then joined in, first harmonising on the chorus and then taking over the lead vocal for the final verse. The queuing punters didn't know what was happening but were enjoying the confusion.

The two Daves finished the song and acknowledged the applause, before Dave turned to his young pretender. 'So what's the big idea, trying to steal my crowd away? It didn't work at the Mean Fiddler and it's not going to work tonight.'

'Face it, Grandad. Dave Masters' best work was in the '70s, when he was closer to my age. It makes sense that if they're looking for the real Dave Masters experience, they should come and see me.' He turned to the queue and added, 'I'm playing at the Royal George, show starts at nine o'clock. If you bail on this old codger you'll have time for couple of pints before I start – better beer, cheaper ticket, better singer.'

'What's your problem, pal?' asked Dave, squaring up to the younger man and trying to calculate how youth and experience would balance out if it got physical. He didn't want that – he couldn't risk injuring his hand before the performance – but if it did turn nasty, he knew it wouldn't last long; Carl would see to that. 'I've worked hard to build this audience. Go and find your own crowd, quit stealing mine.'

'It's a free country, mate. I'm just making sure everyone knows where to find a young and exciting version of Dave Masters when they get fed up with an old man who has to take the keys down to hit the high notes.'

'Who says I can't hit the high notes?'

'It's not your fault, mate. I'm sure I'll make it easy on myself too when I'm your age. It's nothing to be ashamed of, it's just the law of the jungle – the old beasts back down or get taken out by younger, stronger animals.'

'Yeah? Do I look like I'm backing down? Let's have a Dave-off. We'll sing a song together – one verse and chorus each – and they can vote with their applause.' The crowd seemed to approve;

they hadn't even got in yet, and already it was a memorable evening.

'All right, you're on. I choose "Jack of Hearts". Do you want to go first or second?' It was a good choice by the lad, a song from the early days to illustrate his point about youthful energy. Even so, Dave was confident; he knew that he sang the song better now than he did back then.

'After you – you won't want to follow me.' Dave wanted to hear what he was up against first, just in case he had to up his game.

Vagabond Dave started, and he was better than Dave expected. He had a strong voice, although his guitar-playing wasn't much more than okay. He carried the tune well enough and got a decent round of applause when he finished. Dave jumped in with his guitar, immediately adding more complexity and texture to the playing, bringing out more of the melody. He'd played this song solo so many times over the years that it was second nature to him. Vagabond Dave had sneakily taken the key up from the recorded version, but Dave didn't want to leave himself open to the charge of moving it down, so he stuck with it. He attacked the second verse with vigour, making eye contact with the nearest members of the crowd and working the audience in a way that his rival hadn't managed. If this was going to be decided by applause, he had to connect. By the time he hit the chorus, he was nicely warmed up and finding the ambiguous mix of free spirit and melancholy at the heart of the song. He threw in a final guitar flourish at the end and took the – considerably louder – applause. Looking around, he saw that Vagabond Dave and his mate had already left, so he addressed the delighted crowd.

'Ladies and gentlemen, I hope you enjoyed that, I hope you enjoy tonight's show, and I hope there's now no doubt about who really is the best Dave Masters in town.' With that, he headed inside to cheers and applause. The rest of the band had all been watching from the doorway, and there was a lot of laughing and back-slapping as he made his way past.

'That was amazing!' enthused Chris.

'How did you know he wasn't going to be better than you?' asked Shaun.

Dave just fixed him with a glare and said, 'I'll pretend I didn't hear that – nobody does Dave Masters better than me, you lot should know that by now. After that, we have to be brilliant. More importantly, how many times has Chris gone to the loo so far?' The tally was on ten, which Dave thought gave his guess of twelve a fighting chance.

When Tony arrived, the band quickly filled him in on what their leader had done.

'Brilliant. I'll be on to the music press tomorrow – if someone prints it, booking the next round of gigs will be a cinch. Nice work, Tom.' His words said he was happy, but Dave could tell from his face that he wasn't entirely pleased. Doubtless he'd be hearing all about it when the others weren't around.

A couple of last-minute calls of nature pushed Chris's tally up to fourteen, and then it was showtime.

Before launching into the opening number – "Feelin' Alright", still holding strong – Dave addressed the crowd. 'Good evening, Marquee. I hope those of you who got here early enjoyed the efforts of our youth team. Now the main attraction can show you how it's really done.' He could see a few puzzled looks but also good-natured laughter from those in the know. The rest would hear about it soon enough, and then doubtless claim to all their friends that they witnessed the Dave-off themselves.

When they got to "Jack of Hearts", Dave introduced it with, 'Here's one that I've already played tonight,' again prompting a cheer from those who were there, man. Maybe it was the adrenalin from the showdown, but Dave was flying tonight, playing and singing as well as he had in the band's short time together, possibly as well as he had in the last five or ten years. Dying had definitely got him out of his slump.

At the end of the night, as the band celebrated with a beer and, for Shaun, a blonde, Tony walked into the dressing room with a record bag bearing the Ultimate Records logo.

'Prezzy time, lads,' he said. 'Ultimate are going to be releasing Dave Masters' last album in a couple of weeks, and they agreed that I could have some advance copies for you to start working on. I persuaded them that without the real Dave Masters to get out and promote the album, your shows were the next best thing.'

Dave and the others hastily took the records and poured over the track listing, while Tony carried on. 'It's up to you what gets added to the set list; you leave the business to me, and I'll leave the music to you.'

As expected, the next day Tony phoned to talk about the showdown in the queue.

'Bit of stupid risk, wasn't it? What if he had turned out to be really good?'

'It wouldn't have mattered. They're my songs – even if he was a better singer than me – which he wasn't – there's no way he could have sung my songs better. He looked, what, twenty years old? He hasn't got the life experience to connect those songs with an audience. I was always going to win.'

'Well, it's all worked out nicely, anyway. I was talking to Stuart Maconie at *NME* this morning, telling him about the Dave-off. He loved the idea of two tribute acts vying for dominance and he's going to write about it. We'll pay for an advert for the October tour on the same page – bigger venues, more like those last two London shows. The audience is growing steadily, it's time to push things up a notch.'

With Tony sounding happier, Dave decided to mention something he'd been thinking about. 'I've got more good news, Tony. I've started writing again.'

A brief silence before Tony answered, an air of reservation in his voice. 'I thought you were all written out; that's what you told me.'

'I did, I was. But now I've got my muse back. Can we add some of those songs into the set?'

There was no hesitation this time. 'Absolutely not – how are we going to explain that to the punters? "Welcome to a show celebrating the music of Dave Masters; here are some songs that none of you have ever heard but which we think Dave might have written if he was still alive." Look, you're a tribute act now and you're earning good money, plus you're getting paid from the trust fund for your old recordings. Why ruin it?'

'Talking of the trust fund, if we're selling so many records, why am I still getting the same monthly payments as before? Shouldn't I be getting more?'

'You are getting more; you're getting the extra income from the tribute act. Which brings us back to the songs; you can't do the new material.'

'But I'm an artist! They're my songs and I have to get them out there.'

'Well, we can publish them under Tom Mulvaney's name and look for other artists to record them, but unless Tom Mulvaney is going to walk away from the tribute circuit and start from scratch as himself – which as your manager I wouldn't recommend – there's no way. Dave Masters is dead, and that means he can't be writing new songs.'

Dave wanted to argue, but he could see Tony's point. When he got himself into this, he hadn't even considered that he might start writing again. He'd been so sick of the business, it had been inconceivable that he'd want to go back to it. If he'd known he'd regain his enthusiasm for playing, he wouldn't have killed himself off; then again, if he hadn't killed himself off, he wouldn't have got his enthusiasm back. It was a Catch-22, and now he had to just live with it. He'd keep writing the songs – it wasn't something he could turn on and off – but it looked like there was no way to get them out to the public.

A couple of days later, the band reconvened for rehearsal. Dave had been disappointed when he'd listened to the album; none of the original songs were as good as he had remembered. Even "Blood and Rust", which Dave had considered to be quite profound at the time, now sounded like an old man moaning about how rubbish it is to be in decline. If only Dave could have swapped out some of these with the songs he was writing now.

'Well, "Steppin' Stone" is good,' offered Chris. 'If it gets decent airplay, it could work for us.'

'What about the Steve Winwood cover, "Back in the High Life Again"?' asked Shaun. The band was less convinced about that one but agreed to work it up and see how it sounded. Apart from that, the rest of the album – including all the Dave Masters originals – were quickly dismissed. If anything else got released as a single they could reconsider, but for now they all agreed that the Dave Masters who recorded this album seemed a shadow of the artist responsible for their regular set.

'It just goes to show, doesn't it?' offered Martin. 'It's hard to keep going in this line of work – it takes its toll.'

Shaun rose to the bait. 'It doesn't have to. There are lots of artists who have kept going and stayed creative.'

'Name three,' replied Martin. 'Name three who have been going for as long as Dave Masters without going off the boil.'

The others were looking interested now. 'The Rolling Stones?' suggested Ollie. 'They've been going thirty years or so. *Steel Wheels* is a great album.'

Martin shook his head. 'Is it, though? I mean, it's okay, but would you put it in the same league as *Exile on Main Street*? Or *Let It Bleed*? "Mixed Emotions" was a good single, but how far back do you go to find another one? "Start Me Up" was ten years ago. They've survived, but only by turning into a caricature of themselves.' Dave had to agree: he'd spent a lot of time deciding on *Let It Bleed* as the sole Stones album to bring into his new life; he hadn't even considered any of their '80s releases.

Shaun put his head back and thought. 'David Bowie, he's constantly changing – you can't call him a caricature of himself.'

'Yeah, but he's doing that Tin Machine thing now,' said Martin. 'Dink likes Tin Machine, which pretty much proves Bowie's off his game.' It was a fair point; Dink had tried to play Bowie's heavy rock side project on the tour bus; it hadn't lasted two tracks. 'Any more?'

'McCartney?' offered Chris.

'Two words for you: "Frog Chorus".'

Dave was surprised at how much he wanted to disprove Martin's theory. 'Okay, I've got one: Richard Thompson. He's never been a high-flyer with the charts, but the critics love him. And the only guitarists who don't rate him don't know what they're talking about.'

Martin looked like he might accept that one, until Ollie interrupted. 'Didn't he walk away from the music business in the '70s and live in an Islamic commune for a few years?'

Martin made his ruling. 'Okay, it's a no to Richard Thompson. We're still waiting for a single example of someone sustaining a meaningful artistic career for twenty years without walking away or going off the boil.'

'What's your point?' asked Dave, a little hurt at the band's assessment of his last album, even though he shared their opinion.

'My point is, even if Dave Masters' last album is a disappointment, that doesn't change how good his best work is. Tom, do you still listen to McCartney?'

'I listen to the Beatles, and his earlier solo stuff.' It was true: he'd picked the *McCartney* album, along with *Wings Over America*, for his streamlined record collection.

'"Frog Chorus"?'

'Of course not.'

'Right, and if you went to see a McCartney tribute act, would you want them to play "Frog Chorus" or "Maybe I'm Amazed"?'

'"Maybe I'm Amazed", obviously.'

'Obviously. And knowing that he went on to do "Frog Chorus" doesn't change how great a song that is, does it? We judge artists by their best work; we can write off the mistakes and misfires as the price for finding the gold. Everyone makes mistakes in real life, but we don't just judge people by their worst moments; we look at the bigger picture and focus on the good things. Let's help our punters to do that by giving them what they've come to hear. I say the new songs have to earn their way into the set list. If they add something, great; if not, stick with what's working.'

'But... but when you go to a gig you expect the band to play songs from the new album; it's how they promote their latest product.'

'But it's not our product! Our product is the live show. Why water it down? It's not as if we even earn anything from the record sales. We're promoting Dave Masters at his best, not the sub-standard leftovers.'

Dave stopped himself from pointing out that he did earn royalties from the record sales. Without that fact, he couldn't argue with Martin's logic, and he had to agree with the assessment of his latest work as sub-standard. Admitting it to himself stung a bit, though, not least as the songs he was writing now were so much better.

The critics, generally speaking, took the same view. The reviews were kinder than they would have been without Dave's tragic death, but the overall consensus was that, remarkable title track aside, the album mixed merely half-decent cover versions with disappointing originals. "Steppin' Stone" scraped into the top ten, which at least gave them the chance to put it into the show. Dave had also persuaded the lads to work up a version of a Ry Cooder cover from one of the '80s albums, giving it more of the classic Dave Masters sound than Dave had managed at the time. He had always felt bad about letting himself be led away from his original vision for that track, and this was a chance to put it right.

Stuart Maconie's article about the Dave-off was great publicity. He had tracked down some of the punters who were there, and everyone agreed that Dave – Tom – had seen off the younger version. Cindy's favourite part, which she had taken to quoting, was, 'Tom Mulvaney (or Dave ReMastered in the crazy world of Tributeland) squared up to would-be usurper Miles Silvers (Vagabond Dave) and fixed him with a gimlet-eyed stare. "Let's Dave-off," he whispered, in tones so intimidating that grown men lost their bladder control and women went weak at the knees.' Cindy kept joking about going weak at the knees after that, usually when Dave made innocuous comments about needing to buy milk or whatever. The band had loved the article too, not least because at least one grown man – Chris – had needed the toilet straight after the confrontation.

Alongside the feature was an advert for October's tour, at venues like the Bierkeller in Bristol, the Oxford Playhouse and the Riverside in Newcastle. Although Dave Masters had gone off the boil, things were hotting up nicely for the Dave ReMastered Band.

CHAPTER FIFTEEN

For a while it looked like he was going to lose Martin. After the London dates brought the mini-tour to completion, the hesitant bassist had returned to work and a meeting with the personnel department. From his account of things he had been completely honest, laying his dilemma out for them; on the one hand, he was living out his musical dreams: playing great music to packed houses and potentially earning a living from it. On the other, it lacked the security of his regular job. He knew he had to commit one way or the other but still didn't know which way to jump.

It sounded like his employers were as keen as Dave to keep Martin. They offered him a promotion – with salary bump – to lure him away from the bright lights and the road. When he still wasn't sure they offered six months' unpaid leave, at the end of which his old job (not the promotion) would still be waiting for him. Martin had jumped at the chance to keep playing, and Dave just hoped that the next six months would be enough to persuade him that his future was in music.

Tony had booked a busy schedule for their month on the road. Twenty dates in twenty-five days, from Brighton to Stirling and several points in between, all at venues with six hundred or more capacity, and finishing with their biggest show yet,

Camden's Electric Ballroom. Jym and Dink were still on the case, now joined by a sound engineer called Ben. Cindy had even arranged to take a few days off work and join them for a handful of gigs. The rest of the band had greeted this news with laughter, saying that Cindy was checking up on Dave and that he'd have to behave himself. In the past, if a girlfriend had asked to join up with a tour, Dave always dissuaded them. Even Cath, when they were married, had understood that the road was his place of work and not an extension of their marriage. That was his argument then, and it was partly true that he wanted to focus on the music, but it was also a convenient excuse to maintain his unfettered road lifestyle. Now that he was with Cindy, he wasn't interested in one-night stands; he just knew he'd be glad to see her again.

First stop was Swindon, where they held "Steppin' Stone" back until the encores and the audience responded well. The Ry Cooder cover, "The Very Thing That Makes You Rich (Makes Me Poor)", didn't get much response at the start, but as Dave and Shaun built the interplay between guitar and keyboards, cranking up the intensity of the instrumental passages as the song built, it rapidly won the audience over. "Back in the High Life Again" got a decent response, but Dave still felt that they hadn't quite got it yet. They hit the beers, safe in the knowledge that with only a short hop to the following night's gig it wouldn't be an early call for the tour bus the next day.

Oxford was another great gig, although with one unusual element. One fan, a tall, skinny lad, possibly not quite out of his teens, just stood at the front staring at Dave for the whole gig. Whenever Dave tried his old frontman tricks to bring the lad out of himself and into the experience, nothing worked. Dave moved on and made sure that the other 649 paying customers were having a good time. "Steppin' Stone", now promoted to second song of the night, continued to cement its place in the set list, while "Back in the High Life" still wasn't clicking.

'Did any of you notice that bloke down the front, the one who hardly moved all night?' he asked after the show.

'The one who just stared the whole time?' asked Chris. 'Yeah, what was that about?'

'Dead-Eyed Freak Boy?' added Ollie. 'Yeah, I saw him. I wondered if he was tripping on something; he seemed pretty intense.'

So, it hadn't been his imagination. Maybe it was just one of those weird gigs that crop up from time to time. On to Birmingham and, hopefully, a more normal show.

But Dead-Eyed Freak Boy was there again in Birmingham, standing in a similar position and behaving in much the same way. The band laughed about it, but Dave couldn't see the funny side. If this bloke wasn't enjoying the show, why travel thirty-odd miles to come twice in two nights? Despite Ollie's suggestion, it didn't look like he was having any kind of drug reaction that Dave had seen before (and coming from the '70s, he'd seen plenty, even if booze had always been his own drug of choice). He tried to laugh it off, but nagging concerns kept creeping up on him. Dave knew he wasn't anywhere near the same league as John Lennon, but what if this guy was another Mark Chapman? What if he had some bizarre fixation on the real Dave Masters and was transferring it to his musical doppelganger (ironically, actually the real Dave Masters)? If things escalated, no one would ever know that Dave Masters had joined Lennon in the pantheon of murdered stars, they'd all think it had happened to some tribute singer called Tom Mulvaney.

As they left the gig that night, Shaun sloping off with a couple of local girls who had inveigled their way backstage, Dave saw Dead-Eyed Freak Boy hanging around at the stage door. Positioning himself between Martin and Ollie, he avoided eye contact (despite Freak Boy's attempt to fix him with, as Stuart Maconie might have put it, a gimlet-eyed stare). He successfully negotiated the short distance to the tour bus without meeting an untimely end but didn't risk looking out of the windows until they were safely on the road to their lodgings. He often retired to his room when they reached whatever low-rent establishment Tony had spent as little money on as possible, but this time he sat around and had a drink with the others. He didn't want to let his mind dwell on where all this might be going.

The next day, Dave found some time before they hit the road and phoned Tony.

'Tom, hi, how's it going? Jym tells me that the audiences are lapping it up.'

'Yeah, for the most part. Did he mention Dead-Eyed Freak Boy?'

The briefest of pauses, before Tony answered. 'Yes, I think he said something about it. I wouldn't worry – you know how some fans are. He won't be able to get in tonight anyway: it's a student union gig. Take the night off worrying and just enjoy the knowledge that I'm subsidising your audience tonight, along with the rest of the tax-payers.'

Dave scoffed. 'Come off it – since when did you pay your taxes?'

Tony had been breezy and dismissive, but that brief pause had worried Dave. He knew Tony well enough to recognise him gathering his thoughts before answering: he wasn't as blasé as he made out. From past experience, Tony's desire for Dave not to be put off his performance (translation: for everyone, particularly Tony himself, to get paid) would come ahead of any real danger he might be facing; the risk to Dave was something Tony would happily accept. There was one more thing Dave wanted to bring up, unrelated to the possible stalker.

'I'm still writing songs, by the way.'

'Fine. I'm still saying you can't play them.'

It was Jym's turn to drive the tour bus, so Dave took a seat at the front alongside him.

'So, you told Tony about Dead-Eyed Freak Boy,' he began.

'Yeah, I'm sure it's nothing, but I just wanted to run it by him.'

'What did he say?' Dave wondered whether Tony would have been so breezily dismissive with someone else.

'He told me to keep an eye on things. Look, he won't be able to get in at Leicester, and after that we're in Sheffield, which hopefully moves us out of his range; if he's based somewhere between Swindon, Oxford and Birmingham, Sheffield's a hell of a long way just to stare at someone.'

Dave hoped Jym was right. The tour was moving steadily north – they had a rest day after Leicester, and Sheffield was followed by Newcastle and Sunderland, then another free day before the Scottish leg of the tour – Stirling, Glasgow and Edinburgh. Better yet, Cindy was meeting them in Sunderland. She was due to arrive in time for the gig, enjoy the day off with Dave and then come along for all three Scottish shows. As long as he could avoid being murdered or abducted until then, that is.

As predicted, there was no sign of Dead-Eyed Freak Boy in the crowd at Leicester, and Dave even won the pool on Chris's bladder. The student crowd went for the show with youthful abandon, and Dave was pleased when they showed some appreciation for the show's subtler moments, such as "The Very Thing That Makes You Rich" and "Feel Like Going Home".

He had, for once, forgotten about Dead-Eyed Freak Boy until they were leaving the gig. But there he was, waiting at the stage door.

'Tom, Dave, whatever you're calling yourself!' he shouted. Dave's pulse quickened; this was escalating. Putting Jym between himself and the stalker, Dave hurried to the bus, terrified about what might be about to happen.

Dead-Eye was still shouting. 'Wait! I only want to talk.' Dave had no intention of letting this go any further, so he scurried onto the bus and found a seat on the opposite side. Dink was brusquely removing Dead-Eye from the area. He had dodged a bullet – mercifully, only a metaphorical one – but this was getting serious. He hadn't had to deal with stuff like this when he was a proper rock star, never mind now he was just a pretend one.

While the rest of the band partied in Shaun's room, Dave went to his own room and pulled out his notebook. He poured out his feelings in the form of song lyrics. What was going on in Dead-Eye's head? He tried to put himself there, to imagine being that obsessed with someone. Before long a dark and brooding inner monologue had emerged. It was still rough around the edges but had definite potential. He was calling it "Standing Staring". Maybe he'd turn it into a dark, twisted love song, move it away from the stalker angle and towards romantic obsession – that would be easier for an audience to connect with. Not that there was any prospect of an audience getting to hear it. Dave understood Tony's reasons, but he still hoped to wear him down eventually. He had never expected new songs to rise from his empty grave. Now that they had, he owed it to his artistic legacy to let the world hear his new creations. He had to make it happen.

The drive from Leicester to Sheffield was a good hour and a half or, in the language of the Dave ReMastered Band, at least two albums. Today was Ollie's turn to soundtrack the start of the journey. A familiar organ pattern came out of the speakers. Dave looked up, delighted and noticed that Shaun had pricked up his ears too, though, judging from the look on his face, he was intrigued at something he hadn't heard before.

'Ollie,' said Dave. 'I didn't know you were a fan of the Band. Go to the top of the class!'

'Thanks, Gramps. I just wanted to make you old-timers feel at home.' That last comment got a rousing cheer from the rest of the lads, always happy to pile on when people tried to make Dave and Jym feel old.

'There are benefits of advanced years,' said Jym. 'I saw this lot at Wembley in '74.'

'I must have developed good taste before you,' added Dave. 'I saw them in '71 at the Royal Albert Hall. Some of us are destined to be trendsetters, while others just follow in our trail.'

'Says the man who makes a living imitating someone whose best days were nearly ten years ago.' For a moment, everyone held their breath, unsure whether Shaun had overstepped the mark. Dave was aware that everyone was waiting to see how he'd react.

'I resent that,' he said. 'Dave Masters' best days were more like fifteen years ago, not ten.'

Ollie and Dave settled down to an in-depth discussion about Levon Helm, the Band's drummer and, it turned out, a mutual favourite. Despite Dink's hopeful cries of 'Veto!' from the driver's seat, nobody else was in any hurry to get rid of the Band, so *Music from Big Pink* stayed the course. When "The Weight" started, Dave, Ollie and (less successfully) Jym tried recreating the harmonies, much to the delight of the others. A hush fell over the bus at the start of "Long Black Veil", and everyone was drawn in by the unfolding narrative of a poor boy hanged for a crime he didn't commit.

'Great song,' said Martin at the end.

'I don't get it, though,' added Shaun. 'The judge said he'd be okay if he had an alibi, and he was in bed with his friend's wife. If telling the truth gets you out of trouble, why stay quiet?'

'Maybe he didn't want to lose his mate.'

'He can't be that bothered about the friendship, not if he's at it with his mate's wife behind his back.'

'No, you're missing the point,' said Chris, joining the discussion. 'He didn't keep his mouth shut for his mate's sake, he was protecting the woman he loves, keeping her from being exposed; it's a noble sacrifice.'

'Noble?' asked Martin. 'What's noble about doing his mate's wife? Isn't the friend entitled to know what's been going on – wouldn't you want to know?'

'Fair point,' conceded Chris. 'I'd want to know. Noble is maybe stretching it a bit.'

'But what does the husband gain from being told?' asked Jym. 'If she's not going to do it again, coming clean won't benefit anyone. The husband won't trust her and it will just get in the way of them moving forward and rebuilding. Some guilty secrets should stay secret, to protect the innocent. Sometimes a lie that works is better than a truth that ruins everything.'

There was silence for a moment as the others pondered Jym's observation, which was broken by Shaun. 'Never mind that, I still say he's being a bloody idiot. It's certainly not best for him, is it? Think about it: if he's dead, he'll never get to bang her – or anybody else – ever again. How's that good?'

'Shaun,' said Martin, a chuckle in his voice, 'I know you might find this hard to believe, but there are more important things in life than shagging.'

'You reckon? We're hard-wired to look for the next shag, aren't we? Darwin and all that – we have an instinctive need to pass on our DNA. To do that, we need to shag as many women as many times as possible.'

Ollie saw the flaw in Shaun's argument. 'So, if your constant shagging is all about passing on your DNA, why do you use condoms?'

'Are you mad? I don't want to have to deal with kids, do I? Anyway, that's not a problem for you, is it, Sticks? What does a drummer use for contraception? His personality.' Ollie grinned and shook his head while the others laughed. You could always rely on drummer jokes to bring the band together.

CHAPTER SIXTEEN

They arrived at their hotel in the middle of the afternoon. While the crew went to sort out the gear, the band wanted to know what there was to do in Sheffield on a Sunday afternoon and didn't seem impressed by Dave's tongue-in-cheek observation that they could go to church if they wanted.

'I'd rather rack up a few more things to confess.' Shaun grinned.

The lads drifted off in ones and twos, agreeing to all meet up later for a curry – past experience meant that Dave and Jym knew exactly which curry house to suggest. Dave stayed behind and went to his room to tinker with his latest song. At first he struggled to focus, his mind constantly circling back to the conversation on the bus. He had been on the road at Shaun's age and taken much the same approach to women, although he saw things differently now. Even once he met Cath he hadn't changed, reasoning that what happens on the road stays on the road. And, unlike Shaun, condoms weren't really a consideration; back then there was no AIDS to worry about, and other than an occasional dose of the clap, there were no consequences for the blokes. Dave thought about his growing relationship with Cindy; as a younger man he wouldn't have lasted five minutes with her – she wouldn't have put up with his cheating and he'd have lost interest long before she let him anywhere near her. The young Dave wouldn't have understood Cindy's reticence or even cared about it if he did; he'd have given up and moved on to the next girl within five minutes. He had never given a second thought for how his actions affected Cath or the other women; now the thought of hurting Cindy was unbearable, and he genuinely didn't want anyone else. Why trade what they had for a meaningless one-night stand after a gig?

He wandered down to reception to use a payphone, but Cindy wasn't in. It was a Sunday, so he knew she wasn't working, but maybe she had gone round to Nicky's. Oh well, he could try again later. The truth was, for all the joking from the lads, Dave was really missing Cindy. Despite his best efforts, there were times on the road they had to go several days without talking. It would be so good to see her again in Sunderland.

Going back to his room, he forced himself to concentrate on his reworking of "Standing Staring", shifting the song's focus to obsessive, unrequited love. By the time he met the others in town he was really pleased with how it was shaping up. Surely Tony would see songs as good as this deserved to be recorded. Maybe an album by the Dave ReMastered Band, songs inspired by Dave Masters? The lads, with the possible exception of Ollie (who had already done session work), would be beyond excited at the prospect of getting into a real studio.

When Dave arrived at the curry house, the crew were already there, setting about a large pile of poppadoms. The rest of the band soon arrived, and the waiter came to take their order. Dink was easily coerced into proving his manhood by ordering a Phall, which led to much amusement as his meal was punctuated with more sweat than a James Brown gig and more toilet visits than Chris on the first night of a tour.

The conversation turned towards Cindy's imminent arrival. Shaun helpfully observed that some men of Dave's age had trouble getting started and offered to attach jump leads to his own testicles if Dave wanted a bit of help. Dave assured him that wouldn't be necessary. Chris asked if Cindy was bringing Nicky along, and looked a little disappointed that she wasn't. At the London gigs, the two girls generally came along together, and Dave had suspected for a while that Chris liked Nicky. He kept telling him to give her a call once they were back in London, but the lad hadn't plucked up the courage yet.

Jym, as he often did, started talking about the tours he'd worked on over the years. Martin, Shaun, Chris and Ollie had started playing Jym bingo – Jymgo – which involved each naming five classic rock acts and scoring a point for each name that Jym dropped over the course of the tour. Martin was currently winning 3-1-0-1.

'Of course, being in Sheffield I should mention that I was a roadie for Joe Cocker in '82.' Dave noticed Shaun raise his eyebrows in silent celebration. 'What a bloke he was. He could drink you lot under the table even in his sleep. Proper singer, he was.'

'None taken,' said Dave, to general amusement.

Jym grinned. 'I didn't mean it like that. You're pretty good yourself, Tom, I'll give you that. I'm surprised you decided to go into the tribute lark, to be honest – the way you sing and play, I would have thought you could be out there making music under your own name.'

'Why *are* you doing a tribute act, Tom?' asked Chris. 'I mean, Jym's not wrong, you're a great guitar player and we've all heard you strumming away in your room and writing songs. Why not do your own thing instead of playing someone else's music?'

Dave paused; that was a difficult one. Playing his own music was important to him – more important than he'd realised when he decided to become dead – so how could he justify what they all thought he was doing? He ran through his mental checklist of his cover story: years as a sideman and session player, never getting the break he had hoped for. 'Oh, I know my place. I tried all that when I was younger and I didn't get anywhere. I've made a living with sessions, but if this lets me play to decent audiences at the front of my own band, there are worse compromises than only singing Dave Masters' songs. I've always been a fan, after all.'

'How many times did you see him play?' asked Ollie.

'I couldn't tell you: I've lost count of the number of Dave Masters' gigs I've been to.' That was true, but he'd never actually seen any of them; he'd been too busy playing the starring role.

Dave tried Cindy again once they got back to the hotel, even though it was late, but there was still no answer. She was probably down the King's Head or round at Nicky's. He didn't mind that she'd gone out – after all, she can hardly spend a month waiting by the phone on the off chance that he called – but he was disappointed to have missed her again. Without the post-gig adrenalin surge, sleep came easily. Tom Mulvaney was definitely a better sleeper than Dave Masters had been; maybe he just had a happier life.

The next day he finally managed to get hold of Cindy. He gave her the call-phone number and she rang him back. They chatted for ages, with her telling him what she'd been up to (she had been down the pub, with Nicky, last night) and asking about the gigs. He told her about the escalation of things with Dead-Eyed Freak Boy after the Leicester gig, and she asked if he was worried.

'No,' he lied. 'I mean, as Jym says, there has to be a limit for how far he's going to travel to stare at me. We're not expecting him to make it up to Sheffield, and certainly not for the Scottish leg of the tour.'

'Well, be careful. Don't let anything happen to you before I get there, you know?'

'What, so it's okay for something to happen then? Are you hoping for a good view?'

'I didn't mean that.' Dave smiled. From her tone of voice, he knew she'd have hit him affectionately on the arm if she'd been here. 'I mean, don't let anything happen, because I love you.' Her voice put on a mock-dismissive tone for the next bit. 'And because I'm looking forward to the shows – it'd be such a bummer not to see you and the boys at least once more before he takes you out.'

They carried on chatting, getting a bit soppy in a way that Dave was glad none of the band, particularly Shaun, could overhear. Once Cindy finally rang off, Dave checked his change and then made another call, this time to Tony. The news wasn't great: the new album wasn't selling well, and there was talk about not releasing any more singles. As far as Ultimate were concerned, the Dave Masters bubble was on the verge of bursting.

'But the Best Of is still in the album charts; can't they keep promoting that?'

'Oh, they're happy to keep taking the money for it, but they reckon it's reached the stage where everybody knows about it now. It should tick over with sales, but it's not worth their time or money to promote, especially with nothing else to release afterwards. The cupboard is bare now, and to be honest they're not lamenting the fact. We're not going to get any more help from Ultimate, but at least your live shows will still help drive album sales. You just keep reminding people how good the real thing was, rather than your pale imitation.'

'But I am the real thing!'

'Yeah, but only we can know that, or there'll be some very awkward questions. Oh, by the way, I think we've found a buyer for your old house. We're still haggling over a price, but we're not too far off. I wish you hadn't put that clause in your will to give half the proceeds to Cath.'

'It was the least she deserved. She could have fought me for it when we divorced but she wanted to keep things civil. If this makes her life a bit more comfortable, I think she's earned that for everything I put her through.'

'True, but I'd still prefer a bigger lump sum in the trust fund. We burned through a lot of money covering the costs of your disappearance. Your new identity didn't come cheap, you know.'

'About that, who was Tom Mulvaney? Was he the body they found with my ID, or was that just some other dead guy?'

'I didn't ask and I don't want to know. If you're smart, you won't go looking down that rabbit hole either.'

The Leadmill was a great venue, although the band were getting used to this size of room and seemed less impressed than they would have been a few weeks ago. Chris's nerves were no better than usual, but that was all part of the band's routine now; if he ever got over his stage fright, it would probably throw the others off their game. As Dave showed his tour pass at the door, he looked carefully around. There was no sign of Dead-Eyed Freak Boy, but Dave couldn't quite bring himself to believe that he'd seen the last of him.

He found Jym, smoking at the sound desk with Ben.

'Afternoon, fellers. Everything all right?'

'Will be once we've sound-checked, boss,' replied Ben. 'Shall I send Dink to round up the boys?'

'Yeah, let's get this done.' He drew Jym to one side. 'I don't suppose there's any sign of our unwelcome hanger-on, is there?'

'Dead-Eyes? No, no sign so far. I told you, he won't come this far north. We've seen the last of him for the time being.'

'Yeah, I'm sure you're right. Just keep an eye out, though.'

With that, he made his way up to the stage, strapped on his Strat and started playing while he waited for the others. He exchanged a few technical comments with Ben, but they were happy with the sound long before the others turned up. Dave picked up the Ovation so Ben could start getting the levels right for that. He started strumming the opening chords to "The Weight", which was still on his mind from yesterday's journey. He could see Jym nodding along approvingly. He started singing, and as he reached the first chorus, Shaun joined in with a tinkling piano line which wasn't far off Richard Manuel's playing on the original. By the time they reached the next chorus, Martin and

Ollie were locked into the groove, with Chris manfully finding a part for his harmonica. Given that half the band had barely heard the song a couple of days earlier, they didn't make a bad job of it, even surpassing Jym and Ollie's attempts at harmony vocals. They finished the song, to applause from Jym and Ben.

'Ah man, I wish we could add that to the set,' said Chris.

'No can do,' said Martin. 'If Dave Masters didn't play it, we can't play it. Anyway, we've already got one Band cover with "Stagefright", haven't we?'

Ben's voice cut sardonically over the PA. 'That was lovely, now can we get on with some work? I've got levels for the electric and acoustic guitars. Can we do the drums now, please?'

The band set themselves to the painstaking task of balancing all the instruments, getting the sound just right. After the drums, Shaun's keyboard and organ were put through their paces before finally Martin's bass was given the Ben treatment.

'That's great, lads,' said Ben via the PA. 'Do you want to do something as a band now?'

'Okay, lads, any requests?' asked Dave. 'Anything we could do with running through for tonight's show? How about "Back in the High Life Again"?'

'No, I've got a better idea,' said Shaun. 'Join in when you get it, boys.' With that he started on a piano riff which Dave immediately recognised. He joined in with the lead guitar line and the rest of the band quickly picked up the pace behind him and he threw himself into the vocal. It was the Faces track "Cindy Incidentally", and the lads in the band were all grinning, delighted that Shaun had found another way to wind Dave up about Cindy's imminent arrival. At the end of the run-through, Ben announced he was happy. The band trooped off to the dressing room for the final countdown to the show.

What a show it was. From the first number ("Stagefright") to the last ("Trouble on My Mind"), they had the audience right where they wanted them. Even "Back in the High Life Again" went down well, and Martin concluded afterwards that they seemed to have found their way into making it work at last. The rest of the band were flawless, and Dave masterfully played all three of his instruments: guitar, voice and audience. By the time they took their bows the five sweaty musicians were basking in the glory of a job well done. Even better, if Dead-Eyed Freak Boy had turned up, Dave hadn't spotted him, not in his customary place to the right of the stage nor anywhere else.

Backstage was the usual happy, messy chaos, with Shaun looking to perform his Darwinian duty. Dave and the others left him to it, although Chris seemed to be taken with a sweet little blonde girl who was hanging on his every word. Dave hoped that he wasn't going to make a habit of picking up girls after gigs. Shaun may relish the debauchery of rock 'n' roll, but Dave didn't think Chris was that kind of bloke; he could do with something a bit more real than the shallow thrills of a one-night stand.

Eventually, they headed for the minibus. They were laughing and joking, Chris had his arm round the blonde and Shaun, typically, had a girl on each arm. Dave was relaxed and happy, looking forward to winding down, when a figure loomed out of the shadows: Dead-Eyed Freak Boy.

'Please, just let me talk,' he started, grabbing Dave's forearm and gabbling on before anyone else had the chance to react. 'I know I've been acting weird, and I know you don't know me, but… I think you're my dad.'

CHAPTER SEVENTEEN

For a moment Dave struggled to make sense of the words. He was Dead-Eyed Freak Boy's dad? He opened his mouth a few times but no words came out. He felt like he was underwater with everything moving in slow motion. He had a son.

Jym grabbed his arm. 'Come on, Tom, onto the bus. Let's split.' Dave let himself be guided into a seat. Whether by accident or design, the others were giving him space. Had they heard what was said? Jym went back to talk with Dead-Eyed Freak Boy (or should Dave start calling him Junior?). He shook his head to clear it, trying to instigate the change from shell-shock to thinking. The lad was, what? Eighteen or so? He was the right age to have been conceived when Dave was making the most of his on-the-road opportunities. Frankly, back then he made Shaun seem like Cliff Richard. Dave's old joke about not knowing if he had any kids didn't seem quite so funny now. He had a strong sense that this could change everything for him, one way or another.

The bus got going and Jym came and sat himself down next to Dave.

'You all right, mate? I heard what he said. Could it be true?'

'Maybe. If he is mine, though, it's the first I've heard of it.'

'Just a chancer, do you think? Someone trying it on? Or maybe he believes it and it's his mum that's spinning a line.'

'Or it could be true. I don't know what to think, Jym.'

'If you want my advice, forget about it for now. Get back to the hotel, have a drink and get your head clear for Newcastle. All right?'

Dave didn't hang around with the lads that evening, going straight to his room. He wanted to talk to Cindy but wasn't sure what to say. How would she react to this? The whole absent-father thing wasn't a great look. No, that's not fair; he couldn't be blamed for neglecting a kid he hadn't even known about for eighteen years; Cindy would see that. Either way, he wasn't going to bring it up over the phone; she'd be here in two days. They could talk then once he'd had time to get his thoughts straight.

Sleep wouldn't come. His mind kept going back to Dead-Eyed Freak Boy (though now it felt wrong to keep calling him that). What did he want from Dave? Was he looking for a relationship, money or just some closure? Despite having never wanted children, now he found himself wondering what he'd missed out on. What about things with his own father? If he could start from scratch and remake that relationship, what would he want from it? A bit more honesty and understanding – going both ways – would have been good. It was too late for that now, but did it have to be too late for him and his own new-found son, if that's who he really was?

As he was getting on the minibus the next morning, Jym pulled him aside.

'Look, I didn't say this last night, but I've taken that lad's details. Entirely up to you, but if you want to get in touch with him, I've got an address and a phone number. I told him to leave you alone to get your head round things and I'd see if you wanted to talk. I haven't made any promises on your behalf, but hopefully he'll back off a bit and give you time to take it all in.'

'Thanks, Jym. Appreciate it.' Dave paused for a moment,

reluctant to ask the next question and make everything a little bit more real. 'Do you know his name?'

'Ronnie.'

Ronnie. Good name that, like Ronnie Wood or Ronnie Lane; the kind of name he might have chosen.

The gig at Newcastle Riverside was tough for Dave. He was professional enough to deliver, even though his head was all over the place, but a nagging feeling told him he wasn't quite on top form. His lack of sure-footedness must have been infectious, as collectively the band weren't quite on it either. The audience all enjoyed themselves, and it was a perfectly decent performance, but their standards had become a lot higher than that. Dave was annoyed with himself when they came off stage, knowing he was to blame.

'Sorry, lads, I let the team down today.'

'Happens to the best of us, Tom,' said Ollie.

'I thought you weren't your usual self,' said Martin. 'What's up?'

Dave shook his head dismissively. 'Don't worry about it, just stuff on my mind. I'll try to be more professional tomorrow night.'

'I know what it is!' cried Shaun. 'Cindy gets here tomorrow – the old man's trying to save his energy so he can keep up with a younger woman.' The others cheered playfully, but all Dave's anxieties over the Ronnie situation spilled over at last.

'What's your problem, Shaun?' he exploded, squaring up and balling his fists. 'I had a bad gig; it happens. It's nothing to do with Cindy.'

'All right, all right, calm down, Grandad. I think it's great that you can still pull someone like her; I'll be happy if I'm doing the same when I get to your age.'

Martin interjected, 'The world doesn't revolve around your dick, Shaun.'

A mischievous glint came into Shaun's eye. 'You'd be surprised, mate. I'll tell you what, though: I'd be quite happy to have Cindy revolving around my dick. Can you send her over once you've finished with her, Tom?'

That was too much. Even before he realised what he was doing, Dave launched himself towards Shaun, fists swinging wildly. Shaun had a good fifteen years on him, but he wasn't a big man and Dave fancied his chances. Ollie, with a drummer's perfect timing, had anticipated the moment and got between the two of them. As Dave let himself be bundled away, he could hear Shaun's voice.

'It was a joke – can't you take a joke? It was a compliment; I'm saying your girlfriend's fit!'

Dave was going to say something back, but Ollie got in first. 'Ignore him. He's a great player, but the bloke's a prick. Leave him until you've both calmed down, for the sake of the band if nothing else.'

It was good advice. Dave decided to make his own way back to the hotel and again went straight to his room, avoiding the others.

When Dave got to the bus the next day, last one on as usual, the mood was subdued. He could tell that everyone had been talking about last night. That was the other side of life on the road: the camaraderie and banter was great, but when bandmates got on your nerves there was nowhere to hide.

Shaun made his way over to Dave's seat.

'Just wanted to say sorry, Tom, about last night. I didn't mean to hack you off and I didn't mean to disrespect Cindy.'

Dave looked him in the eye. He looked bashful, as if he was genuinely sorry about what happened rather than just saying what the others had told him to (although the line about disrespecting Cindy sounded more like Martin or Chris). He decided to take the apology at face value. 'Don't worry about it, Shaun. I was wound up about not playing my best gig and I wasn't in the mood. You were being a tit, but I over-reacted. I'm sorry. All good?'

Shaun smiled with relief and shook Dave's outstretched hand. 'All good.'

Newcastle to Sunderland was one of the shorter journeys on the tour, meaning there wasn't likely to be time even for a whole album. Ollie's choice, a band called the Long Ryders, was new to Dave. It would have been right up his street on another day, but he barely noticed the music, his mind constantly probing the subject of Ronnie. Jym also chose this journey to break the news to everyone that Tony had booked another show on what had previously been a free date. Instead of a day off after Liverpool in a week's time, they would now cross the Pennines to play York University, then all the way over to Cardiff for the following night. It was a lot of extra travel, but an extra show meant an extra payday, and another chance to build their live following.

They checked into the hotel and Jym offered to meet Cindy's train at the station. Dave wanted to go himself, to see her that bit sooner, but he knew he could do with a lie-down. Half an hour later, there was a knock on Dave's door. He looked at his watch; it was far too soon for Cindy. Had she got an earlier train? He tried to keep the disappointment off his face when he saw who it was.

'Not who you were hoping for?' asked Martin, which suggested that Dave hadn't succeeded.

'Yeah, no. Don't worry about it. Come on in. What can I do for you?'

'I just wanted to check you were okay, mate. I thought the gig was all right last night – not our best, but not bad. But you really weren't yourself afterwards. Everything's all right with Cindy, isn't it?'

'Nah, it's not that. I've just got stuff on my mind, that's all.'

'Anything you want to talk about?'

Dave took in Martin's expression. In some bands, sharing personal problems would be to invite gossip and ridicule. If this had been Shaun offering, he would have been much more suspicious, but that didn't seem like Martin's style. As far as Dave could tell, it was a genuine offer to help.

'Not just now; Cindy's good with this stuff. I appreciate the offer, though, and I may take you up on it another time. Cheers, mate.'

Martin accepted the rejection with good grace and went to find the others. Dave was really coming to appreciate what Martin brought to the band, on and off stage. At the start he had thought Chris was the glue who held the others together, but the longer he spent with them the more he realised it was Martin.

It was late afternoon when the next knock on the door came, and this time there was no disappointment. Cindy leapt through the doorway and into his arms, propelling him backwards into the room to collapse – conveniently – on the bed. Damn, she smelt great.

'I've missed you so much,' he started.

'Shut up and kiss me.'

'Righteo.'

Cindy came with them to the soundcheck. She had been worried about getting in the way, but Jym had provided her with an access all areas pass and said she was welcome to sit at the sound desk with Ben. As long as she didn't talk to him while he was sorting the levels, she'd be fine.

With Dave in good spirits, it was a much better show. It was the first time Cindy had heard them play "The Very Thing That Makes You Rich", and afterwards she said it was her favourite of the night. It was a judgement that earned approving nods from Martin, Ollie and Jym. Jym told her about the time he was part of the crew on a Ry Cooder tour of Europe, but nobody scored a point as he had mentioned it several times before.

Dave and Cindy didn't get a lot of sleep, but they weren't complaining. They did a lot of talking too, and Dave filled her in on the Ronnie situation.

'The poor lad,' said Cindy. 'What did you say to him?'

'Not a lot – I didn't know what to say. Jym got me his contact details, but I'm not sure what to do. I'm not even sure if he really is mine. Maybe it's better if I just leave it.'

'You can't; you have to talk to him, for his sake.' Dave was surprised at how adamant Cindy was. 'Think how big a deal it must have been for him to come and find you; it took him a few shows even to say anything – this is huge for him. The least you can do is help him uncover the truth. If he is your son, you've still got choices, but if you ignore him, he's got nothing – not even certainty.' She went suddenly quiet and turned away from Dave. He leant over and realised that she was crying.

'Hey – what's up?' She resisted when he tried to turn her towards him, so he spooned up behind and wrapped his arm around her. She allowed him to pull her towards him and hold her tightly, and that's how they stayed for the rest of the night.

They were woken by a repeated banging on the door. Normally Jym just came in to shake Dave awake, but in deference to Cindy he was being more circumspect. Dave called that they'd be down at the bus soon, as Cindy sat up and rubbed her eyes. When the two of them eventually stepped blearily onto the bus, the others raised an ironic cheer, and Shaun politely enquired whether they had slept well. Dink was about to select some music when Chris suggested that they let their guest choose. Cindy rummaged through her bag and pulled out a cassette.

'Now then,' said Jym. 'Normal rules apply: this can still be vetoed off, but Cindy showed last night that she's got good taste – in music if not in men – so let's give her a chance.'

Cindy had chosen a World Party album, one that Dave had heard a few times round at her flat. During the second track, Jym said he could hear the Stones in it, adding that he had toured with the Stones in '79, prompting Shaun to shout, 'House!'

Cindy's choice lasted to the end of the album, no mean feat, although some of the lads slept through a lot of it. The next offering, Dink's choice of *Bat out of Hell*, soon woke everyone up. It was a rare instance of one of Dink's selections lasting the whole album.

It was a long journey to Stirling, several albums' worth. Billy Joel's *An Innocent Man* (Shaun's pick) was better than Dave had expected, and Martin's choice of the Proclaimers – he said they had to get in the mood for Scotland – proved to be a rousing success. For his turn, Dave managed to get most of Johnny Cash's *At Folsom Prison* on, with the death-row countdown "25 Minutes to Go" particularly well received. There was general agreement that Cash's version of "Long Black Veil" wasn't as good as the Band's, though Shaun liked the fact that someone in the crowd cheered the revelation of the singer sleeping with his friend's wife.

They had an evening off before the following night's gig at the university's McRobert Theatre. They were staying at a B&B in a town called Bridge of Allan, a stone's throw from the campus. On the suggestion of the landlady (who took an instant liking to Cindy), Dave and Cindy headed up to the university to stroll around the loch. It was, as promised, a beautiful setting. Once they were safely away from everyone else (apart from the ducks), Dave brought up the previous night.

'So, do you want to tell me what those tears were about?' he asked gently. 'I was worried.'

She leaned into him, squeezing his waist with her arm. 'I know I made a big deal about you not being open when we first met, but there's stuff I've never told you. One of the reasons why Alex leaving me...'

'Alex?'

'Pet Shop Bastard.'

'Right, of course. Carry on.'

'One of the reasons Alex dumping me hurt so much is that it wasn't the first time I've been badly treated by a man. When I was young – like, still at school – I started seeing this older guy. One thing led to another and I got pregnant.'

Dave didn't say anything, giving Cindy room to tell the story her way.

'Anyway, he wanted nothing to do with it. He said I'd get in trouble if I told anyone about him. He offered to pay for me to get rid of it, but I just couldn't. He said if that was my choice, it was nothing to do with him anymore. My parents moved me away to stay with my auntie down in Bournemouth for a few months, and when the baby was born we… we gave her up for adoption.' Her voice was barely a whisper now, and Dave's heart broke for her. How had Cindy faced all that when she was so young? 'I think of her every day – every single day. They wouldn't let me trace her, so I've got no idea where she went or what kind of life she's living; I don't even know her name. I just worry that she'll think her mother didn't want her. And I did – oh, Tom, I so wanted her.' Tears streaked her face now, and she buried her head into his chest, digging her fingers into his shirt. He held her tight, stroking her head. He didn't know what to say but suspected that words weren't what she wanted from him right now.

Eventually, Cindy came up for air. The hysterical crying had passed, with just the occasional sob punctuating her words.

'That's why you have to help poor Ronnie. If he's had no father all this time, you've got to at least give him answers. Even if they aren't the answers he wants, he deserves to know, just like my little girl deserves to know that her mum loves her, though she never will.'

Dave promised to get Ronnie's details from Jym. Cindy's revelation had put his situation in context, but there was another reason why he wanted to hear Ronnie's story: over the last day or so it had occurred to him that he had been trying to connect Ronnie's birth with the misadventures of his past life, but those were the misadventures of Dave Masters. As far as everyone else – including Ronnie, presumably – was concerned, he was Tom Mulvaney. Unless Ronnie somehow knew about the fake suicide, there was no way he could be Ronnie's father.

CHAPTER EIGHTEEN

Despite being a seated venue, it was another great gig. The short hop down to Glasgow the next day left plenty of time to surprise Ronnie with a phone call. It turned out that he lived in Reading, which they were due to play in just over a week, so Dave arranged to meet him on the free day after the gig.

The next couple of days rushed by. Dave loved having Cindy there, in stark contrast to his previous firmly held views of girlfriends and tours. Once she caught the train back home, the rest of the tour loomed ominously. Two weeks was nothing on the road, but two weeks without seeing Cindy again seemed huge. They had talked more about Cindy's secret, something that she hadn't told anyone before. Dave felt privileged that she trusted him with it.

Once Cindy was gone, Dave threw himself into songwriting again. He was particularly pleased with one he was calling "Rockabye", a tender song of reassurance in the face of nameless terrors. More than anything, that was what he wanted to provide for Cindy.

The next day he phoned Tony to update him on Ronnie. Tony was concerned at first, but once Dave pointed out that Ronnie almost certainly thought Tom Mulvaney, not Dave Masters, was his dad, he could hear his manager relax.

'So, if you don't think he's your son, why even meet him?'

'Because he deserves to know that I'm not his dad, that this isn't him being rejected.'

'Well, it's up to you, but I don't see what you get out of that. I suppose it's worth meeting him just to make sure he doesn't know who you really are. If he does, we can't let him go round telling people.'

'What's that supposed to mean? You're not going to get your dodgy mates to take him out, are you?'

'Relax. They're not my mates, and that wasn't what I meant. The only person I've ever had killed off is you.'

Once that was out of the way, they returned to the topic of Dave's new songs.

'So how about this,' Dave suggested. 'Why don't we – the Dave ReMastered Band – record the new songs in the style of Dave Masters? It would give us something to sell at gigs.'

'No point. Nobody is interested in a tribute band performing their own material. They only want you to do Dave Masters songs.'

'But these are Dave Masters songs!'

'We know that, but no one else will – and we can't let anyone find out, not ever.' Tony wasn't budging, and to be honest Dave hadn't expected him to. Time to plant a seed – Tony would be more likely to go with it if he thought it was his own idea.

'Yeah, you're right. it's just so frustrating; Ultimate are losing interest due to lack of material, and we're sitting on a potential gold mine of unreleased material. If I'd recorded these songs back in the day, they would be falling over themselves to put out another album. If only we had something like this in the can to offer them.'

'If, if, if. You might as well say if you hadn't spent most of the '80s pissing your talent away, or if you hadn't recorded a turgid final album. Or here's one: if you'd got your mojo back before asking me to kill you off, that would have been a game-changer. But you didn't, and now it's too late; it's not happening.'

Dave bit his lip. He'd all but spelled out his plan to Tony. If he made joining the dots too obvious, Tony would never go for it. He was going to have to be patient.

Cardiff, Manchester and Bristol – the first time Dave had played the Bierkeller in years – came and went, with the band going from strength to strength. The next gig was Reading, and then his meeting with Ronnie.

Ronnie was already in the pub, nervously nursing a pint, when Dave arrived.

'I would have got one for you,' he said. 'But I didn't know what you'd want.'

'No, you're okay – I was going to buy you one.' Dave got himself a drink and they found a secluded corner.

'This place is always dead at this time of day,' said Ronnie. 'I thought we could talk without being interrupted.'

'So, why do you think I'm your dad?' Dave sat back in his chair and took a long look. Ronnie looked nervous, like this was a job interview or something. He was dressed a little more smartly than at the gigs; he had obviously made an effort. Dave hoped he was doing the right thing in shattering the boy's hopes.

'Well, he – you – was never around, I literally have no memory of my father. Mum always avoided answering questions about why I didn't have a dad. She fell ill last year…'

'I'm sorry to hear that. Anything serious?'

'It turns out it wasn't, but we didn't know that at the time. I think it scared her that she might die without ever telling me, so she opened up. She said that my dad was a man called Tom Mulvaney. When I saw your name in that article in *NME*, I wondered if you could be same one. I started digging and realised you were about the right age. She hadn't mentioned anything about you being a musician, but she said my dad ran with a dangerous crowd. There were a lot of crooks involved in music in the early '70s, weren't there?'

Dave thought back to certain notorious managers from back in the day. He'd been lucky to have someone like Tony steering him clear of all that. Then again, in view of Tony's recent activities, who knew how clean his manager had really been?

'True, but I wasn't really part of that scene. How old are you, Ronnie? When were you born?'

'April 1972, so what were you doing in July 1971?'

'Playing music and shagging. To be honest, I could have fathered several children back then without knowing, but the rest of your description doesn't sound like me. Sorry.'

'You're sure you weren't involved on the fringes of organised crime? Mum said that my dad had dangerous friends, that he had aspirations to climb higher but he was hardly the kind of man whose name is spoken in whispers. A low rung on the ladder, she said.'

'Well, I wasn't on the ladder at all. The closest I came to organised crime was my first band, who were just criminally bad. How's your mum doing now? Better, I hope.'

'Yeah, as I said, the scare turned out to be nothing serious. I didn't tell her I had tracked you down because she always said I was better off having nothing to do with you. No offence.'

'None taken – not least because I don't think I'm the Tom Mulvaney you're looking for. Look, my advice is to go back to your mum and ask if her Tom Mulvaney was a musician. If she says yes, then by all means come back to me and we can look into it again. If he wasn't, then like Dylan says, it ain't me, babe.'

Ronnie's shoulders sunk. Dave felt for the kid, and felt guilty too; he had a sneaking suspicion that Ronnie's dad was the Tom Mulvaney whose identity he was now using. It wasn't exactly a common name, and with a criminal background he could easily have fallen foul of Tony's dodgy contacts. The worst thing was that however hard Ronnie searched, he'd never find out that his dad was already dead, because there was no paper trail to his death – it had been replaced by the death of Dave Masters. Even though Ronnie wasn't his son, he couldn't help but feel responsible for him, particularly for the fact that he'd never find the answer to the biggest question in his life.

He knew that Cindy had been on tenterhooks about the meeting, so he phoned her once he got back to the hotel.

'How did it go? Do we have to start calling you Daddy?'

'I'm not the dad. And even if I was, you calling me that would be a bit weird, wouldn't it?'

'Fair point. But you're sure you're not Ronnie's father?'

'The more he told me about his Tom Mulvaney, the more I knew it wasn't me. None of the details matched. If I have got any children out there, Ronnie isn't one of them.'

'The poor love. How did he take it?'

'He was all right. I mean, you could tell it was a blow, but we parted on good terms. I left the door open for him if anything points back in my direction, but I don't think we'll be hearing from him again. How have you been doing?'

'Oh, the same old. Nicky's coming with me to the Camden gig when you get back to London. I wish I could come back on the tour before you come home – those few days in Scotland were great.'

'The highlight of my tour. Well, that or the time we drove off before Dink was on the bus, and he chased after us swearing for a hundred yards or so.'

'So, it's close between me and a sweaty, sweary roadie, is it?' Dave could almost feel the playful smack on the arm over the phone.

'Yeah, I guess you'd better up your game next time we see each other.'

No matter how long or short a tour is, the end always drags. Everybody starts thinking about home and just wants the last few nights out of the way. Not that Dave and the band were phoning in the later shows, far from it, but when they came off after Brighton on the 26th of October, they were relieved to be heading back to London for the triumphant final show at the Electric Ballroom, Camden. It was twice the capacity of their previous London shows and far bigger than anywhere they had played before. Dave made a mental note to go high in the sweepstake for Chris's guts.

They drove through the night after Brighton, so they could sleep in their own beds. Jym delivered the musicians to their homes, then set off with Dink and Ben to safely store the minibus and the gear.

It was nearly 3am by the time Dave pushed open his front door. He dumped his bags on the sofa and headed straight for bed, pulling off clothes as he went. All he wanted right now was some sleep. As he climbed beneath the sheets, he realised there was already someone there. Cindy rolled over, stirring from her slumber.

'Hello, you,' she purred. 'I didn't want to put off seeing you any longer than I had to.' She put her arms around him and kissed him. 'I'm not expecting anything – I know you must be shattered – I just missed you and I wanted to be held tonight, you know?' Dave did know, and he felt exactly the same.

After her experience out on the road, where she had been accepted as part of the touring party for a few days, Cindy was keen to come with Dave to the soundcheck and asked if Nicky could come along too. Dave didn't see why not and said he'd get Jym to arrange passes.

'Is Nicky seeing anyone?' asked Dave over breakfast.

Cindy looked at him suspiciously. 'You know I was joking when I said we could have a threesome after the Del Amitri gig, right?'

Dave laughed. 'Yeah, no, not like that. I was just thinking, would she let us set her up with Chris? He's a decent bloke –

hardly ever gets up to anything on the road, and I think he's quite sweet on her. He seems like the type who would prefer something steady to Shaun's endless one-night stands.'

'I think you might be right. He was always nice with me, making sure I was okay if you weren't around.' She saw Dave's raised eyebrows and hit him playfully. 'No, not like that. I'll see what she thinks. She could do with meeting someone; it's been a while for her.'

When Cindy went off to work, Dave found himself thinking again about Tom Mulvaney, the man whose name he had taken. The business with Ronnie had made him realise he knew nothing about the person he was living as. What if the real Tom had skeletons in his closet that Dave should be aware of? He knew better than to ask Tony again, but he needed to know more.

It was the afternoon of the gig, and everyone was hanging out in the dressing room waiting for the soundcheck. Cindy and Nicky were chatting with Dave and Chris, Shaun was instructing a bouncer about what type of girl to allow backstage, while Martin and Ollie were discussing their favourite rhythm sections.

Matty the bouncer put his head round the door, looking for Dave.

'Excuse me, mate. I've got a lady here who says she needs to talk to you.'

'To me?' asked Dave.

'Yeah, she said she had to talk to the one who is playing at being Dave Masters. That's you, right?'

All the other conversations had stopped now, with everyone suitably intrigued. Dave told Matty to show her in, completely unsure what to expect.

The lady walked in, looking elegant and composed. Her clothes were expensive, but not showily expensive: a real class act. She was also Dave's ex-wife.

'Hi,' said Cath. 'Can we talk?'

Dave was aware of Cindy edging closer to his side, on guard against this mysterious rival. Cath acknowledged Cindy's presence with a glance and added the word "alone" to her request.

'What's going on, Tom?' asked Cindy. 'Who is this woman?' Her hackles were up now.

'Yes, *Tom*.' Cath emphasised his assumed name, making it clear that she knew it didn't really belong to him. 'Tell her who I am.' What the hell was she doing here?

Dave took a deep breath. 'Cindy, this is Cath, my ex-wife. Cath, this is my girlfriend, Cindy.' The ladies nodded greetings, though Cindy didn't seem happy. 'Cindy, do you mind giving me a few minutes so I can find out what she wants?'

'Should I be worrying, Tom? Is something going on?' There was a hint of rising panic in Cindy's voice; Dave took her to one side.

'You know I've changed; you know you don't have to worry about me. I haven't seen Cath since long before you and I got together. I've no idea why she's here, but you have nothing to worry about. She doesn't want me back, and even if she did, that's not what I want. She's my history; you're my future. Okay?'

Cindy nodded but didn't look entirely reassured.

Dave gave Cindy a hug and followed Cath out to the bar. He caught Nicky's eye and asked her to look after Cindy.

Cath had found a couple of bar stools, well away from all the staff.

'You're looking good, Dave. Or should I call you Tom?'

'How did you find out?'

'You're not going to deny it, then? Isn't that what you usually do when you get caught in a lie?'

Dave shrugged. He couldn't see where she was going, so maybe he should just let her get there in her own time.

'Was it Tony's idea? I bet it was – fake your death and rake in the money from increased record sales. Am I close?'

Dave nodded. 'Pretty much, though it wasn't really about the money; not for me, anyway. I didn't want to be me anymore, so Tony took care of it. How did you find out?'

'How did I find out? We were married for six years – I recognised you straight away at the funeral.'

'Why didn't you say anything then?'

'What was the point? You're not my responsibility now.' Her voice softened after that. 'And I knew how unhappy you were, how unhappy you'd been for years. I had a clean start, and if you wanted the same, who was I to make trouble? One question, though: the blonde girl – Cindy, was it? – how much does she know?'

'A lot and none at all. She thinks I'm Tom Mulvaney, she's got no idea who I really am. Then again, she knows the real me pretty well. She knows I split up from someone called Cath, she knows I was to blame for the break-up and she knows about my long history of unfaithfulness, because I told her about it before we got together. She also knows I'm a changed man.'

'And are you? A changed man? Apart from the name, obviously.'

'It seems weird saying this to you of all people, but yeah. I think I've finally grown up. She's the only one I want – no on-the-road conquests, no one-night stands. I'm all in at last.'

Cath smiled, reminding Dave of how good things had been when the first got together, before he started messing her around. 'I'm glad. If you're serious about that, she's a lucky woman. Be careful, though, I suspect she won't give you as much leeway as I did; from the way she reacted to me, she either doesn't trust you or she's been burned before.'

'The latter, definitely; as for trusting me…' Dave completed the sentence with a shrug.

'Anyway, that's not what I came here to say, so I'll get to the point. It's your dad, Dave. He's dying. Not straight away – we're talking months rather than weeks – but he's dying all the same. Here's the address of the care home.' She handed him a slip of paper. 'I know things weren't great between you two, but it's now or never to put that right. It's none of my business anymore, but you'll regret it if you don't try. I thought I owed it to you to let you know.' She stood up from the stool and held out her hand. 'I won't kiss you goodbye, in case it upsets Cindy. Thanks for giving me half of the house; that was kind of you, and unexpected. Good luck with Cindy, and good luck with your dad.'

Dave didn't know what to make of his meeting with Cath – he told Cindy she just wanted his signature for some legal stuff – so he put it out of his mind for now. He had a show to focus on. Tony had styled the gig as a triumphant return to their home patch and that's exactly what it was. Dave had put all the favourites into the set list. "Back in the High Life Again" was now one of them. When Dave had recorded it, it was wishful thinking on his part; now, tonight, in front of a packed crowd of 1,500 fans, all there to see him, to hear his music, he sang it with a euphoric sense of fulfilment. Dave's eye fell on Cindy, dancing with Nicky down at the front. She caught his eye and grinned that crooked grin of hers, the one that melted him every single time. After years of miserable struggle and underachievement, both personally and professionally, his life was back on track. Even if he had had to die to make it happen.

The band came off stage after no fewer than four encores. The last of them came after the venue had put the house lights up and the audience had refused point blank to leave. Dave had to come out with his old Ovation and play the solo version of "It Ain't Me Babe", even though he didn't recognise himself in the lyrics anymore. When he joined the others in the dressing room, the beers were already flowing. Tony lobbed a bottle in Dave's direction.

'Fantastic, lads,' said Tony. 'Best I've seen you play – that month on the road has done wonders for you. Get used to venues like this, because there are more on the way. Take a break now and get yourselves ready for December. I'm not booking another tour yet, but we can do a handful of gigs around Christmas to make the most of the silly money that people will pay to book a hot band – which right now is precisely what you are.'

Cindy and Nicky came in at that point, and Cindy threw her arms around him despite the fact he was a hot sweaty mess. Dave noticed that Nicky sidled slyly towards Chris and started chatting and laughing. Cindy gave him a kiss then pushed a piece of paper into his hand.

'You were brilliant – of course,' she said. 'But I think you should see this.'

He looked at the flyer. 'Seriously? "London's finest Dave Masters tribute act, Vagabond Dave and the Troubled Minds".' There was a set of dates listed, all at bigger venues than Vagabond Dave had played before. Nothing to compete with the Electric Ballroom, but the Dublin Castle, the Half-Moon: all the best small venues in London. While Dave had been out conquering the country, Vagabond Dave had been moving in on his home patch.

'Have you seen this, Tony?' he asked, thrusting the flyer towards his manager.

'Yeah. After you showed him up, it seems that Vagabond Dave realised he needed a band. He's recruited well, to be fair, and they're not bad. The thing is, the only venues that are booking them are the ones we've outgrown. Let them have the Half-Moon and don't worry about it; they're not in your league. Anyway, I have a feeling Vagabond Dave will be disappearing soon.'

CHAPTER NINETEEN

Dave and Cindy were enjoying a lazy morning before her shift at Quicksave. They were playing records, but Dave's thoughts kept drifting back to his conversation with Cath. The thought of his dad dying without him at least attempting a reconciliation was unbearable, but what could he do? The risk of exposing what he'd been up to these last few months was just too dangerous. He couldn't even tell Cindy what Cath had really wanted, because he knew she'd insist on coming with him to see his dad, and then he'd have the whole different surnames thing to explain. It was too complicated, and yet he wasn't sure that he could live with the knowledge that he'd let the old man pass away without reaching out to him.

The phone rang and Cindy picked it up.

'Good afternoon, Cindy, my love,' said Tony. 'Is your uglier half around?'

'I'll have you know he's a very handsome man,' joked Cindy.

'If you say so; he's certainly punching above his weight with you.' Cindy admitted that was true – she told Dave later it would have been rude to have argued – and handed over the phone. 'Hi, Tom. Can we talk in private? I've got an idea. For your ears only, if you get my meaning.'

'I get the picture, yeah.' He turned to Cindy. 'Tony wants to talk business. Do you mind popping back to yours for a bit and I'll come find you when he's done?' Once he heard her front door shutting, he spoke again. 'Right, it's just us. What did you mean last night about Vagabond Dave disappearing? You're not planning something with those dodgy mates of yours, are you?'

'What's the matter with you? Last night you played the best gig of your life – well, Tom Mulvaney's life, anyway – and now you're accusing me of I don't know what. How long have we been friends? You should know me better than that. All I meant was that he's had the city to himself; now we're back, he won't find it so easy to get an audience. Anyway, that's not what I wanted to talk about.'

Dave couldn't keep the smile off his face as Tony outlined "his" plan. He'd decided that they really needed some new product to keep the record company interested. A tribute band album was a non-starter, but long-lost Dave Masters tracks, supposedly recorded at the height of his success, would be a different prospect. Tony wanted to put Dave into a studio and let him record the new stuff but to claim it dated back to the late '70s.

Tony continued, 'The thing is, how convincing can you make it on your own? I know you're a guitarist, but you can play the other instruments too, can't you?'

'Lead and rhythm guitar is no problem at all. Bass and keyboards, I'm not as much of a virtuoso as Phil and Simon, but I can do an approximation of their style. I think I can carry it off. Drums might be trickier. I'll give it a go, but they might be a bit rudimentary.'

'Well, we can't afford to let anyone else know. One word out of place and this whole thing could come crashing down. You're up for it, then?'

'It's a great idea, Tony. I wish I'd thought of it first.'

The prospect of the album helped Dave to push the news about his dad to the back of his mind. He told himself that even if he found a way to talk to the old man, there wasn't really anything either of them could say to make up for the ill-feeling of twenty or more years.

Nothing much was happening between Chris and Nicky, partly because Chris was so shy and partly because he was making the most of the post-tour downtime by visiting family. Dave and Cindy were talking about how to speed things along once he got back.

'We could invite them out on a double date, you know?' suggested Cindy. 'Nice restaurant, plenty of wine, then I can say I feel a bit poorly and would Chris mind walking Nicky to her place while you take me home.'

'That's a bit manipulative, isn't it?'

'Excuse me, Mr Let's-set-them-up.'

'Fair point. I take it that Nicky's keen.'

'She thinks he's sweet, and to be honest, it's been so long since she's had a feller, I think she'd consider Shaun if he asked her.'

'Blimey, we'd better get things moving – Shaun isn't what Nicky needs.'

'Shaun isn't what anyone needs, though Nicky would probably take a one-night stand just for the sake of getting some action.'

Dave had something else to take care of. He wanted to know just what he was up against with Vagabond Dave. Roping Martin in as his wingman, he set out to the Dublin Castle to see what the young upstart had to offer.

Paying on the door, Dave was glad to see that it wasn't a sell-out, but it was still a decent showing. Martin went to get the drinks in while Dave secured a spot to one side of the venue, not too near the front. He wanted a good view of the band, but he also wanted to be able to take in the audience – and, of course, not to be spotted from the stage.

Vagabond Dave came out, clutching his battered acoustic. Where the Dave ReMastered Band wore authentic-looking approximations of the real group's stage gear from the '70s, the

Troubled Minds were a garish exaggeration, and Dave wasn't convinced that some of the sidemen weren't wearing wigs. The one authentic touch was Vagabond Dave's leather waistcoat, which looked just like one of Dave's own stage favourites from back in the day. He had looked for his when he was sorting out stage gear for Dave ReMastered, but it hadn't turned up anywhere. He resented Vagabond Dave for finding such a close match.

'Dublin Castle, are you feeling *alllll riiiiighhhhht?*' bellowed the young impersonator, starting the gig in a way that Dave never had in his entire career but still getting a raucous response. 'Are you ready to roll back the years and rock with the Masters?' Dave exchanged glances with Martin, who grinned back at him and rolled his eyes.

Annoyingly, the music was pretty good. Vagabond Dave had passed lead guitar duties to one of the band, and the lad wasn't half bad. Whether he had an original bone in his body was unclear, but at the very least he was a competent copyist, which was all this particular gig required. The solos slavishly followed what Dave had played on the original records. Whereas Dave's current band had grown as musicians and were now recreating the old songs as living, growing entities, the Troubled Minds were aiming at carbon copies and getting pretty close. Vagabond Dave's vocals were good too. Dave had really wanted to be able to dismiss his rival as a jumped-up chancer, but he had to admit he was doing a decent job; too good a job on "Yesterday's Man". It was one of Dave's early songs, born out of frustration with his dad. The aggressive, accusatory lyrics made Dave feel ashamed at his part in putting up the barriers that had kept them apart for all these years.

Martin and Dave left before the set was over, and exchanged notes on the tube home.

'Well, there's no one in their line-up that I'd swap for who we've got, but they were actually pretty good,' said Martin thoughtfully. 'That said, the bass player nailed "Out of My Depth". I hope that doesn't mean my place is under threat.'

Dave laughed and reassured Martin not to worry. They agreed that while the drummer was better than Jonjo, he wasn't a patch on Ollie, and that the keyboard player was note perfect for most of the time but couldn't make the solos sing the way Shaun did.

'What about the guitarist?' asked Martin. Dave trotted out the line about being a copyist but no more, which had Martin nodding in agreement.

'We already knew about the singer – he's good musically but doesn't connect emotionally with an audience. The weird thing is, I think they're selling something different to us. We try to recreate what it was like to see the real Dave Masters Band; they're selling a distorted memory – all primary colours, the '70s seen through the eyes of someone who wasn't ever there. I don't think they're something we need to be worried about.'

Dave nodded thoughtfully. Martin was spot on with his assessment of the differences; he just hoped his final conclusion was right too.

They chatted more generally, about how well the tour had gone and whether it had helped Martin to decide if his future was on stage or in an office. He frowned at the question, pausing before answering.

'I just don't know. I mean, I'm loving it, and that last gig was unbelievable – if I went back to just doing this as a hobby, I'd never get that kind of rush again. I kind of get why the real Dave Masters topped himself: having played massive shows – much bigger than our ones – it must have been soul-destroying to drag himself around tiny venues again. But if someone that talented can see it disappear, what are my chances of staying on top? Not that I'm anywhere near the top, but you know what I mean.'

Dave nodded but stayed quiet.

'If I can make this last, that's brilliant, but if the next few months is all I get, just a collection of great memories, that's not so bad. I'm not saying I won't stay, but going back to my job is certainly safer.'

'Do you want safe?' asked Dave. 'Sometimes you have to take a risk and jump in.'

Martin smiled and shrugged. He still didn't know.

The morning of the Del Amitri gig came, and Cindy was full of flu. She stayed in bed while Dave fussed around looking after her. There was no way she was going out tonight.

'Should I give our tickets to Nicky, see if she can find someone else?' asked Dave. 'It's a shame that Chris is still away, this would have been perfect for the two of them.'

'No, I don't think she could ask anyone else this late, and she won't go on her own. Anyway, you wanted to see Del Amitri too – you two have a good time and make sure to bring me back a tee-shirt.'

Dave was meeting Nicky at the tube station, and as he left, Cindy snuffled a goodbye.

'Have a nice time and look out for Nicky. Don't let her cop off with anyone I wouldn't approve of. And don't forget my shirt!'

Nicky was quiet at first; it occurred to Dave that he'd never spent much time in her company with just the two of them – it was always in a larger group and always with Cindy. He managed to draw her out of herself and they chatted about music on the way down to Hammersmith.

Dave sold the spare ticket to a tout and they went inside. Nicky bought a tee-shirt, which reminded Dave of his promise to Cindy, so he bought one too. Nicky headed straight to the ladies and came out wearing her new purchase, which she proudly modelled for Dave. He laughed and said it looked great, trying not to look too closely at her bust, now tightly decorated with the faces of Del Amitri. They turned out to be a great live act, with a sound that had one foot in America and a nice rhythmic push and pull, ticking all the right boxes for Dave. They even did a version of "Maggie May", which Cindy would have loved.

They played a song that Dave hadn't heard before, but from

the audience reaction it was something of a favourite. Nicky told him afterwards that it was the latest single. It was a cynical lost-love song – their stock in trade, it seemed – with a clever lyric, finding different ways to come back to the same phrase about spit in the rain. All in all, it was a great gig that would only have been improved if Cindy had been well enough to make it.

It was raining when they left Hammersmith, but not too badly. It was a different matter coming out of High Barnet tube station, with rain hammering down and ricocheting off the pavement like a hundred rim shots. Nicky paused to spit comically in the rain, before singing the refrain from that song. Dave joined in, on the singing if not the spitting, and they laughed as they ran from one sheltered shopfront to the next, trying and failing to reach Nicky's flat without getting completely soaked. Dave accepted Nicky's offer of a drink, hoping that the rain would ease off before he completed his own journey home.

Nicky peeled off her sodden jacket, which had soaked through to her tee-shirt underneath. It was clinging revealingly as she stretched and twisted to free her arms from the sleeves. Dave allowed his gaze to linger just a moment longer than he should have done, and he thought she saw him looking. With her wet hair she looked deliciously dishevelled; Dave felt something stirring and he remembered how much he had always fancied Chrissie Hynde back in the day.

Nicky held his gaze, again for a moment longer than was safe. She swept a strand of bedraggled hair from her eyes, which somehow made things worse. It seemed an unconscious, unplanned movement, but if she had been trying to seduce him, she couldn't have played it better. Dave was transfixed, caught in the headlights and trapped between what he knew he should do and his growing desire.

Nicky was the first to break the spell, putting down her jacket and turning away awkwardly. 'I'll, um, go and get some dry clothes. I'm afraid I've not got anything that would fit you – I'll get you a towel, though.' She went into her room, leaving the door open. Was that an invitation? Don't follow her, get the hell out before it's too late. He hesitated too long and Nicky came back, towel in hand. Dave had hoped that she'd throw on a sweatshirt, or at least dry herself off a bit before coming out, but there she was, still wet and clingy and gorgeous. The lads from Del Amitri were all over her front, making Dave ache with jealousy. He'd give anything to be safely back in his flat, but he'd also change places with that tee-shirt in a heartbeat. He willed her to toss the towel to him rather than come any closer. She didn't. She walked slowly across the room, maintaining eye contact and holding it out to him. His heart was pounding now and he hoped he had it in him to resist, that he was a better man now than in the old days. Nicky seemed different, more purposeful, since fetching the towel. He wasn't sure, but he got the impression that she had done a quick moral inventory and decided she was okay with whatever happened next. He couldn't count on her to pull out of this; it was all up to him.

Dave reached out for the towel and their fingers touched, ever so slightly. It was like a charge of electricity running through the two of them. She looked hungrily into his eyes, and any lingering doubt was gone; Nicky wanted this. What did Dave want? He tried to think about Cindy, about his promises to her, but she wasn't here now and Nicky was. Ten years ago, five years even, he wouldn't have thought twice, but that was a lifetime ago. He wasn't that man anymore, was he?

CHAPTER TWENTY

It turns out he was precisely that man. He was lying in Nicky's bed, listening to her deep, contented breathing as she slept, and he hated himself. Had he thrown away the best thing to happen to him in years for the sake of a casual fling? Not just any casual fling: a casual fling with Cindy's best mate. He couldn't have betrayed her more if he'd tried. It had taken so long for her to trust him, to get past the way men had treated her in her past; how could he ever get that back after this? He thought he'd changed, but even with Dave Masters dead and gone, Tom Mulvaney had turned out to be just as big a bastard. That lyric from last night, about love disappearing in the rain, floated mockingly into his mind.

What about Nicky? What would she be expecting? Would she see this as a one-off, or the start of something? He knew it wasn't happening again – there was no question about that – but would Nicky see it that way? Would she back away quietly or make things difficult? Dave didn't know whether to be honest with Cindy about what had happened, or just hope she never found out. The thing is, silence was only an option if Nicky signed up to it too.

Dave's instinct was to get up, get dressed and go back to his flat before Nicky even woke; send the message that there was no future with him. Then again, it could leave things dangerously uncertain. They had to talk this through, but he wanted to get back to his flat, just in case Cindy called round in the morning and found him missing. For a man with countless infidelities under his belt, he felt surprisingly out of his depth. There were so many routes through this that led to disaster, and he wasn't sure there was even one that got him safely through to the other side.

He took a deep breath and gently shook Nicky awake. Her eyes opened slowly and a smile crept across her face.

'Hello there,' she purred. 'Are you back for more?'

Dave sighed. 'Nicky, we've got to talk. Tonight was a mistake, a huge mistake.'

She sat up, hair dry now but still dishevelled. She clutched the bedcovers to her chest, covering her nakedness, and sat up in bed. 'Ah,' she said. 'Now you discover your conscience. It's a bit late, don't you think?'

'I know, I feel dreadful.'

'Thanks a lot – was I that bad?'

'No, no no no. It was amazing, you were amazing. If it wasn't for Cindy…' He let the sentence hang, unfinished. What he had said was only partly true. The sex had been great, but something had been missing. By the standards of casual shags, it had been spectacular; compared to what he shared with Cindy, it was empty and hollow. 'She's the love of my life. I've been really unfair to you, put you in a terrible position—'

Nicky giggled. 'Actually you put me in several positions, but I wouldn't have called any of them terrible.' She composed herself when she saw that Dave wasn't seeing the joke. 'Look, I'm a big girl; I knew what I was doing. I just wanted to feel that I could still attract someone. I never thought it would be you – I hadn't planned this – but… well, you felt the tension between us, the chemistry, didn't you?'

Dave nodded, closing his eyes against the pain of the admission.

She put a hand on his arm, like Cindy did; the similarity made him wince. 'What do you want to do now?'

'I've got to go home. If Cindy calls round in the morning and I'm not there—'

'Are you going to tell her? About last night?'

'Are you? She'll be devastated if she ever finds out.'

Nicky sighed. 'It would destroy her.'

'I can't tell her, can't do that to her. She's my world.'

'Even with a massive secret at the heart of your relationship?'

He just shrugged. Nicky didn't know that there was already an even bigger lie in the mix, although not one so steeped in betrayal. They agreed not to say anything. For Cindy's sake, they would pretend that Dave had seen Nicky safely back to her flat then carried on home. He felt bad about deceiving Cindy, but the consequences of doing anything else were too unbearable to imagine.

Nicky paused at her doorway as he was about to leave.

'Do you think if you'd met me first, before Cindy, if you'd moved into my building, not hers, we might have got together?'

Dave shrugged. 'Who knows?' But he knew. For him it had always been Cindy.

Holding his breath, Dave turned the key in his front door. All the way back from Nicky's he had been worrying about running into Cindy. What if she'd let herself into his flat and was waiting for him to come home? How would he explain being so late? Should he have stayed at Nicky's all night, claimed that he'd slept on the sofa to avoid the rain? He moved cautiously into his flat, looking for any sign of Cindy's presence. He didn't spot anything: maybe he'd got lucky and she had stayed in her sick-bed. He put down the tee-shirt he had bought – the same design as the one that had clung so irresistibly to Nicky. He knew already that every time he saw Cindy in it, he would be reminded of his broken promises, of becoming again the man he thought he'd left behind. He was tempted just to throw it away, to say he'd forgotten, but he couldn't bring himself to add another deception to his charge sheet. He poked his head around the bedroom door and turned on the light. There was no sign of Cindy, and he realised he had been holding his breath. She'd never know how late he got back; all he had to do now was not give the game away and he might just get away with this. Back in his old days, this was the point where all guilt would have left him; it only counted as cheating if you got caught, right? That wasn't how he felt now. He'd never worried about Cath, but he knew what this would mean to Cindy. This time he couldn't just shrug the blame away.

The next morning, he knocked gently on Cindy's front door and let himself in.

'Are you up?' he called, quietly enough not to wake her if she was still asleep.

'In here.' Her voice came from the bedroom, still croaky. He poked his head round the door, putting his hand over his nose and mouth.

'Are you still infectious? Do I need a hazmat suit?'

Cindy laughed, which promptly set her off coughing. Dave started to move towards her, but Cindy held her hand up and waved him back.

'I'm okay – keep your distance; it's not worth you getting ill as well. How was the gig? Did you and Nicky have a good time?' The last question stung, stabbing him like a dagger, but he knew that wasn't what Cindy meant.

'Yeah, they were really good. They even did an old Rod Stewart song, from his Faces days. Here, I got you that tee-shirt.' He tossed it across the room to her and tried to look happy as she enthused about it.

Nicky was a bit distant the next time he saw her, but Cindy was there too, so maybe she was trying too hard not to give anything away. Cindy was pushing him to arrange that double date with Chris, which now seemed like Dave's idea of hell, but he couldn't think of a good excuse to get out of it.

One way or another, Chris finally got the hint and got together with Nicky. Cindy was pleased, Chris was delighted and Nicky certainly seemed happy. Dave was trying to avoid situations where he was alone with her, and as a result he could only guess how much of that was genuine and how much a convincing cover. He was pretty sure she knew nothing else would happen with him, but he didn't want to risk giving her any false encouragement.

Dave knew he had to keep the pretence of normal life going, to carry on as if nothing had happened. He was tortured by what he'd done, but he couldn't let that show. After working so hard to take down his barriers and be open with Cindy, it was agony to find himself watching every word again. He knew it would get easier; at least that's what he kept telling himself.

There was also the lost album to plan. Looking through the songs he had been writing, he reckoned he already had seven or eight good enough for the album, as well as some covers of a suitable vintage that he'd like to add to the stage show. He still needed to write a few more, but he was well on the way to an album to be proud of. There was a definite split between the songs written before Nicky and the ones he was writing now. There was a joyous spirit to most of the former, while the latter reeked of guilt and regret. It would make a more diverse and emotionally satisfying album, but he'd have traded that in a heartbeat to blot the night with Nicky out of his past. He'd already played Tony some of the new songs, and Tony agreed that they were up there with the best of his old stuff. Dave wasn't sure how easy it would be to make them sound like they were recorded in 1978, but if that was what it took to get his new material out into the world, he'd give it a go.

Once Tony had booked a recording studio, Dave told Cindy he'd be busy for a few days with something Tony wanted him to do.

'Oooh, sounds secretive. You've not got yourself another woman on the side, have you?'

Dave felt his whole body tensing up. She didn't know something, did she?

'Why would you say a thing like that?' he blurted. 'You know I wouldn't do that to you.' He was being aggressively over-defensive and he knew it.

'Hey, I was only joking, you know? I know you wouldn't cheat on me.' She came over to him and put her arms around him. Dave hated himself. 'You've been so good to me, so patient. If I really thought you were plugging your guitar into someone else's amp, I wouldn't still be here, would I?'

'No, I'm sorry. It's just that I know what that means to you and I didn't like the idea of you imagining me like that, even for a moment.' Least of all with your best friend. 'I over-reacted, okay? It's just that you're so important to me – you're my world.'

'And you're mine.' She kissed him. 'Now shut up and put the kettle on, unless that's going to get you all upset as well.'

The day of the first recording session arrived. They started with Dave teaching Tony what he needed to do with the desk. It wasn't long before Tony was at least competent at pushing the buttons, but in terms of setting up mics and getting everything ready for Dave to play, he was no help at all. Eventually there were ready to record.

'Let's do a guide vocal and acoustic guitar track to begin, then we can start building.'

They started with "Your Eyes Shine", a song Dave had written for Cindy early on in their relationship. He tried to push past the complicated mess of his current feelings and remind himself of how he had felt in those early days. He had some ideas for the bass and keyboard parts, and he'd put a nice solo on over the top. He held back with the drums, hoping to emulate the kind of sparse accompaniment that either Vince or Ollie would have added. After several hours recording all the different parts, they got together in the control room to listen to what they'd done.

'No,' said Dave. 'It's not right. We've not got it.'

'Do you want to try again? What is it that's not working – the keyboards? The drums?'

'Bass and keyboards aren't as good as Phil and Simon would have done, but they're passable, and I'm fine with the guitars. The drums are a different matter. I can keep time, but I'm just tapping along where Vince would be living the gaps between the beats, finding all the grace notes.'

Tony was nodding solemnly, as if he understood the musical discussion.

'But that's not the worst of it; the biggest problem is the sound. It's lifeless – cold and dead where we need it warm and living.'

'Well, I'm doing the best that I can,' huffed Tony. 'This is all new to me: I've never been involved in the recording process before. You always took care of making the music, and I took care of selling it, remember?'

'I know – I'm not blaming you. I'm coming up short as well. The problem is that neither of us are record producers. I can hear exactly what I want it to sound like, I know what I need from each instrument, but I don't know how to set the studio up to get it. Are you sure we can't bring in a producer without letting him know what he's working on? What about Clive? The production wasn't the problem with the last album.'

'And then when this album comes out and he recognises all the tracks, what then? It's too risky. If anyone finds out what we've done, we're both for it. Whoever it was would have to keep their mouth shut afterwards. Who would you trust with our secret?'

Dave had no idea. All he knew was that he had to get these songs into the world. Since they had killed him off, he had realised that music – writing, performing and recording – was what he did; it was in his blood. He'd thought he could walk away from all that, but he was wrong. They had to make this work.

'We've got to do something.'

Tony put his hand on Dave's shoulder. 'Leave it with me, I'll have a think and get back to you. This isn't the end, it's just a setback. These songs are so good, we have to find a way to sell them.'

CHAPTER TWENTY-ONE

Dave didn't hear anything from Tony for a few weeks, so he got on with normal life, spending time with Cindy and writing songs when she was at work. His sense of guilt was getting easier to live with. He still suffered from sporadic flares of remorse, but at least he managed to shift his focus elsewhere a lot of the time. Maybe eventually – a few months, a few years – he would be able to live his life without thinking of it at all. He hated that one of his triggers was when things were good with Cindy. He felt like he'd poisoned the best thing in his life, and part of him was afraid it would never feel right again. At least he was finding it easier not to act weirdly around Nicky. Things were going well with her and Chris, who seemed like a new man: more confident, more at ease with himself.

Then there was his dad. It ate him up that even with time running out, there was nothing he could do to make things right between them. His sense of guilt and powerlessness floored him whenever he thought about the old man. Partly as a reaction to that, he had decided to take control over something else: his lack of information about Tom Mulvaney. With the help of yellow pages, he set out on a mission. He was standing in the middle of Barnet, checking the address that he'd scribbled down. 34C

Commercial Road, it had said. 32 was a Chinese takeaway, 34A a laundromat with 34B a flat above it by the look of things. 36 was a dry-cleaners. As far as he could tell, there was no 34C.

'Excuse me, love.' Dave stopped a woman pushing a pram to ask. 'I'm trying to find 34C – Frank Dixon Investigations. Any idea?'

'Try the alleyway next to the Methodist Church, it leads to a courtyard behind the laundry. Maybe something's back there.'

Dave thanked her and found the Methodist church a couple of doors further down. Weeds were growing through the paving slabs in the litter-strewn alley. It didn't smell great, and Dave was glad to reach the end, where it opened out. There was a battered-looking static caravan on the far side of the courtyard. Moving closer he read the sign in the window: '34C Frank Dixon, Private Investigator. Please knock loudly.'

It didn't exactly instil confidence, but he'd come this far. He knocked and waited, then knocked again a little louder. Eventually, once he had reached the stage of hammering on the door there were signs of movement inside and the door swung open.

Much like his caravan office, Frank Dixon had seen better days. He was wearing crumpled clothes with food stains down his shirt – Dave hazarded a guess that the Chinese takeaway at number 32 may have been responsible for those – a stubbly, blotchy complexion and a tangle of unkempt salt-and-pepper hair.

'What do you want?' growled a voice rich in catarrh.

'Are you Frank Dixon?'

'Who's asking?'

'A potential client.' Those were obviously the magic words, and Frank immediately overcame his charm bypass.

'In that case, yes, I'm Frank Dixon. Very pleased to meet you – come in, come in. Sit down and tell me what the problem is.'

The caravan smelled stale, which made sense when Dave saw the sleeping bag and the unwashed dishes in the sink. He took a chair at the small table while Frank rummaged in a suitcase for a notebook and joined him.

'Before we start, how does this work?' asked Dave. 'I mean, are you bound by confidentiality or something?'

'Yes and no. You're not legally protected and I can't hide behind the law to avoid answering questions in court. In practice, what my clients tell me stays between me and them. If you've done anything iffy, that's none of my business as long as you pay my bill. If you were to stitch me up, things might be different and the gloves would be off. I'll lie to the police if I have to, but I won't lie in court.'

Dave paused; it was probably as much as he could have hoped for. 'Fair enough. I want you to find someone. Well, find out about someone: he's dead. Well, technically he's still alive, but I'm pretty sure he's dead really.'

'Right, this sounds like it might be an interesting one. Tell me all about it, and we can discuss my terms.'

Dave explained how – for reasons he didn't want to go into – a friend had arranged for him to take a false identity. He wanted to find out more about the man whose life he was living. He didn't mention Ronnie specifically, but said he had reasons to think Tom had been on the fringes of the criminal world eighteen to twenty years ago.

'Look, if Tom Mulvaney was killed so I could take on his identity I need to know. And I want to know as much about his life before that as you can find out. Does that sound like something you could help me with?'

Frank pursed his lips. 'Yes, I would have thought so. How long have you been living as Tom Mulvaney?'

'Since April.'

'Okay, so anything further back than that will be the real Tom rather than you, the phan-Tom.' He looked to see if his weak joke got a reaction, but Dave wasn't in the mood to indulge him. 'Give me as much info as you've got – national insurance number, stuff like that – and I'll get onto it. I'll want £100 a day, plus expenses, and I'll keep you updated as and when I find stuff.'

Dave looked around at the tatty caravan. '£100 a day? Are you telling me that rent is expensive round here? £50 a day.'

'I don't have to take this case, you know.'

'Yeah, and there were other private investigators in the phone book. Can you afford to turn business away? £50. Take it or leave it.'

'Plus expenses?'

'Plus expenses – reasonable ones.'

Frank's gnarled face creased into a smile. 'Done. £50 is my usual rate anyway. It never hurts to try, does it?'

Dave left his phone number for Frank and warned that from time to time he was away from home for a few weeks, but he'd pick up any messages eventually.

Tony had booked another London show, at the Hackney Empire – where Dave's fake death journey had started – towards the end of the month, then sporadic gigs in decent-sized venues around the country in December. These were the biggest shows the band had played yet, at famous old venues like the Manchester Free Trade Hall and Glasgow Barrowlands. The last date of the year, just before Christmas, was the most exciting of all: Hammersmith Palais. Not quite as prestigious as the neighbouring Odeon, but it was still a pretty special gig and Dave could hardly wait. When they came off the last tour they had been road-sharp and tight as a drumhead. Dave didn't want to lose their hard-earned reputation, so they had to get up to speed again.

He was the last to arrive at the rehearsal room. The others were tuning up and catching up with one another's news.

'Tom might know,' said Ollie as he put down his guitar cases. 'What's happened to that Vagabond Dave bloke? When we were out on the road he was playing virtually every night in London, but he seems to have disappeared now. Do you reckon we've scared him off again?'

This was news to Dave, and he wasn't sure how to react. Had Tony done something? Just how far was his manager willing to go to protect his investment in Dave?

'No idea, I'm just glad he's not around. Anyone who wants to play the part of Dave Masters needs to be a lot better-looking than that skinny runt.'

'Says old man Mulvaney,' added Shaun, grinning in anticipation at Dave's response.

Dave ignored him, pulling a sheet of paper from his pocket and sticking it to the wall. 'Anyway, here's the set list for the next round of shows. It's much the same as we were playing before.'

'Well, that's no surprise,' said Martin. 'Dead men can't exactly expand their repertoire.'

If only you knew, thought Dave. In a few months' time you might have to reconsider that statement.

'I know, but I'm more than happy for us to try the songs in a different order, work out some new combinations. Feel free to make suggestions, but let's get to work on freshening everything up first. Any requests?'

'Something lively, one of the rockier ones,' suggested Martin.

'How about "I Saw Her Standing There"?' added Chris.

Shaun grinned wickedly. 'And just who would you be thinking of when we do that one, Chris – the lovely Nicky, perhaps? We all know what you mean!' Ollie even followed the line with a couple of rim shots and a crash on the high hat.

Dave grinned. Chris was Shaun's new target for relationship-based mockery. Martin had a theory that Shaun found it threatening when other men were willing to commit to the long term (which for Shaun meant two consecutive nights), that the idea of staying with the same woman for longer than it took to perform the Darwinian imperative was difficult for him.

'So how did a fox like Nicky end up with a wet weekend like you?' Shaun wasn't letting it go.

Chris just shrugged his shoulders and grinned. 'I don't

know and I don't care; I'm just glad she did. You should try it sometime.'

'Did you all hear that?' Shaun was almost laughing as he spoke. 'Chris just told me I should give Nicky a try! Maybe I will – don't be surprised if she doesn't come back to you once she's had a real man.'

'That's not… I meant you might give commitment a try,' stammered Chris.

'Too late; I heard what I heard!'

'Leave it, Shaun,' Martin weighed in. 'You're out of order. Again.'

'Well, he made the offer; it would be rude not to give her the once-over.'

'Okay, lads, that's enough.' Dave took charge. 'The only thing needing a once-over is the set list, so let's get started. "I Saw Her Standing There": everybody ready? A-one, two, three, four.'

Tony had been in touch again, telling Dave to meet him at a studio in North London at 9pm on Tuesday night, where he would explain all. Tony was waiting in the foyer when he arrived.

'Right, I've come up with a plan, and I think you're going to like it.'

'Does it let me get my music out under my real name?'

'Hopefully. I've got a producer in the control room of Studio 2, he's set the room up – have you prepared all the songs you want for the album like we talked about?'

'Yeah, I've worked out vocal and acoustic guitar parts for all of them, though we'll need a lot more than that to do them justice.'

'Don't you worry about that; we'll do them justice all right. Come and meet the producer, and don't say anything about who you really are unless I do. Just follow my lead and be Tom Mulvaney, okay?'

They walked down the corridor, past the empty Studio 1 and to the door of Studio 2. Tony paused at the door. 'Remember, you're Tom and you've never met this man before, okay?' Before Dave could answer, Tony opened the door and stepped through.

'Alan,' said Tony. 'This is Tom Mulvaney.' Dave looked and there in front of him was Alan Sharkey. He hadn't seen his old producer in more than ten years, and those years hadn't been kind to him. He looked smaller, and greyer, like he had shrunk into his clothes. He was still neatly turned out – he had always been a fastidious man – and his eyes still had a sharp glint, suggesting that his mental faculties may not have diminished along with his physical stature. The boys in the band had always joked with Alan about his attention to detail, whether it was mics in the studio, the pin for his tie or his longhand write-up of each and every take. Just-so Sharkey, they had called him.

Alan had produced all of Dave's most successful albums. After the debut album didn't yield a hit single, Ultimate brought Alan in for the follow-up, *Flying Wild*. Alan was Dave's fiercest critic in the control room, always ready to challenge him if something wasn't as good as it could be. He was a perfectionist, but one with the knack of bringing more out of Dave than he thought was there. He had been at the helm for the next three albums, including the live one, but had been unavailable for 1979's *Don't Walk, Run*. After that Tony had always tried to match Dave with the latest trendy producer, the one most likely to sprinkle commercial fairy dust on Dave's sound in the pursuit of those elusive hit singles. Dave had always wondered whether Alan was offended that they'd never gone back to him, although his reputation now was as someone whose best days were behind him.

'Pleased to meet you, Tom,' said Alan, holding out his hand. 'I'm not really sure why we're so cloak-and-dagger, but I'm sure Tony has his reasons.'

They shook hands, with Dave nervously saying something about being a big fan of Alan's work, before Tony cut in.

'Right, we've got the studio all night but we want to work fast. Alan has already set everything up, so once Tom plugs in we can check the levels and get going. Here's the plan. Tonight, possibly going on to tomorrow night if we have to, we want to record an album's worth of demo tapes – just acoustic guitar and vocal. We're not trying to make a finished track, just a good, clean, working demo to build on later. All good?'

They made good progress. They started with Dave playing through the song once while Alan recorded it. If both men were happy, they would move on to the next song, but more often than not they would do two or three takes.

'It takes me back, doing it the old-fashioned way like this,' Alan said. 'Usually these days everything is digital – I couldn't believe it when Tony said he had a singer-songwriter who wanted everything done properly.'

By early morning, they had recorded most of Dave's new songs, as well as the covers he had picked out for the album: Richard Thompson's "Withered and Died" and the Who's "The Real Me". The last one had been a bit of a joke choice, given Dave's current circumstances, but it was also the kind of track that Dave would have chosen back in the day. The three men sat together in the control room for a playback of the last tracks they had worked on, and then Alan turned his intense gaze on Tony.

'Now, Tony, do you think you would care to tell me what this is really all about? I don't know what's going on, but I know you didn't go to all this trouble just to make a demo tape for an unknown singer, no matter how good he's just demonstrated himself to be. I've got my suspicions, but perhaps you'd tell me who Tom Mulvaney really is.'

Tony and Dave exchanged looks. Dave shrugged slightly and Tony nodded his head.

'Alan, I've lied to you – as you guessed. When I tell you the truth, it puts our safety in your hands. Please hear me out, and if you're not happy about what I'm proposing, I hope you'll at least keep quiet about it, for all our sakes.' Alan's face wasn't giving anything away. Dave hoped that Tony knew what he was doing.

Then again, there was no one Dave trusted more with his songs than Alan Sharkey.

'Dave Masters isn't really dead. I faked his death so Dave could escape his old life and start a new one, as Tom Mulvaney.' If Alan was surprised, he didn't show it. Tony continued, 'It was only meant to be a way of giving Dave a nice little boost to his pension pot. The trouble is, he couldn't keep away from playing, and then he started writing songs again. We need to find a way of getting the songs out there without revealing that we've been involved in a criminal deception all this time.'

'Do I take it that these demo tapes aren't the end of your plans for these songs?'

Tony nodded his assent. 'Not at all. The demos are just phase one. Next, we need to turn them into fully worked tracks for you to find in your archives. We can present them as long-lost Dave songs that he recorded with the band round about 1978. I'm arranging for the original backing band – other than Davey, of course, God rest him – to come in and make them sound as much like a classic Dave Masters' album as possible.'

'What about solos?' asked Dave. 'I can't just put a solo on the demo without hearing what the others are playing too.'

'I thought of that – obviously we can't bring Dave Masters back from the dead, but if he's not available, then the next best thing would be someone who has shown night after night that they can recreate his guitar sound while playing the part of Dave Masters in the UK's leading tribute band.'

'And do you think this tribute player will agree?' asked Alan.

Tony started laughing, 'I would have thought so – he's sitting right here in the room with you, Alan.' They talked some more about the practicalities. Tony suggested they only play the musicians a few tracks at a time rather than the whole set of demos. That way they wouldn't have to explain the sudden appearance of new material if Dave wrote any more gems. Alan had more questions, prompting Dave to narrate the chain of events that had led to

Dave ReMastered and his renewed love of performing. He also asked Tony – less successfully – for details about how he pulled off Dave's "death". Eventually he came to the crucial question.

'You've said what the stakes are if this is discovered. Why should I expose myself to that kind of risk? I understand what each of you stand to gain from it, but why should I get involved? What's in it for me?'

Tony paused before answering. 'Good question, what's in it for you: two things. First of all, money, lots of it. You saw the kind of numbers we got for *Vagabond Life*. If we can put out an album of previously undiscovered Dave Masters songs from his golden age, we can clean up. You can have a lump sum or royalties on the album, whichever you prefer. Either way, you'll have a financial stake in the success, the kind of reward your talent never got back in the day. Secondly, I was wrong not to bring you back for Dave's later albums. This is your chance to resolve your unfinished business with Dave's music. What do you say, Alan? Are you going to help us to bring these songs to life?'

Alan looked sternly at Tony. 'Once upon a time, I'd have jumped at the chance to work with this man again, and to do it legally. And while the money is very appealing, that's never been my motivation for getting into the studio.'

'I'm happy for you to work for nothing, if you prefer.'

'Oh, don't be an idiot. Of course I'm not working for nothing – if I do this I shall want to be paid handsomely, if only to make up for all those dreadful albums I never got the chance to save.' He turned directly to Dave here. 'Based on your recent work, I wouldn't have been interested in working with you again. But these songs are different. You've found whatever it was that you lost in the '80s. I'm in and I'll keep quiet, but I have conditions. If we are discovered, you keep me out of it. Tony, you can find the demos in your archives or Dave's, not mine. That way I can say I don't remember recording them with Dave at the time. If the truth comes out, I'll be able to deny being involved. And I want a lump sum up front – £50,000 should do – plus a double royalty on the album. Do we have a deal?'

Dave looked instantly towards Tony. He was happy to give Alan whatever he wanted, but he knew Tony, who never gave away more than he had to, would make a counter-offer.

'£30,000 and no royalty.'

'£40,000 and the normal royalty. It'll mean you don't have to go to someone else who wouldn't do half as good a job as me, and you won't have to let anyone else in on your secret.'

Tony smiled. 'Done. If you two want to finish off the demos tomorrow night, I'll start tracking down the rest of the band.'

CHAPTER TWENTY-TWO

Recording the demos with Alan went well, though Tony was still trying to arrange getting the rest of the band together. Vince was happy to drop everything to be involved, while Phil could only be there over a long weekend or during school holidays. Simon was the hardest to pin down. He had just finished a tour with Roger Waters and wanted a break, but he liked the idea of getting into the studio with his old friends again. Away from music, Dave couldn't shake off the fear that everything with Cindy could fall apart at any moment. Even for someone as practised in infidelity as him, it was hard not to let his fears affect the way he was around Cindy.

The Hackney Empire gig came and went, with the band on top form. Chris's new-found confidence ruined the toilet sweepstake and he was playing brilliantly too, the best anyone could remember from him. Dave kept nagging Martin about how good the stage felt, trying to make him see what he'd be giving up if he went back to his day job. Frank Dixon, meanwhile, was making progress. He'd followed some leads on the real Tom Mulvaney that confirmed the connection with organised crime. He'd have to tread carefully, but he was sure it wouldn't be long before he was in a position to make a full report.

Then, in the gap between Hackney and the first of the regional gigs, Dave got the news he was waiting for. Vince, Phil and Simon were going into the studio at the weekend. He wanted to share his excitement, but he knew it was another secret he'd have to keep from Cindy. The studio was booked for all day Saturday and Sunday. They weren't expecting to get it all done in one hit, and Tony had lined up some more studio time for the New Year, but at least they could make a start.

Dave arrived first, waiting outside until Alan arrived. Once in the control room, Dave could barely sit still. The official line was that he was Alan's assistant. Tony had insisted that the guitar overdubs waited until the others weren't there, just in case Dave's playing jogged anyone's memory. Dave thought that was a bit over-cautious, but he didn't argue and left his guitars at home.

As his former bandmates started arriving, it was fascinating for Dave to see how they had changed in the missing years. It was frustrating too, greeting them as strangers rather than friends, not being able to reminisce and to catch up with one another. At the same time, he didn't want to get too close, just in case anyone recognised him.

Phil was the first to arrive, casually dressed and with a much-receded hairline. The ease with which he sauntered in said musician, but the clothes said secondary-school teacher, which was what he was now. He said hello to "Tom" but was more interested in catching up with Alan.

'I couldn't believe it when Tony called,' he was saying. 'I mean, I never knew there were any of Dave's old songs out there. I guess you've heard them – are they good?'

Dave swelled a little with pride to hear Alan's response. 'Up there with his best, if I'm honest. I wouldn't be here if I didn't think there was something worth working up. I'm glad you and the boys all agreed to do this.'

'Yeah, it's just a shame we didn't do this when Dave was still around. He'd have loved this.'

Alan smiled a knowing smile. 'Oh, I'm sure he'll be listening. Let's just make sure we do him proud.'

Vince was next. He told the others about the funeral and said that Dave's death had really knocked him for six.

'Even though I hadn't seen him in a couple of years, he was like a brother to me. Well, that's what I thought – his death made me question all that. I had no idea he was feeling so low; I keep asking myself what else I could have done to help him. I feel like I let him down.' Phil gave Vince a huge hug, reassuring him that it wasn't his fault. Dave wished he could do the same.

'Look,' said Phil, 'Dave pushed everyone away towards the end. This wasn't a cry-for-help-gone-wrong suicide, was it? He wanted it to work. If he was that determined to kill himself, what could anyone have done?'

'I could have tried.' Vince's eyes were glistening now, and Dave turned away. Partly to hide his own reaction but mostly because he was too ashamed to keep looking. Vince had deserved better from him. He had thought that faking his death would only affect him, but he could see now how wrong he had been.

Simon was the last, looking a little more flash than the others – sharper clothes, sunglasses indoors – as befits a man who had become one of the sought-after sidemen for the rock cognoscenti. Once he got in with Phil and Vince, though, all airs and graces vanished, and they were just three lads from Birmingham who had gone on a glorious adventure together. They started jamming, playing some of the old material, and Dave was aching to join in. Once again, he was reminded of what his faked death had cost him.

'Right, if you've all quite finished reliving your yesterdays, shall we get down to some work?' Alan called them to attention. He proposed a way of working: he would play the demo of a track for everyone to listen to, then pipe it into their headphones for the musicians to join in with. They could do a couple of takes all together, then individually record overdubs as needed to build up the track. It was much the way they had worked in the old days, although back then Dave played along for the group takes. The question of guitar overdubs came up, and Alan explained Tony's plan.

'We'll keep as much of Dave's demo work as we can, but if we need to add anything else – including solos – Tony has arranged a stand-in from a Dave Masters tribute act. I've heard him play and he's got Dave's sound pretty well. It's not ideal, but short of discovering that the real Dave Masters isn't dead, it's the best we're going to get.' That wasn't the first thing Alan had said that worried Dave; perhaps he wasn't cut out for keeping secrets.

'Can't this session guy come in with us, so we can play the track properly, solos and all?' asked Simon.

'I don't think so,' replied Alan. 'Tony wants to hear whether you guys can still cut the mustard together before he commits to another session musician's fee.'

'Yeah, that figures,' said Phil. 'Tony always had one eye on the bottom line. Okay, let's get started.'

It went even better than Dave had hoped. His old friends knew his music better than anyone, and their instincts were almost always spot on. If he didn't like something, the kind of thing he would have changed back in the day, he told Alan in the control room and let the producer steer the band right. It was frustrating to be one step removed from the process, but also exciting to see and hear the songs coming together.

As the lads were packing up their gear at the end of the second day, Dave heard them remarking how much they had enjoyed themselves. Simon asked the others if they were ever tempted to get back out on the road. Vince said he'd happily tour again if the work materialised, but Phil was adamant that those days were behind him.

'I had a great time, but you've got to know when to walk away. Anyway, it turns out I enjoy teaching even more than I enjoyed being in a band. It's funny how things work out.' Dave admired him for that; after all, he had tried walking away from music and found it a lot harder than he had expected.

Before the next session, there were the Christmas gigs to take care of. Manchester went brilliantly, Glasgow was the most electric atmosphere yet, and Cindy and Nicky came up for the gig in Wolverhampton. Dave sensed some tension between Nicky and Chris; Cindy had noticed the same but reported that Nicky hadn't said anything to her.

The mood was strained again before the Hammersmith Palais gig. Chris arrived in a foul mood, barely saying a word during the soundcheck and keeping his distance from the others. Anything that anyone said got a short response from him, and Martin was kept busy preventing Shaun from antagonising him.

A little before showtime, Dave cornered Chris in the dressing room.

'Something's up, mate. What is it? If you let me know I might be able to help.'

Chris squirmed and wouldn't meet Dave's gaze. 'It's nothing, really. Look, I don't want to talk about it, all right?'

'Okay, first and foremost, you're a mate. You're worrying me and I want to look out for you.' He knew there was no way to say the next bit without sounding heartless, but it had to be said: 'And I need to know you're clear-headed and focused for the gig tonight. This is our biggest show yet; we can't stuff it up. Are you going to be okay to play?'

For a moment Chris looked like he might react badly, but that passed and Dave saw that Chris understood what he was saying.

'Yeah, yeah; I'll hold it together. I'm sorry, Tom, I get how important it is. I'll park my personal issues and be professional.'

'I know you will, mate. And later, if you change your mind about talking, the offer's still open. I'm concerned for the gig, but I'm more concerned about you.'

Chris was true to his word; he played a great show – they all did. Afterwards they came off, hot, dripping with sweat but happy. The last show before Christmas was in the bag and it was time to celebrate.

Cindy made her way backstage, but Dave noticed that Nicky wasn't with her.

'No Nicky tonight?' he asked. Cindy shook her head, although her eyes told him there was more to this that she didn't want to say. Shaun must have picked up on it, and he took the opportunity to wind Chris up.

'Nicky not here, Chris? That's a surprise for a hometown show. Has she got tired of you already?'

Chris was gritting his teeth, and Shaun kept on going. 'I said she was out of your league. Has she dumped you, then? Found someone better?'

Suddenly Chris launched himself across the room, fists flailing in Shaun's direction. Martin and Ollie, who were closest, dived in to keep them apart. Shaun didn't respond in kind, but neither did he back away. He looked like he was enjoying the reaction he'd provoked.

'Hit a sore nerve, did I? She has dumped you, hasn't she?'

'Yeah, and you'd know all about it, wouldn't you?' snarled Chris, tottering between fury and tears. Dave had never seen him like this before. 'Last night she told me all about what you two got up to the other weekend. You just couldn't leave it alone, could you? You couldn't bear for someone else to have a girl that you hadn't had.'

'Well, you invited me to give her a go, remember? It's not my fault if now she knows what a real man is like.'

Chris tried to launch himself again, but the others were still holding him back. Shaun kept going. 'It's embarrassing enough that she preferred shagging me, but the fact that you're not even in her top two shags from this band must hurt.'

'What?' Chris looked genuinely confused at the last comment, while something in Dave's heart turned to ice. Shaun couldn't know, could he? Or had Nicky been with Martin or Ollie?

'Yeah, she had me the other week, and before that she had Captain Old over there. I notice he wasn't good enough to make her dump you, but she told me he had some good moves for an old feller – better than you, anyway, quick draw.'

Chris spun round to face Dave. 'Tell me it's not true. I can believe it from Shaun, but tell me that you didn't go behind my back with my girlfriend.'

'It wasn't like that,' pleaded Dave. 'She wasn't your girlfriend at the time. It was before you two got together. Remember that Del Amitri gig? It all happened after that. It was only one night and it was before you started seeing her. I promise.'

Chris paused to process the new information, and Dave was aware of the rest of the band's stunned faces looking at him. Actually, that wasn't quite right: they were all looking past him. He half-turned just in time for a palm to slap across his face. Cindy had hit him, and this time it wasn't affectionate and it wasn't endearing. Turning to face her, he saw sheer fury on her face.

'After everything you said, everything you promised, you go and sleep with my best friend. I believed you, Tom Mulvaney!'

'Look, let's talk about this – not here, not in front of everyone. Let me explain.'

'Oh, you want to explain, do you?' She sounded raw, pain spilling out with every word. 'Are you going to tell me how good Nicky was? What she did for you that I couldn't? Was it really just that once, or have the two of you been at it ever since, laughing behind my back?'

'No, really, it was just once and I felt awful.'

'I bet you did. That was why you did it, I suppose, because you knew how awful sex with Nicky would be.'

'Cindy, I promise—'

She slapped him again, the sting rebuking him as she continued her verbal assault. 'Don't you ever say that word to me again, Tom

Mulvaney.' She was clenching her teeth and he could hear from her voice that she was battling to hold back her tears. 'I'm done believing your promises. You're welcome to Nicky, or whoever else you've been banging when you're out on the road. More fool me for ever believing you could change your ways.' With that, she stormed out. Dave went to go after her, but Martin stopped him.

'Not now, Tom. Give her time. She won't be thinking straight tonight.'

CHAPTER TWENTY-THREE

When Dave got home after the gig, he stood on the landing between his front door and Cindy's. Even though it was gone midnight, he considered whether or not to knock. Perhaps Martin was right about giving her space tonight. He wasn't sure what he could say anyway; it had only been once, but that was once too often. He had gambled on her never finding out, and lost big. His reasons for not coming clean were – he thought – motivated by not wanting to hurt her rather than just trying to get away with it, but now that she knew, his silence made the betrayal look worse. He wasn't convinced that there would ever be a right to time to try to explain, but he was sure it wasn't tonight. Reluctantly, wearily, he turned towards his own flat and went inside.

He didn't sleep much that night and rose late the next day. As soon as he was dressed, he went next door. He still wasn't sure that it would do any good, but it was better than doing nothing. He knocked and knocked, but there was no reply. Was Cindy in there, ignoring the front door? Perhaps she had already gone out to work, or just gone out to avoid him. Maybe she hadn't even come home last night, staying with a friend to keep out of his way. His first instinct was to phone Nicky to see if she knew anything, but she was the one friend Cindy wouldn't have gone to.

Lacking any other viable options, Dave turned to the only thing he had left, his music. He sat in his flat, playing his guitar and pouring out his feelings. He hadn't planned to start writing, but a song started to emerge. Based around the repeating line "Through My Fingers", the first verse told of meeting a girl, running his fingers through her hair, then progressed to celebrate her body responding to his touch, and finally how his own stupidity led to it all slipping away from him. It was the story of their relationship. If he'd been able to distance himself and look at the song with a professional focus, he would have recognised it as one of the best songs he'd ever written, but he was too close to think like that. She was gone; what else mattered?

His phone rang later that afternoon. Part of him wanted to just let it ring unanswered, but what if it was Cindy? He picked up the receiver and said hello.

'Tom?' It was Nicky. 'I heard what happened. I'm so sorry.'

Contradictory feelings ran through him. He didn't blame Nicky for their night together – he took the responsibility for that – but why couldn't she have kept her mouth shut?

'Why did you tell Shaun of all people? You know what he's like. If it comes to that, what were you doing sleeping with him in the first place?'

'I know, I know. Chris was away, Shaun walked me home from the pub and one thing led to another. I think he just liked the idea of getting with me to mess with Chris.'

'No kidding. But why did you tell him about us?'

'It slipped out. He was pushing me to compare him and Chris. He was so big-headed, so certain he was better in bed. I wanted to put him in his place a bit, so I said he may have been better than Chris but he wasn't the best in the band. After that, he wouldn't let it lie; he kept asking and asking until I gave in and explained what I meant. I made him promise not to say anything, though.'

Dave snorted. As if Shaun was ever going to keep that promise.

'Have you heard from Cindy?' he asked.

'No. Martin phoned me to say what happened after the gig. He's worried about… well, pretty much everyone: you, Cindy, Chris. Have you heard from any of the others? I haven't had the nerve to contact either of them. I wasn't even sure if you'd want to talk to me after I ruined everything for you.'

'Never mind that, this isn't the time for recriminations. Any idea where Cindy might have gone? She's not answering her door.'

Nicky couldn't think of anywhere, so Dave started saying goodbye, prompting Nicky to blurt out something else.

'Look, if Cindy has gone and we're both single now, maybe we could—'

Dave didn't even reply; he just put the phone down so they could both pretend he hadn't heard.

The next few days followed a similar pattern. Dave didn't like to go out, in case he missed Cindy coming or going next door. After a couple of days, he heard footsteps outside followed by a knock on his door. Hoping that it might be Cindy, Dave leapt to answer it. He took an involuntary step back when he saw that it was Chris. What was he here for – answers? Explanations? Violence?

'Chris, mate, I'm so sorry…'

Chris held his hands up. 'Relax, I'm not angry with you. I've thought a lot and I get that you did nothing wrong; well, nothing to me anyway. I'm sorry for losing it like that after the gig.'

They made a cup of tea and sat down to talk. Dave asked if there was any chance of him and Nicky getting back together (he didn't mention her phone call), but Chris said he couldn't get past the cheating. Right now he was still angry with her, but he knew that even if that changed he'd never be able to trust her again. Dave nodded sagely, hoping that Cindy wasn't somewhere saying the same thing about him. They agreed that Shaun was the main troublemaker, going out of his way first to sleep with Nicky then to rub it in Chris's face.

'She confessed what she'd done – with him, not with you – the night before the gig, and I'd brooded on it all day. That's why I was in such a state when I arrived. I didn't want to let you down, so I swallowed it all, put all the feelings into my playing, but when Shaun kept pushing afterwards, I couldn't keep it in.'

'I don't blame you. And, by the way, good job on stage: no one in the audience would have known anything was wrong. You'd be surprised how many successful bands are made up of people who can't stand the sight of each other off stage.'

'Thanks, but I can't do that. I'm here to say I'm leaving the band, effective immediately. I know there are no more gigs coming up for the next month, so hopefully it gives you time to get someone else in. I'm hardly irreplaceable – you'll easily find someone better than me. I just want you to know there are no hard feelings.'

Dave tried persuading Chris to stay, but his mind was made up. He couldn't play in a band with Shaun anymore and he wasn't going to make Dave choose between them. From a musical point of view, Shaun would be harder to replace, but Dave had no doubt who he'd rather spend days on the road with. Still, as he had said to Chris, there were plenty of bands who survived despite hating each other, and him and Shaun weren't at that stage, not yet. He'd have to get Tony to find a new guitarist.

Tony phoned to give him the dates for the next recording session with Phil, Simon and Vince, and said he'd booked Dave in with Alan the day before, just in case there were any new songs to demo before the main session. Dave told Tony about Chris's decision and he said he'd find someone. Not long after Dave put the phone down, it rang again.

'Tom, how are you doing, mate?' It was Martin.

'I've been better. I haven't seen Cindy since the gig, and have you heard about Chris?' Martin had heard, and that was why he was calling.

'Look, there's no easy way to say this, but I'm going to leave too. I've loved being in your band, but it feels like it's all splintering now. I can't throw away a safe, well-paid job for the sake of something that could be on the verge of collapse. If you can't find a replacement, I'll happily stay on until the end of February, which is my deadline for going back to work, but I'd rather go sooner than later if I can. I've had enough of Shaun, to be honest. I'll miss playing with you, and I hope you'll keep in touch. Thanks for giving me the chance to live out my dreams, for a while at least.'

Dave tried to talk him out of his decision, but even before he started he knew it was hopeless. What a week. He'd lost Cindy – which trumped everything else – but now he'd lost half of his band as well. Not just that, but the half of the band he liked the most. Thank God that the recordings were going well, because it felt like everything else in his life was falling apart. He called Tony back and said to find a bassist too.

Dave and Alan got "Through My Fingers" on tape, and Alan promised that they'd get the band to work on it the next day.

'That sounded pretty raw when you were singing it,' observed Alan. 'Is it about Cath, or someone new?'

'Someone new. I may have a new identity, but I'm still making the same mistakes. Maybe I'm just too old to learn from them.'

'Look, you're an artist; different rules apply. You have to make mistakes like that to fuel your artistic output. This song's fantastic – if you'd behaved yourself in the first place, you'd never have written it, would you? The end justifies the means.'

Dave bit his tongue, thinking that it didn't really work that way; he'd written plenty of good songs when things with Cindy were good. Even if Alan was right, he'd rather have Cindy back and never write another song again. They started discussing the arrangement, and Alan suggested a keyboard solo for it. Dave put his foot down: this one had to be guitar. Not least because he couldn't face Shaun playing the solo live, not on this song.

Dave got back from the recording session to find a visitor in his flat: Cindy. She stood up as he let himself in and held her hands up to shush him before he could speak.

'Don't say anything, just listen.' Her tone wasn't angry, but it was flat, without a hint of affection. The sparkle in her eyes was gone too, which broke his heart all over again. 'I've spoken to Nicky and she's told me what happened between you.'

'And it just happened, it wasn't planned, I…' She held her hand up again and he immediately fell silent. This was Cindy's show; he was going to let her run it her way.

'I know, and I know it was just the one time, but that's not the point. You told me about your past and you swore you had changed. You said you'd never do to me what the other men in my life had done, then you went and did it. How can I believe anything you said to me? How can I know what was really going on in your head when we were together? I promised myself a long time ago that I wouldn't stay with a man I can't trust. I wish we could put this right, but how can I ever trust you again after what you did?'

'I don't know, but can't we at least try? Sleeping with Nicky was the biggest mistake of my life; if I could take it back, I would. Tell me what you need me to do and I'll do it. Please, give me one more chance and I'll never betray you like that again.'

Cindy actually laughed. 'Can you hear yourself? You know who you sound like, don't you? You sound like you a few months ago, when you convinced me to trust you and then slept with my best mate. How can you expect me to take that seriously?' Dave hung his head, ashamed at the knowledge that everything Cindy said was fair comment but still hoping for a reprieve.

'It's over, Tom,' she said. 'I'm sorry; what we had was great while it lasted. I've already moved out of the flat, and I'm not telling you where I'm living now. Don't try to find me; I just want to put this behind me and move on. I hope you can do that too.'

And with that she was gone, taking Dave's last best hope of happiness with her. What a Merry Christmas it was going to be.

part three

AND I FELL BACK ALONE

JANUARY 1991

CHAPTER TWENTY-FOUR

What should have been his first Christmas with Cindy turned out to be his worst ever. Staying in alone, wallowing in sad records and alcohol had been the extent of his festivities. Despite the song's Christmas theme, he should have known better than listening to Joni Mitchell's "River", but it had never felt so apt. He thought of Cindy, wherever she was, and imagined her tears, knowing he was the one who had made her cry.

He remembered the family Christmases growing up, the good and bad ones. His mum, lighting up the house with her laughter when he was little, then him and his dad endlessly clashing after her death, Auntie Vi trying to keep the peace: 'Just for one day, please!' He wondered what Dad would say about how things had gone with Cindy: probably tell him he'd been a bloody idiot again. He'd be right, too. Dave had rarely seen his father's point on anything before; maybe if he wasn't locked into this pretence of death things might be different between them now. But one of them was nearly dead, and the other already was, officially at least; another example of him being a bloody idiot. It was all too late.

In early January, Frank Dixon phoned again. He had completed his investigation and wanted to hand over his report. Dave was glad of the distraction and headed over to the caravan-cum-office immediately. Frank opened the door wearing a different shirt from the last time Dave had seen him, but somehow with an identical food stain down the front, as if it was some kind of corporate logo.

'So, what have you got for me?' he asked.

Frank handed over a large, plain envelope. 'It's all in there. Tom grew up in Coventry, mixing with the wrong crowd and getting his card marked by the police. There was a turf war and he found himself in court as a witness. Whatever he said was going to upset one side or the other, but based on his evidence one of the top men was acquitted. That earned him credit with one firm but made him a target for the other.'

'What happened next?'

'Well, he disappeared from Coventry not long after the court case, probably moved by his new friends for his own protection. It wasn't easy, but I managed to track him down. He was mixing with dodgy types all over – Leeds, Stoke, Carlisle – and did a couple of short stints in prison – it's all in there – before heading home to Coventry about a year ago. He must have thought that after so long it was safe for him to come back. He was wrong; crooks have long memories and whoever he was running from obviously remembered why he ran. As I say, the detail is all there – along with my invoice, by the way – but that's the short version.'

Dave thanked him and wrote a cheque. Frank said to let him know if he needed anything else. That evening, Dave read through the report a couple of times. Tom Mulvaney was just small fry in the world of crime, and even tried to go straight towards the end by the sound of things. Who knows, if Tony's contacts hadn't been looking for someone for Dave to become, maybe he'd still be alive today. Did that make him responsible for Tom's demise? He certainly felt responsible to Ronnie.

The phone rang three, four times before Ronnie answered.

'Tom, hi. I wasn't expecting to hear from you again. I still haven't found any other Tom Mulvaneys.'

'About that, there's something I need to tell you.'

Dave came clean to Ronnie, mostly. He told him about taking a false identity, and that he was almost certain that the life he had stepped into was that of Ronnie's father. He gave a brief summary of Tom's life and offered to send a copy of Frank's report. He hesitated when Ronnie asked who Dave really was, tempted momentarily to tell all, but he thought better of it. When he put the phone down, he was surprised at the sense of relief; it was good to draw a line under something. At least Ronnie had a happy ending of sorts.

A few days later he was back in the studio. Vince, Phil and Simon had finished half a dozen tracks in their previous session and Alan hoped to complete their contributions to the album in the three days set aside for this block of recording. Dave and Alan decided to leave "Withered and Died" with just Dave's acoustic guitar, but all the other tracks featured the three sidemen. Just like the old days, they instinctively got what Dave wanted, adding texture and nuance that were all he could have dreamed of. This really had been a special band, just like the Dave ReMastered Band were becoming until Shaun's libido broke it apart. One of the songs in this session was the cover of "The Real Me", and the lads did Dave proud, particularly Vince, who flailed around his kit like a man possessed.

'Who knew, after all these years of fading into the background?' joked Simon.

'He always had fireworks like that up his sleeve if he needed them,' added Phil. 'He just never felt the need to show off.'

'It's all about the song,' said Vince. 'I play what the song needs, and this needed a bit of flash.'

Dave and Alan exchanged grins in the control room. 'It's one of the reasons I picked it,' said Dave. 'I wanted to finally let him unleash the beast.'

'Well, he's certainly done that. I never knew he had it in him.'

'I did.'

The musicians were frustrated not to be able to hear the completed tracks, guitar solos and all, but Tony had been adamant that Dave shouldn't play while the others were there. By the end of the three days, there were twelve new old Dave Masters' songs in the can, the whole album just waiting for guitar overdubs and a final mix. Alan exchanged farewells with the three musicians and everyone promised to keep in touch, though their lives all ran on different paths now. Phil turned down Simon's offer to put his name about if he wanted to get back into the business – as much as he'd enjoyed these sessions, he was done with that life. Vince wrapped the others in one of his bearhugs and soon the trio were gone.

'Happy?' asked Alan.

'You're the producer, you tell me. What do you think?'

'I think we've just recorded your best album yet. Certainly the best since you started working with, shall we say, lesser talents in the control box.'

Dave grinned. 'I think you might be right. Of course, there's the guitar overdubs to go yet. That idiot from the tribute act could still mess up everything up.'

They agreed to book the studio again in a week or so. Before that, Dave had a first rehearsal arranged with his newly reconstituted band. Tony assured him that he had found a couple of musicians who were perfect to step in for Martin and Chris. Dave wasn't entirely convinced, but Tony had come up trumps with Ollie, so he gave him the benefit of the doubt. Ironically Shaun, who had caused all the problems, was now the only surviving member of his original ReMastered band.

Dave, Shaun and Ollie were jamming, waiting for Tony to arrive with the new recruits. Dave was trying to be breezily cheerful, but things were still tense between him and Shaun. He was furious that Shaun had mentioned his liaison with Nicky in front of Cindy, but he knew he had to get past that; he couldn't afford to lose another band member.

The door opened and Tony walked in with the two new musicians. There was something naggingly familiar about one of them, but Dave recognised the other instantly.

'You have got to be joking!'

Tony ignored his outburst. 'Dave, Shaun, Ollie, this is Miles and Declan, the new members of the Dave ReMastered Band.' Shaun and Ollie exchanged glances, unsure why Dave was so worked up.

'Well, that's a nice welcome,' said one of the two, a lad in his twenties with long hair and a passing resemblance to Dave in his glory days.

'Miles and Declan should already know most of the material – they've been playing in another Dave Masters tribute band for the last few months.'

'Vagabond Dave!' cried Shaun, pointing at the one who had spoken.

'The very same, but you can call me Miles – when we're off stage, anyway.'

'Tony, is this some kind of a joke?' asked Dave. 'Three months ago, he was trying to steal my crowd; now you want to bring him into my band?'

Tony shrugged. 'It all makes sense. You need a rhythm guitarist; he plays rhythm guitar and he already knows the material. Declan played bass with the Troubled Minds, so he's in the same boat. I thought you'd be pleased they won't be starting from scratch.'

From what Dave remembered from their spying mission, Martin had rated Declan, so that wasn't too bad, but he wasn't happy about bringing Vagabond Dave into the line-up, even more so if he had a natural ally in the form of Declan.

Miles held out a hand to Dave. 'It's Tom, isn't it? Look, I know we got off to a bad start, what with the busking and everything, but that's show business – dog eat dog and all that. You won that round, but now by combining our bands, taking the best of each, we can be bigger and better than either of us were on our own. With two Daves to share the singing, it'll be amazing.'

Dave took a moment to process what Miles had just said. 'Two Daves sharing the singing? Excuse me?'

'It makes sense. We've both got an audience, my fans will want to hear me singing Dave Masters, your fans will want you, so let's give everyone what they want. How are we going to divide up the songs between us?'

Dave felt his fists bunching; he couldn't believe the lad's nerve. 'Are you serious? We divide them up like this. I sing the ones that Dave Masters sang, and you sing Davey O'Keefe's backing vocals. I'm the only Dave Masters in this band, and I'm the only Dave Masters we need.'

'With due respect, mate, you're getting on a bit.' A half-smile spread across Miles's face, just asking for a punch or two to remove it. 'That's fine for his later songs, but he recorded his '70s stuff when he was more my age. I can bring the youthful verve that you've lost. In Vagabond Dave, we hardly played any of the '80s songs anyway – we stuck to the good stuff. We did "Feel Like Going Home" and the other hits, but apart from that we didn't bother with anything after *Don't Walk, Run*.'

'I can still do all the old stuff perfectly well, thank you very much. We did a Dave-off before, remember, and I was so much better you didn't even stay to the end.'

'Yeah, but that was when I was just starting; I've sharpened up since then. I still think I should sing the older stuff.'

The two Daves were standing toe to toe, glaring at one another.

'So has Vagabond Dave broken up then?' asked Shaun, directing his question to Declan rather than risk being caught in the crossfire of the frontmen.

'Nah, well, maybe – I mean, if Miles and me come and join you, it leaves the others in the lurch a bit, but you guys earn more than us, so the move makes sense. Tony was happy to juggle both acts before, but he'd rather lose us than you. I'm just glad I play the right instrument to fill one of your gaps.'

Dave turned away from Miles, taking in what Declan had just said. 'What do you mean, Tony was juggling both acts?' He turned to face the manager. 'I thought you said you were going to chase Vagabond Dave off?'

Tony smiled. 'Not exactly. I said I'd take care of them, and I did: I signed them. While you were away on tour, I put them to work on the London circuit, and once you came back, I sent them off to play to Dave Masters fans in Europe. I hadn't realised what a nice little earner tribute bands can be – no need to build an audience from scratch, just tap into all the existing fans who can't see their favourites anymore. I'm going to look out for other tribute bands – it's a growing market.'

At least Dave now knew that Tony hadn't resorted to violence, but it still felt like a betrayal to have taken on another fake him.

'Okay,' said Dave. 'But this isn't a merger of two bands; this is two new people joining an existing and very successful one. He's here to play rhythm guitar, not to be lead vocalist.'

'Co-lead vocalist,' corrected Miles.

'*Backing* vocalist. Tony, tell him.'

All eyes were on Tony. For a moment, Dave wasn't sure what he was going to say. After everything they had been through together, he couldn't believe that Tony wouldn't side with him on this. Then again, if there was more money to be made doing it Miles's way, Tony was capable of anything.

Tony turned to Miles. 'Tom's right. It's his band you're joining, and he's the lead singer.'

'But you said—'

'I said I'd see what he thought, and you've heard what he thinks. Take it or leave it: a share of bigger paydays as a sideman, or stay as you are singing lead to smaller audiences. You're the best fit to step in on rhythm guitar, but I can find someone else.' Before Miles had a chance to respond, Tony turned to Declan. 'You're happy to move across either way, aren't you, Dec?' The eager response left Miles in a very weak bargaining position. Not only was he not getting his own way in the new band, but he'd need to rebuild his old one if he held out.

'If you put it like that, I agree. I still think we should combine, though – Vagabond Dave ReMastered, with two vocalists. It would make a great publicity angle.'

'Not happening,' snapped Dave. 'I'll give you a trial, no more, to see how it works out. After everything you've pulled in the past, you need to prove yourself.'

Miles looked like he was about to protest further, but Tony jumped in quickly. 'And that's fair enough. Look, you're all good musicians. Why don't I leave you to do what you do best and play some music? Once you stop arguing and start playing, you might find more in common than you realise.'

They started with the older material that everybody knew. Declan was as good as Dave remembered, although perhaps a little too rigid in following the original records, while Miles's playing had improved a lot since the last time Dave saw him. The rehearsals were going well, with Declan particularly proving open to direction.

'Feel the groove, Dec. Don't be tied to what's on the record. That's your starting point, but it's got to feel right. Sometimes on stage you have to vary it a bit to keep it sounding right – you're a musician, not a copying machine.'

Miles had more of a tendency to argue his point when Dave tried directing him, but his playing was okay when he shut up and got on with it.

They took a break, and Ollie and Shaun sidled up to Dave.

'What do you think, boss?' asked Shaun.

'I think they can both play. Declan seems like the next best thing to Martin. I'm not sure about Miles's attitude, though. What do you two think?'

'Pretty much that,' agreed Ollie.

'Depends what their girlfriends looks like, doesn't it?' said

Shaun with a grin. Dave turned away without responding and went to find a cup of tea.

They stuck to the old material that day, and Dave said he'd get Tony to send over a cassette with the whole set. Miles and Declan were told to familiarise themselves with the new songs and they would start on those at the next rehearsal.

Tony phoned later that evening to find out what happened after the heated start.

'I knew you guys would work it out – you're all pros after all.'

'That's not the point, Tony. Why didn't you tell me who you had lined up to take Chris's place?'

'Because I knew how you'd react. Miles is a bit full of himself – as if I was ever going to let him share the vocals with you – but I had to hint that you might be open to the idea just to get him in the room. Tell me he's not a decent rhythm guitarist, and I'll start looking for someone else.'

He had a point. Dave hated being played by Tony, but it wasn't as if it was the first time in his life – lives – that had happened. He wasn't entirely convinced that Tony wouldn't have folded on the shared vocals, not if the discussion had gone differently, but he'd never know, would he?

'That leather waistcoat he wears on stage…'

'Yeah, that was yours. I gave it to him when I wanted him to take me on as manager. He's a big fan, so the thought of having something that belonged to Dave Masters almost made him wet himself.'

'But it was mine.'

'Yeah, but you're dead.'

'One more thing: tell Miles he's got to cut his hair. We've never done lookalikes and I'm certainly not having someone in the band who looks more like me than I do.'

Tony chuckled. 'Fair point, leave it with me. Oh, and Alan tells me that you're almost done with the fake album. Just the guitar overdubs to go. Is that right?'

'Yeah, we're making a start on it tomorrow evening, then Alan's going to do the final mix and you can tell the record company that the golden goose is still laying, even though he's been dead for months.'

'Music to my pockets.'

Dave had wangled a key to the studio, and let himself in. He took out his Ovation and plugged in. After tuning up, he started singing a few of his own songs. "Through My Fingers" made him think again of Cindy and everything that he'd thrown away. He did a run-through of Joni Mitchell's "River", an earworm track for him since Christmas. After that, he found himself strumming something else. It wasn't until he reached the vocal that he recognised it: one of the songs from that World Party album Cindy had impressed the tour bus with. It was a bleak, hopelessly resigned song about a love affair that died; no surprises why it had come into his mind just now. The title told his whole story: "And I Fell Back Alone".

Dave allowed his guitar to build in intensity, pouring his feelings into his playing. There was no solo, no instrumental break, just a slow, steadily swelling expression of regret until he came to an end. The lyrics seemed the perfect summary of where he was, of what he'd lost and what had never really been his to start with. They had been doomed from the start: Cindy wanted him to be open and honest, and he hadn't even been able to tell her his real name. Then, when his commitment had been tested, he had failed dismally. He couldn't change who he was, and ultimately that meant he would always be falling back alone. He just felt bad about putting Cindy through it all. She deserved better and he hoped she'd find it, even if it wasn't going to be with him.

When he finished, he noticed a light on in the control room. Alan had arrived.

'Hey, Alan, I didn't notice you come in.'

'No problem. That one was good, what was it?'

'Nothing, just playing about.'

'Okay. Are you ready to start? As you've got the acoustic out, do you want to take a pass at "Rockabye", or shall we go for an electric solo?'

"Rockabye": the song about his desire to protect Cindy from the monsters of her past. He'd have to tackle it eventually, but not yet; not when he was still raw from turning out to be the worst monster of all. 'Let's get the electric out and cut loose. How about "The Real Me"?'

CHAPTER TWENTY-FIVE

With the album finished and nothing happening in Dave's personal life, he threw himself into whipping his new band into shape. At the next rehearsal Declan had clearly done his homework and was note-perfect on all the new (to him) songs. He was a little too perfect at times, still rigidly copying rather than listening and reacting, but Ollie was taking him under his wing and helping him work on that. Miles, still with his Dave Masters hair, was less co-operative. He'd certainly listened to the songs, airing his opinion on how bad many of them were, but he hadn't learned his parts. Most of the session was spent with Dave having to teach him different chord changes and rhythms.

'Look,' said Dave after another abortive attempt at "Steel Strings", 'if you don't want to be here, we can find someone else.'

'I want to be here, I just don't think we should be wasting our time. The fans at our gigs go wild for the classic material, so why bother with the rest? Give the punters what they want: Dave Masters in his pomp, not second-rate leftovers.'

'You know what the punters want, do you? Is that why we played Hammersmith Palais while you were still in pubs and clubs?'

'Yeah, well, you had the better band, I'm not denying that. You're a much better lead guitarist, and Ollie and Shaun are a step up from what we had. But now we've got the best players all together, if we drop the filler we'll be unstoppable. And I still think you should let me sing some of them.'

'Look, I'll make this simple for you; either knuckle down and learn the full set, or sling your hook and we'll find someone else who will. This is my band and I don't need some cocky little kid with his thumb up his arse telling me how to run it. Do you think you can handle that?'

The two of them glared at each other for a minute, the others waiting to see who would back down. Miles blinked first, turning away and beginning to strum his part for "Steel Strings", miraculously getting it right for the first time in ten attempts. At least Declan seemed to be a good fit, but the constant friction with Miles was rubbing off on everyone; rehearsals never got close to the easy-going atmosphere of the early days.

'It's not working, Tony.' As soon as he got home from the rehearsal, Dave had picked up the phone. 'Whenever we start teaching them the songs from the later albums, he whines about it not being what the fans want – as if I don't know my own audience! Declan's fine, but Miles is a nightmare. He won't accept that I'm in charge – *and* he hasn't got his hair cut yet.'

'Look, I've booked a few gigs for next month. Stick with it for those and see how he does. If you're still not happy after that, we'll get rid of him, but at least give it a go.'

Dave could see he wasn't going to get anywhere, so he changed the subject. 'Did Alan tell you we've finished the overdubs?'

Dave could hear the glee in Tony's reply. 'He was like a kid at Christmas; said you were playing up a storm. He's doing the final mix over the next few days and then we'll take the tapes to Ultimate. Any thoughts on what you'd like as the first single? No promises, but I'll see what I can do.'

If Dave thought there was a song that would bring Cindy back to him, he would have pushed for it, but he knew it would take more than songs to undo what he had done. 'Just make sure it's one of mine rather than a cover. I want to remind people of Dave Masters the songwriter, not the "gifted interpreter of other people's songs".'

Music wasn't the only thing on his mind, of course. He had been doing a lot of thinking about Cindy. He doubted she would listen to him even if he managed to track her down, but he had to try. He had placed personal ads in the music papers – "Cindy Incidentally. I wish I'd known then what I know now. Please call me. Tom" – but so far she either hadn't seen it or wasn't interested in responding. He had to try something different.

He picked up the telephone and dialled.

'Frank? Hi, it's Tom Mulvaney. I've got another job for you.'

Frank had asked him for as much information about Cindy as he had. Dave gave Frank the address of her old flat in Barnet and told him about the King's Head and working in Quicksave until she disappeared from his life, but stressed that he had already tried all of her local contacts. He mentioned the aunt in Bournemouth as well, just in case that helped.

'Well, I think I can squeeze you in among my busy caseload. For a higher rate, I can prioritise you and put the others on the back burner.'

'Busy caseload? How many cases are you working on at the moment, Frank? Honestly.'

'If I take this one on, that will bring it up to… let me see… er… one.'

'Same fee as last time then?'

'Plus expenses?'

'Reasonable expenses.'

The first date with the new line-up was fast approaching, and Miles was slowly, reluctantly, falling into line. He still baulked at cutting his hair but agreed to put it in a ponytail for the show.

Even he could see that having a Dave Masters lookalike playing someone other than Dave Masters could confuse the audience. He tried telling Dave that the set list was all in the wrong order, but Dave shut the discussion down straight away.

'Look, I know you had your set list and it was working for you. Ours has worked really well for us too. It's tried and tested. Let's see how the first few gigs go and we can consider changes once we're up and running. I don't run the band as a dictatorship – Ollie and Shaun will tell you that – but I make the final call. Stop fighting me every step of the way and maybe I'll start listening to you.' Dave wished he had stood up to Tony and got rid of Miles when he had the chance, but there was no time now before the tour. He'd have to make the best of it.

Tony's tour schedule took them, plus Jym, Dink and Ben, on a two-week jaunt around the country. They were playing a mixture of the same venues as last time, plus a handful of bigger ones. In Bristol Tony had booked the Colston Hall instead of the Bierkeller, in Nottingham they were playing Rock City, and in Glasgow they were back at the Barrowlands. Ticket sales were strong and these were rooms that took two thousand or so fans at a time. It was great to be back at some of the venues from his best days, even if it was just for single shows. Back then he could sell out multiple nights at each venue, but it was still a massive step up from the Jericho and the Georgian Theatre.

Shaun was explaining the tour-bus music policy and the three-veto rule.

'You mean we all get a say?' asked Declan. 'In the Troubled Minds, Miles always chose. Most of the time we listened to nothing but Dave Masters.'

'Didn't you hear enough of that on stage every night?' asked Ollie. 'I mean, it's great music, but it's boring sticking with one thing all the time.'

'That's what I've always said,' added Shaun, lasciviously.

Dave was at the back of the bus, taking all this in. He was beginning to wonder if one of the reasons he found Shaun's attitude to women so irritating was because it was like being confronted with a younger version of himself. He didn't recognise that person anymore, although recent events made it clear that he wasn't so far beneath the surface.

'The others weren't Dave Masters fans before I pulled them together,' explained Miles. 'I wanted them to know the material back to front.'

Dave could hear the mischief in Shaun's voice as he responded. 'In that case, shouldn't we be playing some of Dave Masters' later albums in the bus, so you and Declan can get to know them properly?'

Miles looked horrified, but Declan steered the conversation smoothly away from conflict – perhaps his playing wasn't the only thing he had in common with Martin. 'We know what we're doing now – we never rehearsed so hard in the other band. Who chooses the first album of the tour then?'

Dink was the first to react. 'Me, and you're going to love this, *Rock and Roll* by Motorhead.'

'Veto!' called Ben.

'Is "Ace of Spades" on that one?' asked Ollie.

'No.'

'Veto.'

Dave, Jym and Shaun raced to wield the decisive third veto (Shaun won, his youthful reactions beating the two older men), and Jym announced that it was Ollie's turn to try his luck. Dave usually enjoyed Ollie's selections, and he struck gold this time with a John Hiatt album that Dave had back at the flat. Hiatt had assembled an all-star backing group of Ry Cooder, Jim Keltner and Nick Lowe. Jym voiced his approval, though the younger lads hadn't heard it before.

Settling back to enjoy John Hiatt, Dave reflected on what he had learned. Miles had been a bit of an authoritarian in the other band: that wasn't a great surprise. And Tony wasn't wrong about him being a serious Dave Masters fan; at least he had that going for him.

Later in the journey, Dave moved seats and went to sit alongside his new guitarist.

'So how did you get into Dave Masters?'

'My older brothers had all of his records. I grew up loving the early stuff, but once he started messing with his sound to stay relevant, it just wasn't the same.'

Dave smiled; Miles was only echoing his own thoughts about his later work. 'True, but there are still some good songs, once you get past the production.'

'I know!' Miles was getting animated. 'I saw one of his last gigs before he died, just a small place in Oxford. His playing was amazing. Hearing the more recent songs stripped back made me appreciate them more – well, some of them. His quality control dipped towards the end.'

Dave wanted to argue and defend himself, but again he knew there was something in what Miles was saying. His body of work was marred by a lot of the '80s material. At least the album he'd just finished showed that he could still produce great music, even if the rest of the world would see it as the last gasp before his '80s decline rather than a long-awaited return to form.

The band checked into their accommodation while the crew went to set up. Dave wanted to phone Cindy, and the fact that he couldn't, not today or any other day, brought back the darkness that never seemed far from him now.

He was interrupted by a knock on his door, which turned out to be Declan.

'All right, Tom,' said the bassist, looking a little awkward. Dave ushered him in, making an effort to be friendly and welcoming; if Declan hadn't played a venue as big as the Colston Hall before, he might need some guidance to get his head into performance mode.

'I wasn't sure whether to say anything, but I'm really excited about being in this band and I don't want anything to go wrong.'

'I'm sure it won't. Your playing in rehearsal is great, much more relaxed and natural now. You'll be fine.'

Declan smiled gratefully. 'Thanks, but that's not what I mean. Miles thinks I'm on his side – your band versus his band, that kind of thing, but I'm not. You should know, he's got something planned for tonight.'

This didn't sound good. What was Miles up to? 'Go on.'

'You remember the argument about sharing the vocals? He's planning on doing it anyway. On the songs that we used to do – some of them, at least – he's planning on crashing the lead vocal. If you don't get out of his way, he's just going to sing along with you, hoping you'll be the one to back down. He thinks that once you hear how well he captures Dave Masters' voice, you'll see he was right and do whatever makes for the best show.'

'Did he now? Thanks for telling me Declan, I appreciate it. It can't have been easy, going against your mate.'

Declan shuffled his feet. 'We were never big mates – he always kept himself slightly above the rest of the band. Shaun and Ollie – and you – all seem great, much more friendly than the Troubled Minds. I hope you and Miles can sort things out, but if you decide to get rid of him, please don't ditch me too just because I arrived with him.'

Dave promised that Declan's place in the band would be based solely on his own merits, and that so far he hadn't seen anything to make him worry on that account. He had one request, though.

'Don't tell Miles that I know what he's planning, okay? I can deal with him, but I want to see whether or not he actually goes through with it.'

CHAPTER TWENTY-SIX

Miles behaved himself at the soundcheck. Afterwards, Dave went to give Ben a copy of the set list while the others went back to the dressing room. Declan was nervous, but nothing compared to Chris's early days. Shaun regaled the others with tales of just how bad Chris had been, conceding that he'd always pulled it out of the bag once he got up on the stage. Miles wasn't saying much, giving no indication of whether he'd go through with his planned coup.

Before they went on, Dave gathered the musicians together for a final pep talk. 'Look, I know it's the first time the five of us have played a show together, but we've got this. You all know your parts, it's tried and tested material, and a lot of these people have been out to see us before. This is our audience.'

'It's Dave Masters' audience, surely,' interjected Miles.

'Yes, it's Dave Masters' audience, but he's gone so we're looking after them for him. They've come to hear us play his music. Remember, we work together on that stage and we send everyone home happy. All ready?'

'Let's rock!' shouted Shaun, prompting laughter from the Ollie and Declan.

'Too right – let's rock,' agreed Dave, before leading them out to the wings.

The first number was "Steppin' Stone", much to Miles's displeasure. The audience was loving it, singing along right from the word go. This could be a great night if Miles didn't wreck things.

'Thank you, Bristol,' said Dave at the end of the song. 'We're the Dave ReMastered Band. This is "Double Down on Love".' The song crashed straight in to the lyrics with no introduction, and he was about to jump straight in when he became aware of Miles singing his heart out ten feet to his left. Miles got less than a line into the song before stopping and looking dumbstruck. He was singing, but his mic wasn't on – only the band could hear him.

'One, two, three,' called Dave, and started the song properly, with the rest of the band sharply following his cue. Miles didn't look happy but soon fell in on guitar. The next song was another early one, "Jack of Hearts", but Miles didn't sing, prompting Dave to look through the darkness towards the sound desk. He pointed at Miles than up in the air. He thought his rival had learned his lesson and could probably be trusted with backing vocals again. He'd briefed Ben when dropping off the set list, marking which songs he thought Miles might play silly buggers on, and Ben had been ready to cut his mic at the first sign of trouble. During Shaun's keyboard solo, Dave drifted across the stage. Turning his back on the audience so no one would see the look on his face, he spoke into Miles's ear.

'Your mic should be back on, but if you try anything like that again, Ben will silence it for the rest of the show. Just be a professional and do your job. Last chance.'

From that point on, Miles behaved himself. He played and sang only where he was supposed to, although he hardly radiated enthusiasm. There would be words after the show, but this would end one of two ways: Miles fell into line, or Miles said goodbye. Dave had never let anyone mess his music up, and now Cindy was gone, his music was all he had left.

The recriminations began as soon as they reached the dressing room, and the others started on Miles before Dave could even open his mouth. Shaun was furious, accusing Miles of making them all look like idiots; Ollie hadn't been sure what had happened from the back of the stage, but once the others brought him up to speed, he was livid. Dave let everyone blow off some steam, then stepped in.

'Right. Here's what's going to happen. Miles, first of all, you owe your bandmates an apology. Whether you think you should be singing lead or not, you can't mess them around on stage like that. Secondly, either you knuckle down or you leave the tour; it's as simple as that. Which is it going to be?'

Miles muttered something about staying, but he didn't look particularly enthusiastic. To be fair, he seemed more embarrassed than anything.

'And have you something to say to your bandmates?'

Shaun and Ollie were glaring as he offered an apology so quiet it could have been written by John Cage. Dave would have to keep an eye on things; even if Miles behaved from now on, he'd already destabilised the band's happy dynamic. Everything could easily come crashing down.

Later, as the others made their way to the hotel bar, Dave asked Miles to wait with him in the lobby.

'What is it?' snapped Miles. 'Haven't you made me look stupid enough tonight?'

'I'd say you did that to yourself, but let's move on. We've got off to a bad start and I'm phoning Tony tomorrow to fill him in, but I meant what I said about giving you another chance. You're a decent player but you're going to have to earn your stripes with the others. Show them that you can pull in the same direction as the rest of us. This is my band; if you can deal with that, we can work together. What do you say?' He was tempted to extend his arm and offer Miles a handshake but wasn't confident that Miles would accept it. The two of them locked eyes for a long moment, before Miles shrugged and brushed past Dave, heading for his room.

When they climbed into the tour bus the next morning, Jym reminded everyone that it was Miles's turn to choose the music. Even before he opened his mouth, Ollie and Shaun just shouted, 'Veto,' with Dink (who was next in line to choose) wasting no time to add his voice to theirs. Unfortunately, his choice of Hawkwind's live *Space Ritual* album was vetoed off almost as quickly, allowing Jym to put on Fleetwood Mac's *Rumours*. It chilled everyone out nicely, although "Oh Daddy" gave Dave another jagged reminder that he still hadn't found a way to stop the clock running out on his relationship with his father.

When they stopped for petrol, Dave found a payphone and called Tony, telling him all about Miles's attempted coup.

'Well, well, well, I wasn't expecting that. Shall I sack him?'

It was tempting, but Dave had promised Miles a last chance. 'Not just yet. I've told him he's on his last chance. Start thinking about possible replacements, but I'd rather not throw a new guitarist in mid-tour if we can avoid it.'

'Okay, I'll put out feelers and see who might be available. By the way, Ultimate have decided on the first single from the lost album: it came down to either that Who song or "Shadow Life".' "Shadow Life" was a song that he'd written in the gap between messing up with Nicky and Cindy finding out. It was sung in the first person, from the perspective of someone trying to carry on as normal but terrified of being found out. It was a good song, but Dave wasn't sure how he felt about singing it every night.

'And?'

'They've gone for your one.'

'It's a bit dark and broody, isn't it? Wouldn't something more up-tempo be a better first single?'

Tony chuckled. 'I thought you wanted the songwriting royalties. Anyway, even the suits could see they can't just keep releasing covers as singles; they want to remind people what a great songwriter you are too. They're putting it out in a couple of weeks, so you'll be able to add it to the set list. If I can get some advance copies of the album, I'll pass them on to you, but I haven't had any joy on that front yet.'

Dave's next call was to Frank Dixon, or rather his answering machine.

'Hi, Frank, Tom Mulvaney here. Just checking in for a progress report. I'll try again when I get the chance.' He hoped Frank would have some good news. He still wanted to make things right with Cindy, but what if she didn't want to hear what he had to say?

The next day was a rest day, and Dave finally got hold of Frank, who said he'd had a breakthrough. Dave felt his heart quicken, but his excitement didn't last long.

'Well, I say breakthrough, that's overstating it a bit. I've found the aunt in Bournemouth.'

'And?'

'And she's dead, so that's not a lot of use. It's opened up some other leads to follow, though. I'm sure I'll find her if I keep at it.'

Miles was nowhere to be seen for most of the day. Jym said he'd taken himself off into town and hadn't been seen since. If it wasn't for the fact that he hadn't checked out, Dave would have suspected that he'd cut his losses and gone home. The others were in the hotel bar, with Miles the main topic of conversation.

'You know him best, Declan,' said Shaun. 'Do you think he'll toe the line?' Before Declan could answer Miles walked in, wrapped up against the cold in a thick winter jacket and with a woolly hat on his head. All the conversation stopped, with everyone looking at the prodigal rhythm guitarist.

'All right, Miles,' said Dave, breaking the ice.

'Look, I know you all hate me right now, and I know I was a tit.' It was a promising opening. 'The thing is, I've been a Dave Masters fan ever since I was a kid. When he died, I convinced myself that I was the best person to keep his music going. When I found out about you,' he nodded towards Dave, 'I got jealous.

Once Tony took me on as a client, I was determined to overtake you, to become more successful. When he asked me to join your band, I thought I could steal them from you, but that was before I saw you on stage. You're a much better Dave Masters than me. If you'll still have me, I want to try again. I'll play Davey O'Keefe to your Dave Masters and I won't try to upstage you.'

'Yeah, nice words, but how do we know we can trust you?' asked Ollie. 'How do we know you won't try something else the next time you get a microphone in front of you?'

'Fair question. I knew you'd need a sign that I was serious, so…' His hand went up to his head and slowly pulled off the hat. Not only had he got a haircut, losing the classic long-haired Dave Masters look, he'd even dyed it to match the pictures of Davey O'Keefe from the old album covers. 'I can hardly take over as lead singer when I look more like one of the sidemen, can I?'

It took a moment, but the others slowly started grinning, then laughing, and soon Miles was accepted back into the fold. It wouldn't last, of course, unless he backed up his claims on stage, but at least the wounds were beginning to heal over.

The rest of the tour went much better. Miles was as good as his word and seemed to be enjoying himself on stage; he had even given Dave the long-lost leather waistcoat as a peace offering. It took a while, but after a couple of shows Dave was reassured that they were a happy camp again. Miles was even allowed to pick music for the tour bus, with a Maria McKee album proving particularly popular with everyone except Dink. A few tracks in, a guitar line woke Dave up like an electric shock.

'That sounds like Richard Thompson,' he said instinctively.

'Yeah, it's him,' said Miles. 'He guests on a few tracks on the album.' Dave was pleased with himself; he'd always said he could recognise his favourite's playing a mile off. He was in good form on this one, too, and Dave made a mental note to add the album to his own collection when he got the chance.

The tour finished, although Tony had booked a few more isolated gigs to keep them working. He'd been busy on other things too: news about previously unheard late '70s Dave Masters material was leaking into the music press. *Q* magazine covered the story, remarking that if a lost cache was going to be found, these dated back to the ideal time: late enough for him to have honed his songwriting but before he lost focus and began second-guessing the market. The official story was that it was material Dave and the band had recorded between 1977 and '78 during gaps in their American touring schedule. For some reason, the songs were forgotten when it was time to record 1979's *Don't Walk, Run*. Tony claimed the tapes came to light when clearing Dave's home for sale. Once he realised what they were, he set about preparing them for release, knowing that it wasn't fair to deny Dave's devoted fans for any longer than necessary. Alan was quoted in the article too, rather cheekily commenting that he remembered the sessions as if they were only a few weeks ago. Alan also remarked on the maturity of Dave's songwriting, saying that these songs showed an understanding of life that seemed to elude him in the material that followed in the early '80s. There was no critical appraisal – no one apart from Tony, Alan and, presumably, the Ultimate suits, had heard the completed album yet, but it was still being hailed as one of the most anticipated releases of the year. Not that Tony had given Dave the chance to hear it yet.

'As soon as I get vinyl copies from Ultimate, I'll pass them on. The fact that they think you're dead is making it hard for me to say why I need advance copies. You'll be happy, though, I promise. I just wish we could stop Alan dropping hints every five minutes. If he's not careful he'll blow the whole thing wide open. I might have to have a word with him.'

'Oh, come on, no one is going to think twice about it. I mean, it's like I said about the funeral; the fact that everyone thinks I'm dead means people will ignore him. I checked all the lyrics carefully; there's nothing to date them beyond the late '70s. I just want to hear the songs – are you sure that you can't let me have a copy from the master tape?'

'No way. Ultimate are treating this like the crown jewels – it's a full lock-down until the release date. You'd want to tape it for the band to rehearse from, and can you honestly say you trust the others not to leak it? You'll just have to be patient this time. Trust me, though, you're going to love it.'

"Shadow Life" came out as a single, and if it was anything to go by, the album was going to be fantastic. Alan had done a terrific job with the sound. Dave could almost picture his younger self, along with Vince and the boys, playing along with it. Midweek sales figures suggested another smash hit.

The band reconvened for another live show, this time at Leicester's De Montfort Hall. They had been rehearsing "Shadow Life" and added it to the set list, though the rest of the album was still an unknown quantity. When Miles arrived at the tour bus, he seemed particularly excited.

'I know it's not my turn, but you've all got to hear this – I mean, really, you've got to hear this.'

'I was going to put some Supertramp on,' protested Shaun.

'Never mind that, I've got the new Dave Masters album. It's not officially for sale for another few days, but a mate who works at HMV let me have it early. I taped it last night.' No one protested as he pushed the cassette into the player. Dave was as excited as everyone else.

Tony had been right: Dave and the band loved it. It could easily have been recorded back in the '70s, when he was still full of fire and talent and self-belief. The first track, "Drain the Glass", was a swaggering paean to seizing life and squeezing it for all it was worth, written in his first flush of renewed songwriting, when he was seeing everything through Cindy-tinted glasses. "Worth the Wait" was another song from the same time, about finding true love after numerous false starts. Dave would need all his professionalism to perform that one after everything that had happened since he wrote it. There were several songs on this album that could make his life difficult for a while.

Then there were others that weren't. The Who cover came next, blasting out powerfully, and the reaction from the bus was immediate.

'We have *got* to do this one!' exclaimed Ollie.

'What a monster – I love it,' added Shaun.

Dave could see what they meant; quite apart from the irony of the title, he had thought when he picked it that it would make a great opening number live. Listening again to Vince going to town on the drums made him wonder how Jonjo would react – it was exactly the kind of playing that he'd always wanted to indulge in, albeit executed to a much higher standard. Dave thought that Ollie would make a good fist of recreating Vince's chops, though.

The rest of the album continued to go down well. The line from "Withered and Died" about sneaking out from a good friend's bed stabbed him afresh, but it wasn't as if he hadn't lived it countless times in his old life. Dave particularly enjoyed how much Miles loved "Get Out of My Way", an angry rocker written in response to Miles's audience-stealing in his Vagabond Dave days. Every track sounded better than Dave had dared to hope. Late on side two, though, the second-to-last track was something he didn't remember recording, a naggingly familiar refrain picked out on the acoustic guitar. Eventually, with a dreadful sense of recognition, he realised what he was listening to.

The wounded resignation of his vocal hit him right in the guts, and the pained lyrics which had so perfectly expressed his desolation when Cindy left were just as devastating now. It was the World Party song, way too modern to have been covered in 1978. How had it found its way onto the album? This could ruin everything.

CHAPTER TWENTY-SEVEN

No one seemed to recognise the song, but it was surely only a matter of time. Was there anything he could do to get it off the album? Dave was struggling to focus his thoughts, struggling to make sense of this latest development. How had it happened? He had never even recorded the song.

His first instinct was to phone Tony as soon as possible, but he soon decided that would be a mistake. He was growing increasingly concerned about Tony's criminal connections; Dave was the only person who knew Tony's role in all of this, the only one who could point the finger at him. Tony's friends had killed Tom Mulvaney once, so who was to say he wouldn't ask them to do the same again? He had to find out what had happened, which meant his first call should be to Alan.

He tried phoning him from a call box when they arrived at the venue, while Jym, Dink and Ben were setting up the gear, but had to leave an answering-machine message.

'Hi, Alan, it's Tom, Tom Mulvaney. Look, we need to talk about the album. I'm playing a gig tonight but I'll try you again tomorrow. Please take the call; this is really important.' There didn't seem to be anything else he could do, so he tried to forget about the rogue track and get his head into show mode.

His professionalism kicked in and it was a decent show. "Shadow Life" went down well, as did all the usual highpoints. Now that Miles had adjusted to the idea of being Davey rather than Dave, he was actually proving to be a good rhythm guitarist, and his enjoyment of the music added to the playfulness of the stage show, which was no bad thing.

Miles tried to get the new album on again for the post-gig drive home, but Dave successfully argued that they should keep the rota and veto system going. It was his turn next, so he opted for something he was confident would avoid vetoes and occupy the stereo for the best part of an hour. Some classic Rolling Stones did the job, and even Dink kept his veto in his pocket. The last track stung though, reminding him that with Cindy gone he had lost his last, best chance of getting what he wanted.

The next day, Dave phoned Alan again. This time his call got an answer.

'Dave.'

'It's Tom, remember?'

'Oh, it's all right; I'm alone in the house. It's not as if anyone is listening. How did the gig go?'

'Never mind that, we've got a problem. How did "And I Fell Back Alone" end up on the album? It wasn't on the track listing we agreed.'

Alan chuckled. 'Oh, that. You were halfway through the Joni Mitchell song when I arrived for overdub day, so I just started recording. When you went into the other one, I was glad I had. It was so good I couldn't bear to leave it off the album. It was a bit naughty of me not to tell you, but it was meant to be a surprise, a treat for you.'

'But it's not my song.'

The line went quiet. Eventually, Dave had to break the silence.

'Alan? Are you still there?'

'Yes, yes; still here. I didn't recognise it, so I assumed it was a new one of yours. Whose song is it?' The breezy, affable tone in Alan's voice was gone now.

'A band called World Party.'

'Never heard of them. Would they be an old band form the '70s, one of your obscure favourites? Can we pass this off as an innocent mistake?' Hope was playing a double-header with fear in his voice now.

'No. They're current and the song wasn't even written when my album was supposed to be recorded. This blows our whole 1978 backstory. I don't know how Tony is going to react.'

'Haven't you told him yet? Maybe he could stop the record going to press?'

'It's too late, copies have already been shipped. One of the guys in my band got hold of one through a mate, which is how I found out. Once someone recognises the song, there are going to be some very awkward questions.'

'Oh dear, I am so sorry; I just wanted to get another great song on the record. Look, let me have a think and a chat with Tony, in that order. I'm sure we can work this out somehow.'

Dave wished he could share Alan's optimism. They could hardly write it all off as coincidence. It occurred to him that people would assume World Party had somehow stolen the song from him, not the other way around, but that was no consolation. His own songs were precious to him; if someone suggested he hadn't really written one, particularly one as stunning as "And I Fell Back Alone", he'd be furious. The fact that he was putting another songwriter in that position made him almost as uncomfortable as the prospect of being found out.

Later that day, Dave's phone rang. He snatched up the receiver and answered; it was Tony.

'What a bloody disaster,' he began. 'What were you thinking of, cutting a track that wasn't even written back in the late '70s?'

'I didn't!' How was this his fault? 'I was just playing in the studio while I waited for Alan to arrive. I didn't know he recorded it, let alone stuck it on the bloody album. I'm fine, by the way, thanks for asking.'

'Never mind that, how do you think I am? The record goes on sale tomorrow. I can hardly go back to Ultimate and get them to recall all the copies, can I?'

'Can't you? I mean, if no one ever hears the song…'

'It will never work; for one thing we'll never get all the copies back and someone somewhere will hang on to a copy in the hope it becomes a valuable rarity in the future. No, we're stuck with the album as it is.'

Tony fell silent, but the tone in his voice hadn't been good.

'So what's the plan?'

'I don't know,' he snapped. 'I'm still formulating it. Step one will be getting our story straight; step two will be damage limitation, making sure that this doesn't expose what we've been up to for the last year.' He paused, then started speaking in the slow voice that Dave recognised as Tony sorting his thoughts by speaking them aloud. 'The good thing is we've got plausible deniability. Neither of us were there for the recordings – officially at least.'

'I was there!'

'No, no, you weren't. Dave Masters was there, back in '77 and '78, but you're not him. Tom Mulvaney wasn't there and neither was I. If we stick to the story, there's nothing to link either of us to the recordings.' That was a fair point. Nobody knew he was the real Dave Masters, so nobody would be directing any questions towards him. It was still a potential nightmare, but a nightmare that wasn't – yet – pointing in his direction.

Tony was still speaking. 'At least Alan left the track with just you – I mean, Dave – on it, so Vince, Simon and Phil won't be asked about it. I'll talk to them anyway, make them see it's not in their interests to rock the boat. The only person in the firing line is Alan. I'll have to make sure he knows what to say and what not to say. He could claim it was a demo that was with the completed tracks, that he assumed it came from the same sessions. Yeah, that might work. Whatever you do, don't panic: we can ride this out. A bit of controversy about the album might even help sell a few more copies. The only worry is Alan; he's a great producer, but I'm starting to think he's not cut out for keeping secrets; did you hear the stuff about it feeling like he was in the studio only a few weeks ago? He needs to understand just how high the stakes are, for all of us. I'll take care of that. As for you, keep gigging and just carry on as normal.'

Dave could see Tony's point. If there was a weak link in this conspiracy, it was Alan.

Despite Dave's best intentions to carry on as normal, his mind kept restlessly switching from one of his problems to the next. More than ever, he wanted the reassurance that Cindy used to give him. He phoned Frank to see if his investigation had turned anything up (it hadn't). The next day he went out first thing to buy his own copy of *Lost Masters* – the title that Tony had persuaded the record company to give his latest masterpiece. He had to admit, it sounded really good, the best he had sounded in years. It helped that his songwriting was back on point, if he said so himself, but thanks to Alan everything about this album was just perfect. Well, almost everything; side two track six felt like an unexploded bomb.

For the gig at Croydon's Fairfield Halls, there had been some discussion as to whether the band members should just make their own way there, with it being relatively close at hand, or all take the tour bus. In the end, remembering Martin and that first-ever gig, Dave had decreed that they should all go together on the tour bus. This time it was Ollie who used his choice to put *Lost Masters* on.

Despite Dave's protests, the band insisted on having a run at "The Real Me" during the soundcheck. He made it clear that they weren't adding any material to the set until it was properly rehearsed: if there was one thing a tribute band couldn't afford to be it was ragged or obscure (Shaun pointed out that was two things, the cheeky git). Even so, Dave was enjoying their enthusiasm and their desire to include the new songs. He had started to feel the same way himself, despite his mixed feelings about the Cindy-inspired ones.

"The Real Me", even in its under-rehearsed form, sounded pretty good. Alan had suggested replacing the horns on the Who's original with block chords on the organ, and Shaun had clearly been listening carefully. Ollie let himself off the leash on the drums, drawing exclamations of delight from his bandmates, while Declan did a passable impression of Phil's passable impression of John Entwistle.

'Again!' roared Shaun once they had finished.

'No, let's do another one – how about "Get Out of My Way"?' suggested Miles.

Dave brought the discussion to a close. 'No, if Ben's happy with the levels, we'll call it a day there. Leave something in the tank for the show itself.'

It was a good show, and backstage everyone was buoyant. Dave was quieter than usual, but the rest of the band were celebrating another success along with the prospect of playing the new material. There were a couple of weeks before they were due to play again, and Dave had promised that they could start working on the new songs. Ollie, Declan and Miles were arguing good-naturedly about which of their favourites ought to go straight into the set, while Shaun was otherwise engaged, this time with a cute redhead.

Dave was aware of some disturbance outside the dressing room, with the raised voice of one of the bouncers calling for someone to stop. Suddenly the door burst open and a burly figure barrelled into the room. Dave recognised him instantly; it was Vince Preston. He scanned the room and locked eyes with Dave. A smile spread quickly across his creased face and two steps later he enfolded Dave in a huge bear hug.

'It's bloody you, isn't it?' he whispered in Dave's ear. 'I knew as soon as I heard the guitar overdubs. I'd know your playing anywhere, Dave.'

CHAPTER TWENTY-EIGHT

The bouncer was still standing in the doorway, looking unsure what to do. If Vince had been aggressive, things would have been different, but reckless hugging was outside his usual remit of things to deal with. Dave whispered to Vince, 'No one here knows – say nothing,' then reassured the bouncer that it was just an old friend paying a surprise visit.

'Guys,' he said, addressing the rest of the band, 'this is Vince. We did session work together, back in the day.'

Miles did a double take. 'Vince? As in Vince Preston? Are you Vince Preston? You are, aren't you? Bloody hell – you played with Dave Masters!'

The others exchanged looks, seemingly shocked that a proper rock musician was among them, but generally managing to keep their cool a lot better than Miles. Vince casually accepted that, yes, that's who he was, and, yes, he had played with Dave Masters, which prompted Miles to launch into a thousand fan-boy questions, much to everyone's amusement. Vince tolerated his frothing for a while, before turning away to talk to the others.

'Where's the drummer?' Ollie made himself known. 'Good job tonight, man. Really good job.' Ollie grinned and thanked him, clearly delighted with praise from the person he was paid to imitate.

Dave pulled Vince into a corner of the room, away from the others, surgically removing Miles and asking for some privacy. Reluctantly, Miles retreated. Over Vince's shoulder, Dave could see Ollie receiving a high five from Declan, presumably in honour of his celebrity endorsement.

'So what the hell are you doing here?' asked Dave. 'No, wait, let's not get into it now. Did you drive here?'

'Yeah.'

'Right, let's save the catch-up until there's no one to eavesdrop. Can you give me a lift back and we can do our talking in the car?'

Once that was arranged, Vince good-naturedly let Miles inundate him with questions about life in the Dave Masters Band, although the guest looked happier talking drum minutiae with Ollie. When not getting technical Vince was sharing anecdotes, such as the time they locked an American radio DJ out of his studio during a toilet break and took over his show, playing their favourite album tracks – plus a heavy rotation of Dave Masters songs, obviously – until the station's security guards broke down the door with fire axes. As a result, they were banned from appearing on all radio stations in Colorado, a ban which still stood to this day. Even Shaun and the redhead took an interest, once they came up for air.

When Jym announced that the gear was all loaded and they were ready to roll, the others reacted with disappointment at parting from Vince. Shaun announced that he was going home with the redhead, and Dave made his own apologies, saying he was also going to give the tour bus a miss for the trip home and catch up with Vince instead.

'Don't think much of yours.' Shaun grinned.

'How dare you,' deadpanned Vince. 'I'm not that kind of a girl.'

Once the tour bus drove off, Dave and Vince set out to retrieve Vince's car. They chatted about the show – Vince had been impressed with the band, particularly Ollie, and he approved when Dave told him Ollie was a Levon Helm fan. He laughed at Dave's description of Jonjo in the first incarnation of the tribute act. Vince offered his spare room for the night and they put Dave's guitar case into the boot.

'It's so good to see you again,' said Dave as they drove off. 'You're looking well.' He was too. After seeing Vince in an emotional state at the funeral, the happier setting of the recording studio had given Vince the chance to relax and be more himself. Vince seemed to have enjoyed holding court in the dressing room – some things never changed – but Dave was still uncertain if he'd be quite so happy once he heard everything Dave had done to deceive him, along with the rest of the world.

'Yeah, I could say the same for you, given that you've been dead for nearly a year. What the hell is that about?' There was a sense of bewilderment in his voice. Dave had been dreading this: how was he meant to explain what he'd done? He wasn't even sure himself, all this time later. In truth, he'd made one big decision, and then found himself taking countless smaller steps leading on from it. Each step made sense at the time but it was hard to explain the journey as a whole.

'I just couldn't face the life anymore; I didn't want to be me. You remember what it was like back in the '70s: everything we'd dreamed of. Then it all started drifting away: gigs were getting smaller, reviews getting snottier, and then Ultimate rejected my last album and cancelled my contract. One disastrous gig pushed me over edge and I agreed to Tony's plan.'

'Now that's the one thing that makes sense – I thought Tony would have been behind all this. It was his idea then?'

'Richard Thompson's actually, Well, indirectly.' He saw the look of confusion on Vince's face and told him the whole story: the Hackney Empire gig, the song, the burger bar conversation and the events that led to him walking out of his own life. 'Once I said I was in, Tony put everything in place and here I am. Fair play to him, it did revitalise my career, just like it was supposed to.'

'That's what worries me; are you sure he's got your best interests at heart in all this? I mean, he's making more money this way, and even though you're seeing some of that, it's a bit drastic – it's not like you can go back to being you.' Dave could see the concern on Vince's face, and he had put his finger on one of the truths that Dave had tried not to think about for the past year. Vince was a genuine mate, someone who had always had his back; Tony was all about the bottom line. Had his plan been about rescuing Dave from a miserable life, or just maximising his own income?

'Who knows? Back then I wasn't thinking about that, I just didn't want to be me.'

Vince chuckled. 'You didn't want to be you, so you set yourself up as your own tribute act? Talk me through that one.'

'Yeah, that surprised me too. I started living a normal life again, parts of me that had got lost came back and I just had to get up and play again. I couldn't risk being recognised, so I hid in plain sight. If I reminded anyone of myself, well, that's what tribute acts are meant to do. It was just meant to be for a bit of pocket money, but then it started building and next thing I know we're playing decent venues again – better ones than before I stopped being Dave Masters.'

'And what about the lost album?' asked Vince, checking his mirror as he pulled into the outside lane on the dual carriageway. 'Where does that come in?'

Now the story was more painful. 'I found my muse again. Getting out from the industry, meeting normal people and living a normal life unblocked my songwriting.'

Vince was nodding. 'Those songs were good enough to have been from back in the '70s, but some of the lyrics didn't fit. Someone new?'

Dave knew he'd end up telling Vince all about Cindy, but he wanted to leave that till later: he still had to make him understand why he'd deceived him along with everyone else. 'Yeah, but I did what I always did and lost her. I thought it was going to be different this time, but…' He shrugged, hoping to let the gesture finish his sentence, before realising that Vince had his eyes on the road and hadn't seen it.

'Yeah, I got that from "Shadow Life". Sorry to hear that, mate; you could do with the stability. I never understood why you didn't make more effort when you had Cath.'

'I was young and stupid. At least now I'm not young.'

They stopped at a red light, which allowed Vince to turn to look directly at Dave. 'I was devastated when I heard you'd killed yourself. I was blaming myself, second-guessing how I could have made a difference. I felt like I'd let you down when you needed me.' His voice was breaking a little.

'You never let me down, mate.'

'So how could you let me – everyone – think you'd topped yourself? Didn't you know how many people would be completely messed up? I don't mean fans like your guitarist: I mean real people who actually knew you and loved you. Didn't you stop to think about how it would affect us?' Dave thought there was an undertone of anger cutting through the grief in Vince's voice.

Dave shook his head. 'I don't know what I was thinking. If it's any consolation, seeing you and my dad at the funeral opened my eyes, but by then it was too late. Tony wouldn't let me tell anyone; he said that if people found out what we were up to, we could both get in a lot of trouble. How did you know, anyway – was it really the guitar?'

Vince's eyes twinkled as he replied. 'How long did we play together? I'd recognise your playing anywhere. As soon as I heard the finished album, with overdubs supposedly done by some tribute band player, I knew what I was really listening to. I started checking the listings for your gigs, and once I found one, I decided to come out and see for myself. I didn't recognise you when you were helping Alan in the studio, but as soon as you walked out on stage, once I knew what I was looking for, it was obvious. Who else knows?'

'Alan, obviously, and Cath – she recognised me at the funeral but didn't say anything. She came to find me later to tell me my dad was ill.'

'Yeah, I heard about your dad. How is he?'

'No idea. How can I go and visit him when he thinks I'm already dead? Like you said, I'm stuck as Tom Mulvaney now. You didn't tell anyone, did you, about me?'

'No, I wanted to tell Simon and Phil but thought I'd check you out first. Maybe it's better I don't; as you say, the more people who know, the more chance someone lets it slip. I haven't told Mary yet, but I'm going to. I spent too many years watching you screw up a marriage to start keeping secrets from my wife.'

By now they were pulling into Vince's driveway: a semi-detached in Beckenham. It was a far cry from your typical rock-star pad, but it seemed like a nice, respectable place. Apparently, Vince and Mary had moved back to be nearer to her parents a couple of years ago and it was close enough to London if Vince found session work. Mary had already gone to bed, so Vince and Dave opened a bottle of whisky and caught up with one another's lives. Dave told him all about Cindy, about messing everything up, about the false alarm with Ronnie, and the private detective. Vince told him about his career since Tony stood the band down. He didn't often get to play live these days but still got enough session work to put food on the table.

'It made a nice change, tonight, being backstage after a gig. There's nothing like a bunch of musos kicking back after a job well done.'

Dave couldn't resist: 'The old joke has come true: what do you call someone who hangs around with musicians? A drummer.'

Vince rolled his eyes. 'Always the drummer jokes.' He was smiling, though, and soon the two old friends were reminiscing about gigs and sessions, and the practical jokes that had accompanied them.

'Do you remember how careful Alan was about filling in his

session logs?' said Vince.

'Yes!' exclaimed Dave. 'And that time we hid his fountain pen, so he'd have to use a biro.'

'He was almost in tears – "it's not the same, it's like asking Hendrix to play a tennis racket".'

'I never knew anyone so obsessed with penmanship as that man. Good producer, though.'

'Great producer, one of the best.'

The next morning, Mary had left for work by the time Dave surfaced so Vince gave him a lift to the train station after getting his phone number so they could keep in touch. He could get a fast train to Victoria, and from there take the tube all the way back to High Barnet. He bought a copy of *Q* magazine and started flicking through it. Lemmy from Motorhead was on the front cover – which would have pleased Dink – along with Queen and someone called the Cowboy Junkies. Turning to the reviews section he found that *Lost Masters* was one of the main reviews. Dave grinned when he saw they had given it the maximum five stars – a rare accolade, and three more than they had given "Steel Strings", the only one of his albums to come out between *Q*'s launch and his apparent death. He was barely able to keep the grin off his face as he read the review:

> Fans who only know Dave Masters from his patchy '80s work, or – worse still – from his lacklustre posthumous album, could be excused for wondering what all the fuss was about when he died. *Lost Masters* is what the fuss is about.
>
> Recorded in 1977 and 1978, these tracks have spent the intervening years gathering dust in Masters' own personal archive, beyond the memory of his regular collaborators and beyond the knowledge of his record label, until now. Freshened up tastefully by original producer Alan Sharkey,

who worked with Masters on his career-defining four album run of greatness, these showcase everything that his fans loved about the sadly departed Masters. He's equally at home cutting loose on tracks like "Drain the Glass" and "Get Out of My Way" as he is opening his heart on "Through My Fingers" or the number-one single "Shadow Life". As ever, his choice of covers – The Who, Richard Thompson – shows impeccable taste, although he manages to breathe something of himself into each of the borrowed tunes.

Knowing that his life would ultimately end in suicide adds a poignant irony to some of the songs – the album is bookended by "Drain the Glass" (a celebration of living in the moment) and "I'd Do It All the Same Again" (asserting that past choices, good and bad, make us what we are). Most poignant of all is "And I Fell Back Alone", a sparse outpouring of solitary despair. It seems to so prefigure Masters' sad demise that it's hard to believe it was written and recorded more than a decade before that tragic event.

The Who cover is "The Real Me", which begs the question, who was the real Dave Masters? Guitar hero with few betters outside the very top division? Underrated songwriter who deserved to be placed alongside his heroes Thompson and Townshend? Gifted interpreter of others' material? In truth, he was all of the above and more. This collection of songs that inexplicably slipped through the cracks deserves to stand alongside the very best of his work, adding to the too-late realisation that he is one of the great lost talents of British rock.

Dave read the review through a few times and found himself quite overcome. Even when he'd been producing those 'career-defining' albums in the '70s, he'd never had a write-up like that. Maybe it did take death – real or apparent – for people to truly appreciate him. Were they just being kind because he was dead? Surely not

– they had slated *Feel Like Going Home* as an album, and that came out after his supposed death. A sense of frustration at the wasted years of the '80s swept over him, briefly overtaking the positive feelings that the review had initially prompted. There was no doubt that he'd lost his way, but he was back on track now. He'd proved that he could still produce work to stand alongside the best of his old stuff. Now he had to find a way to keep doing it.

CHAPTER TWENTY-NINE

He was disappointed to find no messages on the answering machine when he got home. He hadn't expected Cindy to reach out, but he was hoping for something from Frank, or that Tony might have seen the Q review. He picked up the phone and called his manager himself.

'I'm reading it now – it's great, isn't it? I was just about to call you.' Tony's voice was all sunlight and happiness.

'Did you read the bit about it being hard to believe "And I Fell Back Alone" was written so long ago?'

'What? You're joking – where does it say that?' There was panic in Tony's voice now, which, Dave had to admit, he was quite enjoying.

'Relax, they don't make the World Party link. It's towards the end.'

'Ah yeah, I've got it now.' There was a pause while Tony obviously digested the relevant part of the review. 'Oh, that's all right – they just meant it foreshadows your suicide. Don't do that to me, you cheeky swine, I thought we were in trouble.'

'Who are you calling a cheeky swine? I'll have you know I'm one of the great lost talents of British rock. Q magazine says so.'

Tony was laughing now. 'Not so fast, Dave Masters is the great lost talent, you're just someone who sounds like him. When are you going start adding to the set list?'

'We're rehearsing the new songs next week. We're already doing "Shadow Life", but I'm not sure how many others to put in – it'll take a while for people to get to know album tracks. The lads are itching to have a go at "The Real Me".'

'Just as long as you don't start playing the World Party one. Let's try to sweep that one under the carpet.'

Dave popped into the King's Head that evening, hoping to run into Chris or Martin, who still drank there sometimes, but they weren't in. He called in at the video store on his way home and rented a couple of movies. Since Cindy's departure, he had never quite got the social life thing going again. It was partly because the band had taken off and taken him out of the routines he had been establishing, and partly because his little social network had centred around Cindy. Without her he was just filling time between gigs.

The next day he called in to the newsagents to see if the music weeklies were carrying reviews for *Lost Masters* yet. His eye was drawn to the *NME* front-page headline: "Dave Masters Mystery". Snatching up the paper he flicked through the pages, looking for the promised article.

'Oy!' came the shout from behind the till. 'Are you going to buy that or just rough it up so no one else wants it?' Dave absent-mindedly reached into his pocket and deposited 65p on the counter as he walked out. There was a bus stop almost directly outside, so he sat down and continued his search.

It was Stuart Maconie again, the man who created the Dave ReMastered buzz with his story about the Dave-off. This time he was querying how Dave Masters in 1978 had managed to record a version of a song that Karl Wallinger of World Party wouldn't claim to have written until a full twelve years later. The article made reference to near-identical tune and lyrics. Wallinger flatly denied any plagiarism: 'It's my song! I can't explain how he wrote my song before I did, but I've never heard his version before.' They had even got a quote from Alan Sharkey: 'What can I say? Dave was always a writer ahead of his time.' Tony wouldn't be pleased with that one. Dave felt bad for Karl Wallinger, but no one was going to believe the 1978 recording copied the 1990 one. He avoided phoning Tony, hoping that somehow this latest development might pass him by.

Deep down, he knew that wasn't realistic. Sure enough, by the evening the story had graduated to the television news. Karl Wallinger was doubling down on his – legitimate – claims to the song, saying he could go into details about the particular relationship that inspired it, although he didn't want to do so publicly, for the sake of the other party involved. There was also unfortunate footage of Alan, getting doorstepped by reporters as he left his house.

'I have nothing to say,' he was bleating, the fear visible in his eyes. 'I have no idea where Karl Wallinger heard the song, but Tom – I mean Dave – got there first.' Dave flinched; had Alan really let both names slip out together? Dave's phone rang almost as soon as the news moved on to something else.

'Are you watching the news?' snapped Tony.

'Yeah. Did I hear him call me Tom?'

'You certainly did. I told you we couldn't rely on him holding the line.' Dave could hear the anger in Tony's voice. 'The damn fool – I'm going to have to get into this now.'

'What are you going to do?' Dave had the feeling that he wasn't going to like whatever answer Tony came out with.

'Damage limitation. First of all, I'm going to remind Alan to watch his mouth. Then I'm going to get in touch with Karl Wallinger's management. If I let them talk me out of legal action, we could put out a joint statement saying we can't understand how it's happened, but we're prepared to accept that two talented artists genuinely came to create similar work independently. We can say it's like monkeys writing Shakespeare, but instead of being a theoretical possibility, it's actually happened this time.'

'Hang on a minute, are you comparing me and Karl Wallinger to monkeys or to Shakespeare?'

'What do you think? Look, I've got calls to make. You go off and have a banana or something and let me get on with my job.'

The next day was a rehearsal day. Before Dave even got his jacket off, Miles was asking about his time with Vince Preston. It was hard to shake him off, even though Dave played it down as just a catch-up with an old friend.

'That's just it – you never said you were friends with one of Dave Masters' bandmates.'

'Yeah,' added Shaun. 'We just thought you were a boring old bloke who had knocked around the music industry without ever amounting to much. Who knew you were a boring old bloke who had knocked around the music industry and actually met someone sort of famous?'

The others laughed at that, and Ollie pointed out that he was the only one to receive the seal of approval from his counterpart in the Dave Masters' original band.

'Only because Simon Tilley has never heard me play,' retorted Shaun.

'Never mind all that,' replied Dave. 'Let's get down to rehearsing. I think we should add the album tracks into the set gradually – one or two at first and see how they go down. We can always add more if the audience seem to want them. Any suggestions for where we should start?'

As expected, "The Real Me" was unrivalled as the first choice. The rest of the votes were split between the livelier options of "Drain the Glass" and "Get Out of My Way", or the more melodic and thoughtful "Through My Fingers" and "Your Eyes Shine". Dave agreed that they should work on all of them, and see which ones were sounding best, although the thought of singing the last two still prompted conflicting emotions for him.

'Did you guys see all the fuss about "And I Fell Back Alone"?' asked Declan.

'Yeah, who would have thought Karl Wallinger would go stealing songs?' added Shaun. 'I mean, I know he wears his influences on his sleeve and he loves the old rock classics, but to nick someone else's song and pass it off as his own? I thought he was better than that.'

'How did he even know about the song?' asked Miles. 'I've heard everything Dave Masters has ever recorded – B-sides, the lot – and I didn't know these songs existed. If it was in Dave's personal archive, how did Wallinger hear it?'

'Who cares?' added Declan. 'Why don't we play it? It's a great song, and the controversy means everyone will know about it.' The idea seemed popular with the others, though Dave had his own reasons for shutting the discussion down.

'No need for you guys to waste time rehearsing it,' retorted Dave. 'It's just voice and guitar. If we were going to do it, it would just be me.' The others looked crestfallen as they realised he was right. Dave took the opportunity to move things on. 'Now, "The Real Me". From the top.'

Dave caught the TV news later that night, and there was more footage of Alan failing to deal with questions about the *Lost Masters* recordings.

'Look, I'm just a record producer who was given some old tapes to clean up. I don't know anything about plagiarism or fake recordings, okay?' Fake recordings? Why had he said that? He was falling to pieces. If they weren't careful, he'd go too far and reveal everything. Dave knew that Tony would have picked up on Alan's latest indiscretion, so he didn't bother phoning him. He went to bed that night wishing that the whole problem would just go away. When he awoke it had got an awful lot worse.

According to the radio, Alan Sharkey had been found dead in his house. He left a typed suicide note apologising to his wife and children for not being a stronger man. Dave felt physically sick. Had Tony laid his threats on too thick? Had he scared poor Alan to the point of killing himself? Ironically for someone who had famously committed suicide, Dave couldn't imagine anyone feeling so desolate that they actually went through with it.

Dave phoned Vince, hoping to find some comfort in shared memories of Alan. Vince's voice sounded heavy with emotion, and Dave guessed that he'd already heard the news.

'I can't believe he's gone,' said Dave.

'Can't you? Really?'

Dave hesitated; he hadn't been expecting the accusing tone. 'I mean, he was as happy as he's been in years working on those songs. Don't tell me that you saw this coming?'

'Of course I bloody didn't, but I don't believe the suicide story either. Are you seriously telling me that you do?'

Dave felt the room lurch. What was Vince saying? If it wasn't suicide, Vince must think that someone else had killed Alan. Was Tony capable of that? Had Tonys "damage limitation" involved those dubious friends of his? Was Alan another life lost on his account?

Once Vince realised Dave wasn't going to say anything, he carried on, his emotions tumbling out with his words. 'A typed suicide note, Alan? Are you serious? That man never typed anything if he could help it; he'd have hand-written it, immaculately. I'd bet pounds to pennies he never wrote that note. Someone killed him, I'm sure of it.'

'Who?' Dave knew the obvious conclusion was Tony, but somehow he wanted Vince to be the first to say it.

'Well, you're the expert on fake suicides, aren't you? What have you got yourself mixed up in, Dave? How could you do it – to Alan of all people, lovely harmless old Alan?'

'I didn't! I wouldn't! The first I knew of this was a few minutes ago from the radio.'

'Do you expect me to believe that?' Vince was shouting now.

'What happened to you, man? The Dave I knew could be a tit, but I never had him down as a murderer.'

Dave's voice rose to match Vince's. 'I'm not! I can't believe you'd think that of me. You know me better than that.'

'I don't know what to be believe anymore. You've changed, man.'

'I've changed, have I? What about you? Don't forget, you owe your career to me. If I hadn't taken you on, you'd still be playing pubs in Birmingham and working on a building site somewhere.' All the emotion about Alan was coming out as anger. Vince, on the receiving end, was giving as good as he got.

'Here we go, you always thought you were better than the rest of us – singer-songwriter guitarist egotist. I never thought you'd add murderer to your list of credits.'

'*I didn't!* Why are you so thick you can't see that? If that's what you think of me, go fuck yourself.' With that Dave slammed the phone down. His heart was pounding and his mouth parched and dry. He realised that somewhere during the phone call he had stood up, so he sat himself down and tried to get his raging emotions in check. He was already regretting the things he had said to Vince. How could Vince think he was involved in murder? Then again, Vince wouldn't have expected Dave to fake his own death. He'd make things up with Vince, but maybe he should give them both time to calm down first.

Dave stayed in most of the day, afraid to stray from his phone in case Tony called and afraid of a knock at the door, just in case Tony had decided that Dave was another unnecessary risk, part of the problem rather than a vital cog in the money-making machine. Late in the afternoon, the phone finally rang. Dave snatched it up.

'Tony?' he yelped.

'No, it's Frank, Frank Dixon. I've got some good news at last.'

It took Dave a moment to take that in. For the first time in weeks he had forgotten all about Frank and his investigation.

'How good is good? I mean, I'm not having the best day in the world.'

'I've found her. I've got an address and everything. I've written it all up as a report for you. Can you come round to the office sometime tomorrow? Or I could post it – up to you, but if you come round, you could pay me the last part of my fee at the same time.'

He'd found her. Dave hadn't thought that anything was going to salvage today, but this was genuinely good news. 'That's fantastic, Frank. Thank you so much. Yes, I can get over there tomorrow morning.'

'Don't make it too early, or you'll be waking me up. Not before eleven, okay?'

It didn't balance out the news about Alan, but a sense of relief and anticipation was a welcome change to the darker feelings that had swamped his day so far. Finally, he was in a position to start making things right with Cindy.

His mind was still churning everything over when he went to bed, and unsurprisingly he didn't sleep well. He tried drinking to help him drift away, but his thoughts kept returning to Alan Sharkey, imagining the fear in the old man's face as Tony's nameless associates arrived to take care of business. Had they typed the suicide note themselves or stood over him and made him do it? How much warning would he have had – would it have been instant and painless, or did he know what was coming? So many questions, and the only thing Dave was sure of was that this had gone way out of his control.

He awoke, bleary-eyed and groggy. His head was pounding. No, wait, it wasn't his head: it was the front door. Someone was knocking loudly, hammering on the door. That realisation shook him awake. Was this Tony's goon squad? Was this how Tom Mulvaney was going to die for a second time? He scrambled out of his bedroom just in time to see his front door splinter open. Half a dozen uniformed police officers rushed through, one holding some kind of battering ram device.

'Tom Mulvaney?' the lead policeman barked accusingly. Dave nodded blankly. 'You're under arrest, mate.'

part four

THE REAL ME

APRIL 1991

CHAPTER THIRTY

Dave woke up, fully aware of where he was. That was a good thing; for the first few days, the realisation that he wasn't in his own bed, in his own flat, had been a soul-crushing start to the day. He rolled over onto his back, wincing at the tuneless symphony of ageing bedsprings, and opened his eyes. Ricky was still asleep, and other than his bed there was no noise, which meant he must have beaten the rising bell. It wasn't a peaceful quiet, though; there wasn't much about his current home that encouraged peace or restfulness. He climbed gingerly down from the top bunk, doing his best not to disturb Ricky. He made it to the floor, but the next bit was trickier: peeing quietly into the tin bucket the two men shared when confined to their cell. He managed to aim for the side, rather than the noisier option of firing directly into the pool of their shared urine (at least neither of them had produced anything more substantial last night). Ricky stirred a little at the noise but didn't wake; it was funny what you got used to. Dave had been lucky with his cell-mate. Ricky, like him, was on remand waiting for his trial. He was little more than a kid whose mates broke into what they thought was an empty house. The way he told it, it had been the first time he'd ever done anything like that, but when they all ran, he had been the one who got caught. Dave had seen the fear in his eyes when he was shown into the cell, the tension in every muscle. Once Ricky realised Dave wasn't a hardened con and was unlikely to batter him for speaking out of turn, he began to relax a bit. Dave had shown him the ropes and guided him into life inside Pentonville Prison, giving him the benefit of his vast experience – all of two weeks' more time inside than his young cell-mate.

It wasn't long before the rising bell, so Dave sat himself down at their table rather than disturb Ricky by climbing back up. A lot had happened since his arrest. The charge was conspiracy to commit fraud, with Tony named as co-defendant. Not that the police had found Tony yet; he had disappeared, clearing out the trust fund as he went. Dave wasn't sure how Tony knew about the imminent arrests, but it stung that he hadn't bothered to warn him before vanishing. Evidently Alan hadn't trusted Tony either, leaving a letter in the care of his solicitor with instructions to deliver it to the police in the event of his death or disappearance. He had revealed everything about the fake recordings, although not about Dave's real identity. As far as the police were concerned, he was still Tom Mulvaney. That had proved to be a problem, as Tom's past activities meant that the magistrate wouldn't even consider bail, hence his current residency at HMP Pentonville.

The day of his arrest was still a haze of images rather than a coherent memory. He'd been in a state of shock for most of the journey to the police station, and the whole business of mugshots, fingerprints and form-filling felt like it was happening to someone else. The police asked Dave lots of questions about Alan, as if they thought he was involved in his death, but the only charges so far concerned the recording of the album. Despite knowing he was innocent of Alan's death, he still felt guilty, and he got the impression that the police shared the view that he was responsible. Running away from his old life had seemed like a good idea at first, but it had created more problems than it solved. There were so many loose ends he needed to tie up – Cindy, Frank's report, his dad – and he was stuck in prison with no way to do anything about any of them. Cath had said his dad had months to live; if he went down for fraud (which seemed inevitable) his dad would be gone by the time he finished his sentence.

'Morning, Tom.' It was Ricky, stirring from his sleep.

'Morning, Ricky. I didn't disturb you, did I?' He nodded towards the bucket in the corner.

'Nah, you're all right. It's a big day for you today, isn't it? Meeting your brief, yeah?'

A high-flying barrister had got in touch to say she was keen to take Tom's case pro bono. His solicitor wasn't sure why such a generous offer had come out of the blue but had strongly recommended Tom to meet with her and make the most of it. His day in court was still a couple of weeks away, so there would be plenty of time for her to get to know the details of the case and work out his best defence.

'Yeah, this afternoon. I'm not sure what she'll be able to do, though. My case doesn't look great, does it?' As far as he could see, his freedom was less likely than a Beatles reunion.

By now the wing as a whole was waking up, with guards moving from cell to cell unlocking doors and letting the prisoners out for breakfast.

Two months on remand had taught Dave not to make eye contact with other prisoners over breakfast. Along with Ricky, he went to collect his food and take it back to the cell. Both Dave and Ricky made a point of keeping their distance from the serious cons whenever possible. Some of them were all right, but others could be unpredictable. Keeping your head down and avoiding trouble was the best policy.

Ricky was expecting his weekly visit from his mum that afternoon. At first her visits had been upsetting, reminding the lad of what getting caught had cost him, but he was coping better now. Dave had had a few visitors since arriving at Pentonville, but no one on a regular basis.

He had hoped Vince might come, to give him the chance to make things up after their last conversation. The other one at the top of Dave's wish list was, of course, Cindy, but he knew that wasn't likely. Martin and Chris had brought tales of the implosion of the Dave ReMastered Band. Martin was still friendly with Shaun (Chris, understandably, not so much) and he filled Dave in on Shaun's account of things.

'Apparently that Miles bloke tried to talk the others into staying together, to keep the band going. He said it was for your sake, but Shaun reckons he just wanted to seize the Dave ReMastered brand for himself. Even when he backed down and said they could go out as Vagabond Dave, the others weren't keen.'

'They all knew it wouldn't be the same without your guitar,' added Chris. Dave smiled and asked what was wrong with his singing that they wouldn't miss that. He said he appreciated the others' loyalty in not signing up with Miles.

'Loyalty? Shaun?' scoffed Chris. 'Are we talking about the same bloke? He hasn't waited around – him and Declan have started recruiting musicians for a Supertramp tribute act – they're growing beards and everything. Even if you get off there's no band for you to come back to.'

'What about Ollie?' asked Dave.

'He was the first to get another gig: he auditioned for some girl singer getting ready to tour her first album. He's rehearsing now and then he's on the road for the next couple of months – they're on a major label, so he's getting decent money.'

'Well, good luck to him. I can't expect anyone to wait around when I might not be out for a few years.'

Chris's face fell. 'Don't say that. You might get off – I mean, it was all Tony's idea, wasn't it?'

'Yeah, but if they can't find him, I'm left holding the baby. I knew what I was doing: I recorded the demos knowing that Tony would pass them off as Dave Masters; I did the guitar overdubs knowing the same. A judge might take pity on me and give me a lenient sentence, but it's only me in the dock and they need someone to take the blame.'

The lads agreed that it was Tony who deserved to take the fall for the fake album, but they could see that the courts were unlikely to be so inclined towards sympathy.

'Here's the thing that I can't get my head round,' said Chris after a pause. 'You wrote those songs on the fake album, right?'

'Right.'

'If you could write songs as good as that, what were you doing wasting your time as a tribute act? Why weren't you out on the circuit playing your own stuff?' Dave had no answer to that, not one that wouldn't have led to more difficult questions.

There had been two more visitors apart from his former bandmates. Jym had come during Dave's first few days in Pentonville, bringing gifts of tobacco – he said he knew how valuable a bit of snout could be inside. He had filled Dave in on the chaos of unpaid bills that Tony's disappearance had caused. Jym himself, along with Dink and Ben, were out of pocket for the last run of gigs, though Jym made sure Dave knew that he wasn't blaming him for that. An old friend had managed to get him onto the crew for a Fairport Convention tour, so he was still solvent.

'Anyway,' said Jym, 'my experience of Tony Broadway has only cost me a bit of money; you've lost more than that. How did he talk you into it?'

Once again, Dave struggled for an answer. 'I don't know, I guess the idea of actually getting to record my songs – even if no one would know they were mine – was too good to turn down. Stupid really.'

'Well, keep your chin up, mate. Half the music industry is looking for Tony – he owed money left, right and centre before he vanished. Hopefully someone will track him down before you go in front of a judge. If they can throw the book at him, maybe they'll go easier on you.'

The only other visitor was the most unexpected: Frank Dixon. At first Dave thought he was looking for his final payment, but when he mentioned the money, Frank waved his apology away.

'Don't worry about that – I know you've got no access to funds right now. I mean, if things change and you're able to pay, great, but you've got bigger things to worry about. How are you holding up? Anything I can do to help?' Dave had toyed with idea of getting Frank to look for Tony, but he wasn't sure that the private detective, for all his talents, would be any more successful than the police. Also, he owed Frank enough money that he couldn't pay. Frank verbally filled Dave in on what he'd found out, and agreed to keep hold of the report until Dave was in a position to do something about it. Dave thanked him. If only Frank had finished his investigation a few days earlier, before the arrest.

A private room had been set aside for Dave's meeting with the barrister. The guard offered to stay for the barrister's safety, but she sent him away, stating that her client's right to confidentiality was too important to compromise.

She was about Dave's age, give or take, and looked impressive in an expensive suit. Maybe it was that first skirmish with the guard, but she looked like she didn't let people mess her about. Dave liked her, though he still had a nagging suspicion that she may somehow be connected to Tony and his mysterious friends.

She introduced herself as Penelope Soper and settled into the chair opposite him, taking a legal notepad and pen out of her briefcase.

'So, how does this work?' he started. 'Why did you offer to take my case? I mean, thank you – I appreciate it – but what's going on?'

She gave him a long, appraising look. 'I'm here to try to keep you out of prison, if that's okay with you. I've read all the case notes and I gather that you're not denying taking part in the recordings or that you knew how they were going to be passed off. Even with that being the case, I think I've got a strategy that might get you off altogether.'

'I don't understand, I did what they said I did – how can you get me off?'

She smiled and changed the subject. 'I forgot to mention, I believe you know my son. I'm Ronnie's mother, and I know that I'm not talking to Tom Mulvaney. Would I be right in thinking that your real name is Dave Masters?'

CHAPTER THIRTY-ONE

Penelope was smiling, enjoying the shock she had just given him.

'Relax, the guard can't hear us, and everything you say to me is confidential. I couldn't tell anyone without your permission even if I wanted to, or I'd be struck off. I want to help you, but I have no intention of giving up my livelihood. First question: am I right?'

Dave sighed and admitted the truth.

'I thought so; it was the only thing that made sense of all the pieces of this puzzle. Second question: apart from me, who knows?'

'Tony, wherever he is.'

'Tony Broadway?'

'Yes, and Cath, my ex-wife. Alan knew, God rest him, and Vince.' Penelope's eyes narrowed, seeking clarification. 'Vince Preston, the drummer from the fake album.'

Her eyes pinned him to his chair with their intensity. 'Right, let's get one thing straight, you are to stop referring to it as the fake album. You can call it by its title, *Lost Masters*, or call it the lost album or the last album or just the album, but don't ever call it the fake album. People hear fake and think fraud; letting that terminology go unchallenged makes you look guilty.' His first impression of Penelope was reinforced: she was formidable.

'Do you think that any of those people are likely to come forward and offer that information to the police, or to tell someone else?'

'I wouldn't have thought so.'

'Not even your ex-wife? Has she got any axes to grind?'

Dave shook his head. 'No, we parted on good terms. She recognised me at my funeral but didn't say anything. I only found out later, when she came to let me know my dad was ill.'

'And Vince?'

Dave hesitated. Before their last phone call, he would have trusted Vince with his life. If only he knew what had been going on in Vince's head since they'd last spoke. 'He recognised my playing from the album and came to find me. Best friend I ever had, though we had an argument before I was arrested and didn't leave things well. But I can't believe he'd give me up.'

She made a note. 'How sure are you of that?' Dave could only shrug. How sure was he of anything anymore? 'Right, well, let's hope you're right; it's vital that nobody finds out who you really are before the trial. You're being tried as Tom Mulvaney and that suits us fine. If you have the urge to unburden yourself with anyone else, resist it. I don't care if it's a cell-mate, a visitor, even the prison chaplain. Nobody else can know who you are. Is that understood?' Dave nodded weakly, unable to argue even if he'd wanted to. 'Good. Now, tell me everything about how you came to be here – right from the beginning.'

Dave went through it, from the painful winding-down of his career and the Richard Thompson gig, all the way through to his rapid success as Dave ReMastered and rediscovering his gifts as a songwriter. She asked a few clarifying questions along the way and took notes as he spoke. Eventually, she asked if he had any questions for her.

'Just one, the one I asked at the beginning. Why are you helping me?'

She smiled, with what seemed like genuine warmth breaking

through her professional demeanour for the first time. 'Because you told Ronnie the truth. Partly I wanted to see you for myself, just to confirm that you really weren't my Tom Mulvaney, but the fact that you went out of your way to help a young man you had no connection with tells me you're not all bad – certainly, it says that you're a better man than the real Tom Mulvaney.'

Dave muttered something about not knowing about that, but Penelope was having none of it.

'You certainly are better than him. He was a charmer and a rogue and frankly I was old enough to have known better when I met him. He was also a criminal who went on to do terrible things to people who didn't deserve it. That was why I tried to keep Ronnie from knowing anything. Eventually I realised it wasn't my decision to make; I had to let Ronnie choose for himself. He thought he'd found his dad and was crushed when you said you weren't the right Tom Mulvaney, but he kept on looking. If you hadn't got in touch again, he'd have spent the rest of his life searching. He'll never meet his father, but he's got some closure, thanks to you. This is my way of saying thank you.'

Before Penelope left, Dave told her about Frank Dixon, the unpaid bill and what it was for. She wrote down Frank's details and said that she'd take care of it; Dave could pay her back once she managed to get him off. She shook his hand before leaving and reminded him again to keep his true identity a secret.

Dave arrived back in his cell and saw that Ricky was back from his visit.

'How did it go, with the brief?' he asked.

Dave smiled. Penelope had given him hope. He couldn't see how she was going to get him off, but she seemed confident. He didn't want to say too much – he was taking her instructions seriously – but being asked the question had made him realise that he actually believed in her.

'Really, really well. How was the visit from your mum?'

'Now, do you remember the C chord I showed you last time?'

Mac's brow furrowed, but Dave knew to wait. Mac got frustrated if he wasn't given time to think for himself, and he didn't want a frustrated Mac to deal with.

'Like this?' The burly prisoner put his fingers on the guitar neck in what he hoped was the right position.

'Nearly – move the finger on the A string down a fret, the second one.' Mac made the adjustment. 'Go on, sound it out.'

Mac ran his plectrum across the strings and grinned at the result.

'That's it, well done. Now combine that with the other three, and you can have a go at "I Saw Her Standing There". Shall we play it together?'

It was a much-simplified version and they were taking it at about half pace, but with Dave singing along it was stuttering but recognisable. Mac's scarred, grizzled face broke into a huge smile at the end of the verse. Dave had approached the governor, Mr Hutchings, and asked for permission to teach guitar to some of the prisoners as part of the prison's education programme. He had found out that there were a couple of acoustic guitars knocking around, and now he had a dozen or so pupils who each met him once a week. Originally, it had just been an excuse to get his own hands on a guitar again, but he soon found he loved the pleasure his students got out of it. The governor had said how finding a sense of purpose helped keep the prisoners out of trouble inside, and Dave was beginning to see that in the reactions of prisoners like Mac.

'Now, remember to practice those chord shapes between now and the next lesson. I know it's hard not having an actual guitar to practice on, but the more familiar you get with putting your hand in the right positions, the smoother you'll make the changes when you're playing. We've got a few minutes before we finish. Anything else you'd like me to show you?'

'Just play something – play a sad one.'

'Okay, here's a Dave Masters song, I think you'll know it.' Everyone in the prison knew his story: it had been all over the newspapers, the tribute singer who made a fake album. There was a certain amount of admiration for his audacity, but also some prisoners – and guards – who made it clear that his celebrity status, such as it was, wouldn't help him inside. There had been some dicey moments and more than a few sleepless nights where he felt like he was trapped in a nightmare. Strangely, the guitar lessons had helped. Mac had been one of the first prisoners to walk through the door, which itself had been a frightening experience for Dave. Mac was a long-termer serving serious time for offences that Dave really didn't want to know too much about. The rumours he had heard terrified him, and Dave's first thought when he saw Mac's huge, meaty, tattooed hands was that they seemed more suited to violence than making music. In his initial eagerness to help, Dave had upset Mac, talking down and disrespecting him as Mac saw it. Fortunately, once Dave found the right level, things improved and they started to make progress. That made Mac happy, and Dave discovered that being in Mac's good books made an awful lot of things in prison go better.

Dave strummed the opening chords to "Let You Go". He'd hated the song for so long, but since messing things up with Cindy he'd found new meaning in it. This time, at last, he was the one being left behind, the one whose lover only wanted freedom from them. For the first time in years, he felt like he could sing it honestly. Well, Cindy had got her freedom, even if his was still hanging in the balance. He picked a solo, sparse and emotional, closing his eyes as his fingers went to the strings, pouring emotion into the familiar pattern of notes. When he finished, he pinched the bridge of his nose and pretended not to be crying. He wasn't sure, but he thought Mac may have done the same. He knew better than to ask him about it though.

Mac was the last of Dave's students for the day, so the guards escorted the two of them back to their respective wings. There was free association in the wing for an hour or so before it was time for Dave to collect his evening meal to take back to his cell. Dave found Ricky playing cards with some of the other remand prisoners.

'Hey, Tom,' called one of them, a car thief called Ned. 'How was Mad Mac today?'

'Doing well. I keep telling you there's a sensitive musician in there.'

'Is that a sensitive musician who killed a man by feeding him into an industrial mincing machine?' asked Doug the pickpocket.

'Allegedly,' added Ned. 'They never proved that one.'

'Only because Mac fed the evidence to his dogs. Have you ever asked him about that stuff? You know, spice up the guitar lessons by including a bit of truth or consequence.'

'I don't want to risk the consequence,' said Dave. 'It's safer to stick to guitar and let the crimes of the past remain in the past. Did he really do that, though, with the mincer?'

'You sure you want to know?'

Dave thought for a moment. 'No, let's change the subject. What have you lot been up to?'

'Doug had a meeting with his brief,' said Ricky.

Doug took up the tale. 'Yeah, he's not optimistic. He wants me to plead guilty to get a shorter sentence, but I want to fight it – they messed with the evidence, I'm sure. I mean, I'm not saying I didn't do it, but they can't prove I did it. Why should I go down for that?'

'But you did it.'

'Yeah, but they can't prove I did it. That makes all the difference.'

'Did you hear about Andy Mattacks?' said Ricky. 'His trial finished today.'

'And?'

'Eighteen months.'

'So, what happens now? Will they move him off to one of the other wings?'

Ned and Doug laughed. 'No, he doesn't come back here,' explained Doug. 'They never put you back where you're settled. They'll have taken him miles away – up north, or deep in the south-west or somewhere. Once you're found guilty, they just make it harder for people to come and see you and they don't give you the chance to say goodbye to your mates. We're not people, remember, we're society's problems to be kept out of decent people's way.'

'So when your trial finishes…'

'One way or the other, you'll not be seeing me. I'll either be free to go, or I'll be in a van up to some other nick where I'll be fresh meat for the hardnuts. Why do you think I want my lawyer to fight the charges? A sentence is a sentence, long or short; you still have to go through the same initiations and shakedowns in a new place. If there's a chance of avoiding that, I'll give it a go.'

It hadn't occurred to Dave that his sentence wouldn't be served at Pentonville. He knew that remand prisoners got privileges that the convicted men didn't, but he had got used to the regime here, and Mr Hutchings seemed pretty fair. He wouldn't go as far as to say he enjoyed it here – the feeling each night when the cell door slammed shut never went away, and the humiliation of having his life dictated by a bell and men in uniform still burned – but he had made some friends, and the guitar lessons even made him feel useful. What would it be like if his new governor didn't let him teach guitar? How would he fare without the protection of someone like Mad Mac the Mincer? The confidence Penelope inspired seemed perilously fragile now. He couldn't see how she could get him off. Nobody had falsified evidence; there was no one to crack under her cross-examination. The bare facts told the whole story: he had made the fake – sorry, the lost – album and been part of the conspiracy to pass it off as genuine. Then there was the question of Alan's murder. They had no evidence against him, but Penelope has warned him that the prosecution might use the fraud trial to go fishing, hoping something would come up in court that would let them throw the more serious charge at him. That would really raise the stakes for

Dave. The Johnny Cash track, "25 Minutes to Go", came back to his mind; he felt like the latter stages of the song, where the prisoner's desperation was reaching fever pitch.

Back in the cell that night Ricky was reading a book from the prison library while Dave lay on his bunk thinking.

'Tom? You all right, mate?'

He didn't answer at first. He wasn't all right. The conversation with Doug and Ned was still weighing heavily on him.

'Tom? You was sighing and stuff. You okay?'

He hadn't realised he had been sighing. 'Oh, don't worry about me, Ricky. Just thinking, you know?'

'Yeah, I know. You don't want to be doing that, mate. Not in here.'

'Do you ever think about what's going to happen after your trial?'

'I try not to. I mean, I'm going to plead guilty. My brief reckons there's a chance I get away with a suspended sentence and a fine – first offence and all that.'

'And if not?'

'Then I'm screwed. I'll have to do the time and try to keep out of trouble, but I get scared when I think about it, so I don't think about it. I try to think about what I'm going to do whenever I get out instead.'

'And what are you going to do?'

'I won't go breaking into houses, that's for sure. My cousin works as a decorator; he said he could take me on. I'd have to move, though – he lives out in Kent. That might not be a bad thing, getting away from the people who got me into housebreaking.'

'Hang on a minute, you're going to be a decorator? A former housebreaker going into different people's houses every day: isn't that going look suspicious?'

Ricky laughed. 'Yeah, that's what I said. My cousin's cool, though, he said that what his customers don't know won't hurt them, just so long as I don't start nicking again. He says everyone deserves a second chance, but if I blow that, he won't be giving me a third one.'

That sounded about right: everyone deserved a second chance. Tom Mulvaney's life had been Dave's second chance, and look what he'd done with that: made the same old mistakes when it came to women, and then made a whole new set of mistakes on top. Even if Penelope somehow managed to get him off, it was hard to see how he could pick up the pieces and make a third chance for himself.

CHAPTER THIRTY-TWO

Dave tried to push his fears down, focusing on the day-to-day rather than the terrifying future. Mac and his other pupils were making mixed progress, but even those who forgot everything from one lesson to the next seemed to enjoy their time together. As for him, holding a guitar in his hands made him feel alive, even if he only got a few minutes at the start or end of each lesson to properly play. Doug's trial date came and went. Despite the supposedly dodgy evidence, he was found guilty and sent down for three years. Dave felt sorry for the bloke, even if he'd brought it on himself.

Doug's place as Ned's cell-mate was quickly filled. A young lad called Warren, on remand like the rest of them. It was his first time and he was clearly terrified. He could have done a lot worse than Ned for a cell-mate. Ned could be cynical and opportunist, but unless you crossed him (or left your car unattended) he was all right. He took Warren under his wing and, along with Dave and Ricky, helped him to adjust to the Pentonville experience. Warren reminded Dave of Ricky when he first came in: same age, more or less; same haunted eyes; same questions. Maybe everyone was like that at first; maybe he had been too.

'So how does visiting work?' asked Warren during free association.

'It's different for remand prisoners than convicted ones, but there's still a limit,' explained Ned. 'Cons only get three or four visits a month. We can have up to seven visits in a week, but no more than ninety minutes in total, so in practice you won't get through that many people. They tell you who wants to visit in advance, so you can say whether or not you'll see them: I mean, you don't want to use up all your time with some bloke from the pub and then have to turn away someone more important.'

'Yeah,' Ricky laughed, 'my mum took up all my time last week and then I had to say no to Winona Ryder.'

'Heartbreaking,' deadpanned Dave.

'It was – Winona cried for hours,' said Ricky. 'No, seriously, though, it's not usually a problem. For me it's mainly my mum who comes, once or twice a week.'

'My wife came once, but I told her not to come again,' added Ned. 'She wanted to bring the kids, but I said no. What's it going to do to them to see their dad in a place like this? Sometimes visits do more harm than good, reminding you what you've left behind.'

Ricky shook his head. 'Nah, I don't agree. I know what you mean – I used to be in pieces after my mum's visits – but after a while you learn to handle it. Now the stories my mum tells me – how my little sis is doing, what's happening at work – that's my anchor to the outside world. That's how I remind myself that what happens inside these shitty walls isn't my whole life. I'm stuck here for now, but I won't be forever. Seeing Mum reminds me that there's someone who sees me as more than just a prisoner number.'

'What about you, Tom?' asked Warren. 'What do you think about visitors?'

Dave had to think for a moment before replying. 'I'd be happy to have them, but I don't have anyone who cares enough to come, not more than once. After the novelty of the first couple of weeks, no one came back.'

'No family?'

There was his dad, of course, but how could he begin to explain that one? 'No, I've got an ex-wife and that's about it. I was hoping that some of my bandmates might come more often, but I don't blame them for keeping their distance.'

'Bandmates? Were you a musician then?'

A smile stretched across Ned's face. 'Of course, you don't know, do you? You're in the presence of a celebrity. Do you remember that story about the dead rock star and the fake album?' Warren nodded, his eyes switching back and forth between Dave and Ned. 'This is the man who sang and played on the fake tapes.'

'Allegedly,' chimed Ricky with a grin.

'Nothing alleged about it,' said Dave. 'It was me, guilty as charged. I had a good twenty years as a session musician, found a bit of success as a tribute act, then let my manager persuade me to make those recordings. Not that I took a lot of persuading, to be fair; I've only myself to blame.'

The conversation moved on. Ricky and Ned answered more of Warren's questions about prison life, while Dave found himself thinking again about visits. The bit about no one caring was a bit self-indulgent; Jym had promised to come again once Fairport finished their run of live dates. To be honest, he didn't really mind that no one came to see him; apart from Vince and his dad, the only person he wanted to see was Cindy, and she hadn't been interested when he was free. Why would now be any different?

He was making his way back from the latest guitar lesson, this time with Toxic Tim the Peterborough Poisoner, when a guard called out.

'Mulvaney! Over here.' He dutifully followed the shout to where Mr Nicol was standing with a piece of paper in his hand. 'I was just on my way to deliver this. You've got a visitation request for later in the week.' He thrust the paper towards Dave and walked away without any further words. It had been weeks since his last visitor; who was it this time? As he read the name on the slip, he couldn't believe what he was seeing.

He avoided association time and went straight to his cell. He needed space, time to think. He looked at the name on the slip again, checking that he hadn't imagined it or read it wrong the last dozen times. What did she want? Why now? Maybe she had found someone else and wanted to let him know personally. Maybe she just wanted to laugh and tell him this this was the universe's way of evening the score, paying him back. He didn't even dare to hope that she wanted him back, I mean, his circumstances had hardly improved since she dumped him in disgust four months ago, had they?

When Ricky and the others found out about Dave's impending visit, he dodged their questions. Ned was the pushiest, carrying on long after Ricky and Warren backed off.

'So, who is she then? Family or friend? Or more than a friend?'
'Leave it, Ned.'

'Why should I? There's not much to talk about in here, so when there's something new it's your duty to share it with your mates. What are we talking about? Should I hang around near the visitors' room – is she an eyeful worth catching?'

'I said leave it.' He could feel his jaw clenching.

'Oooh, I think we're touching a nerve. I know: she was your girlfriend until you got arrested, but she hasn't been to visit you in all this time. She's one of those good-hearted types who thinks it's kinder to dump you in person than by letter, not realising that the whole room will be listening in and hearing every humiliating word. I'm right, aren't I? Take my advice, Tom, tell her you won't see her. You'll thank me in the end.'

Dave's fists were balled now. It was all he could do stand up and walk away. He headed back to his cell, ignoring Ned's baiting as he went. He could hear Ricky sticking up for him, having a go at Ned.

When Ricky came to the cell a bit later, he asked how Dave was but soon realised Dave didn't want to talk, backing off and giving him space to brood. She'd already broken up with him, so it wasn't what Ned thought. He just couldn't understand why she was coming.

A small wooden table was the only thing between him and the empty chair opposite. He fidgeted nervously, one of a couple of dozen prisoners scattered around the room. Some of the others chatted among themselves while they waited, but Dave couldn't take his eyes off the door that the visitors would soon be walking through. He couldn't wait to see Cindy again and yet at the same time he was dreading it. Should he change his mind, say he wouldn't see her? Maybe he wouldn't like what she had to say. But if he didn't meet her, he'd never know; surely that would be worse, wouldn't it? He just wished she'd arrive and get it over with.

The bell rang, and the guard opened the door. Wives, parents and friends started filing in, scanning the room to spot their loved ones. As more and more people came through with still no sign of Cindy, Dave began to panic. He had nearly changed his mind; what if she'd done the same? Maybe at the last moment she realised she had nothing to say to him after all. The thought terrified him, almost as much as the thought of having to face her again.

Then she walked in and Dave momentarily held his breath. She looked good. She had let her hair grow longer, but her eyes still peeked through that fringe. When he had teased her about it, back when they were together, she admitted that she liked to hide behind it, enjoying the barrier between her and the rest of the world. Dave hated the fact that the fringe wasn't the only barrier between them now.

She sat down opposite him, looking about as awkward as he felt.

'Hey, you,' she said. She was trying to be casual but Dave could hear the effort in her voice.

'Hi. You're looking great.' She didn't answer. 'I mean, it's great to see you. I kept hoping you'd come, but I never thought you would.'

'You've lost weight,' she said at last, still not quite managing the easy-going, playful tone of their previous life.

'Yeah, prison food – it doesn't really encourage binge-eating, if you know what I mean.'

'I bet. It suits you, though, the weight.'

'Maybe I should have come here sooner.' She actually smiled, albeit briefly. 'Why did you come?'

Her eyes locked on to his through the fringe. 'We need to talk. Is what the papers say true? Did you really record the lost Dave Masters record and pass it off as his?'

Dave sighed, glancing around to see how close the guards were. 'Yeah,' he said quietly. 'It was Tony's idea. He said we'd sell more copies of another album by Dave Masters than one by an unknown tribute act. He said I sounded close enough to the real thing that we'd never get caught. That was before the producer decided to add a song that wasn't released until after the real Dave Masters died, which he couldn't possibly have heard, obviously.'

'Yeah, about that. Why that song?'

'Do you need to ask?' She didn't answer, just kept looking at him, daring him to be honest. 'Okay, because when you left, I realised that I had nothing that I cared for anymore. I threw myself into the recordings because it kept me busy, but all I could think about was how stupid I'd been. I felt more alone than I'd ever felt in my whole life – more than when Cath left me, more than anyone had ever made me feel. I'm not saying that I didn't deserve it, but it broke me. Music has always been how I deal with emotions, and that song nailed it.'

'So, you really did write all the songs on the album, apart from the cover versions?' Dave nodded his reply. 'Once I heard they were your songs, not the real Dave Masters', I started listening more carefully. Are they about me, about us?'

Dave nodded again. 'Most of them, yeah.'

'When did you write them?'

Dave wasn't sure where this was going. 'Some were after we broke up, some were before… well, before I stuffed things up.'

'You mean before you slept with Nicky.' The sharpness in her tone was another slap across his face.

'Yeah. And some were after… what I did, but before you found out. Basically, getting together with you unblocked my songwriting, and even after we broke up it stayed unblocked.'

'Is that all I was then? A way to get back to writing songs again?'

'God, no! You made me feel like a real person, got me in touch with myself again. First I wrote because everything was so good, then I wrote to deal with how I felt about messing up. You were my muse, which was brilliant, but you were so much more than that.'

He looked in her face for any sign that she believed him, but he couldn't read what was happening behind her eyes, a fact that stabbed at him.

'So, that single, "Shadow Life"?'

'After Nicky, before you found out.'

She nodded, as if it was what she had been expecting. '"Your Eyes Shine"?'

'Before everything. I mean, after we started, but before everything else. It was one of the first songs when I started writing again.'

'"Rockabye"?'

'After we started getting close – after you told me about…' he paused, deciding how to refer to her lost baby, 'about your past.'

'But before you shagged Nicky?'

Dave winced again. 'Yes, before that.'

'What about "I'd Do the Same All Over Again"?' she said the title accusingly. 'How does that fit in? Is that one about what you did?'

'God, no. I wrote that long before things happened with Nicky. That one isn't even about you. Well, it is a bit. It's about all my other mistakes, all the decisions and wrong turns and how they led me to where I was when I wrote it, which was in a pretty good place. It was saying that I wouldn't change those mistakes because they led me to you. There are mistakes since then that I would change, and Nicky is top of that list.'

'Really, top of the list? More so than, oh, I don't know, taking part in criminal fraud and getting yourself arrested?'

Now it was Dave's turn to fix Cindy with his gaze. 'In a heartbeat. Given the choice of you and prison, or freedom without you, they could lock me up for years. I know it doesn't work like that, that you're not coming back, but I mean it. Losing you is the biggest regret of my life.'

She held his gaze and for a long time didn't speak. Dave didn't speak either, figuring that if she needed time to process what he had said, he wasn't going to rush her.

Eventually she spoke again. Dave wasn't sure but he thought there was a softer tone to her next question. '"Through My Fingers"?'

'After you found out. The next day, in fact.'

She started crying. Dave reached out his hand to take hers, but the guard called out, 'No touching.' They both instinctively pulled their hands back and she fished some tissues out of her bag.

'I knew I'd need these, you know?' she muttered, and Dave tried to smile reassuringly. 'When I heard all those songs and realised they were about me…' she paused to wipe her eyes, 'I started to think about it all again. I got past the anger and thought that maybe you had meant all those things you said. I tried making sense of all the different lyrics – how the same man who wrote "Shadow Life" could write "I'd Do the Same All Over Again"; how the happy love songs fitted in with the guilty ones. When I found out about you and Nicky I thought I'd been stupid, that you'd just been lying to me all along. Listening to those songs I started to wonder if it was that simple, I wondered if you really had been telling me the truth.'

'I did – I was.' Dave had never wanted to be believed more in his life.

'But you still slept with Nicky, didn't you? How am I meant to get past that? Why do that if you loved me so much?'

He'd asked himself the question a thousand times and he still couldn't come up with an answer. 'I don't know. Even at the time, part of me was screaming to leave but I didn't. It was only that one time – even after we split up, it never happened again.'

'I know, I spoke to Nicky.'

'So have you two made up?' If she could forgive Nicky, maybe she could forgive him too. Cindy's response shot that hope down.

'Hardly. She was my best friend and she slept with my boyfriend. How am I meant to trust her after that? How am I meant to trust you again?' Her eyes were glaring now, daring him to respond.

'I know,' he said at last. 'I don't blame you – I wouldn't trust me either. For what it's worth, you were – are – the love of my life and I'd do anything to get you back. But I can't take away the pain I caused, or the way I betrayed you. I really am sorry.'

Her gaze softened, but the way she looked at him was still miles away from the way she used to.

'Thanks for being honest, anyway,' she said eventually. 'The answers you gave, about the songs, have helped. I can make more sense of it all now, even if that can't get us back together.'

Dave smiled weakly. 'I know we're over, but if I've helped you to move on, then I'm glad about that. I really never wanted to hurt you.' She nodded, and smiled sadly. 'There's one more thing I can do for you. Go see my barrister, she'll have something for you. Tell her who you are and that I sent you for the report.' He could see from Cindy's face that she was confused. 'Trust me, just do it. Her name's Penelope Soper and she'll know what you're talking about. Go see her, please.'

CHAPTER THIRTY-THREE

He sat down again, tapping his hands repeatedly against the legs of his suit trousers. Then he stood up for the tenth or twelfth time and paced, not that there was a lot of room for pacing in the small holding cell. The Old Bailey: in terms of name recognition, it scored as highly as the Royal Albert Hall or Madison Square Garden, but it wasn't a venue he had ever expected to play. He sat down again and tried not to fidget. Seconds later, he was on his feet, as he heard the heavy door being unlocked. Penelope walked in, wearing robes and a lawyer's wig over her dark suit.

'How are you doing?' she asked. If her smile was supposed to calm his nerves, it wasn't up to the job. 'The suit looks good on you.'

'I know how to wear a stage costume, though I'm not sure I could pull off that wig of yours.' He smiled weakly. 'I thought I knew all about stage fright, but this is something else.'

'Just relax, all you have to do today is confirm your name and then say not guilty when they ask how you plead. Apart from that, leave everything to me for most of the trial. Are you sure you're happy with my plan?'

'If you think it's my best chance of not going back to prison, yeah, I'm happy.'

'I mean, are you sure about the consequences afterwards? We won't be able to put the genie back in the bottle.'

Dave knew what she meant. He looked her in the eye. 'The consequence I'm most concerned about is not going back to prison.'

'Fair enough. It's risky, but I think we can pull it off. One more thing, don't forget they're still hoping to turn something up that links you to Alan Sharkey's death.'

'But I didn't – I couldn't – kill anyone.'

'I know that, and I'll take care of it if they try to imply that you did. It's my problem, not yours, but when we put you in the witness box, be careful not to give the wrong impression. Come on, we mustn't keep the judge waiting.'

A few minutes later, Dave was escorted into the court by two policemen and led to the dock. Penelope was there, sitting at a desk in the front row facing the bench and whispering with the younger lawyer assisting her. Across the aisle from Penelope was, Dave assumed, the prosecution lawyer. He was tall and thin, with small steel-rimmed glasses perched on top of a beakish nose. He reminded Dave of one of his old schoolteachers, which wasn't a good start. He had a couple of assistants, and they all exuded an air of smug confidence.

Dave took a moment to look around the room. The jury box was still empty, but the public gallery was full; nice to know he could still pull a crowd. Ironically, there were no more people here than had come to see him play at places like the Jericho or the Georgian Theatre, which was partly what had got him into this mess. He scanned the gallery for familiar faces. Jym and Chris were there, sitting together. They smiled encouragingly and Chris gave him a thumbs-up. He tried to respond with a smile, but his mouth refused to assume the position; he was too uptight, too scared. He saw a worried look pass across both of his friends' faces. Chris whispered something to Jym, who nodded. Chris looked as nervous as Dave, his complexion the same as before one of their early gigs. For a moment he had a vision of Chris having to run out of the court in the middle of proceedings, and that tricked his face, fleetingly, into a genuine smile.

Then he saw her, sat a few rows behind Jym and Chris, and his heart almost stopped. Cindy had come. What did that mean? She noticed him looking and smiled, making a tiny hand-waving motion with her fingertips. Again, he tried to smile but wasn't sure how successful he'd been. He hadn't seen her since that prison visit. He had hoped she might come to the trial, but now that she had, he wasn't sure if it was really what he wanted. Somehow her seeing him get sent down would just make it worse.

One of the court officials addressed the room. 'All rise.'

The judge walked in, all robes and wig, like he'd stepped out of the eighteenth century. He settled himself on his throne-like chair and nodded to the official, who continued. 'The case of the Crown versus Mr Thomas Mulvaney. Mr Justice Penhaligon presiding.' The two lead counsels, Penelope and the beaky man, Patrick Creaveny-Walsh, identified themselves, and then it was Dave's turn. He was asked to confirm that he was Thomas James Mulvaney of Flat 8, Squire Court, High Barnet.

Dave leant into the microphone. He usually preferred to get the opening number out of the way before talking to the audience, but that wasn't an option this time. 'I am.'

Next came the charges. As instructed by Penelope, he pleaded not guilty, which meant it was time for the jury to be brought through and sworn in. Penelope had warned him to expect the jury to be looking at him a lot, particularly early on. She told him not to play to them – that was her job, not his – but to try to look normal: not too emotional but not too cold either. The prosecution would want the jurors to think of him as a criminal. Her job was to make them see him as a person.

The judge had a few words for the jury before, at last, he called on the counsel for the prosecution to make his opening remarks. Creaveny-Walsh stepped forward.

'Ladies and gentlemen of the jury,' he began confidently. He was a natural frontman, the Mick Jagger of the courtroom. 'We are here today to hear a case of fraud and conspiracy where only one conspirator is present. The absence of his partners in crime should not prevent you from holding him to account for their collective crimes. I am sure that the counsel for the defence will try to argue that others are the true villains of the piece, but I shall be presenting evidence to prove that this is not the case. As you will hear, the defendant deliberately sought to pass himself off as the late rock musician,' he followed the phrase with a slight snort of contempt, 'Dave Masters, deceiving both the Ultimate record company and the many fans of Mr Masters by passing off his own, inferior, songs as original works by said artist.'

He carried on in a similar vein for some time, laying out the details of the case and casting Dave – or rather Tom – in the starring role. Tony and Alan were both mentioned, with the clear implication that the three of them were equally to blame for the scheme. The fact that both were beyond the reach of the law – one of them permanently – shouldn't stop Thomas Mulvaney from answering for his crimes. He said they would hear from expert witnesses who would demonstrate that the recording couldn't possibly have been made in the 1970s as claimed, from the police, from a representative of the record label and even from one of the musicians who took part in the recordings. Dave's stomach lurched at that point. When Penelope had shown him the prosecution's witness list, his eyes had got stuck on that one name. He still couldn't believe it, even after she explained what was going on.

Eventually, after nearly an hour, Dave got the impression that Creaveny-Walsh was winding up.

'This is a crime against art, a crime against the music industry and a crime against the very fans who are the life-blood of that industry. I will demonstrate that the accused committed an act of criminal deception, that this deception caused material, financial harm to others, and that he sought to gain financially from doing so. For the sake of the many victims of this terrible, calculated act of deceit, we must act decisively and convict those responsible. That only one of them stands before us today, should not sway you from your duty. You must make him answer for his crimes.'

When it was Penelope's turn, she took a different tack.

'Members of the jury, you've heard a lot from my learned opponent, but I'll make this brief. Thomas Mulvaney is a simple man who wanted to make music, to share his music. He hasn't caused any harm. There is no victim here, and there is no crime. The prosecution will try to argue otherwise: that's his job. Your job is to weigh the two different versions of events and to decide which of them you believe. To borrow a phrase from one of Dave Masters' heroes, Bob Dylan, everything else is just blowing in the wind.' With that she nodded her head respectfully to the jurors and returned to her seat. If Creaveny-Walsh's opening was like a prog-rock double album, all side-long songs and self-indulgent instrumentals, Penelope was the Ramones: short, sharp and straight to the point. He wasn't sure that she had countered the accusations that Creaveny-Walsh had stacked up against him, but if likeability counted for anything Penelope was ahead.

The prosecution's first witness was Nigel Toppinger, the head suit at Ultimate. Creaveny-Walsh's approach with witnesses seemed similar to his opening remarks: taking his time, asking question after question to gradually build up the impression he wanted to create. Nigel seemed happy to talk at length, saying how devastated everyone at Ultimate had been about Dave's death, and how they had felt a responsibility to his fans to put out the lost album. They touched on the commercial implications of the death, the way that Dave's old albums had started selling again, and the compilation album's excellent sales figures.

'So, in that environment, how would you describe the

commercial potential of a new album of previously unheard Dave Masters songs?' Creaveny-Walsh cued up the question.

'Songs dating back to his '70s heyday? It was as near to a certain best-seller as you get in this industry.'

'And it was something that a fraudster would have reason to believe you would pay handsomely to get your hands on?'

'Absolutely, and we did.'

They went on to cover the discovery, a couple of weeks after release, that all was not as it seemed, how "And I Fell Back Alone" couldn't possibly have been recorded by Dave Masters, as the original version wasn't released until May 1990, a month after Dave's death. Creaveny-Walsh asked Nigel how he had felt when he discovered that he had been deceived.

'I was furious. I had been duped into deceiving Dave Masters' loyal fans, tricking them into paying their hard-earned money for nothing more than a convincing imitation. If we had known the truth, we would never have released the record.'

When Penelope got to her feet, she was warm and friendly with Nigel, inviting him to repeat what he had said about Dave's long and productive relationship with the record company. As Nigel waxed lyrical about Dave's twenty unbroken years of partnership, she cut him off.

'Unbroken? Is it not the case that in March 1990, just a few weeks before his tragic death, you terminated Dave Masters' contract with Ultimate, refusing to release the final album required by that contract?'

Nigel stiffened in the witness box. 'Erm, yes, that's correct. At that point his sales had been steadily declining for some time and we decided the album just wasn't good enough to be released on the Ultimate label; we have standards to maintain.'

'And what changes were made to that album before you eventually released it as *Feel Like Going Home*, just in time for the Christmas market?'

Nigel was squirming now. 'None.'

'None at all?'

'None. Well, we changed the title to make the most of the hit single, but other than that it was the same album.'

'The same album that you had previously decided wasn't good enough for your meticulously high standards; I see. And going back to *Lost Masters*, when you discovered that it wasn't what you had thought, did you remove it from sale, to protect your customers from buying,' she checked her notes and quoted his earlier phrase, 'nothing more than a convincing imitation?'

'No. No we didn't.'

'Why ever not, if you were so concerned with the standards of the label and protecting your customers?'

'We had money invested in it, and we thought some people might be curious to hear it, knowing the truth about what it was. It was our last chance to make some money out of Dave Masters, so we let it run.'

'Your last chance to make some money out of Dave Masters.' She turned and looked to the jury with raised eyebrows. 'I see.'

Creaveny-Walsh asked a few more questions, but Dave got the impression he was just trying to soften the impact of Penelope's cross-examination, making sure that her exposure of Nigel's motives wasn't the last thing the jury saw. He looked across to see how it was going down with the jury, but he just couldn't read this audience.

The next witness was an Inspector Smallwood, a police officer who was mainly there to tell the jury the contents of Alan's letter. Alan had outlined being approached by Tony Broadway and asked to record a new artist he was working with. At the first session, Tony had given the instruction that the recordings had to sound like the work of Dave Masters and admitted that they would be passed off as such. Creaveny-Walsh allowed the policeman to state that, according to Alan, the only ones aware of what was happening were himself, Tony and Tom Mulvaney. The three other musicians involved believed that they were working on genuine demo tapes left behind after Dave Masters' death.

'Demo tapes?' asked the judge.

Creaveny-Walsh fielded the enquiry. 'A common practice in the music industry, m'lud. A simplistic, rough take on a song before it is given a fuller arrangement. In this instance, the demo version contained just acoustic guitar and singing.'

'Thank you, Mr Creaveny-Walsh; I am indebted to your knowledge of the world of rock music.'

'I'm afraid, m'lud, that I have no such knowledge outside of this case; I'm more of a Mahler man myself.' Of course you are, thought Dave; elitist snob.

Creaveny-Walsh moved on, inviting Smallwood to outline Alan's account of recording "And I Fell Back Alone", along with the resulting media storm. Alan had apparently written that he then received threats from the conspirators warning him to stick to his story and take it to his grave. Alan had mentioned Tony's criminal connections and how they made him fear for his life.

When Penelope got her chance with the witness, she didn't hang about.

'Inspector Smallwood, you said that Alan Sharkey feared his fellow conspirators might take steps to silence him. Could you read the part of his letter where he suggests that Tom Mulvaney might be part of such an act?' The inspector shifted on his feet, looking towards Creaveny-Walsh as if for help.

'It's not a difficult question, Inspector Smallwood. You've told us that Alan Sharkey commented on Tony Broadway's criminal connections; can you tell us where in his letter he suggests Tom Mulvaney might be part of a plot to kill him?'

'I... can't.'

'I'm sorry, why not?'

'Because... because Alan Sharkey only comments that he feared Tony Broadway might have him killed. He lays no such accusation against Tom Mulvaney.'

The judge intervened at this point. 'Ms Soper, your client is not on trial for murder. There is no charge against him concerning the death of Alan Sharkey.'

Penelope beamed. 'Thank you, your honour. You are, of course, entirely correct. It must have been the line of questioning that my learned opponent pursued with the witness that confused me. I'm sure that the jury will remember there is no suggestion of Tom Mulvaney having any part in such offences. Inspector, are there any parts of the letter where Mr Sharkey says anything about his experience of working with the defendant on the tapes?'

Inspector Smallwood looked relieved to move on to less difficult questioning. 'Yes. He says that the two of them worked well together, that Tom Mulvaney had a good understanding of Dave Masters' sound and that when the band came in to record their parts, Mulvaney was an invaluable aid in recreating that sound.'

Creaveny-Walsh looked happier about that, even if his attempt to smear Dave with Alan's death had been scuppered, Penelope had handed him further evidence of Tom's part in the fraudulent recordings.

'And one last question, Inspector: who does Alan Sharkey say was the brains behind the plan to create this so-called fraudulent album?'

'Tony Broadway.'

'Not Tony Broadway and Tom Mulvaney?'

'No, Ma'am, just Tony Broadway.'

'Thank you, Inspector. No further questions.'

An expert in sonics was next, dazzling the jury with complex equations and talk of signal decay. He talked about the vintage equipment in the studio but highlighted the tell-tale signs that revealed the tapes to be modern recordings. Creaveny-Walsh limited himself to a few gentle prods if the boffin drifted down a technical cul-de-sac, finishing by asking what likelihood, in his professional opinion, there was that the album might have been recorded in the 1970s.

'None at all.'

'Your witness, Ms Soper.'

Dave thought he saw the boffin steeling himself for Penelope's assault.

'Mr Harrison, are you a music fan?'

He visibly relaxed. 'Yes, yes, I am.'

'Are you a fan of Dave Masters?'

'A little bit, yes. I've got some of his albums.'

'And have you listened to the *Lost Masters* album? As a fan, I mean, not in a professional capacity.'

'Yes. I bought a copy when it came out – I was keen to hear it.'

'And what did you think, as a fan?'

He grinned. 'It was good – really good. I enjoyed it.' Dave wasn't sure how this would help the case, but it was a welcome ego boost.

'And, before you heard suggestions to the contrary, did you have any suspicion that the recordings were anything other than what they were purported to be?'

'No, none at all. I should emphasise that this was before I had started conducting any of my scientific analysis.'

'Understood, Mr Harrison, nobody is calling your professional credentials or capabilities into question; the defence fully accepts your technical findings. I merely wanted your opinion on the artistic merit of the recordings. No further questions.'

Creaveny-Walsh's next witness was the one Dave had been dreading. Vince Preston took to the witness box and swore his oath. He looked to the dock and made eye contact with Dave. Dave tried to read his expression, to work out if he still felt the way he had in their last phone conversation, or if time had softened his anger. He had no idea – Vince might as well have been wearing a mask; either way, it felt weird having his oldest friend as a witness for the prosecution, a witness against him.

When Vince was asked to confirm that he was a professional musician. He briefly made eye contact with Dave, who knew they were both thinking the same thing: all the drummer jokes over the years. For a moment he thought he caught a hint of warmth, of humour in his old friend's eye.

'That's right. I'm a drummer. Some people – ignorant people – would say that's not the same thing as a musician, but what can you do?'

The jury and the public gallery laughed, while Creaveny-Walsh scowled. He invited Vince to talk about his twenty-year association with Dave Masters, then asked how he came to be involved in the *Lost Masters* recordings. Vince explained that he had been asked by Tony.

'Did Mr Broadway say anything at that time about pretending the tracks were recorded in the 1970s?'

'No. Well, we suspected something was up, because he told us not to tell anyone what we were doing. When the album came out, we realised that he was pretending that our part dated back to 1978 as well as Dave's, but by then we didn't want to make trouble. The three of us agreed to keep our heads down and keep quiet. After all, it was us playing on the tracks and it was Dave singing, so where was the harm?'

'Or so you thought.'

'I'm sorry?'

'It was Dave singing on the track, or so you thought.'

'Yes, exactly.'

'Apart from yourself, Simon Tilley and Phil Chambers, who was present at the recording sessions?'

'Alan Sharkey was there, as well as his studio assistant.'

'And do you see that studio assistant here in the courtroom?'

'Yes.' He pointed. 'Over there, the defendant.'

'And what did the defendant's duties in the recording studio consist of?'

'Occasionally Alan would send him through to the studio

itself to adjust microphones or move a baffle wall, but generally he stayed in the control room with Alan. I could see them through the glass, discussing things.'

'He was involved in shaping the recordings?'

'It certainly looked like it. Alan has always been open to other people's ideas – he doesn't mind who comes up with something as long as it's the right idea for the record.'

'So, is it fair to say that the defendant played a significant part in the creation of the *Lost Masters* album?'

'Yes, I'd say that was fair.'

'Thank you, Mr Preston. Your witness, Ms Soper.'

Penelope got to her feet. Dave knew this was the crucial moment of the trial. His mouth was dry and his palms were sweating. If Penelope was as nervous as him, she wasn't showing it.

'Mr Preston. Once you, Simon Tilley and Phil Chambers had finished recording your parts, was the album then in its completed state?'

'No, not at all. They still needed to record some guitar overdubs before the final mix.'

'Guitar overdubs? I thought you were using the guitar part from the demo tapes.'

'That was just the rhythm part. It still needed the lead guitar parts that Dave would normally have added in the studio with the rest of us.'

'And who was going to provide the lead guitar part?'

'Tony said that he was going to bring in the guitarist from a Dave Masters tribute act. We were all curious to hear how close this guy would get to Dave's style, but none of us were there when he actually recorded.'

'Were you optimistic about him recreating Dave Masters' style?'

'Personally, no. It was something we discussed a lot. Tribute acts are about recreating something that already exists. That's very different to coming up with new material in the same style. I wasn't convinced at all.'

'And when you heard the final album, what did you think?'

'I knew that the guitarist wasn't just some copyist. He was the real thing.'

'You mean he did a convincing job of playing in the style of Dave Masters?'

'No. I mean he was Dave Masters. As soon as I heard his playing, I realised that he was the real Dave Masters.'

There was a collective intake of breath in the room. Creaveny-Walsh was on his feet in an instant. 'Objection!'

The judge looked at him, inviting him to explain, and Dave saw him realise that he didn't know exactly what he was objecting to, other than being blindsided by the revelation. The judge turned to Vince.

'Mr Preston, could you clarify your last remark? Do you mean that it is your belief that the guitar part was played by Dave Masters, rather than by Tom Mulvaney?'

'No, your honour. I mean that the man sitting in the dock, the man you refer to as Tom Mulvaney, is in fact my old friend and bandmate Dave Masters.'

CHAPTER THIRTY-FOUR

The public gallery was abuzz. Even after a life on stage, Dave had never been more aware of being the centre of attention. Penelope had talked to him about this moment, about not looking alarmed but being a point of calm in the storm. It took the judge a moment or two to restore order. Dave forced himself not to move, and certainly not to look towards the jury. He just kept his eyes fixed on Vince, sitting calmly in the witness box.

Creaveny-Walsh got back to his feet and opened his mouth to say something, but the judge silenced him with a raised finger.

'This is most irregular. I shall adjourn the proceedings for half an hour, and I shall see lead counsels in my chambers at once.' With that he sprung to his feet and swept out.

'Is it true?' asked one of the guards, leading him back to the holding cell. 'Are you really Dave Masters?'

Dave hesitated. Did Penelope's instruction not to tell anyone still apply? The guard carried on. 'Only, if you are, could I get an autograph? My Auntie Sarah's one of his – your – biggest fans.'

The other guard, who was a bit older, cut him off. 'That's not really appropriate, John.' He paused for a moment before adding, 'That said, if you are the real Dave Masters, I'm a big fan. I saw you at Hammersmith back in '74. Great show.'

Dave turned and grinned. 'My lawyer would probably want me to say "no comment", but thanks.'

A few minutes later, Penelope was let into Dave's cell.

'Well,' she said. 'Creaveny-Walsh was a bit upset.'

'Just a bit?'

'Foaming at the mouth, almost literally. He accused me of planning this – as if I'd do such a thing.' She raised her eyebrows in Dave's direction, reminding him that she had indeed planned the whole thing, persuading Vince to offer himself as a prosecution witness. 'He said that if I knew something so germane to the case, it was my responsibility to notify the prosecution rather than ambushing him in the middle of the trial. I simply reminded him that it was his witness who had the information, and asked why he hadn't made me aware of such a significant fact. I said I had no idea and I was just fishing.'

'And you certainly caught something,' added Dave.

'That's what the judge said. He also said he was considering ruling a mistrial, but when I hinted that I was open to that, and that the DPP might assign a different prosecuting counsel, Creaveny-Walsh insisted that the trial proceed. I reluctantly agreed. To cut a long story short, we've got maximum impact from the news that you're Dave rather than Tom, without anyone being able to accuse me of withholding information. We're in with a chance.'

Back in the courtroom, the judge restarted the trial. Vince returned to the witness stand and was reminded he was still under oath. Penelope resumed her cross-examination.

'Just in case anyone has forgotten where we left things. Mr Preston, could you repeat the last thing you said?'

'Well, I can't remember the exact words, but I believe I had just identified the accused as Dave Masters, finest singer-songwriter I've ever worked with and a damned fine guitarist.' There were smiles in the jury box, and a chuckle running around the gallery. Dave met Vince's eye and gave him a tiny nod of gratitude.

'Thank you, Mr Preston. No further questions.'

Creaveny-Walsh was on his feet in an instant.

'Mr Preston, why didn't you offer this information at an earlier stage? Such as in any of the many meetings we had in advance of the trial?'

Penelope was on her feet. 'M'lud, I'm sure this can't be the case, but it certainly sounds like my learned friend has been coaching witnesses.'

Vince answered before the judge could intervene. 'Well, you told me just to answer the questions that you asked, not to drift off the point or get bogged down in unnecessary details.'

'Unnecessary details! You knew that the accused was really Dave Masters and you thought it was an unnecessary detail? Why on earth didn't you say something sooner?'

'What was it you said to me? You have been practising the law for over twenty years, while I spent that time hitting things for a living; I couldn't possibly be expected to know which facts are legally significant and which aren't. I was to keep my answers strictly to the point, so I did. You should have asked, mate.'

The gallery was laughing more loudly this time, very much at Creaveny-Walsh's expense. The judge stepped in to put him out of his misery.

'Mr Creaveny-Walsh, do you have any further questions for your witness? I fail to see how this particular line of questioning is going to lead to further insight, entertaining though it may be.'

Creaveny-Walsh returned to his seat and sat down abruptly.

'I believe that Mr Preston was the last witness on the prosecution's list.' Creaveny-Walsh nodded curtly. 'In which case, I think we will adjourn until Monday morning. Both sides will need time to assimilate today's unexpected developments. When we resume on Monday I will ask if the prosecution has any more witnesses or whether it wishes to rest. Court adjourned.'

Dave went back to Pentonville for the weekend, but the news from the trial got there before him. As he was marched back onto his wing, he heard a few shouts of "Dave" from his fellow in-mates. Even one of the warders made a joke about it being nice to see him standing there. Penelope had warned him not to discuss the trial with the other prisoners, and certainly not to discuss his identity, although he could hardly avoid that – it was all that anyone wanted to talk about.

He took Ricky through the trial, saying how Penelope had made Nigel from Ultimate look like the double-dealing money-grabber he was and how her cross-examination of Vince had unwittingly revealed his big secret.

'So it's true then.' Ricky grinned. 'I'm sharing a cell with a genuine rock star?'

'I don't know about that. More like a faded has-been; the star power ended years ago.'

The morning papers told another story. Every front page proclaimed that Dave Masters was alive and well and on trial for pretending to be Dave Masters. When Dave and Ricky went down to collect their breakfast, Dave was once again the focus of everyone's attention.

'What's the matter with you lot?' said Ricky loudly to the staring prisoners. 'Haven't you ever seen a number-one recording artist in here before?'

Later, during free association, lots of prisoners came over to see Dave, telling him they were big fans, or that they weren't particularly fans but hoped he got off. Mad Mac the Mincer had apparently been boasting about learning guitar from a genuine rock star. Dave was just glad he hadn't taken the deception as another sign of disrespect.

'So, what should we expect today?' Dave asked Penelope, back in the holding cell at the Old Bailey.

'Creaveny-Walsh hasn't submitted any more witnesses, so he

must be going to rest his case. Assuming he can't disprove the notion that you really are Dave Masters, he'll probably go in hard on you in cross-examination. If so, everything depends on how you come across, whether he can paint you as a conniving, deceitful bastard.'

Dave nodded, glad that nobody was going to call Cindy as a witness.

The first of Penelope's witnesses was a familiar face for Dave. Frank Dixon took the oath and had obviously made an effort to be presentable in court; his shirt was clean if not ironed, and he was even wearing a tie, albeit one with fresh food stains on it. Penny went through the basics, establishing that Frank was a private detective and that he had been hired by the defendant in November to compile a report.

'Can you tell the court what that report was about?'

'Yes, he wanted me to investigate the past of a man called Tom Mulvaney.'

'And what name did the accused tell you he was going by?'

'Tom Mulvaney. He told me he was living under a false identity but wouldn't say who he really was.'

'I see. And did he say why he wanted this information?'

'Yes: curiosity. He wanted to know about the person whose identity he was given. He said he was becoming worried that the real Tom Mulvaney may have been killed to provide him with a new identity, and he didn't want that on his conscience.'

When Creaveny-Walsh began his cross-examination, he homed in on that last point.

'Mr Dixon, you say that the defendant didn't want murder on his conscience. From your findings, do you think the real Tom Mulvaney was killed for Dave Masters' convenience?'

'That's a difficult one, he—'

'But he was killed, and then his identity passed on to the defendant?'

'Yes—'

'No further questions.'

Penelope tried to clear that one up, allowing Frank to say that Tom was probably going to be killed anyway for a long-held underworld grudge, and that passing his identity on for money was just a happy bonus for the killers, but Dave was afraid that Creaveny-Walsh had successfully landed a blow against him.

Penelope only had one other witness, Dave himself. The public galleries were packed; Penelope said that people had started queuing hours before the doors opened. It wasn't the first time Dave had been the hottest ticket in town, but never quite like this. Penelope had been through her line of questioning with him, so he knew exactly what she wanted from him at each stage.

'Could you state your name, please?'

'I've been living as Tom Mulvaney, but my real name is Dave Masters.'

'And how long have you been living as Tom Mulvaney?'

'Since April 1990.'

'Could you tell the court why you decided to adopt a false identity?'

'I was fed up with being me, fed up with the way things had gone. My personal life was a disaster, my records sales were dwindling, I'd stopped writing decent songs and my record company didn't want me anymore. My manager, Tony Broadway, said faking my death would boost my sales, and after one particularly bad gig I thought, what have I got to lose? I wanted to get out and start afresh, to be someone normal, someone who wasn't me.'

'You wanted to be someone else, yet you ended up working as a musician again, playing your own songs in a tribute band to yourself. Can you explain how that happened?'

'It wasn't planned; it just happened step by step. I missed playing, then a friend...' he found Cindy in the public gallery, now alongside Jym and Chris, 'a very special friend took me to see a tribute band and I thought, why not? At that stage it was just for fun and beer money.'

'But it didn't stay that way, did it? Why was that?'

'It turns out, I'm fairly good at being Dave Masters.'

That got a ripple of laughter from the gallery, as well as from some of the jurors.

'You mentioned your manager. What was his role in all this?'

'Well, as I said, faking my death was his suggestion in the first place. Once I realised he wasn't joking, I resisted at first, but eventually I agreed. After that he took care of everything. Before I knew it, he had me driving to Barnet to a flat he had rented for me, with my new identity in an envelope. He was handling my finances via a trust fund that was set up according to the terms of my will.'

'Whose idea was that?'

'Tony's. I wanted to still control my own money, to sign everything over to my new identity, but he insisted it was too risky – that any direct connection between the estate of Dave Masters and Tom Mulvaney could give everything away. He paid me a monthly amount to cover my living expenses. The plan was that when the record sales took off, he'd increase the payments, but somehow he never got round to that. And when he disappeared, he cleared out the trust fund.'

'So you didn't benefit financially from the surge in album sales after your apparent death?'

'I went from owning a six-bedroom detached house in Surrey with no mortgage to renting a one-bedroom third-floor flat in Barnet. I had a small regular income, but I lost control of the money I had in the bank. I wouldn't say that I was trading up financially.'

'And when the tribute act started to take off?'

'Yes, that was different. I persuaded Tony to manage the band, and there's no one better than him at building an act. He was booking shows whenever and wherever he could. I got a decent income from that, on top of the monthly payments from the trust fund, although that was never part of the plan.'

'But Tony was happy for you to do it?'

'Not at first, no. He thought I'd be recognised. I told him I was going to do it anyway, with or without him, and he decided he'd rather help me and take his percentage. In time, he saw it as the perfect cycle: the record sales increased the demand for the tribute act, and if people saw the tribute act, they were more likely to buy my old albums. He even signed another Dave Masters tribute act to his books without telling me.'

'Without telling you?'

'Yes, he did a lot of things without telling me.'

'Like killing Alan Sharkey?'

Dave hesitated. 'I don't know about that; I can only speculate. I do know he was worried Alan wouldn't stick to the story once questions were being asked. And I know that the people Tony used to set up my new identity weren't what you would call law-abiding. Unfortunately, I didn't know any of that until I was already living my new life.'

'How did the *Lost Masters* album come about? Was that part of Tony's plan to make more money out of your apparent death?'

'Yes and no. If he was here, he would tell you it was his idea.'

'Objection!' Creaveny-Walsh was out of his chair. 'The witness can't speculate on how someone else would answer a question, particularly in order to present himself as an innocent.'

The judge didn't hesitate. 'Sustained.'

'Okay, I'll rephrase that. I had started writing songs again and I wanted to record them. Tony wouldn't let me record them as Dave ReMastered. I decided that the best thing to do would be to record them as myself and put them out as recently discovered old recordings. I planted the idea and let Tony think it was his, because I thought that was the best way of getting him to agree.'

'And what was the motivation for releasing the songs?'

'For Tony – based on what he said to me – it was the money. I didn't care about that; I just wanted to get my songs out there, to have people hear what I'd been working on. For the first time in years I had new music I could be proud of. It was killing me not to share it.'

'So, it was your idea to record the *Lost Masters* album, but Tony Broadway was under the impression that he thought of it. Who made all the arrangements?'

'Tony.'

'And what was his part in the recordings themselves?'

'None. He had always left the musical side of things to me, just like I left the business side of it to him.'

'We have heard how "And I Fell Back Alone" exposed the pretence. How did that happen?'

'"And I Fell Back Alone" was never meant to be on the album. I arrived early for one of the last recording sessions – we only had the guitar overdubs left to do – and I was just playing to entertain myself while I waited for Alan to arrive. Without me realising, he turned up and started recording. He thought it was a new song of mine and put it on the album without telling me. I didn't find out until it was too late. I'd like to take this opportunity to apologise to Karl Wallinger: it's a great song that really touched me, and the last thing I would have wanted was for my version to cast aspersions on his talent. I hope that if any future editions of the album are pressed, they will put the appropriate publishing credit on to give him his due.'

'Thank you, Mr Masters. Your witness, Mr Creaveny-Walsh.'

Creaveny-Walsh eased himself out of his seat and prowled in front of the witness box.

'Tom Mulvaney, Dave Masters, Dave ReMastered. You like to play with identities, don't you?'

'Well, I'm no David Bowie if that's what you mean.' The jury enjoyed that one, though Creaveny-Walsh didn't seem to appreciate the joke.

'What I mean is, why should we believe you now? By your own admission, you faked your own death, took another man's identity and then started a new career impersonating yourself. By my reckoning, you were Dave Masters pretending to be Tom Mulvaney pretending to be the deceased Dave Masters who wasn't really deceased. Have I missed anything in your façade of lies?'

Dave went to answer, but the question had only been for the jury and Creaveny-Walsh was already pressing on. 'Why did your marriage break up, Mr Masters?'

There was no point lying; this was all a matter of public record. 'I was a bad husband.'

'In what way?'

'I was unfaithful. I was young, immature and I loved the life of a touring rock musician.'

'How many times were you unfaithful to your wife?'

Penelope was on her feet at that. 'Objection! What possible relevance has that got to the case in hand?'

Creaveny-Walsh riposted, 'Establishing character, m'lud, which I believe is key to understanding the events that have taken place.'

'I'll allow it. Please answer the question, Mr Masters.'

Dave hesitated. How many times had he been unfaithful to Cath? He genuinely wasn't sure how to put a number on it. 'A lot of times.'

'More than one? More than ten? More than a hundred?'

'Yes, more than a hundred.' The reaction around the room told Dave that he wasn't looking good right now.

'It's clear, Mr Masters, that you are what members of my profession would call an unreliable witness.'

'Objection!' Penelope was on her feet immediately. 'That's a judgement for the jury to make, not my learned opponent.'

'Sustained. Mr Creaveny-Walsh, please restrict yourself to questioning the witness rather than telling the jury what you want them think about him.'

'Of course, your honour. Mr Masters, given your extensive history of betraying your wife and the many deceptions that you have entered into in the last year, not least the fact that you started this trial under one name and are now finishing it under another, why should the jury believe a word you have to say about any of this?'

'Because I'm telling the truth.' Dave felt his temper stir and tried to remember Penelope's instructions: don't let Creaveny-Walsh rattle you.

'Do you expect us to believe that you didn't do all this for the money?'

Dave shrugged. 'I can't control what people believe. I can only tell them what I know. When Tony first suggested killing me off, he said it would boost my record sales, but by the time I agreed I just wanted to change my life, to not have constant reminders that I used to be famous.'

'Come on, it was for the money, wasn't it?'

'As I said earlier, I was much more comfortable financially before I was dead. If it was all about the money, I could have stopped years ago. I was doing it for the love of the music, then I stopped loving the music.'

'And it's very convenient that Tony Broadway isn't here to answer any questions, isn't it, Mr Masters? Have you and him made a deal where you play the innocent and then he splits the money later?'

'Objection! Does Mr Creaveny-Walsh have any evidence to support that allegation?'

The judge glared at the prosecution counsel. 'You know better than that, Mr Creaveny-Walsh. Unless you have some evidence to introduce, you will withdraw that question.'

'So withdrawn, m'lud. Let me rephrase that. Mr Masters, isn't it the case that the absence of Mr Broadway in the dock allows you to tell whatever stories you want about your activities in the last year? You arranged for all of your assets to be transferred into the trust fund and you intended to benefit financially from your supposed death. I put it to you again, you were in it for the money.'

'And I can only tell you again that I wasn't.'

'And, as we have established, you are a man with a history of changing his story to suit his circumstances. No further questions.'

Penelope got to her feet and turned to the witness box.

'Mr Masters. My learned opponent has made some strong accusations about money being a prime motivational factor in your actions in the last year. I'd like to ask you about your apparent death. What assets did you hold at the time?'

'I had plenty of money in the bank – I mean, I wasn't a millionaire or anything, but I was comfortable. I had some residual income in the form of songwriting and performing royalties, and I owned a nice big house in Surrey.'

'And was it all put into the trust fund that Tony Broadway was to operate?'

'Almost all. I stipulated in my will that my ex-wife Cath should receive half the money from the sale of the house. Tony tried to talk me out of it, but I insisted.'

'And why did you do that?'

'It had been her house as much as it was mine. When we divorced she could have taken me to the cleaners but she didn't; she just wanted a quick, clean ending. This was my way of saying thank you, and apologising for all the grief I'd caused her when we were married. You've heard the kind of husband I was; she should have left me years earlier.'

'What was the value of the house?'

'I'm not sure what it finally sold for, but I think it was put on the market at £500,000.'

'You gave your ex-wife the equivalent of £250,000 by way of saying thank you and sorry?'

'It was the least she deserved.'

'Well, that doesn't sound to me like the actions of a man who is driven by the acquisition of money. Were you hoping for a reconciliation with your ex-wife?'

Dave shook his head. 'No, there was never any prospect of that. She wouldn't have me back and I wouldn't want her to. We've both moved on.' His eye sought out Cindy in the public gallery. 'There are some relationships I'd want another chance with, but my marriage isn't one of them.'

'Thank you, Mr Masters, no further questions.'

The judge called for the end of the day's session, saying that court would resume the following morning for the closing arguments.

'How do you think it went, Penelope?' asked Dave once he had been escorted out of the courtroom and back to the cells.

'Hard to say. It all comes down to what the jury make of you, and if they believe us or Creaveny-Walsh. If the jury decide they like you, we've got a chance.'

'And if not?'

'Let's just hope they like you.'

CHAPTER THIRTY-FIVE

Creaveny-Walsh was addressing the jury.

'Ladies and gentlemen of the jury; please look at the man in the dock, the accused. Tom Mulvaney, Dave Masters, whatever he has decided to call himself today: this is a man who cannot be trusted. And whatever name he goes by, he has admitted to playing a crucial part in recording the music that lies at the heart of this case. He wrote the songs; he planned, along with the conveniently absent Tony Broadway, to deceive Ultimate into releasing a record that was not what they had been led to believe; he planned to foist that record on an unsuspecting public, to part thousands of Dave Masters fans from their hard-earned money for what they believed to be the work of an artist in his prime. In fact, it was the work of an artist whose talent had long since dried up, a man who was a pale imitation of his former glories. His motivation in all this was to wring a last few pounds out of his failed and ailing career. More than that, he was quite prepared for others to die in order to preserve his secret. Alan Sharkey and the real Tom Mulvaney stand in silent testimony against his all-consuming desire for a final payday.

'Although he pleaded not guilty, you have heard him admit to all the principal charges in this matter. He has admitted to writing the songs; he has admitted to recording them. We have heard how he helped the late Alan Sharkey to guide the other musicians in the studio. Without him, none of this could have happened. He even admits to planting the idea for the whole criminal venture in the mind of Tony Broadway. If Mr Broadway really is the criminal mastermind that he is being painted as, does it seem likely that a mere rock musician,' Creaveny-Walsh spat the words out as if he couldn't imagine a lower form of life, 'would be capable of so manipulating such a towering criminal genius? The accused has also admitted to living the past year under a false identity, that of Tom Mulvaney, and to maintaining that falsehood right up until the point when the veil of lies was ripped away from him in this very courtroom. What does all this tell us? It tells us that Dave Masters is a calculating, deceitful, untrustworthy criminal. He has lied and manipulated to squeeze more money out of his deluded fans. I don't know if any of you are fans of his, my own tastes run to higher things than his tawdry, raucous racket, but how must it feel to hear that someone you admire thinks so little of you that he will go to such lengths to part you from your money? That's what Dave Masters has done – he has admitted as much – and you must find him guilty.'

Dave was reeling. Creaveny-Walsh had laid into him, as Penelope had guessed that he would. Although Dave knew that most of what he said was unfair, there was enough truth in the argument to make him worry. It was true that he had lived a deception for a year; would that be enough to turn the jury against him? Would it have been better to have gone into the trial under his real name? He'd never know, but it was too late now. He just had to trust that Penelope knew what she was doing.

She was on her feet already, standing before the jury and smiling.

'There is much that my learned opponent and I disagree on, but we are agreed that the identity of the accused is a central point for your consideration. We have discovered, you and I both, during the course of this trial that Tom Mulvaney is no mere Dave Masters tribute act, he is Dave Masters himself, and that fact has a major bearing on everything else you have heard in this trial. Tom Mulvaney stood accused of pretending to be Dave Masters, of recording an album of songs supposedly written by Dave Masters and seeking to deceive Dave Masters' fans into spending their money on the work of another, lesser artist. But now that we know the truth, that Tom Mulvaney *is* Dave Masters, the whole case is cast in a different light. Dave Masters stands accused of recording an album of Dave Masters songs and offering it, first to his record company and then to his fans, as an album of Dave Masters songs. The credits on the album sleeve state that the musicians were Dave Masters, Vince Preston, Simon Tilley and Phil Chambers. All of that is factually correct. Whatever Tony Broadway – who always dealt with the business side of things, remember – told Ultimate Records concerning the recording of the album, the only falsehood on the album sleeve is the wrong attribution for the Karl Wallinger song, which no one has disputed was an accident that my client was unaware of until it was too late. No fraud was committed by my client in the making of the album, or in the release of the album.

'In his opening remarks, the counsel for the prosecution described this as, "a crime against art, a crime against the music industry and a crime against the very fans who are the life-blood of that industry". And yet it is hard to find a victim in all of this. Are Ultimate Records the victims? They coldly cast Dave Masters out from their ranks, a decision that led to the breakdown that saw him walk out of his own life. Yet they subsequently released what they thought was his last album, as well as the album of new material at the centre of this case. Did they lose money as a result of his actions? Not at all. Since his apparent death, Dave Masters has had two number-one singles released on Ultimate Records. The compilation *Vagabond Life: The Best of Dave Masters* was a best-seller; the album *Feel Like Going Home*, despite disappointing reviews, was still a greater commercial success than his most recent previous records, and *Lost Masters* sold well before this controversy. Apparently, since Friday's revelation, sales have dramatically increased, earning yet more money for Ultimate Records. If there's a victim in all this, it certainly isn't them.

'Are the fans the victims here? They got exactly what they paid for: an album of Dave Masters' music. More than that, everyone in this courtroom who has expressed an opinion on the album has said it is the best thing Dave Masters has recorded for years. It is hard to see how the record-buying public can be cast as victims here. Whether the music was recorded in 1978 or 1991 makes no difference to its aesthetic quality. This is a court of law, not an arbiter of artistic quality, but there is absolutely no evidence to suggest that anyone was disappointed with what they heard. The only dissent was raised when they thought it wasn't a genuine Dave Masters album, an allegation that we now know to be false.

'The accusation is that my client took part in this deception – which was no deception – with the aim of financial gain. And yet, Tony Broadway, along with Ultimate Records, are the ones who made all the money. Let's not forget that it was Broadway who controlled the estate of Dave Masters after his apparent death. He only paid a monthly stipend to my client, and that stipend was not increased once the sales of *Lost Masters* started to roll in. When Mr Broadway disappeared, he cleared out the trust fund, leaving Dave Masters as the only person not to benefit financially from the sales of the album. Does that make my client sound like a master criminal? It sounds more like the age-old story of an honest, well-meaning musician being taken advantage of by an unscrupulous manager. The prosecution has also sought to smear my client as bearing responsibility for the deaths of Tom Mulvaney and Alan Sharkey, but no evidence has been presented to that effect nor any charge laid against him. You should not allow their respective tragedies to influence your deliberations on this case.

'So, let's sum up. Deception in the case of the *Lost Masters* album? No. Harm caused to others? No. Financial gain as a result? No. Dave Masters has committed no crime and has no charge to answer. Yes, he lived for a year under a false identity, but that is not what he stands accused of today. There may be legal consequences that Mr Masters will have to face in the fullness of time, but they are not the business of this trial. By the very criteria that my learned opponent, the counsel for the prosecution, set out at the start of the trial, Dave Masters is demonstrably not guilty, and it is your duty to return such a verdict.'

A roar of applause rang out from the public gallery. If Penelope was feeling pleased with herself, she didn't show it as she returned to her seat. Creaveny-Walsh went puce and the judge was shouting to regain control of his courtroom. The judge dismissed the jury to their deliberations and the room quickly cleared.

'That was amazing. Do you think we've pulled it off?' he asked, once he was alone with Penelope in the cell.

'Hard to tell. The gallery was with us, but the jury might be another matter.'

'What do you think?'

'I think we'll have to wait and see.'

They didn't have to wait long. Less than an hour later, a court official came to the door and handed a piece of paper to Penelope.

'The jury has reached a verdict. That was quick.'

'Is quick a good thing?' asked Dave.

'It can be. Either the jury recognised that you did nothing wrong or they bought Creaveny-Walsh's account of you as an untrustworthy fraudster. All it really means is that they agreed with each other. It could go either way. Come on, let's get back to court and find out.'

The jury foreman stood up as directed and the judge asked him the question. Dave could feel the blood pounding in his ears.

'Have you reached a verdict on which you are all agreed?'

'We have.'

'What is that verdict?' The gap before the answer seemed intolerable for Dave. Come on, spit it out.

'We find the defendant not guilty.'

Again, the public gallery erupted. Dave turned to the crowd, desperately looking for Cindy. His eyes quickly found Jym and Chris, but she wasn't with them. Why hadn't she stayed? Had she heard enough? Had she decided she didn't care what happened? Those thoughts were soon displaced as he found himself grinning back at his jubilant friends. Relief was flooding through him and he gave himself to his moment of triumph.

The judge, for the last time, sought to regain control of his courtroom. Once a semblance of order had been restored, he said the sweetest words Dave had heard in a long time.

'Mr Masters, you are free to go.'

Penelope was the first person to greet him as he stepped from the dock. He wrapped her in a huge, grateful hug and realised how drained he felt; his arms barely had the strength to squeeze as he thanked her.

'It was a pleasure. I should thank you; pulling off an unexpected win in a high-profile case won't have done my career any harm. I'm just glad we got the right result. One more thing, the press will want to hear from us, but there's something else you should take care of first. Come with me.'

She led him through the corridors of the courtrooms, a maze of turns that reminded him of being led to the stage at an unfamiliar venue. She stopped by a door and beckoned for him to go through.

'What's in there?' he asked. She just smiled and indicated again for him to go in.

Cindy was sitting in a chair in the middle of the room. There was another chair opposite her, so Dave sat down.

'So, you won?' she asked. 'Penelope said you'd only be able to come to see me if you won.'

'Yeah, she got me off. It's good to see you again.'

Cindy smiled. 'It's good to see you too. You scrub up quite well – in a suit and everything. Or is this just another new identity, Dave?' She put lots of emphasis on the name, reminding him of the big deception he had never come clean with her about. 'So, you really are Dave Masters then? That wasn't just some clever trick to keep you out of jail?'

'No, I really am Dave Masters. I'm sorry for another lie, but I had to lie to everyone about that. Everything else I've said to you – all along – has been true. You know all my secrets now.'

'I know. After we spoke in the prison I went home and listened again to the *Lost Masters* songs. Knowing when each of them was written helped me get a better picture of what was going on in your head over the last few months. I know you meant all the things you said to me, before Nicky and after. And thank you – thank you so much – for that report. That meant more to me than anything you could have said.'

'I knew I could never put right what I'd done to you, but at least I could try to help you put other things right. I thought if I could find your daughter, give you something of her life, it might help you. Have you been in touch yet?'

'I wrote to her parents. I explained that I wasn't trying to get her back or to take their place, and that I wouldn't try to make contact with Joni – they called her Joni – behind their backs. Her mum sent me a lovely letter with lots of photos. They're going to tell her about me, and I can meet her, if that's what Joni decides she wants.'

'That's fantastic. I'm so pleased for you.'

'And I'm pleased for you. You're a good man, Tom, I mean, Dave.' They both laughed at the slip-up. 'Which one are you going to be from now on?'

'Dave. It's time for me to stop hiding from the truth and get honest.'

'I like the sound of that. Calling you Dave is going to take some getting used to, you know?'

Dave smiled, then a thought struck him. 'Why do you need to get used to it? I thought we were finished.'

'I always said that I could never go back to a man who cheated on me, and I stand by that. The way I see it, Tom Mulvaney cheated on me with Nicky. Dave Masters may have a history of unfaithfulness, but he's never been unfaithful to me. Tom and me are over, but I can give Dave Masters a chance.'

'Do you mean that?'

'Yes, I don't think you're the same man who cheated on Cath. I'm willing to give it a try, to see how we get on. But if you ever cheat on me again, I'll have your balls for earrings.' Dave laughed, until he saw the look in Cindy's eyes. 'I'm not joking. Don't even try me on this one, you know?'

A month later, Dave and Cindy were sitting in Dave's new car, bought with the advance from his new record deal – not with Ultimate – and listening to a Ry Cooder album on their way back from another visit to Dave's dad. Dave was growing his hair longer again, though he had decided to keep the beard. Neither Tony nor the trust fund money had turned up yet, but at least he was getting his royalty payments – much increased – again.

'Your dad was looking better than last week,' said Cindy. 'I think having you back in his life has made a difference.'

'I don't know about that,' replied Dave, although secretly he suspected that Cindy was right. His first visit had been emotional. Cindy had come along to support him, but she left the two men alone to go through some of their shared baggage. Since then, the visits had been much more social, with the two men learning what Cindy called the emotional language of their new relationship. 'He likes you, though,' added Dave. 'He keeps telling me so. And telling me not to mess it up like a bloody idiot this time.'

'He knows what he's talking about, your dad.' She reached across and turned up the music; it was an instrumental track, gently lilting with Cooder's slide guitar to the fore. 'I like this one. What's it called?'

Dave smiled to himself before he answered, aware of how apt the title was. '"I Think It's Going to Work Out Fine".'

PRESS RELEASE

FEBRUARY 1st 1992

EMI are pleased to announce the release of a new album by Dave Masters. *Dead Man Singing* is produced by Phil Collins and features guest appearances from stars such as Paul McCartney, Karl Wallinger, Richard Thompson and Ian McLagan. Dave's long-standing sidemen Vince Preston and Simon Tilley also appear on the album, along with Chris Breslan and Martin Summerfield, both previously of the Dave ReMastered Band.

Dave Masters will be undertaking an extensive tour to promote the album, leading a band consisting of Vince Preston, Simon Tilley, Martin Summerfield and Chris Breslan. As well as performing at venues such as Hammersmith Odeon, Edinburgh Playhouse and Birmingham NEC, the Dave Masters Band will also undertake a series of smaller gigs in UK prisons, highlighting the work of charities that promote prisoners' access to the arts as part of their rehabilitation.

Producer Phil Collins: 'It's been a privilege to work with Dave. I've been a fan for years, and this is the strongest set of songs he's ever produced – even better than the ones on the *Lost Masters* album. It's an honour to step into Alan Sharkey's production shoes, and I just hope I've done justice to the body of work Alan and Dave built up over the years.'

Paul McCartney: 'It's nice to get to play on some of his songs after all these years of him playing mine, the cheeky sod.'

Karl Wallinger: 'When Dave invited me to take part in the recordings, I didn't hesitate. He's a great talent and it's brilliant that he's back where he belongs. And he's promised not to steal any more of my songs.'

Ian McLagan: 'Dave toured with us back in the '70s, and he hasn't lost that sense of fun and adventure, even if he's better behaved now when it comes to the ladies. It's so good to see him getting the recognition his talent has always deserved.'

Richard Thompson: 'I just hope he's learned not to take career advice from my set list. No good can come from that, for anyone.'

Dave Masters: 'It's been a crazy year, but I'm back to doing what I love and surrounded by the people I love. Not everyone gets to have a second or third chance in life, and I don't intend to waste mine.'

Dead Man Singing by Dave Masters will be released on EMI on March 2nd 1992. The first single from the album, a double A-side "I've Just Seen a Face"/"Cindy Incidentally", will be released on February 14th.

DEAD MAN SINGING: DISCUSSION QUESTIONS

- Dave starts and ends the book as Dave Masters, rock musician, but is he the same man? What has changed for him?
- Why did Dave offer to hold guitar lessons in prison? Do you think the Dave from chapter 1 would have made such an offer? Who benefitted more, him or his students?
- To what extent is Dave saved by Cindy? Would you agree with the statement that he regains his music through her, and that he regains her through his music?
- How much did Cindy's past experiences shape her reactions and decisions throughout the novel? How much does our past shape our present? How can people break free from past hurts?
- Cindy, Cathy and Penelope are all examples of strong women. Did you find yourself reacting differently to each of them? Which did you prefer and why?
- 'Some guilty secrets should stay secret, to protect the innocent. Sometimes a lie that works is better than a truth that ruins everything' (Jym, p139). To what extent do you agree with Jym?
- What do you think the future holds for Dave and Cindy? Will they ever be able to listen to Del Amitri again?

- Dave's relationship with certain songs changes over the course of the novel. Why do you think that is? Can you think of similar examples in your own life? How familiar were you with the music referred to in the book? How did the songs influence the way you engaged with the unfolding story?
- 'We judge artists by their best work; we can write off the mistakes and misfires as the price for finding the gold. Everyone makes mistakes in real life, but we don't just judge people by their worst moments; we look at the bigger picture and focus on the good things.' (Martin, p130). Do you agree with Martin's assertion that artists should be judged on their best work? Does the same apply to people in everyday life?
- What, apart from Dave's supposed death, made it so hard for him to be reconciled with his father?
- Why do you think Dave decided to help Ronnie, even though he couldn't possibly be his father?
- 'There's a thin line between not caring what people think and not caring if you hurt them, isn't there?' (Cindy, p117). Where do you draw the line between being true to your authentic self and being considerate of other people? To what extent are the two mutually exclusive?

To request an extended version of these discussion questions, please go to the contact page of www.stevecouch.co.uk

ACKNOWLEDGEMENTS

This book took a long time to write. It started with a song at a Richard Thompson concert more than 30 years ago, although it wasn't until 2021 that the idea of Dave Masters and his story emerged from that memory.

Every attempt has been made to make the musical elements of the book historically accurate, although there has been some deliberate fudging on my part. The Richard Thompson concert in chapter 1 is an amalgam of two separate shows, a couple of years apart – I did see him at Hackney Empire, and I subsequently saw him perform "Now That I Am Dead", but not on the same occasion. The Del Amitri gig in chapter 19 is also a genuine one, although I left out the fact that Vic Reeves joined them for the encores (it seemed too bizarre and irrelevant a detail for the purposes of my story; like the drummers Dave praises in the book, you only play what serves the song). All release dates of specific songs are, to the best of my knowledge, correct, although the timing of the pub quiz in chapter 5 is two or three months too early for the MC Hammer joke. I apologise to any harem-pant-wearing dance pedants who are offended.

MC Hammer anachronisms apart, getting the music right was a big part of writing this story. I wanted to nail Dave's sound (a

British take on American country rock – The Who and the Faces meet the Band) and wherever possible the specific songs that crop up in the text are carefully and deliberately chosen. If anyone is interested, there are two Spotify playlists that I put together while writing. One is called Dead Man Singing and it consists of the songs in the story, from the first cover Dave plays in chapter one ("Stagefright") to the Ry Cooder instrumental that closes the final chapter ("I Think It's Going to Work Out Fine"). The second playlist, Dave Masters 100, features one track from each of the 100 albums chosen in chapter three, minus Dave's own albums and a few others that aren't available on Spotify. Sadly, it was during the writing process that Neil Young and Joni Mitchell decided to remove themselves from that platform, denying both playlists some important tracks. Spotify also didn't have any version of "Now That I Am Dead", which was originally released on the *Invisible Means* album by French Frith Kaiser Thompson, but if you want to hear the seed that this story grew out of, there are a couple of Richard Thompson solo performances available on YouTube.

There are several people, other than the many musicians whose work fed into my creative process, who I owe a debt of thanks to. My wife Ann and my sons Peter and Dan have allowed me to devote hours to the work, putting up with a near-constant soundtrack of 70s and late 80s music, along with my endless chat about both the music and the writing. Their singular failure to be impressed by my literary aspirations does much to keep my feet on the ground where they belong. My Mum, by contrast, has always been my biggest (though not necessarily my most unbiased) fan, although the boys would be quick to point out that unlike them, she doesn't have to live with me. Mum has been hugely supportive of this book in so many ways. I'm very grateful to her for that, as well as everything else over the years. I love you, Mum. Yes, you will get a free copy of the book.

Several friends have encouraged me along the way, with Lou Porter, Kieran Fahy, Harry Lund and Cheryl Gadsby all reading early versions of the text and providing encouragement, feedback, support and criticism in varying proportions. They all helped me to get *Dead Man Singing* to where it is today. Many other people – too numerous to name – offered suggestions for Dave's record collection without realising what I was asking them, as well as sharing memories of small concert venues around the country which helped me to shape Dave's touring schedule. Tony Watkins' vastly superior knowledge of classical music was invaluable in nailing down Creaveney-Walsh's musical prejudices, although I wouldn't for one moment want anyone to read that as implying that Tony shares that character's prejudices. I mean, he probably does, but I wouldn't want to be the one to expose him.

Friday 13th January 2023 was a lucky day for me. That was when I received the email saying that the Book Guild wanted to publish my book. After years of fruitlessly knocking on agents' and publishers' doors, they won't ever know just how much their decision meant to me. As well as Chloe May who sent that email and wrote the editorial report that made me realise someone had really got what I was trying to do with this story, I should thank Fern Bushnell, Daniel Burchmore, Liberty Woodward, and Hayley Russell for their expert handling of production and editorial matters, Chelsea Taylor for the cover and design of the book and Meera Vithlani for co-ordinating The Book Guild's promotion work. Liz Gordon of Brilliant Fish PR has been an enthusiastic and knowledgeable guide to my own promotional efforts and has also done so much to steer me through the process of letting people know about the book. Stephanie Carr and her team at Troubador made setting up my author website at www.stevecouch.co.uk a simple process, while Skye Price-Elliot totally aced perhaps the toughest of all the required tasks: making me look good in photos.

So many friends have shared my excitement that I can't possibly mention everyone by name. I've been thrilled by how many people seemed almost as delighted as me at the news that this book was going to be published. Apologies to those who are left out, but I wanted to particularly thank the Gadsby family – Jules, Naomi and Hannah, as well as early-reader Cheryl – for their friendship and support for many years and their excitement now. Jules has been excellent company at several Richard Thompson gigs over the years too. Dan Lloyd, one of my friends from Man v Fat Bournemouth, was a huge boost to my optimism while I was trying to find a publisher. His repeated inquiries whether I had any news yet, along with certainty that he'd get to read it as a proper book, helped to keep me going and I'm glad for both of us that he's finally going to get his wish.

As a list of people who I owe a debt of thanks to, this is far too small. There are countless others who have played a part in my writing journey, both before and during *Dead Man Singing*. While getting the book over the line was a huge team effort, any shortcomings that remain in the final version are, of course, down to me alone.

Finally, thank you to you. Whether you're reading this having finished the book, or are just browsing and deciding whether or not to take the plunge (do it! Do it now!), thank you and I hope you enjoy it: that's the point.

ABOUT THE AUTHOR

Steve Couch lives in Bournemouth with his wife and two sons. He has been employed as a youth worker, a writer and editor, a youth football coach, and as a club coach for Man v Fat Football. Career highlights include being paid variously for the following: watching films, playing computer games, going to church, telling lies about the national sport of Denmark, and jumping around in a skip.

Steve shares a birthday with Nick Hornby, the Football League and Paul McCartney's first solo LP. He is a mediocre blues harmonica player and a four-time winner of *Tea Time Theme Time* on BBC 6 Music's Radcliffe and Maconie show.

For more information, please visit www.stevecouch.co.uk